...city-loving book addict, peony obsessive **Katrina**
...dmore lives in Cork, Ireland, with her husband, four
...ive children and a very daft dog. A psychology
...duate, with an MSc in Human Resources, Katrina
...nt many years working in multinational companies
...d can't believe she is lucky enough now to have a job
...t involves daydreaming about love and handsome
...n! You can visit Katrina at katrinacudmore.com

...risty Jeffries graduated from the University of
...fornia, Irvine, with a degree in criminology, and
...ived her Juris Doctor from California Western
...ool of Law. But drafting court documents and
...king in law enforcement was merely an apprenticeship
...er current career in the dynamic field of mummyhood
... romance writing. She lives in Southern California
...h her patient husband, two energetic sons and one sassy
...dmother. Follow her online at christyjeffries.com

P...
Dy...

Also by Katrina Cudmore

Swept into the Rich Man's World
The Best Man's Guarded Heart
Her First-Date Honeymoon
Their Baby Surprise
Tempted by her Greek Tycoon
Christmas with the Duke
Resisting the Italian Single Dad

Also by Christy Jeffries

Sugar Falls, Idaho
A Marine for His Mum
Waking Up Wed
From Dare to Due Date
The Matchmaking Twins
The Makeover Prescription
A Family Under the Stars
The SEAL's Secret Daughter

American Heroes
A Proposal for the Officer
The Firefighter's Christmas Reunion

Montana Mavericks
The Maverick's Bridal Bargain

Discover more at millsandboon.co.uk

SECOND CHANCE WITH THE BEST MAN

KATRINA CUDMORE

IT STARTED WITH A PREGNANCY

CHRISTY JEFFRIES

MILLS & BOON

First Published in Great Britain 2019
by Mills & Boon, an imprint of HarperCollinsPublishers,
1 London Bridge Street, London, SE1 9GF

Second Chance With The Best Man © 2019 Katrina Cudmore
It Started with a Pregnancy © 2019 Harlequin Books S.A.

Special thanks and acknowledgement to Christy Jeffries for her contribution to the Furever Yours continuity.

ISBN: 978-0-263-27246-8

0619

Printed and bound in Spain
by CPI, Barcelona

SECOND CHANCE WITH THE BEST MAN

KATRINA CUDMORE

To Majella, the best little sister in the world!

CHAPTER ONE

THE BEAST PRESSED his snout against Hannah McGinley's car window, the glass instantly fogging up. 'Good doggy, off you go, now,' Hannah called out, trying to sound in control but also cheerful—the last thing she wanted to do was anger this beast any further. Her arrival on the driveway of Château Bonneval had already caused him to run alongside her car like an entry at the Grand National, his incessant barking almost causing her to drive into one of the hornbeam trees lining the long avenue.

As a farmer's daughter from Shropshire, she'd been told time and time again she'd no cause to be so scared, but no amount of cajoling from her family had ever rid her of her terror of even the smallest of dogs, never mind the donkey-sized version staring at her right now as though he couldn't wait to sink his teeth into her.

Looking in the direction of the front door of the château, Hannah willed someone to come out and rescue her. Surely they had heard the beast's hound-from-hell baying?

Not for the first time, Hannah wondered at her decision to agree to travel to France to act as the celebrant at her best friend Lara's wedding blessing. An easy, joyful decision in most circumstances, but not when you had dated and fallen in love with the best man and brother to the groom, Laurent Bonneval, only for him to end it all. And the worst part of it all was that the wedding was taking place in his home—Château Bonneval. Why couldn't it at least be at a neutral venue? Her only hope was that they would be surrounded by others all weekend and she would manage to project the air of calm professionalism she'd been rehearsing ever since Lara and François had travelled to London from Manchester, where they lived, just to ask her to be their wedding celebrant.

Though moved beyond words that they trusted her to perform their wedding blessing, especially given the fact that she was so new to being a celebrant—this would only be her fourth wedding—she'd asked if they were really, *really* sure it was she they wanted to be the one to perform the ceremony. Lara and François had exchanged a tentative glance before Lara had leant across the table of Hannah's local Richmond coffee shop, and touched her arm. 'You've been my best friend since we were seven.' Pausing, Lara had given her a half-smile, one that had asked Hannah to understand, to trust her. 'It would make our day even more magical to have you bless our marriage.'

Tears had blinded Hannah for a moment as she'd remembered how Lara had waded in on her first day at Meadlead Primary School and told Ellie Marshall and her gang to mind their own business when they had interrogated Hannah during the break with endless questions as to who she was, why she was joining the school in the middle of term, why she was so skinny. Frozen inside, confused by everything in her life, Hannah had been taken aback at just how grateful she was to Lara when she'd led her away from her interrogators. For weeks after, she'd remained silent. And while that had garnered her endless suspicious glances and whispered words behind cupped hands from the rest of class, Lara had cheerfully chatted away, her quirky humour and buoyant outlook on life thawing Hannah's numb heart.

That day in the café in Richmond, Hannah had turned to François, her heart as usual jolting in remembrance—some of François's features were so like Laurent's: the thick dark wavy hair, the strong and proud Gallic jawline, the wide, high cheekbones, the clean blade of a nose. 'Will...?' She tried to form the word Laurent, but it stuck in her throat and refused to budge. Eventually she managed to mutter, through a false smile, 'Will having me as the celebrant be okay with all of your family?'

François's eyes were different, a softer, more forgiving blue, none of the striking, pain-inducing brilliance of Laurent's. The care in his eyes had matched his gentle tone when he had answered, 'Laurent is to be my best man,' but Hannah had still felt it like a whip to her heart.

She'd looked away from the discomfort in both Lara's and François's expressions, hating that they had been put in this position. Their wedding should be a carefree celebration, not tainted by the fact that she'd foolishly fallen in love with Laurent, confusing his Gallic charm and romantic gestures for a sign that he'd felt what she did, that he too had wanted more.

In the months after he'd left London to return to the family business and château in Cognac, telling her before he left that he didn't want to continue their relationship, she'd puzzled over the overwhelming effect he'd had on her. The pain, the disappointment, the humiliation had been so engulfing she'd struggled to comprehend it all. Was it the fact that he was the first man she'd ever truly fallen in love with? Which admittedly was pretty tragic at the age of twenty-nine. But up until then, she'd never met anyone who had quickened her heart, who had communicated so much with a glance, who intrigued her.

At first she'd resisted the chemistry between them, her age-old need to protect herself holding him at arm's length. But in truth she'd been changing and had been more receptive to allowing someone into her life. She'd chased security and stability throughout her early twenties, desperately needing the safety of establishing her career in finance and buying her own apartment. But as she neared thirty, she'd realised she wanted more. A more free life, a more optimistic life. One of taking chances and not being so afraid. And into this new way of thinking and daring to dream had walked Laurent Bonneval. The brother of her best friend's new boyfriend. And he'd swept her off her feet. But ten months later he'd left her with a broken heart.

But that heart was now mended and firmly closed to Laurent Bonneval's charms.

Hannah jumped as the beast's tail hit against her door panel as he turned and bounded away, disappearing around one of the château's fairy-tale turrets that sat at each corner of the four-storey building.

She breathed out a sigh of relief. But then her heart plummeted to the car floor. From around the corner, sprinting at first, slowing to a jog when he took in her car, came Laurent, the beast at his side.

Stopping, he raised a hand to shield his eyes from the low evening sun. Behind him his shadow spilt across the gravelled drive, his tall, broad frame exaggerated.

She waited for him to move. Tried not to stare at the fact that he was wearing only running shorts that revealed the long length of his powerful legs and a lightweight vest top that showcased the taut, muscular power of his broad shoulders and gym-honed arms. His skin glistened with perspiration.

Heat formed in her belly.

He moved towards her car.

Her heart somersaulted.

She grasped for the window control and buzzed down her window a couple of inches, only then realising how stifling the car had become as she'd been held hostage by the beast. She longed to run a hand through her hair, check her make-up in the mirror. But she resisted giving him any sign that she cared how she looked in his eyes.

He came to a stop a few feet away from the car. The beast came to heel at his command. 'Hannah...' Her heart pinged at the concern in his eyes. 'Are you okay?'

The low, intimate sound of his voice almost undid her. Memory after memory rushed through her brain— how he used to leave her voicemails that had her blush and giggle. His mouth against her ear when they would be out with others, whispering a compliment, a promise. The Saturday mornings when they used to cycle to their favourite French bakery in Putney Heath and eat breakfast while playfully flirting, her legs trembling when his fingers would stroke her hand, her arm, her cheek, before he would suggest that they head home. His murmured words when they made love afterwards that had swelled in her heart and burst like joyful bubbles in her bloodstream.

Hannah breathed in deeply. She was over him. She had to remember that fact. Her focus now was on deciding which direction her life should take. Stay in her career in finance either in London or Singapore or take the risk of becoming a full-time wedding celebrant in Spain. Her old cautious side told her to hold on to her regular income and secure career but deep inside of her she wanted to be free to make her own decisions away from the confines of corporate life, to make a difference by being an integral part of one of the most important days in any person's life.

She was here to support Lara. To celebrate with her and François. Laurent Bonneval was just a minor aggravation in what should be a gloriously happy weekend.

Now was the time to enact the calm professionalism she'd sworn she would adopt for the weekend. Unfortunately her trembling hands and somersaulting stomach didn't appear to have received that particular memo.

She buzzed down her window a fraction more. Nodded in the direction of the beast. 'I'd appreciate it if you'd lock him away.'

Something unyielding kicked in Laurent's chest at the coolness of Hannah's tone and stony expression. He pointed in the direction of the stables; at his command Bleu ambled away to where he slept alongside the horses.

Hannah's gaze followed Bleu's every step and even when he disappeared from view, her gaze remained fixed in that direction. 'Will he come back?'

He edged closer to her door, crouched over to speak to her in the small gap of the window. 'I heard him barking—I'm sorry if he scared you.'

She shook her head as though to deny any suggestion she'd been scared. 'Is he yours?'

'Yes.'

She grimaced at that. He knew that she was scared of dogs. He cursed himself for not having locked Bleu away. Lara had told him Hannah was due to arrive around this time but Bleu had looked so despondent when he'd led him to his kennel earlier, Laurent had relented and allowed him to accompany him as usual on his evening run. 'Despite appearances, he's as soft as a marshmallow. He just wanted to say hello to you.'

Hannah shook her head, clearly not believing him. 'He's terrifying—I've never seen anything like him.'

'He's a Grand Bleu de Gascogne. He has a very affectionate temperament.' Moving to the car door, he opened it. Hannah's gaze shot back to the corner of the château where Bleu had disappeared and then back to him. He gave her a smile of encouragement. 'He won't come back, I promise. You can trust me on that.'

Her forehead bunched and her mouth dropped into an even deeper scowl.

For long seconds she stared at him unhappily, heat appearing on her high cheekbones, but then with a toss of her head she yanked her handbag off the passenger seat and stepped out of the car.

In the silence that followed he cursed François. When François had told him that Hannah was to be their wedding celebrant he'd been incredulous. François knew of their history, how uncomfortable it would be for them both, but François, usually so sanguine, had refused to change his mind in the face of Laurent's demand that someone else take on the role. His only compromise was his pledge that he and Lara would be present in the château at all times over the weekend to smooth any awkwardness between him and Hannah.

'Your journey—was it okay?'

Hannah shrugged at his question and moved to the boot of her car. 'I'd like to go inside and see Lara.'

By her tone, he knew she was as keen as he was for the others to be present in the château. But once again, his father had decided to make life difficult for everyone around him. He followed her to the boot of the car and lifted out her suitcase. 'François and Lara called me earlier—there's been a change of plans. They're now staying in the family apartment in Bordeaux overnight. Lara tried calling you but she couldn't get through.'

Her expression appalled, Hannah pulled her phone from her handbag, 'I'm having problems connecting to the French network.' Then with an exasperated breath she asked, 'Why are they staying in Bordeaux?'

'Apparently my father had already made a restaurant booking for them and refuses to cancel. He wants to show Lara and her parents some of the city's nightlife.'

Her head turning in the direction of the château, she asked uneasily, 'So who's staying here tonight?'

'Just you and me.'

Her eyes widened with horror.

Irritation flared inside him. He'd known she wouldn't be keen for his company, but did she have to make it so obvious?

But then his indignation sank into guilt. He and he alone was the cause of all this tension. The least he could do was try to make this weekend somewhat tolerable for them both.

Leading her in the direction of the main entrance, he said, 'Let me show you to your room. All of the château staff have this evening off as they will be working long hours in the coming days with the wedding.' Inside the coolness of the double-height hallway of the château, his desperation to take a shower and have something cool to drink abated a fraction. The heatwave hitting most of south-west France for the past week was becoming unbearable. He kicked the front door shut with his heel, knowing he was only trying to kid himself—the weather had little to do with how he was overheating.

This always happened when Hannah was nearby.

Pale pink sleeveless blouse tucked into mid-thigh-length lemon shorts, plain white plimsolls on her feet, thick and glossy brown hair tied back into a high pony-tail, she was all delicious curves and sweetness.

He uttered a low curse to himself. He knew he'd hurt her. She deserved better than him remembering how incredible it was to hold her, to feel her soft curves. But in truth, their relationship had been built on a bed of intoxicating mutual attraction.

He'd seen it flare in her eyes in the moments after they had first met, their handshake lasting a few seconds longer than necessary, neither trying to pull away.

That first day, as they'd sailed on his yacht, *Sirocco,* which had then been moored out of Port Solent but was now moored out of Royan, Hannah had been friendly but he could tell that she was avoiding being alone with him. He'd wanted to shrug off her indifference but in truth her reticence had intrigued him and the intelligence in her eyes and her close friendship with Lara had had him wanting to know her better.

She had turned down his invitation to meet for a drink later in the week.

So he'd orchestrated it for her to attend a dinner party he'd thrown in his Kensington town house. He'd hoped to impress her with his cooking but she'd left early, saying she had an early flight to Paris in the morning. As he'd walked her out to her awaiting taxi, for the first time ever, he'd felt tongue-tied. All night he'd been unable to stop staring across the table at her, her natural warmth that was evident behind her initially reserved nature, her genuineness, her authenticity lighting something inside him. On the few occasions she had looked in his direction, he'd seen that spark of attraction again, but she'd always snatched her gaze away. That night of the dinner party, he'd let her go, without pressing his lips to her cheek as he'd ached to, something deep inside him telling him he had to wait until she was ready to accept the spark between them.

Their paths had crossed several times in the months that had followed. He'd used to playfully remind her that his offer of meeting for a drink was still on the table but she would smile and turn away.

And then, one day, when they had all gone swimming in the Solent after another day sailing on his yacht, *Sirocco*, she'd watched him dive from the rail. When he'd emerged from the water deliberately close to her, her initial frown that had spoken of some deep internal turmoil had transformed into a gentle smile and she'd softly said, 'I think I'm ready for that drink.'

He'd trod the cold English Channel water, grinning widely, not caring that everyone else in the party could see his delight. He'd wanted to stay there for ever, staring into Hannah's soulful brown eyes, his heart beating wildly in delight and anticipation that had been more than about the desire to tug her gorgeous bikini-clad body towards him.

Now he led her up the main marble staircase of the château to the second floor where, at the end of the corridor, he opened the door to her bedroom. Hannah walked inside, her gaze widening as she took in the antique jade hand-painted wallpaper, the Louis XV furniture.

He stayed at the doorway. They had dated for over ten months. The chemistry and intense attraction never waning, escalating in fact. But as they'd grown closer, as his heart had begun to need her, panic had set in. Laurent didn't believe in love and commitment. When he'd been twelve, François ten, his father had left the family home to conduct an affair. The following year his mother had done the same. And in the years that had followed his father had disappeared from the family home at least once a year to continue his affairs. The affairs, the hurt they had inflicted on everyone around them, had poisoned Laurent for ever against any thought of commitment in his own life.

His panic had soared when he'd visited Hannah's family one weekend and seen their love and devotion to one another. How could he ever bring her into the toxic mix of his own family, which was so full of unspoken anger and accusations? And his panic had soared even more when Hannah had told him of her plans to become a wedding celebrant. At first he'd laughed, thinking she was joking. But she'd been serious. The woman he'd thought of as being as career-minded and as focused on success as he was, who had never given any indication that she was looking for commitment, wanted to be the officiator of the institution he'd no regard for—marriage.

Increasingly he'd realised just how incompatible they were despite their attraction and laughter and warmth for one another. And then he'd learnt of his father's stroke and his need to return to Cognac to head up the family business. For years he'd waited on the sidelines to be given the role of CEO, beyond frustrated at the decline in the Cognac House's market share under his father's neglectful leadership. Bonneval Cognac had been in existence since the seventeenth century. It was Laurent's legacy and one he was determined to restore to its rightful place as the most exclusive cognac house in the world. It was a promise he'd made to his beloved grandfather before he died, a man who had despaired at his own son's disloyalty and irresponsibility, not only with the business, but with his own family.

Knowing that there was no future for him and Hannah, Laurent had ended their relationship when he'd returned to France. It had been a gut-wrenching conversation, and he'd seen the pain and confusion in her eyes, but it was not a conversation he regretted. Hannah deserved someone who actually believed in love and commitment. Someone who reflected the love and devotion and stability of her own background.

This weekend would be awkward. But they needed to somehow build a new relationship as their paths would cross time and time again in the future. Maybe having to spend time together this evening was an opportune time to begin that process. He was the one who had messed up by allowing their relationship to become too intense—the least he could do was ensure that the next few days were as painless as possible. For both of their sakes.

'I had planned on eating out tonight—I need to go and check on my wedding present to François and Lara first, but there's a restaurant nearby. Will you join me?'

CHAPTER TWO

HANNAH STUDIED LAURENT and marvelled at his ability to forget the past. It hurt her, angered her, but part of her envied him for it. Wasn't it what she was striving to achieve herself, after all? For a moment she was about to say no to his invite. The last thing she wanted to do was spend time alone with him.

Standing in the doorway, a shoulder propped against the frame, his arms crossed on his chest, his expression untroubled, he waited for her response. He was still the best-looking man she'd ever met. And damn it, she was still attracted to him. As her mum would say, *figgity, figgity, fig*. Well, if he could shrug off the past then so could she. She popped her suitcase on the luggage rack. Flipped the lid open, pulled out her laptop and placed it on the desk by the window, determined to have some control.

Opening up the laptop, she asked him for the Wi-Fi password and, logging in, she said, 'I'm doing an online thirty-day yoga challenge and I want to do today's session now. I'll need a shower afterwards.' She glanced behind her in his direction. 'I won't be ready for at least an hour so don't wait for me if that doesn't suit you.'

'I didn't know you practised yoga.'

She shrugged. 'It helps me to let go of all those small things that irritate me in life.'

He made a grunting sound low in his throat before saying, 'I'll see you downstairs in an hour,' and then walked away.

She closed the door and leant heavily against it. This room, the entire château, was beyond incredible. She'd stolen glances into the endless rooms they had passed downstairs, her breath catching at their delicate elegance.

It was hard to comprehend that Laurent lived here. All alone. She knew from Lara that his parents had moved to a lodge on the thousand-acre estate after he'd returned from England to take up the role of CEO. She'd heard Lara's description of this magnificent château, had known of the world-famous cognac brand, but until now she hadn't fully grasped his family's wealth and standing.

This was not her world. It brought out all the inadequacies she so desperately tried to keep hidden.

Now, more than ever, she was glad that she'd never told Laurent about her early childhood. How could someone who came from this background ever understand her? Not believe she was tainted by it?

She was even more grateful that she'd never fully opened her heart to him, dared to tell him she loved him. She'd felt too vulnerable, too unsure of what his response would be—which should have told her everything she needed to know about their relationship. Though deeply charismatic, Laurent somehow managed to never fully reveal himself or show any vulnerability. For most of their whirlwind relationship she'd been blind to that, too excited by the fact that this gorgeous man wanted her in his life. He'd been attentive and fun with a determined and self-possessed streak she'd found utterly compelling. But he'd never really answered her questions about his background, what he wanted in the future. And in their last conversation he'd told her that he couldn't give her commitment, a permanent relationship.

Thankfully she'd managed to stop herself from pleading that she was happy to keep things casual, knowing that in truth she only wanted to buy more time to persuade him that he could commit. At least she hadn't followed that particular deluded path of trying to change another person.

After her yoga and shower, she changed into a knee-length white shift dress, a narrow gold belt cinching in the waist. Brushing out her hair, she let it hang loose and applied some make-up. About to leave, she paused to stare out of one of the four windows in the room. Below her room, set amidst a wide purple border of lavender, sat a huge swimming pool. Beyond the pool an immaculate lawn ran down to a tree-lined river. Laurent used to talk about that river, the Charente, when he spoke about home, which admittedly was a rare occurrence. In London, his whole focus had seemed to be on his career as a fund manager and the busy social life he'd created in his adopted city. He'd lived life with abandon, hungry to experience new places, new things—she'd travelled more in her short time with him than she'd ever previously done.

Downstairs she busied herself with staring at the landscape paintings of country scenes hanging in abundance in the hallway as she waited for him, and when his footsteps tapped, tapped, tapped on the marble stairs as he jogged downwards, she realised how much she missed his endless energy and enthusiasm for life. She gave him the briefest of smiles when he came alongside her, tried to ignore how good he looked with his damp hair, his pale blue shirt open at the neck worn over lightweight navy trousers, tried to ignore how his freshly applied aftershave flipped her heart with the memory of waking to find him crouched beside her, dressed for work, a cup of tea in one hand, a plate with toast in the other, his brilliant smile turning her weak with happiness.

'Ready to go?'

She nodded to his question and followed him to the front door. As he was about to pull the ancient handle that opened one side of the heavy double oak doors she could not help but ask, 'Will he be out there?'

He turned, confused at first by her question, but then reached out as though to touch her forearm. Hannah jerked back, unable to bear the thought of him touching her. Afraid for how she would react. For the briefest of moments he looked thrown by her reaction before he dropped his hand. Opening the door, he answered, 'No. Bleu knows to stay in his kennel when I send him there.'

Tentatively she followed him out onto the gravelled driveway. 'Did you inherit him from your parents?'

He walked to the side of the château, past a parked four-by-four, and opened the doors of one of the five stone-crafted single-storey outbuildings that were set back from the château. Daylight flooded the building to reveal a silver sports car. Hannah swallowed the temptation to exclaim at its beauty.

'I didn't inherit Bleu but this car I did inherit. My father is an avid vintage-car collector. He moved most of his collection to an outbuilding at the lodge but left this car here as there wasn't enough room for it. He wanted to sell it but my mother persuaded him to keep it within the family. I don't get to use it as much as I'd like to...' he paused and glanced out at the blue, cloudless evening sky '...but this evening is the perfect night to take it for a run.'

Hannah watched him manually lower the soft top of the car, the pit of disappointment in her stomach at his answer having her eventually ask, 'So where did you get Bleu?'

In the initial days and weeks after Laurent had returned to France she'd held out vain hope that he might call, change his mind, her heart slowly splintering apart, but after a month of silence, her heart a void, she'd accepted that it was truly over between them. But somehow, the thought of Laurent choosing Bleu, knowing her fear of dogs, spoke more than a year of silence of him moving on from her.

After he'd left she'd been numb, but eventually, when she'd grown exhausted by the emptiness inside herself, she'd insisted that her heart mend. She'd worked harder at fixing her heart than at anything she'd ever tackled before. She had thrown herself into her work and her training course to become a wedding celebrant. She'd filled every minute of every day with work and exercise and reading and meeting up with friends and family.

Only once had she slipped up and shown just how deeply devastated she was. She'd taken her newly acquired wedding celebrant certificate to show to her parents on the day she graduated from her course. Her dad had been out at the weekly livestock market in their local town, but her mum had made a fuss of her achievement, even opening a celebratory bottle of champagne. In the comforting cocoon of her childhood home, once the euphoria of achieving the qualification had worn off, she'd realised how tired and lonely she really was. And when her mum, with her usual gentle perceptiveness, had asked how she was, the tears had come. Hannah had fought their spilling onto her cheek, not wanting to upset her mum. She'd just nodded instead at what her mum said in response to her hiccuped short explanation before quickly changing the subject to a much happier topic—

her sister Cora's pregnancy and the much-anticipated arrival of the first grandchild into the family.

Later, back in London and alone in her apartment, she'd reflected on what her mum had said and taken some solace from her observation that at least she was risking her heart now and living life as she should be, with its invariable ups and downs, joy and disappointments. Hannah had been taken aback; she hadn't realised that her mum saw through how much she was protecting herself. Which was silly really—her parents were the most empathetic people she knew. Of course they understood why she struggled so much to trust others.

She'd met her parents when she was seven. She hadn't wanted to be in their house; she hadn't wanted their smiles, their kind voices. Their encouragement to eat her food, to play with their daughters, Cora and Emily. She had wanted to be back in her old house. With her birth parents. But the police had taken her away and now she had to live with new people. She'd been so scared. Above all else she'd hated change. Because it meant things might get even worse. She'd known how her birth parents operated, but not these strangers.

Now opening the passenger door for her, Laurent moved to the other side of the car. It was only when they were both seated inside the car that he turned and answered her question. 'I found Bleu one night when out running in the woods of the estate. I heard his whimpering first—the vet believes he ate some poison a local farmer may have put down. He was already an undernourished stray. We didn't think he'd pull through. But he did. He's a gentle giant. But I'll make sure he's locked away while you're here.'

Hannah swallowed at the tenderness of his tone, at the emotion in his eyes. Torn between her deep fear of dogs and the guilt of locking away this poor animal who had been through so much already, she answered, 'No, don't, that's not fair on him. I'll keep out of his way.'

Turning on the engine, which started with a low throb, he turned and regarded her. 'I can introduce him to you if you want.'

She jerked in her seat, instantly terrified. 'No, don't.'

He gave her a concerned look before backing the car out of the garage. When he'd turned it in the direction of the drive he said, 'You never really explained to me why you're so scared of dogs.'

She shrugged. 'I've always been petrified of them, it's just one of those things.' Which wasn't true. She could remember a time when she wasn't scared. But like so much of her early childhood, the story of why she feared dogs was one she'd locked away inside herself years ago.

Laurent's gaze narrowed. For a moment he looked as though he was going to probe further but then, putting the car in gear, he sped off down the drive and out onto the narrow lanes of the Cognac countryside.

The wind whipped against her hair. She tied it back with an elastic band from her handbag. Despite her anxiousness about the entire weekend, for a moment she felt exhilarated as they zipped along and she smiled to herself as the force of the warm air blasted against her skin. The car was small. Laurent's thigh was only inches away from hers. She tried to focus on the low hedges they sped by, the endless bright fields of smiling sunflowers, the gorgeous order of vineyards with their row upon row of vines, and not the way Laurent's large hands clasped the wheel, the assured way he handled the car. They slowed behind a tractor. Hannah felt a jolt of nostalgia for her Shropshire childhood. The rides with her dad out on his tractor. The carefree days filled with her dad's laughter, the late evenings of drawing in bales of hay. But even then a part of her could not help wonder how she'd managed to escape from what came before, wondering if one day she'd have to go back to it.

Laurent slowed as they approached a village. The road narrowed even further to wind its way past pale stone houses with light blue shutters, then a *boulangerie* shut for the evening, a bar with some locals sitting outside who waved to Laurent as he passed by. At the other end of the village he pulled into a narrow driveway, a plaque with the name Villa Marchand on the entrance pillar, the viburnum hedging dense with white delicate flowers brushing lightly against the sides of the car. And then a two-storey house appeared, its blue shutters tied back. Jasmine and wild roses threaded their way up the outer walls, curling around the Juliet balconies on the upper floor. To the side of the house stood an ancient weeping willow tree on the banks of a river.

Laurent parked the car and got out. Hannah followed him to the front door. He opened it to reveal a stone-flagged sitting room, large white sofas surrounding a heavy teak chest that acted as a coffee table. The walls were painted in a soft white; a large grey painted mirror hung over the open fireplace.

'Why are we here?'

He frowned at her question as though he'd expected her to already know the answer. And then, stepping into the room, he said, 'This is my present to François and Lara. A summer home. It's where François proposed to Lara. I'm hoping it will tempt them to visit more often.'

She followed him into the room, leaving the front door ajar. 'You miss François?'

He turned at her question. Her heart lodged in her

throat as his blue eyes twinkled and his wide generous mouth lifted in a smile. 'Don't tell him.'

Before she could stop herself she heard herself say, 'You could always move back to England to be closer to him.'

She turned away from how his expression fell, winced when he said, 'My life is here now. I'll never leave Cognac again.'

Picking up a small bronze figurine of a cat from the side table, she said, 'That's quite a turnaround from before.' She lifted her gaze to study him. 'You used to say that there was nothing here for you.'

'Things change.'

'But not people. They just reveal their true selves to you.'

'I never—'

Regretting instantly the bitterness of her voice, that she'd revealed her upset with him, Hannah interrupted with a forced laugh, 'You're certainly putting my wedding present of a set of organic cotton bath towels into the shade with this villa.'

Laurent shook his head. 'The infamous wedding list.' Pausing, he gave a smile. 'It has caused a lot of amusement amongst my parents' friends.'

Hannah swallowed a giggle, imagining the other guests' bewilderment at some of the items Lara and François had listed. 'I think water filters, recycled furniture and garden equipment for their allotment are very practical gifts to ask for.'

Laurent's eyebrow lifted. 'My father had to explain to a friend of his who's a guest at the wedding what a wormery is. Trust me, it was a very long telephone conversation.'

Hannah smiled, trying so hard to pretend that she was

finding all this easy, a bittersweet thickness forming in her throat at how easily they fell back into their shared humour and banter.

Silence fell between them. Laurent's smile receded. The room closed in around them. She looked away from him. But even then she felt the force of his gaze. Heat grew on her cheeks, a rumble of attraction stirred in her stomach and, when she glanced back at him, it exploded at the rigidity of his expression—his square jawline fixed, his dark thick brows drawn downwards, his mouth stern. She'd at first been drawn to his easy charm but it was this more private, serious-minded side of him—the responsible older brother who was so protective of his only sibling—this self-assured and professionally astute man she'd fallen in love with.

His jaw moved a fraction. The chemistry that had always been so strong, so potent between them was at work again.

She willed herself to walk away, to break the silence, regretting having come here.

His mouth tightened. The knot of fear and anticipation twisted even tighter in her stomach.

'How have things been for you?'

She jolted in surprise at his question. His voice, as always, like warm honey trickling through her insides. For a moment she was about to answer in a similarly low intimate tone, but caught herself in time and instead, with a flourish of bonhomie that took even her by surprise, she walked away, pretending to inspect the books in the bookcase. 'Great. I've been busy. Emily married late last autumn in Granada in Spain. We had a great week there—it really is a beautiful city and it was so nice for all of my family to have spent the time together.' Her forced smile was replaced by a genuine one when she added, 'And Cora had a little girl. She's called Diana. She's gorgeous. I'm totally smitten by her.'

Laurent smiled at her description. For the briefest moment, the old ease that had existed between them flared. Hannah was thrown; her smile faded, and disappeared altogether when she thought of her sisters' happiness. She loved her sisters with all her heart and would never begrudge them anything...but faced with how content they were, how successfully they managed their personal lives, Hannah not only felt lonely but also doubted she would ever manage to achieve a similar happiness.

Laurent winced as the wistfulness in Hannah's expression was replaced with an unsettling sadness. She wanted what her sisters had. Marriage, children, a united family. The things he could never give to her.

He gestured for her to follow him into the kitchen, a sudden urge to keep moving, to be distracted by doing things, taking hold. 'Let me show you around. I had an interior designer manage the renovations and furnish the rooms but I could use your advice as to whether there are additional items Lara would like.'

Hannah walked around the island unit of the hand-painted kitchen, her gaze shifting out onto the garden and the river beyond. 'Have they seen the villa since you redecorated?'

Earlier, when she'd asked why they were here, for a moment he'd been thrown by the fact that she didn't know. Somehow it felt as though she should know everything that was happening in his life. 'Not since their last visit. They had wanted to stay here before the wedding day but I told François that there was a problem with the electricity.'

'When are you going to tell them?'

'I'll give them the key on their wedding day. They can spend their first night here together.'

The weariness in her expression faded and the warmth he'd so adored about her in London appeared. She gestured around her, towards the kitchen and then the garden outside. 'Lara is going to be so happy. She has always wanted a garden of her own. Right now they only have their allotment and that's miles away from their apartment.' In this enthusiasm, her happiness for her friend, he realised how much he'd missed her. He missed this warmth, her laughter, her sheer presence.

Pointing towards a notebook hanging from the kitchen's noticeboard, he said, 'Take a look upstairs and note down anything you think I should get the interior designer to add.' Then, backing towards the garden door that led out onto the newly laid patio, he added, 'I need to check out some work that was carried out in the garden today.'

Outside, he walked across the stone patio—as he'd guessed, the contractor had done a good job—hating his need to get away from Hannah. From her smile. Hating the reality of what he'd walked away from.

He was standing on the riverside steps when she came out and joined him ten minutes later, handing him a bullet-point list in her neat and precise handwriting. She'd listed bathrobes, champagne, Belgian chocolates, decaffeinated coffee and a double hammock. He lifted an eyebrow at that last item.

Hannah laughed and gestured towards the giant willow. 'It'd be fun for them if it was hung from the willow across to the boundary trees. I can see them lying there on their wedding night staring up at the stars before going to bed.' Her voice trailed off and her gaze dropped down to the new wooden rowing boat that he'd asked his interior designer to organise.

Heat radiated from the stone of the river steps. There was a vague creaking noise as the overheated house and earth shifted in expansion. But the heat on Hannah's cheeks, the heat in his belly, had nothing to do with the weather and everything to do with her mention of bed. In London, they would meet after work sometimes in the city, other times he would meet Hannah off her train in Richmond if he'd been travelling that day, with the intention of having a drink or a meal, a visit to the theatre, but more often than not they would head directly home and into bed and only surface hours later to eat before tumbling back into bed until the following morning.

Hannah had always craved chocolate after they had made love. She had a particular love for dark chocolate straight from the fridge. 'Do you still have an addiction to chocolate?'

Her head whipped around at his question, a spark of anger in her eyes. 'I try to stay away from things that aren't good for me these days.'

He forced himself to smile, knowing he deserved that comment.

She folded her arms, stared across the river towards the bank of poplars growing there. She bit her lip for a moment and paused in deep thought before saying, 'Now I know what's missing in the house—I couldn't put my finger on it for a while—family photographs. You should get some framed and placed around the house to add a personal touch. I can send you some of Lara and her family.' She paused and considered him. 'You don't think it's a good idea?'

He rubbed the back of his neck and admitted, 'I can't remember the last time my family had a photo taken together.'

She grimaced. 'Not with your dad being ill and everything.'

He didn't bother to tell her that it was probably close to a decade since they'd had a family photograph taken. In the years after he'd left home, Laurent had rarely returned to Château Bonneval, and when he had his visits had always been brief. Some briefer than others when he would leave almost immediately, completely frustrated when his father would refuse to listen to his advice on saving the business.

He walked down the steps and, pulling the boat towards himself, stepped into its hull and turned to Hannah. 'Let's go for dinner. The restaurant is a ten-minute row down the river.'

Hannah stepped back on the grassy verge and considered him. As she tilted her head to the side her ponytail swept against her shoulder, exposing the arched curve of her neck, and a memory of her giggling when he used to press his body to her back, place his lips on the tender skin of her neck, left him momentarily dizzy. The boat rocked beneath him. He jerked, almost losing his balance.

Hannah laughed. He shook his head at her amusement at his predicament and almost lost his balance again.

When she joined him on board she sat down as clumsily as possible, obviously in the hope of tipping him into the river.

Laurent effortlessly rowed against the light flow of the water and Hannah studied the neighbouring gardens they passed by, seeing in the long and narrow plots the unfurling of family life. A woman on a recliner reading a newspaper while her husband clipped a bay tree. A family of five sitting at the edge of the river eating dinner beneath a huge oak tree and stopping to wave hello as they passed by. Hannah wanted this domesticity but would it ever happen for her?

A surge of anger towards Laurent caught her by surprise. Why had he come into her life? Why, when she'd lowered her defences for the first time ever, thereby allowing herself to fall for a man, had he broken her heart? And as she watched him pull on the oars, his shirtsleeves rolled up, his forearm muscles bunching with each pull, her anger soared even more. She didn't want to be so aware of him, so giddy around him, so vulnerable, and her resolve that she would never let him get to her again hardened.

She needed to remember his faults. He liked to eat strong-smelling cheeses that had made her gag whenever she'd opened his fridge. He took work even more seriously than she did—how often had he cancelled dates or forgotten about them, to her annoyance? And despite his gregarious personality, in truth he was a closed book. She knew so little about his background, his family. And he had a birthmark on his bottom. Okay, so she'd admit that that was actually cute.

'You're starting to scare me.'

She jumped at his voice. 'What do you mean?'

'You look like you're trying to figure out the most effective way of murdering me. In fact, it reminds me of the evening your work colleagues came to a party in my house.'

Their first fight. 'You were over an hour late for your own party. My colleagues were wondering if you were a figment of my imagination.'

His eyes glinted. 'Ah, so, despite your denials to the contrary, you had been talking to them about me as I had suspected.'

I couldn't stop talking about you. I could see my col-

leagues' amusement as I recounted things you had said and done, day after day, but I was too giddy with amazement over you to stop. 'They wanted to see for themselves if your wine collection was as impressive as I said it was.' She smiled when she admitted, 'My senior partner especially. He was rather put out when he saw it was a much more extensive collection than his.'

And then she remembered what had happened that night after the others had left, how Laurent had made love to her in the moonlight that had streamed through the window and onto the floor of his bedroom, his eyes ablaze with passion and emotion.

She dropped her head. Inhaled against the disturbing mix of desire and pain that was grabbing her heart.

'How's work?'

She looked up at his softly spoken question. Had he guessed she was remembering that night on his bedroom floor? Her anger resurged. 'I've been offered a promotion which would involve a transfer to the Singapore office.'

Up ahead on a bend in the river, below a string of lights threaded through trees, a wooden sign on the riverbank announced that they had arrived at La Belle Epoque.

Laurent guided the boat towards the restaurant's river steps, nodding approvingly to her news. 'That's fantastic. When are you moving?'

He shifted the oars inside the boat, wood upon wood making a solid thump, a sound just like the thud her heart gave to his enthusiastic congratulations.

She gritted her teeth and eyed him, not caring at the hurt heat flaming in her cheeks. Did he not even feel a single pang that she would be moving so far away? How could he not realise how torn she was about leaving her family behind?

The move to Singapore was an incredible opportunity, but in truth, deep down, she was scared of being lonely... forgotten by her family.

'Are you going to accept?'

She shrugged at his question. 'Do you think I should?'

He considered her for a moment and then those blue eyes blazed with an ominous energy. 'Is something or somebody keeping you in London?'

She folded her arms. 'Perhaps.'

The blaze in his eyes intensified. 'Are you dating someone?'

She'd been on some dates during the past few months; wasn't getting back on the figurative horse the best way to get over a fall? By dating other guys she'd hoped that maybe she could rekindle the hope and optimism and openness that had been growing in her before she'd met Laurent, but her dates hadn't been a success. She'd felt too wary, had struggled to connect with them. Now she clung to the hope that maybe it was just a case that she'd tried dating too quickly and that with time she would be more open to a relationship...but she feared that maybe she would never find it inside herself to trust a man again. 'How about you? Are you seeing someone?' she countered.

Laurent stood and jumped onto the landing steps, jealousy coiling in his stomach. For the past year he'd immersed himself in work, driven by the need to prove himself as a worthy CEO, but now as he turned to find Hannah's eyes sparking with anger he realised it was also to distract himself from the pain he'd caused her. He held out his hand and Hannah reluctantly took it. When she leaped, her hand tightened for a split second on his but the moment her foot touched the step she snatched it away.

They stood facing each other, the air between them dense with tension.

Hannah's jawline tightened. 'So, are you dating someone?'

'I'm too busy with work.'

'You worked crazy hours in London—it didn't stop you dating then.'

'It's different now.'

'In what way?'

She was testing him, pushing him for an answer and he wasn't sure what her question really was.

'Running a family business is complicated.'

Her nose wrinkled at that.

He pulled in a breath and admitted, 'After what happened between us, I don't feel like dating.'

'Yet?'

Would he ever want to date again? Right now, he couldn't see himself wanting to ask another woman out. But he couldn't admit that to her so instead he simply shrugged.

She looked at him with a puzzled expression. 'You're the one who ended it.'

When he'd ended their relationship, he'd used the excuse of needing to focus on his new life in France. And the fact that they wanted different things in life, namely that he wasn't interested in marriage. He'd kept from her the actual reasons why he would never marry, how his trust in others had been destroyed as a teenager, because to do so would have meant revealing his true self to her, a self he spent most of the time trying to avoid.

They shifted apart at the sound of footsteps behind them. Gabriel, the owner of La Belle Epoque, greeted them warmly and guided them to an outdoor table with views of a weir and an old mill.

Local teenagers were playing in the river, laughing and calling to one another in the evening sunshine.

After Gabriel had taken their order and poured them a glass of white wine each, Hannah smiled as one of the teenagers swung over the river, whooping loudly before landing with an enormous splash in the water, which earned her applause from her gang. 'When we were teenagers and the weather was fine, I used to go down to the river that ran through our land with Cora and Emily to swim and hang out. Did you and François do the same?'

'We spent our summers with my grandparents in Paris.'

She placed her elbow on the table and balanced her chin in the cup of her hand. 'I thought Parisians left the city for the summer. Why didn't they come here?'

'My grandparents moved to Paris after my father took over the family business.' He stopped with the intention of saying no more, but thanks to Hannah's expectant silence he found himself eventually admitting, 'There were arguments. My grandfather didn't approve of how my father was running the business, so they moved away. When we were old enough I asked my grandfather if François and I could spend the summers with them in Paris.'

'Did your parents not mind?'

He couldn't help but give a rueful laugh. 'They were too busy to even notice we weren't around.'

She grimaced but then, ever the optimist, asked with excitement, 'Did you like Paris?'

'We both loved it. François even stayed and finished his final years of school there.'

Her brows shot up. 'Wow, I couldn't see my parents agreeing to that—they even struggled when we left for university. Your parents obviously encouraged you to be independent.'

She was reading the situation all wrong. Not surprising given her background. Once again this evening he felt torn between changing the subject and telling her about his family. Before, he'd never felt that compulsion. In London, he'd been able to block out his past, but being back in Cognac for the past year had stirred up all the memories and emotions of how betrayed he'd felt by his parents' affairs.

'Is everything okay? You seem upset.'

He started at Hannah's words. She'd always been so good at reading his moods.

'Our family life was rather chaotic. I persuaded François he would do better in a calmer environment.'

'Have you always been the protective older brother?'

He grinned at the playfulness of her question. 'Probably.'

Hannah grinned back and then in a flash memories and attraction danced between them.

His throat tightened.

Hannah twisted her wine glass around and around. 'It was a shame you couldn't make Lara and François's civil ceremony in London last week. I know François was disappointed but at least your father was well enough to travel with your mother.'

'I was travelling in Asia—promoting the House.'

She snorted, clearly not buying his answer. 'I reckon, given your views on marriage, that you were simply avoiding the ceremony.'

'That's possibly true too.' Seeing her smile of satisfaction that she'd called it right, he added, 'But before you accuse me of disloyalty or not playing my part, can I point out that there is no tradition here in France of there being a best man at weddings? But as Lara is keen to have her sister as her bridesmaid, to keep some British traditions, I have agreed to be the best man.'

She laughed at that. 'You make it sound as though you have agreed to take a place on a battlefield.'

Was marriage, commitment, trusting in others, so easy for her? 'Did you mind being asked to be the wedding celebrant?'

'I was honoured. What else did you expect?'

He wanted to say that he thought she should have said no to François and Lara. But instead he said, 'Are you actually enjoying the work? It can't be easy combining it with your day job.'

'You still don't understand why I want to be a celebrant, do you?'

'It's not the career direction a young and successful finance director usually takes.'

Their conversation was interrupted by one of the waiting staff arriving with their orders: *salade au saumon et l'avocat* for Hannah, double *carpaccio de boeuf* for himself.

After they had eaten for a few minutes in silence, Hannah placed her cutlery on her plate and said, 'I love being a wedding celebrant because I want to contribute something meaningful to people's lives.' She paused and looked at him with a determined pride. 'I need something positive and uplifting in my life.'

He lowered his own cutlery. 'I'm sorry that I hurt you.'

She sat back in her chair, folded her arms and stared towards the teenagers who were walking home through the meadow on the other side of the river. 'It's in the past.'

'We'll see each other in the future. I don't want to cause you any further hurt.' For reasons he didn't under-

stand he felt compelled to add, 'Nothing has changed…
there can be no future for us.'

Her gaze flew back to him. Anger now sparked in her
eyes. She stood. 'It's been a year. I'm over it… I'm over
you, Laurent. I've moved on. Don't overinflate your importance in my life.'

CHAPTER THREE

THE FOLLOWING DAY, leaving his Sales and Marketing director to wrap up a meeting with the buyers from an international airline in the tasting room, Laurent rushed back to his office located in the recently opened modern extension he'd commissioned last year. Designed by world-renowned architect, Max Lovato, the acclaimed building was his signal to the world that Bonneval Cognac was about to retake its positon as the most exclusive cognac brand in the marketplace.

A wide walkway joined the second floor of the old cognac warehouse to the executive floor of the new building. Max's vision of the walkway resembling a floating garden had been realised thanks to an extensive and lush planting scheme of mature trees and plants that had produced an eye-watering bill.

Laurent rolled his shoulders against the financial pressures that perched there permanently these days like an overloud and insistent chatterbox parrot. Only time would tell if his ambitious and costly expansion and marketing strategy would pay off. If they didn't make the projected sales figures he'd forecast for this year, things could get very difficult. He would even have to seriously consider selling a share of the business. Which in his eyes would be nothing less than abject failure.

His assistant, Mila, rose from her chair when he entered her outer office and gave him an apologetic smile. He shook his head as if to say that he understood why she'd called him out of his meeting—they both knew of old how obstinate his father was.

When he entered his office he gritted his teeth at the sight that welcomed him—his father sitting behind his desk flicking through his paperwork. When was he going to accept his retirement, that Laurent and not he was now the CEO of Bonneval Cognac?

'Ah, Laurent.' His father gave him a smile, the left side of his mouth not rising quite as high as the right. Laurent felt his frustration ease at this reminder of his father's stroke, but it flourished again when his father added, 'You took your time.'

Laurent breathed down his irritation. 'I was meeting with AML Airlines. We're trying to persuade them to carry our XO Exclusif in their first-class cabins.' Seeing his father's sceptical expression, he added, 'Unfortunately we have a lot of ground to make up for the way their contract was managed in the past.'

'It was not our fault that our competitors undercut us.'

He bit back the temptation to laugh bitterly at his father's poor defence and said instead, 'We didn't negotiate the contract renewal properly. We backed them into a corner where they had no choice but to go with the competition.' He paused, about to say that living off past glories and perceived status had no place in today's business world.

For long seconds he and his father glared at one another. But then a discreet cough from behind him had him spin around to find Hannah.

He nodded in acknowledgement of her presence and received a lukewarm smile in response. She was still angry with him for reiterating last night that they had no future together. But he'd needed to say it, for his sake as much as hers—there was too much lingering physical attraction between them, which, thrown into the mix of the crazy emotions that came with a wedding and their forced proximity over the weekend, could lead them to doing something that they both regretted. After their dinner last night they had travelled back to the château in silence and he'd left for work this morning before dawn, leaving a note to say that he'd taken Bleu to stay with his friend Phillippe for the duration of her visit.

'This morning I gave Hannah a tour of the House.' Laurent turned his attention to his father, who added, 'Hannah was all alone in the château when your mother and I returned from Bordeaux. François and Lara were delayed in the city.' His father shook his head in reprimand. 'We can't have our house guests not entertained, Laurent. It's your duty as a host to ensure they're well cared for. I had planned on taking Hannah to lunch now but your mother is insistent that I return to the château— she's getting much too stressed about this wedding. I want you to take Hannah to lunch instead.'

Laurent was about to say no. He'd a string of meetings this afternoon he'd yet to prepare for. But he could tell his father was waiting for him to object. His father relished arguing with him. And he certainly wasn't going to embarrass Hannah by having an argument over who would take her to lunch.

Before he could say anything, though, Hannah stood. 'Antoine, I'll drive you home.' She gestured to his paper-strewn desk. 'I'm sure Laurent is busy.' Giving him a brief smile, she turned towards the door.

His father walked after her. 'I don't need you to drive me. I called François and told him to collect me on his way back from Bordeaux. He and Lara are downstairs waiting for me. You should see more of the town. You can accompany me downstairs on the way. I need to rush, though—apparently François and Lara are late for a meeting with their wedding planner.'

Hannah looked at him helplessly. Obviously waiting for him to argue against taking her. His father, meanwhile, looked all set to have an argument with him. 'It'd be my pleasure to take you to lunch.'

Hannah regarded him curiously. 'You never liked to take lunch in London.'

She was right. In London he'd worked at a furious pace; he still did so here, but he somehow also managed to fit in lunch and regular runs. He regarded Hannah, only now realising how well his new life suited him despite the pressures of his role. Aware of his father's keen gaze on them both, Laurent shrugged. 'I guess Cognac and the way of life here has changed me.'

For a moment he thought Hannah was going to ask what he meant but instead she held out her arm for his father to take.

Laurent grimaced and waited for his father to bat Hannah's arm away, as he did any other offer of help—he'd even thrown the walking stick his physio had given him out of one of the château's windows one day, and had grumbled like crazy when Bleu had gone and fetched it back.

But instead of rejecting Hannah's offer of assistance, his father placed his hand on her arm and Laurent followed them as they moved in the direction of the elevator, his father's limp slowing their progress.

Downstairs, his father chuckled when they walked outside to find François and Lara propped against the fountain in the entrance courtyard, arms wrapped around one another, Lara giggling as François whispered into her ear.

'*Le jeune amour est si puissant*...young love is so powerful,' his father said quietly.

Laurent rolled his eyes. His father certainly knew about love, or, in his case, lust and ego. Had he ever loved all those other women? In his teenage years, Laurent had been certain that his parents didn't love one another. How could they when they'd had those affairs? Yet they'd kept coming back to one another. And now, since his father's stroke, they were closer than ever. His head ached from trying to understand them. *Young love*—his gaze shifted to Hannah. She was the only woman he'd ever come close to loving.

His jaw tightened to see how she was watching Lara and François's playful flirting.

With a shriek, Lara broke away from François and ran to Hannah. The two women embraced, laughing and chatting over one another. Laurent looked away from the delight shining in Hannah's eyes, at the relief lightening her whole expression. It was as though in Lara she'd found a safe and secure harbour. Had she ever reacted like that with him? On occasion, but now, with the distance of time, he could see that even in the depths of their relationship Hannah had held herself back, as though uncertain of him. Why was that? Had she rightly sensed in him a man damaged by his past, a man who would bring her no happiness?

The Bonneval Cognac House was located on the outskirts of the town, its high greystone perimeter wall surrounded by pretty tree-lined roads and the Charente River to the south. When Hannah had driven the ten miles from the château to the House with Laurent's father, Antoine, this morning, for the first time since arriving in France she'd managed to relax, thanks to Antoine's easy company.

He'd surprised her by his quietness. When he and Laurent's mother, Mélissa, had arrived at the château he'd been like a whirlwind of charm and activity. But in the car after five minutes of idle chatter, he'd closed his eyes. She'd assumed he'd fallen asleep but as she'd slowed for a red traffic light as they'd neared the town, he'd said with his eyes still closed, 'I'm sorry for being such poor company. I get so tired at times.'

Hannah had been tempted to reach out and touch him, to respond to the bewilderment in his voice.

'It's okay. I enjoy silence, having time to think,' she'd said instead.

It was a while before he'd responded, 'You're sad.'

Hannah hadn't known how to answer, feeling completely undone by the simplicity of his statement. 'I was before.'

He'd opened his eyes at that, the intensity of the Bonneval blue-eyed gaze faded with him, but still more than capable of seeing through her pretence.

His quiet calm in the car, his attentiveness as he'd guided her around the distillery and the visitor centre had been so in contrast to his combative encounter with Laurent just now that she'd been thrown by the unexpectedness of it all.

Now as she watched Laurent open the rear door of François's car and his father's refusal to accept his offer of assistance to sit into the low seat, she wondered at their relationship.

Then, having waved the others off, Laurent asked her to wait a moment before he disappeared down a cobbled laneway at the side of the reception area.

A few minutes later he was back, now riding a sleek black Italian scooter. He handed her a white helmet to wear and then pulled on a black one himself. 'I have a meeting at two. Travelling by bike will save us from having to look for parking and we'll also be able to bypass the summer tourist traffic.'

This was not how she'd planned for this weekend to work out. At worst she'd thought she'd have to observe Laurent from a distance; now she was about to ride on a scooter with him. She yanked on her helmet, trying not to stare as he pulled off his silver tie and bunched it into his trouser pocket, releasing the top buttons of his white shirt, before pulling on a pair of mirrored aviators. Did he seriously have to look so hot all of the time? Did this man have any down days? Maybe this could be a form of aversion therapy? By spending all this time with him and how it reminded her of her previous heartache, then maybe she would develop an aversion to him.

She swung her leg over the scooter seat, glad she'd opted to wear her navy Bermuda shorts instead of the new white and blue summer dress she'd bought for the weekend. For the past month as the wedding weekend had loomed ever closer she'd found herself constantly drawn to the boutiques near her work at lunchtime. She'd go out with the intention of picking up a sandwich from her local favourite deli, only to find herself in a changing room trying to convince herself that she was only there to buy new things because her existing wardrobe was dated. When in truth this weekend had been the real reason. Her trips to the beautician and hairdresser had also ostensibly been about looking professional for the wedding, but whenever she looked into the mirror, she'd wondered what Laurent would think.

She edged herself back in the seat. As far away from

him as possible, with the intention of holding on to the side of the seat, but Laurent's sharp right turn as they exited out onto the street soon had her clinging to his waist.

From the low-rise modern outskirts of the town they soon entered the old town, Laurent buzzing down narrow cobbled streets, past imposing centuries-old sandstone houses, many with ornate carvings around their doorways, past outside diners sheltering beneath sun umbrellas. They passed tourists staring into the windows of the specialist Cognac and Bordeaux wine sellers and elegantly dressed locals walking with purpose towards lunch dates.

Laurent came to a stop at a *fromagerie*.

From outside she watched him purchase some items while talking animatedly with the young blonde woman who served him. She looked away when the young woman waved out to her, annoyed with herself for feeling jealous.

Afterwards they drove along a maze of deserted alleyways, the restaurants and shops giving way to old stone warehouses, ancient pulley systems hinting at their previous use.

They came to a stop on a grassy bank by the river. Under the shade of a lime tree, he spread out their lunch of cheese, crackers, quince and a bottle of sparkling water each. She smiled and sat a distance away from him, trying not to show how thrown she felt that he'd chosen a picnic for them to share.

Laurent broke off a piece of *reblochon*, placed it on a cracker and handed it to her. At first they ate in silence, the only sound the roll of the river and birdsong from the trees lining the riverbank.

'It's so pretty here.'

Laurent grinned. 'Given your love of picnics, I thought you'd appreciate it.'

She bit into the cheese, trying to focus on the creamy texture and the nutty taste and not how her heart was melting at his warm smile, at the fondness in his voice. For want of a distraction she tentatively prodded the parchment paper of the other cheeses.

Laurent chuckled. 'I promise I haven't bought anything offensive.'

'I'm still terrified to open my fridge door.'

'Even a year later?' he asked, turning, his knee touching her thigh. Despite herself she jerked away.

She caught the disquiet that flashed in his eyes and said, 'Some fears are deeply ingrained.'

He picked up another cracker, placed a thin slice of quince paste and then some creamy Brie on top. She shook her head when he offered it to her, feeling undone by the intimacy of this picnic, the act of him preparing and offering her food.

'Dogs, pungent cheeses and hair down the plughole, I already know you fear all those...anything else you'd like to confess to?'

Reaching for a cracker and loading it with some more of the *reblochon* even though she really wanted to taste the Brie, she admitted, 'After my flight here, you can add turbulence—we were thrown around for a good ten minutes.'

Laurent's expression grew concerned. 'Were you hurt?'

'Luckily I had my seat belt fastened.' She shrugged, trying not to make a big deal of it, but in truth when the plane had been tossed around the sky she'd longed with every fibre of her being for his calm reassurance. And, tragically, seeing him again brought home the sad truth that every night for the past year when she'd come home from work to her empty apartment, she'd longed for his company. It was him she'd wanted when she'd read, heard or seen something that had fired her imagination and had been bursting to share it with someone. But he hadn't wanted her. She had to remember that. She rolled her eyes, forcing a light-hearted tone to her voice. 'I was okay until the guy next to me panicked and grabbed my hand. His grip was incredible. I had to ask him to let go after a while. He'd already told me that he was a fireman from York on the way to see his sister in Bordeaux. You'd think after five years of service turbulence wouldn't worry him.'

Laurent leaned back and threw her a sceptical look. 'That sounds to me like a perfect excuse to flirt with you.'

She was still smarting from what he'd said last night at the restaurant about them not having a future. She hated his assumption that she might even think that that was a possibility, hated that he'd no understanding that there was no way she'd ever allow herself to fall in love with him again, hated that he must have been alarmed enough by her obviously poor attempt to disguise her attraction to him to even say it... Had she given him some unconscious sign? Had she stared at him too much in the boat, been too jumpy around him? So she said, 'He did ask for my number when we landed.'

He leaned towards her, his expression a mixture of incredulous and irritated. 'I hope you didn't give it to him.'

Deciding not to answer his question, just to rile him, she said instead, 'I loved my tour of the Cognac House earlier. Your father was a great host, fun and full of great stories.'

He picked up a cracker and snapped it in two. 'He's always had an eye for a pretty woman.'

Hannah couldn't help but laugh at his disgruntled tone.

'I think we both know that I was a convenient way for him to escape the château and your mother's long list of things she wanted him to do.'

Throwing his head back, Laurent took long annoyed gulps of his water. Confused by how agitated he was at her mention of his father, she felt a desire to try to understand their relationship. She knew from their time together that he didn't have an easy relationship with his parents, his father in particular, but he'd never gone into specifics; instead he'd shrugged and said that his parents were different from him.

When he'd learned of his father's stroke, however, he'd been visibly upset. He had called her in her office, told her what had happened, and that he needed to leave for France immediately. Hannah had gone to his house, wanting to comfort and support him, but he'd rushed about packing, shutting down any attempts she'd made to discuss how he was feeling. He'd barely hugged her before he'd run out to the awaiting taxi. After that day, things had changed between them. He'd grown distant from her. Constantly preoccupied, he'd flown home to Cognac at every possible opportunity.

'He said he's probably never going to be able to drive again.'

Laurent let out a sigh. 'It's what frustrates him most.'

'Losing that freedom must be hard.'

Arching his head back, he stared up at the canopy of the tree for a few moments before saying, 'He's certainly making life hard for those around him.'

After his father's stroke, she'd once suggested to Laurent that she travel with him to Cognac but he'd said it wasn't a good idea. She'd tried to hide how hurt she was, tried to remain supportive, but increasingly she'd known that he was excluding her from his life. Now, having seen his home here, the vastness of the Cognac House, his place as CEO of such a prestigious brand, she understood why he'd seen no place for her here. She cleared her throat, trying to focus on their conversation, and asked, 'In what way?'

Propping himself back on his elbows, Laurent stretched his legs out on the grass. 'For a start he doesn't accept that he's no longer CEO of the House.'

Distracted by the sight of his long legs, the narrowness of his hips and waist in his grey trousers, the gleam of light shining from the silver buckle of his belt, remembering all the times she'd clumsily, desperately, unbuckled his belts in the past, she asked weakly, 'Can he take on another role?'

'And give him a legitimate reason to come in and interfere? I don't think so.'

His shirt was pulled tight across his chest, revealing the outline of taut skin and defined muscle beneath. She shifted on the grass, and against her better judgement angled herself a fraction closer to him, a thrilling sensation flourishing in her limbs. 'All of his experience could be a valuable asset to the business.'

His gaze lingered on her silver ankle bracelet. His blue gaze was darker than usual when he looked back up. 'I don't remember you ever wearing an ankle bracelet before.'

There was a low and seductive timbre to his voice. Her heart turned over. 'I spent the New Year in India. I bought it there as a memento.'

He sat up, leaning back on one arm. 'Did you go alone?'

'The yoga teacher I follow online, Kim Ackerman, was running a week-long course there, so I signed up for it.' She was tempted to add that it was the online videos from Kim, a London-based online yoga superstar, that had kept her sane for the past year—chasing away the memories of him that had threatened to subsume her, replacing her regrets with a more productive mindset of being grateful for what she had in life and the opportunities out there waiting for her to grab hold of. 'It was a spur-of-the-moment decision. I decided I couldn't take any more of the wet weather we were having.' She shifted away from him again, the chemistry between them making her way too jumpy. 'There must be a role in the company your father could take on with all of his experience.'

He ran a hand tiredly against his jawline and for a moment she thought he wasn't going to answer her, but then he said quietly, 'My father almost brought the business to ruin.'

'I didn't realise...'

He shook his head. 'You had no reason to.'

'Am I right in guessing that you have a strained relationship with him?'

He laughed at her question. 'That must be hard for you to comprehend, given how well you get on with your parents.'

Despite his laughter, his voice contained an edge, a disappointment, a hurt that stabbed at her heart. 'It's a shame you don't get along—is it the fact that you've taken over as CEO? In my work I often deal with family businesses. It's not unusual for there to be conflict between generations, especially when the younger one takes over. It's hard for the older generation to let go and for the younger people to listen to advice.'

He eyed her with exasperation. 'Trust me, it has nothing to do with me not listening. The issues between us go back decades.' A tic appeared on the ridge of his jawline. 'Both of my parents had affairs when I was a teenager and left each other. When the affairs petered out they would eventually return.'

Hannah startled at the raw hurt in his voice. 'Seriously?'

Laurent's eyes widened. She flinched at the crassness of her response.

'Would I joke about something like that?'

She shook her head, seeing the hurt in his eyes, her heart pulling, her mind racing to understand what it would do to a teenager to experience such turmoil. Emotion clumped in her throat—anger and sadness and compassion for a teenage Laurent trying to deal with his parents' affairs; upset and regret that he'd never felt able to tell her any of this before now. She leaned towards him, her fingers brushing against his thigh. His eyes met hers. Softly she whispered, 'That must have been so painful for you.'

Bewildered, Laurent felt the electric charge of Hannah's touch, trying to reconcile it with the empathy in her eyes. He never spoke about his past. Why then was he telling this woman whom he knew he needed to keep his distance from? His mind reeling, he knew he had to somehow downplay it all. 'It was chaotic. Escaping to Paris to stay with our grandparents helped to bring back some normality. That's why I encouraged François to stay there.'

'Why didn't you?'

'I came back to Cognac in the hope of persuading my father to hand over the business to me.' He began to fold up the cheeses in their parchment paper, placing them back into the paper bag, thrown by the realisation that it was more than just that. He'd returned because he'd feared for his mother, who had always become with-

drawn and silent whenever his father left the family
home. 'From the age of sixteen I worked in every opera-
tion in the business from the distillery to the warehouses
and Admin. I wanted to know every facet of the business inside out. When I turned twenty my grandfather
and I made one final attempt to persuade my father to
hand the business over to me but he refused. I left for
Paris after that and then London. Staying in Cognac was
pointless. The only reason I'm CEO now is because of
his stroke. It was a decision forced upon him.'

'That annoys you?'

He blinked at her question. He'd assumed his issues
with his father were because of the past, but with Hannah's question he realised it was also about his father's
lack of acknowledgement and recognition of everything
he was doing to turn the business around. 'He doesn't
trust me and questions every decision I make.'

He stood and went to a nearby bin, throwing the bag
of half-eaten cheeses into it.

Hannah was waiting at the scooter when he turned
around. She handed him his helmet and asked gently,
'Are you enjoying the role of CEO?'

That was the first time anyone had asked him that
question, the first time he'd stopped to consider it himself. 'Yes, I am. We're slowly turning the business around.
I've appointed some new talent who are as keen as I am to
see the business thrive. We've a great team with a world-
class product.' He paused as a sense of ease, almost the
freedom of self-determination, swept over him in ac-
knowledging to himself the job satisfaction the role was
giving him. Then his heart lurched at Hannah's smile at
his words, at her obvious pleasure that he was enjoying
the role. For some reason he wanted to include her in the
conversation, to, in a small way, let her know that he still

thought about her. 'I travel a lot with the role. I try to incorporate some downtime in the places I visit, especially to go and see any alternative museums.'

A glint sparked in her eye. 'I bet none have been as exciting as the lawnmower museum we visited in Finland.'

He grinned. 'Well, I did visit a museum of bad art in Berlin and a balloon museum in Perth.'

She gave him a teasing smile. 'And to think how you used to complain when I dragged you to museums in the past.'

'What can I say? You converted me to the more quirky places.' He was tempted to tell her that when he'd visited the museums he had missed her laughter, the serious way she would read out the exhibition notes, loving the peculiar facts.

'I'm jealous. They sound really cool.' Her hand coming to rest on the gear shift of the scooter, she gave him a tentative smile. 'Why did you never tell me about your childhood when we were together?'

'There was never any real cause to.' Which was the truth. But not the full story. How could he tell a woman who had grown up in a textbook happy family the truth of his dysfunctional one? What would have been the point?

'But you have now,' she said.

'In London, I didn't handle our split well. I was distracted by my father's illness, taking over as CEO, wrapping up my affairs in London. I should have explained myself better. I saw how unhappy and chaotic my parents' lives were, growing up. I don't want any of that... I can't give you what you want in life—marriage, commitment.'

'Trust me, Laurent, I'm more than aware of that fact. Anyway, I don't recall ever asking you for those things.' With an angry tilt of her chin, she asked, 'So, are you enjoying being back in Cognac? Do you miss London at all?'

Mixed with the irritation of her question was a hint of wistful hope. Softly, not wanting to hurt her, he answered the truth. 'I feel completely at home here. I hadn't realised just how much I missed Cognac when I was away. It's where I belong. Bonneval Cognac is my legacy. I passionately want to make it a success.' He rubbed a hand at the tension in his neck rather than give into the temptation of reaching over and touching the soft skin of her cheek in a bid to wipe away the frustration in her expression. 'There are aspects of London that I miss greatly, but the decisions I took when coming back to Cognac were the right ones.'

She worked her jaw, unhappy with his answer. 'You say Bonneval Cognac is your legacy but who will inherit the business if you don't believe in love, in marriage? Or will you have children regardless of all that?'

'Look, up until my father became ill, it was never certain I would inherit the business in the first place. I think for now I should concentrate on having a business to pass on. Who actually inherits it is a far-off issue that doesn't concern me right now.'

She stepped back from the scooter. 'François is so eager and happy to marry… How can two brothers be so different in their views on relationships?'

He grimaced at her question. 'When something is wrong in your life, it can make you reject it even more fiercely or the exact opposite—crave it with all your being.' She frowned in confusion so he added, 'Our teenage years were extremely volatile. My guess is that François is looking for security.'

She shook her head and laughed. 'I'm sure François has more reasons to marry than just looking for security.' She paused before adding, 'You really are cynical about love, aren't you?'

He raised a sceptical eyebrow. 'What other reasons would he have to marry?'

She blinked at his question. 'Shared dreams, friendship, companionship, loyalty, commitment...love. Will that do, or do you want me to list even more?'

'And what happens when it all goes wrong?'

'It doesn't have to.'

'More than a third of marriages here in France end in divorce.'

Hannah stared at him, the anger in her expression shifting to frustration and then sad resignation. Pulling on her helmet, she said, 'I need to get back to the Château to prepare for the wedding rehearsal later this evening.'

In no mood to prolong this conversation he jumped onto the bike and fired the engine. They were driving back towards the old town centre, her warm palms disturbingly placed on his waist, when he heard her say, 'Maybe someday you'll meet the right person who'll change your mind.'

CHAPTER FOUR

OUT BEYOND THE dining room, the softly lit swimming pool beckoned Hannah. She shifted in her seat, the silk skirt of her halter-neck dress welding to her legs. What she wouldn't give to stand and run across the lawn, unzipping her dress and tossing it aside, before diving into the water. The cool water would wash away the unbearable heat of the night. Wash away her exhaustion from trying to converse in French. The seating plan for the rehearsal dinner taking place in the formal dining room of the château had placed her at the centre of the long dining table, Nicolas Couilloud, a business associate of the Bonneval family, on her right, a school friend of François's from Paris on her left. Both men had spoken of sport and politics all night and Hannah had struggled to keep up, with her schoolgirl French.

The blissful pool water might also wash away her ever-growing anxiety about tomorrow. The earlier rehearsal hadn't gone to plan. To start with they hadn't been able to locate Antoine and Lara's dad. When the errant fathers had eventually returned to the château Lara's dad had sheepishly admitted that they had gone to visit a friend of Antoine's who owned a nearby vineyard and had stopped to taste some of his cellar. Lara and François had been decidedly tetchy and the whole rehearsal had been conducted with a frostiness in the air. Hannah had tried to lighten the mood but no one else had been inclined to follow her lead. And Laurent's silent and brooding presence hadn't helped matters either. Having him standing beside François and continually stare at her had caused her to stumble over her words.

What if the same happened tomorrow? What if she failed to capture the magic of the event? The wedding celebrant was like the conductor of an orchestra; it was she who would set the tone of the wedding. What if she messed up? Messed up in front of her best friend and the two hundred and fifty influential guests. Messed up in front of Laurent.

She cast her eye around the rest of the table. No one else seemed inclined to leave even though the meal had ended over an hour ago. Would they notice if she slipped away to work on her blessing speech? She still wasn't certain it fully captured the essence of Lara and François's relationship.

The seating plan had placed the younger generation to her left—the tension of earlier forgotten, Lara and François were chatting with their close friends who had travelled from around the world to celebrate with them. And to her right were Lara's and François's parents along with old family friends and associates, all busily chatting.

It was only she and Laurent who seemed like lone islands cast aside from the noisy anticipation that came before a big life event. Laurent was seated at the head of the table. At the pre-dinner drinks on the terrace he'd easily moved between the guests, being his usual charming self. It was only when Nicolas Couilloud had taken him aside and spoken to him that Hannah had seen him tense. He and Nicolas had ended their conversation with much shaking of heads. Instinctively she'd moved towards Laurent wanting to ask if everything was okay but, on seeing her approach, he'd turned away and spoken instead to Lara's sister and bridesmaid, Stella.

Already halfway across the terrace, suddenly without purpose, Hannah had faltered before she'd forced herself to continue, skirting past Laurent and Stella without a glance in their direction, hoping it looked to the other guests as if it had been her intention to step inside the château all along. She'd washed her trembling hands in the downstairs cloakroom, trying not to think about how beautiful twenty-four-year-old Stella looked in her red silk sheath dress with its daring slash to the thigh.

She had to give Laurent his due. He was doing an excellent job at avoiding her this evening. Which she should welcome. Wasn't that what she wanted after all—for them to keep their distance from one another? But it was so at odds with the intimacy of their conversation at lunchtime. Was he regretting having been so open with her?

She closed her eyes for a moment. Suddenly exhausted by this whole weekend. Exhausted by the wealth and culture of Laurent's life now. The opulence of the dining room, the sophistication oozing from the other guests, all reminders of the contrasting squalor of her early years. This wasn't her world. Even after she'd been rescued she'd been brought up in the warm simplicity of country life. Her dad wouldn't know a derivative, a Chagall, the difference between a Saint-Émilion and a Médoc, even if they all bit him on the bottom. And she loved him for that. Love, loyalty, family and his animals were all that mattered to him.

She was also exhausted from being so physically close to Laurent. Not only was she struggling to contain her attraction to him, but after what he'd told her today, opening himself up to her, she stupidly, crazily, felt more connected to him. The very opposite of what she'd hoped to achieve this weekend.

Why was this weekend turning out so different from how she'd imagined it would? Only this evening, Lara had decided, with the encouragement of her parents and in a nod to tradition, that she should spend tonight away from François. So now Lara, Stella and their parents were spending the night with Laurent's parents in their lodge but there weren't enough beds for Hannah to move too. It shouldn't matter but she felt excluded by this change of plans. The vulnerability, that deep fear of disconnection that sat at the core of her being, was being stirred back into life by this weekend and she hated how out of control it made her feel.

She opened her eyes. Blinked at the brightness of the room and then was dazzled by the opulent diamonds hanging from the ears and throat of Nicolas Couilloud's wife sitting opposite her.

Her gaze unconsciously moved up the table, past the other guests, her heart performing an impressive leap to find Laurent staring towards her with concern. She twisted away, trying to tune back into the conversation between Nicolas and a glamorous French movie star seated across the table from him about redevelopment plans in Cannes, where they both owned summer houses, which they were vehemently opposed to, grumbling about the effect on the already chaotic traffic.

Laurent stood. Immediately all of the chatter around the table died as all heads turned in his direction. Was it his height, his powerful build, his ridiculously masculine features that were so exaggerated and beautiful that when people first met him they were often silenced by the need to study him, or was it simply his aura of command that so effortlessly had people respond to his movement?

He gave them a smile. A closed-mouth smile. The smile he gave when being polite. 'Thank you for coming to dinner tonight. I hope you've had an enjoyable evening.' He paused and nodded in the direction of François and Lara, his smile widening in affection. 'But as we have an important and busy day ahead of us tomorrow we need to draw this night to a close.'

The guests nodded, chairs moved backwards, some of the women picked up their evening purses, but all came to a stop when from the opposite end of the table Antoine called out, 'One more drink out on the terrace.'

For the briefest moment a pulse twitched at the side of Laurent's jawline. 'We can party tomorrow. For now, we all need to rest.'

Antoine stood. The entire table swivelled in his direction. 'One more won't do us any harm.'

Now everyone turned back towards Laurent and waited for his response. His eyes narrowed.

Without thinking Hannah stood. 'As wedding celebrant I agree with Laurent. I don't want any of you tired tomorrow.' She smiled at a frowning Antoine. 'I'm expecting you to dance with me, Antoine.'

Antoine's blue eyes twinkled. 'It will be my pleasure.'

Hannah said her goodbyes to her dinner companions and then, after a quick hug with Lara, encouraging her to try and get some sleep, she slipped out of the dining room before everyone else, averting her gaze when she saw Laurent unhappily follow her hasty departure.

Laurent went to knock on Hannah's bedroom door but at the last second pulled his hand away. In the aftermath of their lunch, as the hours had passed by in a blur of work meetings and telephone calls, a chasm had opened up in him as to the wisdom of having been so frank with Hannah. Would she think less of him, knowing his background? Now, after deliberately keeping his distance from her all evening, was he really about to throw all of that good work away? It was an easy question to answer. The tension that had been etched on her face earlier when she'd sat with her eyes closed at the dining table was too profound to ignore.

He knocked on the door. Swallowed when the consideration that Hannah might answer the door in her nightwear dawned on him. Despite himself he smiled at that thought.

The door swung open. Hannah eyed him, her gaze narrowing when it honed in on his smile. She folded her arms. He mirrored the action, propping himself against the doorframe, unbalanced not for the first time at how striking she looked in her figure-hugging knee-length purple halterneck dress that accentuated every glorious curve of her body. The urge to step forward and release her hair from its tight bun had him tense every muscle in his body. 'I had the situation downstairs under control.'

She raised an eyebrow. 'Have you come all the way to my room to tell me that?'

Despite himself he laughed at her deadpan expression. Then, taking in the paperwork in her hand, he said, 'Come outside, there's something I want to show you.'

She shook her head. 'I need to prepare for tomorrow's ceremony.'

'You're nervous about tomorrow.'

She stepped back. 'No, I'm not.'

He pushed away from the doorframe. 'Come outside— what I have to show you might help you relax.'

Shoving a hand onto her hip, she answered, 'For the last time, I don't need to relax.'

Something about the tilt of her hip got to him. Shrugging off his tuxedo jacket, he stepped into the room and threw it onto the back of a bedroom chair. His bow tie soon followed.

She looked at the jacket and his bow tie with dismay. 'What the hell are you doing?'

Her horrified expression only fuelled his need to push her to be honest. 'This damn heat. Prove to me that you're okay about tomorrow by coming with me.'

She gave him a disbelieving look before slamming her paperwork down on the bedroom console table next to her open laptop and then storming out of the door. He walked behind, his eyes taking in the angry sway of her hips as she hurried along the corridor and down the stairs in her high heels.

The château was silent. Earlier, François and he had waved all the guests goodbye, but no sooner had the tailgate lights of Lara's parents' car disappeared in the direction of his parents' lodge when François had raced to his car, shouting that he needed to see Lara one more time.

Laurent had stood watching the trail of François's tail lights, envying his brother's ability to throw himself into love so wholeheartedly. But then he'd shivered despite the heat of the night and prayed that life would be good to François and Lara, that time, and the dimming of passion, the reality of committing yourself to another person for eternity, the lure of others, the selfishness that was at the core of every human being, would not destroy their marriage.

Outside he led Hannah in the direction of the estate's farm. The farm's single and double stone outbuildings were built around a cobbled courtyard, a water pump in

the centre. Opening the door of one of the smaller buildings, he stepped inside, to a chorus of chirping, inhaling
the scent of the heavy blanket of fresh straw on the floor.

She paused at the entrance and gave him a dubious
look. Then as she peered through the doorway her expression lit up. 'Oh, wow, they're so beautiful,' she whispered, taking small tentative steps towards the hen and
her seven yellow fluffy chicks.

Stopping a distance away from them, she crouched
down and watched the chicks stumble around their
mother, chirp, chirp, chirping away. 'When did they
hatch?'

The knuckled wave of Hannah's spine was exposed
by a gap in the back of her dress. He swallowed against
the memories of running his fingers along her back when
she lay beside him, a slow sexy smile forming on her lips
when it was a prelude to sex, a sated smile when it was
in the aftermath. He stuffed his hands in his pockets and
walked to stand next to her. 'Earlier today.'

She stood. 'They're adorable, but why did you bring
me to see them?'

'Remember the endless photos of newborn animals
that your mum sent to you, which you then forwarded
on to me? I thought seeing these little guys might help
you forget about tomorrow.'

She eyed him curiously. 'Do you think I *should* be
nervous?'

'You'll ace tomorrow.' He paused and watched the
chicks stumble away from their mother and then with
a jolt of alarm race back to her as though terrified they
were about to lose her. Then turning to Hannah, the
unease in her brown eyes slamming into his heart, he
added, 'You're amazing. Always remember that.'

Reddening, Hannah gave a faint smile and backed

towards the door. Outside she looked around the near-empty courtyard, a single tractor the only sign of any farming activity. 'I'm guessing there isn't a working farm here any more?'

'There was in my grandfather's time. My father let it go. I've recently employed a farm manager. He's reintroducing some livestock. I want the château to be self-sufficient.'

She nodded to this. 'Good idea.' The night sky was clear, a fat moon shedding bright light down on their surroundings. Into the quiet of the night she said in an almost whisper, as though she was telling him something very intimate, 'The option of moving to Singapore isn't the only one I'm considering. I'm also thinking about moving to Granada in Spain to become a full-time wedding consultant.'

'Really? Your career is in the city. Why would you give up everything you've achieved?'

She shrugged, the long delicate lines of her exposed collarbone lifting and falling. 'I fell in love with Granada when I was there for Emily's wedding. It would be an exciting option, a new start for me.'

He'd always thought of her as being ambitious in the corporate world only. These new ambitions made him uneasy. Unfairly and irrationally, he hated the idea that she was forging a new and unexpected life. 'What about your promotion? Your transfer to Singapore?'

'Granada is only a short flight away and Emily and her husband are planning on buying a holiday home there. Singapore is so far away from everyone I love.' Wounded eyes met his for a moment. Guilt and regret slammed into his chest. Then with a brief grimace she added, 'Do you want to talk about your conversation with Nicolas Couilloud earlier?'

When they had dated, they had been a sounding board for one another over work issues. Hannah's advice had always been solid. For a moment he considered telling her, realising how much he missed having someone to talk to about issues that were troubling him. But talking about work would feel as though they were dropping back into their old relationship. 'It's just a business issue.'

'A sizeable business issue, I'm guessing.'

He gestured for them to walk back through the lightly wooded copse that separated the farm buildings from the château. He tried to resist talking but Hannah's patient silence, the worry, the frustration of his discussion with Nicolas had him eventually blurt out, 'Nicolas is one of my father's oldest friends but he also owns the company who distributes our cognacs. He's vital in our supply chain. He has the whole market sewn up—he has no competitors with the same market reach. He told me tonight that he's going to increase his fees when our contract with him is up for renewal next month.'

They emerged from the shade of the copse. Hannah came to a stop and asked, 'Why?'

'He's citing increased transportation costs.'

'You don't believe him?'

He inhaled a deep breath, frustration clogging his lungs. 'I can't help but think that it has something to do with my father.'

Hannah's eyes widened. 'Surely not. Why would Antoine have anything to do with Nicolas's decision?'

He could not help but smile at Hannah's innocence, part of him deeply envying her for never having experienced the soul-destroying destructiveness of a dysfunctional family.

'Why are you smiling?'

He jolted at the anger in Hannah's voice. Then, shrugging, he walked away, answering, 'Not all families are sweetness and light.'

She caught up with him on the terrace. 'Do you think that I'm that naïve, that I don't understand how people hurt others driven by their ego, by fear, by insecurity? I've seen it time and time again in my work, partnerships falling apart, family businesses not surviving. And do you know what the common denominator in all of it is? A lack of communication, a lack of connection and honesty.'

He sat on the arm of an outdoor sofa and crossed his arms. 'Being an outsider is easy. Try getting mangled up in the politics and personalities and history of a family business—then such logical analysis goes right out of the door. My family aren't like yours...so bloody normal.'

Hannah eyed him angrily before shifting her gaze towards the pool and the river beyond. She folded her arms, her delicate chin jutting out furiously. 'There's nothing normal about my family.' She paused and then added softly, 'My real family.'

Laurent stood. Confused by her words. 'Real family?'

She bit her lip, her gaze refusing to meet his. Silence descended between them. He waited, thrown by the emotion playing out in her expression as she made several attempts to answer his question. Eventually she answered in a faint whisper, 'I'm adopted.'

His brain tried to process what she'd said. 'Adopted?'

Her gaze met his, a flicker of disappointment soon being replaced by anger. 'Yes. Adopted. It happens.'

'You never said before...why not? *Dieu!* Why not?' He knew he was saying the wrong things but frustration, the awful feeling he hadn't known Hannah at all, drove him on, 'Why tell me now?'

She blinked at his questions. 'After what you told me today about your parents… I guess it seemed right that you know.'

He cringed at the now calm softness of her voice, which only emphasised his own angry torrent of questions. He breathed in and out to the count of four, trying to focus on Hannah rather than his hurt that she'd never told him before. He sat on the sofa properly, gestured that she should sit on a chair opposite.

Reluctantly she did so.

'What age were you?'

She raised a hand and kneaded her collarbone. 'Seven.'

For a moment he flailed for the right way to talk about it all. He'd been an insensitive sod up until now and he desperately wanted to get this right. He gritted his teeth against the ball of failure that was rapidly growing in his gut—what type of boyfriend had he been that Hannah had never felt inclined or able to tell him this before? 'What happened?'

For a moment her concentration seemed to be on running her fingertips against the interwoven rattan reeds of her chair. But then she tilted her head in his direction, pride burning from her eyes. 'My birth parents were both drug users. My memories are hazy, as you can imagine, but I remember a lot of parties and being left alone in the house on many occasions.' She stopped and swallowed. Her bottom lip gave a quiver. 'One night the police came and took me away.'

'You were scared.'

She gave a humourless laugh. 'Terrified.'

He fell back into his chair and stared up at the night sky for a brief moment. Then with a sigh he sat forward. 'I'm so sorry, Hannah. I wish you had told me before now.'

'What difference would it have made?'

Her question was a challenge. She wasn't hiding that fact in her direct gaze as she waited for his response, in the tension of her body, one leg wrapping around the other tightly at the calf. Would knowing about her adoption have changed anything? He swallowed and admitted, 'Maybe I would have been kinder…maybe I would have taken better care not to hurt you.'

Hannah's heart crumbled at the softness of Laurent's tone, at the sincerity of his expression. But at the same time her brain stirred in indignation and demanded that she show some pride. 'For crying out loud, Laurent, I don't need your pity just because I was adopted.' She sat forward in her seat, keen to change the subject, keen to bury the past once again, and the vulnerability and emptiness and confusion that arose in her any time she unearthed it all. 'If Nicolas ups the cost of distribution, what will be the impact on the business?'

Laurent eyed her with bewilderment. 'That's not of importance right now.'

She forged on. 'Will you speak to your father about it?'

He paused for a moment, clearly toying with whether to allow her to change the subject, but then with a sigh admitted, 'For all I know my father could be behind this price increase.'

Her mouth dropped open. Was he being serious? 'Why would he do that?'

His expression darkened at her disbelief. Tensely he answered, 'My father didn't want me to take over as CEO. It was my mother who insisted upon it. He would love to see me fail.'

Hannah shook her head. 'Are you sure? Maybe your father knows nothing about it. Why not at least talk to him? Maybe he has some advice he can pass on to you. Surely he doesn't want to see the business struggle… which I'm guessing it will, based on how anxious you looked all night.'

'I did?'

She could not help but smile at his annoyance that she'd spotted his tension. 'Don't worry, no one else would have noticed. But I know the signs—your right eye twitches.'

He crossed his arms. 'It does not.'

She laughed. 'Yes, it does.'

He shook his head but his bright blue eyes gave away his amusement. Then softly he said, 'We did have some fun times together, didn't we?'

Her smile faded. She swallowed at the fondness in his eyes. Despite herself she heard herself admit, 'Yes, we did.'

He gave her one of his wide-mouthed smiles that always reduced her to putty. 'Do you remember the night we went kayaking on Lake Saimaa?'

Hannah smiled in remembrance of the stunning beauty of the crystal-clear Finnish lake and exploring it under the summer midnight sun. 'How could I forget? It was magical.'

'And the time we went snowboarding in Ještěd?'

Hannah grimaced. 'I reckon the locals are still deaf from my screaming.' She paused and threw him an accusatory glare. 'And you were all Mr Cool, zipping around the place, showing off.' She could see that he was about to object, so she interjected, 'Never mind the travel, what I miss is having a gorgeous meal cooked for me in the evenings. You've ruined me to the pleasure of a ready meal for ever.' Only when she'd said those words did she cringe and wonder why she did.

She sighed in relief when he laughed and added, 'And I miss having you there in the mornings to pick out my ties.'

She shook her head. 'I'm still convinced that you're colour-blind.'

He stood and held out a hand to her, to help her rise. She took it, every cell in her body responding to its familiar strength. She went to take her hand away, but Laurent tightened his grip and stepped even closer. For long seconds he studied her, his blue gaze quickening her heart, sending fire into her belly. The scent of lavender hung heavily in the air, almost drugging in its density. In a low voice he eventually said, 'You never answered my question as to whether you're seeing anyone.'

Heat formed on her cheeks. Her throat grew dry. He always had this effect when he stood this close, when he spoke, when his eyes played games with her heart. She lowered her gaze to his mouth. She wanted to kiss him. She wanted to kiss him hard and remind him of everything he walked away from. But instead she whispered, 'Stella is young—don't break her heart.'

He let out a low disbelieving sigh and said in a grumble, 'She's at least ten years younger than me.'

'Eight actually, which is nothing.'

He inched forward, forcing her to tilt her head to meet his stare. 'I'm not interested in Stella.' Heat and chemistry and emotion whirled and twisted around them.

Hannah blinked, trying to shake off the hot need burning through her veins, the cloud of desire that was fogging her brain to everything but the desire to feel his lips, to touch the hard muscle of his body. Just for one more time. What was the harm?

She leant forwards and then up onto her tippy-toes. His eyes darkened. She angled her head, shifted an inch away from his mouth. Her head swam with his nearness, with his familiar scent and heat. With a whimper of annoyance she placed her mouth on his.

It took a few seconds for her to realise that he wasn't responding to her kiss.

He didn't want this.

Shame exploding in her chest, she went to pull away.

But at her movement his arms wrapped around her waist, stopping her, and he kissed her with an urgency that had her instantly on fire. Her breasts, pushed hard against his chest, immediately felt tender and desire trickled through her body like an illicit pleasure. His kiss grew ever more hot and demanding and she met that demand, wanting to punish him. One hand wrapped around his neck, holding him closer, the other ran over the heat of his chest, past the soft leather of his belt and then lightly over his trousers, euphoria spreading through her when he groaned. She wanted to make love with him.

At that thought she broke away.

Panting hard, they stared at one another. What self-destructive part of her would sleep with him? Her ridiculous pride that wanted him to regret ending their relationship?

She flailed for something to say. Eventually she realised she could find a safe harbour in his business concerns. 'What's the worst-case scenario if Nicolas increases his fees?'

Laurent gave a disbelieving laugh. 'You kiss me and then ask a question like that.'

She decided to try to brazen this all out. 'To answer your earlier question, yes, I've been on dates, but none recently. I'm a young woman with desires.' She stopped as she inwardly cringed, before adding, 'I guess this wedding is bringing them out more than usual.'

Laurent's mouth dropped open. 'Are you propositioning me?'

'Are you kidding? It was a kiss. Nothing more. A moment of physical weakness from me. Don't get ahead of yourself.'

Laurent frowned. 'Hannah, you know—'

'Yes, yes.' Hannah interjected. 'Trust me, you were more than clear about our future in London, just as clear last night and again today at lunchtime.' She winced at the bitterness in her voice and decided to change tack. 'Now, putting my professional hat on, can I advise that you speak to your dad? I know how difficult it is to put the past behind you, but surely the future is more important?'

With a look of exasperation he sighed. And then, his expression sobering, he considered her for much too long before asking gently, 'Are you in contact with your birth parents?'

Hannah eyed the main doorway into the château and the softly lit hallway beyond. She swallowed before she admitted, 'They both died. Soon after I was taken away my dad overdosed. My mum died ten years ago.'

'Dieu!'

Her gaze shot back to his, disappointment barrelling through her at the disgust in his voice. 'Not very pretty, is it?'

Laurent grimaced. 'I wish you had told me.'

Hannah edged towards the doorway, suddenly feeling beyond exhausted. 'Just as I wish you had told me about your childhood.' She gestured inside. 'I need to go and check over my paperwork for tomorrow.'

She'd stepped onto the marble floor of the hallway when he called out, 'I thought we had known one another.'

She tried not to wince at the tired bewilderment in his voice. Turning, she nodded in agreement, her heart once again tumbling on seeing him. She forced herself to give him a smile of encouragement. 'Speak to your dad.'

He shook his head. 'I'll find a solution…by myself.'

Her exhaustion washed over her like a fresh wave. 'Do you let anyone into your life, Laurent?'

A deep frown bisected his forehead. 'Maybe it's safer not to let others in.'

She understood why he thought that way. She too carried hurt and pain and ghosts from the past. 'Perhaps it's safer, but I'm guessing it's an unhappier life for doing so.'

CHAPTER FIVE

THE FOLLOWING AFTERNOON, at the entrance to the walled garden, Laurent pulled François to a stop. François eyed him restlessly, keen to keep moving. Placing a hand on François's shoulder, Laurent looked him straight in the eye. 'Relax. Everything is going to be okay.'

François let out a frustrated breath. '*Dieu!* I feel sick with nerves.'

Laurent rolled his eyes, deliberately being obtuse. 'I still don't understand why you're insisting on marrying, but if you are going to do it at least try to relax and enjoy it.'

François shook his head and laughed. 'You're not fooling me, Laurent. I know how much you love Lara. Deep down I know you're happy to see us marry.'

Laurent held his hands up in defeat. 'Okay, I'll admit you two might actually make it work.'

François smiled triumphantly. 'I can't believe you've actually admitted that. You've made my day!' Then, looking down, he scuffed his shoe off the brickwork of the garden path before saying, 'It's good to have you by my side, you know.'

Laurent swallowed, taken aback by the affection in François's gaze. As brothers, they weren't given to displays of emotion. He lifted an eyebrow. 'I'm going to make you pay for it somehow.'

François laughed. 'I appreciate the supreme sacrifice you're making by being my best man.'

Laurent grinned at his brother but then, sobering, he said, 'Whatever my views on marriage, I do wish you and Lara every happiness.' Then taking a key from his tux jacket, he handed it to François. 'My wedding gift to you both: Villa Marchand. I've had it renovated for you.'

His eyes wide in surprise, François weighed the key in the palm of his hands and shook his head. It was a considerable time before he managed to say, in a voice choked with emotion, 'I'm lost for words… I've loved that house ever since I was a boy and Lara fell in love with it too when we visited there last summer.'

Laurent shrugged, trying to pretend not to be choked up at François's delight. 'I know. That's why I'm giving it to you. You can stay there tonight if you wish, rather than here in the château.' He gave François a grin. 'I thought you might like the privacy. Hannah visited the house with me Thursday night and suggested some items that Lara might enjoy, so the house is honeymoon ready.'

François grimaced. 'How are things between you two?'

'Awkward.'

'I saw you out on the terrace last night when I returned to the château.' François paused and threw him a questioning look. 'You seemed very close.'

Dieu! Did François see them kissing? 'What do you mean "close"?'

François stepped back from his growled question. 'You were chatting, oblivious to the fact that I'd walked out to say hello—what did you think I meant?'

Guilt and relief washed over Laurent. 'You should have interrupted us. It would have been nice to chat with you over a drink. And nothing is going to happen between myself and Hannah. Relax.'

'You were so good together—' François shook his head '—but I'm not going to lecture you again on all of that.' His expression hardening, François added, 'Don't hurt her.'

Memories of their kiss last night slammed into Laurent. Turning in the direction of the garden, he said, 'I have no intention of doing so.'

He walked away but when François did not follow he turned at the doorway to the garden to find his brother eyeing him sceptically. When François eventually decided to join him, he said, 'Lara needs Hannah in her life. Promise me that you won't make things any more awkward than they already are. Stay away from her, Laurent.'

Laurent tried to make an acquiescing noise. François raised an eyebrow.

With a sigh, Laurent relented and said, 'I promise.'

Seating had been arranged on the lawns either side of the central cobbled pathway. Bows had been tied onto the rose bushes dense with blowsy blooms that were planted at regular intervals along the herbaceous border, their heavy scent filling the air. At the wisteria-covered archway that led out to the lawns of the château, a pedestal and two gilt chairs had been placed for the blessing ceremony to take place.

Laurent's heart took a sizeable wallop when he spotted Hannah breaking away from a conversation with a friend of Lara's and walking towards the pedestal. Dressed in a knee-length pale pink dress, the fitted bodice emphasising her curves, the skirt flaring over her hips, her hair tied back into a sleek ponytail, she looked both professional and as sexy as hell.

Dieu! Their kiss last night had been unbelievable. Hot, sultry, beautiful. But it'd been too much of a reminder of how much he missed her. And not just physically. It had brought home how much he missed her warmth, her gentleness, her easy presence.

Moving towards the archway, François and he nodded hello to the already assembled and seated guests. But all the while, an invisible force was pulling him towards Hannah, who was checking through her paperwork.

Her gaze shifted upwards as their footsteps neared. She smiled warmly at François and, walking towards him, hugged him tightly. 'Gosh, you look incredibly handsome, François.'

Laurent blinked at the affection in Hannah's voice, at her calm enthusiasm.

François fiddled with the collar of his tux jacket, casting a critical eye down over his suit. 'Is everything looking okay?'

Hannah adjusted his bow tie a fraction. 'There, now you're perfect.'

Then, with an unenthusiastic glance in Laurent's direction, she returned to her paperwork.

He cursed under his breath. Today was going to be as awkward as he'd feared.

The arrival of his parents kept him busy for the next few minutes as he had to encourage his father along the path as he insisted on stopping and chatting to the guests, despite the fact that the ceremony was about to start at any minute. When he then tried to assist his father to sit, his father pushed his arm away, muttering that he wasn't an invalid.

Taking his seat beside François, he tried to tune into the chamber orchestra playing to the side, tried to find some reassuring words to say to François, whose legs were jigging like crazy. But time and time again his attention was drawn back to Hannah, who was going through a constant ritual of thumbing through her paperwork and then looking expectantly towards the entranceway before glancing back to her paperwork again.

Circulate. Mingle. Do his best man and host duties. And stay the hell away from Hannah. That was the plan of action for today he'd formulated in the middle of last night when unable to sleep, thanks to the after-effects of their kiss.

But it hadn't just been their kiss that had kept him awake. It was also the haunted look in Hannah's eyes when she'd spoken about her adoption. He'd caused her enough hurt as it was. He wasn't going to add to that tally by spending time with her, which would only be asking for trouble given the chemistry that whipped between them like a live coil.

His plan of action, which had made sense in the middle of last night, had one major flaw, however. It hadn't taken into account how alone and nervous Hannah would look as she stood waiting for Lara's arrival. He moved restlessly in his chair. Telling himself to stay put. The last thing they needed were wagging tongues from those who knew of their previous relationship.

Once again Hannah's gaze shifted down over the crowd, towards the entrance. A bumblebee flew close to her. She leapt backwards, flapping her hands wildly. The bee got the message and buzzed away. With a grimace Hannah glanced nervously out towards all the assembled guests before her hands gripped the wooden sides of the pedestal, her skin flushing.

Standing, he approached her, deliberately blocking her from everyone else's view. 'I know you are going to do an incredible job...' He paused, knowing he should step away now but Hannah's brown wide-eyed expression, and the way her dress gave a faint glimpse of the valley between her breasts, pierced through all his resolve to keep his distance. 'You're looking beautiful today.'

Hannah's hand shot from the side of the pedestal to switch off the microphone.

Dieu!

Hannah glared at him.

For a moment all he could hear was the orchestra's light playing. Maybe the guests didn't hear him. That brief glimmer of hope was soon dispelled, however, when sudden whoops and claps of approval thundered behind him.

He grimaced in apology. Hannah gave him one last glare before painting a calm professional smile on her face and looking beyond his shoulder as though waiting for a stage curtain to rise. He turned from her. Shrugged at the assembled guests, many of whom they had socialised with when they had visited François and Lara in Manchester and who had let it be known of their disappointment when their relationship had ended, trying to pretend that what he'd said wasn't of significance.

He retook his seat.

Leaning in towards him, François hit him with an exasperated stare. 'So much for promises.'

Hannah knew that it was a bride's prerogative to be late. But she wished with every fibre of her being that Lara would hurry up and arrive. She was already ten minutes late. Which under normal circumstances Hannah wouldn't even notice in the special hum and excited anticipation that came with the waiting for the bride.

Why did Laurent have to come up and speak to her? She'd just about been coping up until then. For a brief few seconds when he'd looked at her with that reassuring smile of his that had her heart turn over, his eyes soft and tender, she'd felt weak with relief that he was there to support her. But then he'd spoken and the dark edge in his voice when he'd said she looked beautiful had unsteadied her. And then the echo of his voice fading out over the sound system had registered. God, she couldn't bear the thought of people speculating incorrectly that their relationship might be back on. And now, there he was, sitting in front of her, looking all gorgeous and brooding in his tux, his black dress shoes shining brilliantly, his long legs spread out in front of him, his blue gaze continually glancing in her direction, making her already frayed nerves unravel even further.

She looked out over the guests and tried to maintain her professional smile. While inside she was a churning mess of emotions. Not only was she thrown by having Laurent so close by, but she still wasn't certain that her speech was any good. Was it just rambling thoughts? Would it have any meaningfulness for Lara and François?

Why did she feel so damn lonely, so vulnerable today? It felt as though a hole were opening up inside her. Would her relationship with Lara be the same once she was married? Had she been wrong in telling Laurent about her adoption? Had it really served any purpose? She'd wanted him to understand that she too knew of broken families. That it didn't have to define you. But she'd failed to explain all of that last night. Maybe her speech today might convey some of what she was trying to say.

Of course, the irony was that even though she believed your past didn't have to define your future, she knew only too well that putting that belief into practice was easier said than done. Some fears seemed to tether you to the past by their force.

Laurent turned in his chair and, looking towards the entrance, said something to François. Hannah smiled at François's nervousness. Laurent shifted around in his seat and for a moment their eyes met. Unaccountably, tears threatened at the backs of Hannah's eyes at the light smile he gave her. The loneliness inside her deepened.

She looked away. She was *not* going to think about how she used to sit in work meetings daydreaming of one day walking towards him, becoming his wife. She used to fantasise about her dress, what her bridesmaids would wear, marrying on her parents' farm and, God help her, making love to her new husband.

Now she pulled back from the impulse to roll her eyes at her own naivety.

A movement at the entranceway had her pause and then she was smiling crazily, tears once again forming in her eyes as first Stella, dressed in a primrose-yellow midi-dress, walked down the path, soon followed by a beaming Lara on her father's arm. Her lace, full-skirted midi-dress was perfect for a summer wedding, as were the rosebuds threaded lightly through her blonde hair tied up in a loose chignon.

When Lara reached François, Hannah's heart swelled to bursting point at the love that shone in both of their eyes, at how they smiled at one another shyly. How glorious to know that you were going to spend the rest of your life with the person you so deeply loved.

Hannah gestured to them to take their seats before her. She returned Lara's excited smile. Hannah gave her ear a quick tug. Lara giggled. Ear tugging used to be their secret way of communicating to one another when in school. One tug indicated a positive reaction, two tugs a negative response.

On François's and Lara's behalf she welcomed all the guests and expressed how honoured she was to be their wedding celebrant. Then, pausing for a moment, she stared down at her speech, praying her love and hope and wishes for them would be adequately reflected in what she was about to say.

'When I was training to be a wedding celebrant I spoke to many friends, colleagues and family about what they felt was the key to a successful marriage. Many people cited love, respect, honesty, trust and kindness as being key. But another word was sometimes used as well, a word that intrigued me, because up until that point I hadn't thought of it as being important. And that word was hope.'

She paused and looked first at Lara and then François, swallowing against a catch in her voice. 'I was lucky enough to be present on the first night that you met. Immediately I could see how suited you were to one another, and the hope that immediately sprang between you. At first came the hope that the other person was feeling the same way, that they would call again. And as the weeks passed, the hope was that the obstacles you faced would not stand in your way—François living in Paris, Lara in the middle of exams.'

Hannah looked out towards the guests. 'What is life without hope? What is love without hope? We need hope to know and believe that everything in life passes. Hope allows us to work together through tough times, knowing there will be a brighter future. Hope makes us more resilient. Hope allows us to dream, to share a vision for the future. Hope is also vital in forgiveness. We all make mistakes in life and hope is central to us learning from that experience and allowing ourselves to move on.'

From the corner of her eye she saw Laurent shift restlessly in his seat. She willed herself not to look in his direction, but as she continued her gaze slowly drifted towards him. 'Hope is integral to daring to dream, daring to believe that the person you have fallen in love with will love you back for ever, will understand and support you, will respect your marriage, will be your partner and friend and confidant.'

She pulled her gaze away from Laurent's tight-mouthed grimace, loneliness swamping her heart like a lead weight. She focused instead on Lara and François. 'Hold tight to your love and hope in one another. With hope you'll conquer whatever troubles life will invariably throw at you. Hope will allow you to share a life that is optimistic and ambitious and fun. They say that marriage is a huge leap of faith, but I actually think marriage is the ultimate song of hope. The hope of believing in the magic of love, in trusting the other person with your heart, in daring to dream of a future together. With all of my heart I wish you a joyful future together.'

She paused. A fat tear rolled down Lara's cheek. Hannah smiled through the heavy emotion clutching at her heart when Lara tugged her earlobe once. Then, pulling herself together, she looked towards Stella. 'And now, before I conduct the exchanging of vows, Lara's sister, Stella, will read a poem that Lara and François have chosen to be part of today's celebration.'

Moving down the lawn towards the river where the wedding photographs were to be taken, Laurent smiled when his mother held back from the rest of the wedding party to wait for him.

'It was a beautiful ceremony.'

He nodded in agreement when she took his arm, trying to mask how much Hannah's speech had unsettled him. Hope. It was a concept he'd never considered before. He was an achiever, ambitious for his career. But the hope Hannah had spoken about during the ceremony, the hope of shared dreams, of trusting in others, did he possess any of that?

He and his mother walked in silence until his mother finally said, 'It's nice to finally get to meet Hannah.'

He studied his mother, wondering where this conversation was going.

'I'd like you to meet someone, marry one day too.'

Laurent stared at his mother. This chat was not following the normal pattern of their conversations, which usually revolved around business and social events and the practicalities of everyday life. They *never* spoke about anything personal. He was about to give a glib reply but the emotion of the day, seeing François so happy, recalling his conversation with Hannah last night had him ask instead, 'Why did you and Papa stay married? Why were you both so unhappy that you had affairs?'

His mother came to a stop. Stared at him with consternation. 'I'm not sure that's really a question for today.'

'Did you ever really love one another?'

His mother winced, but then, rolling her shoulders back, she answered, 'We married too young. We allowed our selfishness, our restlessness, our own insecurities and frustrations to get out of control—your father should never have taken over as CEO of the House. It didn't play to his strengths. From the first day, he struggled in the role and was deeply unhappy and overwhelmed, but he wouldn't admit to any of that. For me, it was hard to accept that the man I married wasn't the person I thought he was. I thought I was marrying an ambitious CEO when in truth I'd married a man more interested in buying and selling cars. But neither he nor I could accept that fact. We were too proud and we also felt the weight of family history and expectations. It soon became a vicious circle of us taking our disappointments, our frustration and hurt, out on one another. And on you two boys.'

Hard, confused anger rose up from deep inside him. 'When you and Papa walked out on us we never knew when you would return, or indeed if you ever intended to.'

His mother looked at him helplessly. 'I thought having one parent at home would be enough.'

He bit back a bitter laugh and shook his head in disbelief. 'And that was supposed to make up for the fact that I knew one of you was away with other people, enjoying life. At least you had the decency to only do it the once, whereas Papa must hold a world record for infidelity. Was it the same woman all of the time or do you even know?'

His mother blanched and then, looking down towards the lake where his father was talking with Lara's parents, said in a barely audible voice, 'You need to speak to your father. There are things he needs to explain to you.'

In the distance, walking in their direction from the lake, François called out, 'Mama, you are needed for the photos. You too, Laurent. And has anyone seen Hannah?'

His mother looked at him expectantly. As though waiting for a response. His gaze moved back towards the walled garden. Hannah was standing at the archway talking to an old university friend of François's from Paris. He heard her laughter and then she was waving him goodbye. She turned in Laurent's direction and even from this distance he could see her hesitate in coming down the path to join the rest of the wedding party.

He turned to his mother. His anger dimming at the plea in her eyes, at the age spots on her cheeks he was only noticing for the first time. 'You and Papa seem happy together now. Why is that?'

She gave him a regretful smile. 'With experience we have learnt not to hurt one another. Your father's pride and need to be in control is less of an issue and I've adjusted my expectations of him. He's a good man. I wish we both had been less worried about status in the past and focused on what was important—our family.'

Laurent ran a hand against the tautness in his neck. Studied his father giving directions to the photographer as to where he should position the waiting bride and groom. 'Are you certain being in control isn't still an issue for him?'

His mother laughed lightly, observing what was unfolding between his father and the harassed-looking photographer too. 'He can slip back into old habits like the rest of us sometimes.' She paused and grimaced. 'Speak to him, Laurent. Let him explain himself. He struggles knowing you have such a poor opinion of him.'

Taken aback, he stared down at his father, who was now slowly limping towards Lara's parents. He swallowed against a lump in his throat. Then, turning in Hannah's direction, he saw that she'd turned away and was walking back through the walled garden. 'I should go and tell Hannah that she's needed.'

He could tell his mother wanted to say more. But he needed to get away; he needed breathing space. And to his alarm he realised he wanted to be in Hannah's company right now. He needed her calmness, her ability to distract him from even the worst of his thoughts with her smile, her quick-witted humour.

He bolted up the path, close to breaking into a jog. Hannah was heading along the path towards the predinner drinks reception on the terrace when he caught up with her. 'You're wanted for some photographs.'

She looked at him as though she didn't believe him. 'I am?'

For a moment he wondered if the small pearl earrings

she was wearing would feel as smooth to his touch as her skin. And suddenly the need for lightness, to hear her reassuring laughter, grabbed him. 'You're one of the stars of today's celebrations, of course you're wanted for the photos. Especially when you are looking so beautiful.'

She eyed him suspiciously but then, with a look of curiosity, asked, 'Is everything okay? You don't seem yourself.'

She was right. But he didn't want to talk about how unsettled he felt by his conversation with his mother. 'You have that effect on me.'

She stared at him wide-eyed for a moment but then, throwing her head back in laughter, she threw her hands up. 'That's the cheesiest line I've heard in a very long time.'

She walked away from him in the direction of the river. He watched her for a moment, cursing his inability to think straight, his pulse upping a notch when he took in the sway of her hips and those much too sexy strappy sandals in the same shade as her dress that had distracted him throughout the wedding ceremony. When he caught up with her he said, 'Well done on a great job. The ceremony was excellent.'

'Even to a wedding cynic like you?'

He smiled at the scepticism in her voice. 'You don't have to personally believe in something to be able to identify brilliance.'

A hint of a smile flashed on her mouth. 'Just don't try broadcasting that to the other guests, will you?'

He swallowed a chuckle. 'Sorry about that. I hadn't realised the microphone was on.'

For a moment her gaze met his and they shared a moment of private amusement that flowed over him like calming balm.

In the distance, they could see the wedding party.

François and Lara were leaning against a tree barely taking notice of the photographer, who was circling them, snapping them from every possible angle. Lara's parents and Stella were watching them, nibbling on canapés.

And then he spotted his mother and father, a distance away from the rest of the wedding party, talking intently, their bowed heads almost touching.

He came to a stop. And stared towards them.

'Something is definitely up.'

He started at Hannah's words. And was about to deny that anything was wrong, but then his mother ran a hand against his father's cheek, the tenderness of the movement catching Laurent by surprise, and without thinking he admitted, 'My mother believes that I should speak to my father about his affairs, that he needs to explain things to me.'

'You don't want to?'

'Who in their right mind would want that conversation with a parent?'

'It might ease the tension between you. It might help you understand what happened back then. It could be your opportunity to explain how it affected you.'

She was right, but the anger inside him didn't want a rational explanation. Waving in response to the photographer's beckoning for them to join the others, he said, 'They're waiting for us.'

Shading her eyes from the glare of the sun, Hannah nodded and then, her gaze shifting towards his parents, who were now accepting glasses of champagne from a waiter, said quietly, 'They seem so close now, it's hard to believe that they both had affairs and that their relationship survived it.'

Hannah swivelled around to study him when he gave a dry laugh. With a disbelieving shake of his head, he explained, 'I was thinking that exact same thought.'

Hannah rolled her eyes. 'The synchronicity of our thinking strikes again.'

The pearly white eyeshadow on her eyelids glittered when she blinked and his heart quickened at her soft smile, at the amusement sparkling in her eyes. They used to joke when they were together about their frequent simultaneous thoughts. From wanting a glass of wine all the way to ideas in the bedroom. He breathed in at that thought, remembering that dark winter's night he'd answered his intercom close to midnight to Hannah, and as he'd gone to open the door had fantasied about her wearing nothing but her overcoat. He'd opened the door to find her wearing her killer black heels and knee-length white woollen coat. She'd walked past him, dropping her coat onto the floor, and he'd watched her walk naked up the stairs, turning once with a flirtatious smile.

With the photographer's beckoning becoming ever more frantic, he reluctantly led Hannah down towards the river.

'So, what did your mum say?'

'That their affairs stemmed from their unhappiness, primarily due to my father not coping in his role as CEO.'

'You don't sound convinced.'

He shrugged, not knowing what to think.

'Put yourself in his position. You've wanted to be CEO from a young age—how would you feel if you were now failing, realising that you weren't capable of the role?'

He let out an angry breath. 'I certainly wouldn't go and have an affair as a way of coping.'

Hannah nodded. 'No, I don't think you would either. But I think you'd struggle to accept it—just as anyone else would. I'm not saying you should forgive your father. But maybe you should try to understand him.'

He was about to argue why he should do anything of

the kind, but Hannah interrupted and said, with empathy shining in her eyes, 'Not for his sake, but for yours. Don't let your parents' mistakes hold you hostage to the past.' As they neared the others Hannah said softly, 'If you want to talk later I'll be here for you.'

Aware of François's narrowed and unhappy gaze as he watched them on the path he said, 'François told me to stay away from you.'

'And Lara warned me to keep well away from you,' Hannah admitted with a grimace.

Coming to a stop, he said quietly, 'We should really listen to them.'

For a moment she looked as though she was about to agree with him, but after some consideration said, 'I think what we had between us deserves better than that. I know it's over between us and I accept that fact, but avoiding each other...' She paused and shrugged. 'It seems childish but also a disservice to how close we once were.' Reddening, she looked back down to the river. 'I don't know if that makes any sense to you.' Then nodding towards François, who was now beckoning for them to join them, she added, 'Why don't you ensure that the photographer takes a photo of your family and Lara? You can get it printed and place it in Villa Marchand for when they come back from honeymoon.'

Nodding, he placed his hand lightly on the small of her back and together they joined the others, his plan of action to stay away from Hannah crumbling in the face of her softly spoken truth—what they had in the past, the friendship and fondness, the connection between them even now, deserved better than easy avoidance. Spending time with Hannah might be dangerous and an emotional minefield but it *was* the right thing to do.

CHAPTER SIX

WITH A DEEP SIGH, Lara stepped out of her high heels and leaned against the wall of the château. 'Do you know what this reminds me of?'

Having similarly divested herself of her own shoes, Hannah closed her eyes and lifted her face to catch the last rays of the setting sun. 'When we used to hide at the back of the school in year seven during break?'

'Exactly! Mrs Wilson was certain that we were up to no good.' With a chuckle Lara added, 'Remember how she used to try to smell our breaths to check if we'd been smoking?'

'When in reality we hid there to make up stories and games about an imaginary zoo.'

Hannah opened her eyes in time to see Lara roll hers. 'All of the other girls thought we were so dorky. I guess we were really.'

Shifting closer to Lara, Hannah rearranged some of the rosebuds that were working their way loose from Lara's fine hair and said, 'I'm guessing you refused to allow the hairdresser to use any hairspray to fix these in place?'

Lara gave Hannah a teasing smile. 'We all have to do our bit for the environment.' Both Lara and François worked for environmental agencies. They had met when

François had visited Manchester to spend the weekend with an ex-colleague who now worked with Lara. In both their professional and personal lives, they were passionate about protecting the planet.

'François told me about Laurent's gift.'

Hannah's heart tightened at the emotion in Lara's voice, the tears shining in her eyes. 'Are you pleased?'

Lara gave her a beam of a smile. 'Thrilled and stunned. It has made today even more incredible. Buying our own house was always going to be a challenge on our salaries. Villa Marchand is everything I ever dreamed of in a home, even before it was renovated. I can't wait to see it later. And of course it has such special memories of our engagement. François is already thinking that we should move here permanently. I suppose we could look into the possibility of working remotely for our current employers or apply for positions in Bordeaux.'

Hannah took a step back. 'Leave England?' She tried not to show her disappointment but then blurted out, 'I'll miss you so much.'

'And me you…but flying to Bordeaux from London would almost be as quick as getting the train to Manchester.'

Lara was right, but, still feeling unsettled at losing her best friend to France, Hannah asked, 'But what's the rush. Why move now?'

'We need more room. We're only able to afford a one-bedroom apartment in Manchester at the moment.'

Hannah was about to ask why that was a problem when up until now she and François had loved their apartment in Didsbury, but then Lara gently laid her hand on her stomach.

'Oh, my God! Are you pregnant?'

Lara nodded, her cheeks flushing, her eyes sparkling

with tears. 'You're the first to know. I'm only seven weeks pregnant. We've agreed to wait a little while longer before we tell others but I wanted you to know. I could never keep a secret from you, could I?'

Hannah pulled Lara in for a hug and whispered, 'I'm so, so happy for you.'

Lara, so much smaller than Hannah, dropped her forehead against Hannah's collarbone. 'Promise you'll come and visit me if we move here.'

Hannah pulled back at the doubt in Lara's voice. 'Wild horses couldn't keep me away.'

Lara grimaced. 'With Laurent being so close by... I wasn't sure how you'd feel about visiting here.'

Hannah wasn't certain how she would feel about visiting either. The stirrings of panic shifted in her stomach as she imagined having to pretend not to be affected by Laurent time and time again. But she couldn't let Lara know any of that. Slipping back into her shoes, she indicated that they should go back to the reception. Earlier when Lara had pulled her away from the ballroom after the marathon celebration dinner, muttering that she needed some air, François had warned them to be back within ten minutes for the slideshow that Stella and their Manchester friends had compiled and which was about to show against the side wall of the château, next to the walled garden. Hannah had been as keen to escape; a three-hour meal seated at the same table as Laurent had made her decidedly jumpy and exhausted from the constant adrenaline rush that came from observing him and the moments when their gazes would meet, a pointless harpoon of desire and connection piercing her heart.

Heading down the path in the direction of the walled garden, Hannah said, 'We'd better get back to the slideshow before François sends out a search party.'

'You're spending a lot of time with Laurent today.'

Hannah felt a brief but intense burst of annoyance and then guilt at the worry in Lara's voice. 'No more so than with anyone else.'

Lara raised a disbelieving eyebrow to that.

After the official photos had been taken they had walked up to the drinks reception together and had stayed chatting, talking about work and travel. And over the long dinner, when many at their table had swapped seats to chat to others, Laurent had invited her to come over to his side of the circular table to join his conversation with Lara's mother.

'There's nothing behind it other than the fact that we still get on. I have dreams of my own to follow—you know that.'

'The move to Singapore I understand but your idea of moving to Spain doesn't make any sense. What's in Spain for you?'

Hannah laughed. 'Spanish men!'

Lara shook her head, a ghost of a smile on her lips.

'I have dreams, Lara, ones that don't contain Laurent. I'll always be fond of him. I can't switch off completely the friendship we had. Yes, he hurt me, but I have good memories too. I want to remember those, learn to have a new type of relationship with him now. I'll need to, you know that. We have years ahead of us of seeing each other, especially if you move here.' She paused and gave Lara a reassuring smile. 'But I have moved on.'

For long seconds Lara eyed her, clearly weighing up whether she should believe her or not. Hannah forced herself to maintain her reassuring smile, but it hurt her cheeks and her heart to do so; it was hard to smile when doubt was mocking what you were trying to convince yourself and others of.

* * *

Laurent chuckled when a baby photo of Lara popped up on the wall of the château. Her fine, wispy blonde hair was standing on end, and the writing on her mud-stained jumper—TROUBLE—was an apt description for the mischievous glint in her eyes as she lunged towards a wary sheepdog with muddy hands. And then he groaned when an unfamiliar picture of himself and François in the bath appeared. He looked about three, François, a year old. Both of them were smiling wildly at the camera oblivious to the crowns of bath foam on their heads, which Laurent guessed, given the grin on their father's mouth as he knelt beside them supporting François with a hand against his back, he'd placed on his sons' heads.

His father looked so young, so carefree in the photo. It was hard to reconcile him with the man who had become so irritable and secretive in later years. Hannah's question as to how he would react if he wasn't capable of running the business came back to him. He stared at a new photo, this one of him pushing François in his pram, his hands barely able to reach the handles. Five previous generations of Bonneval sons had successfully run Bonneval Cognac; it undoubtedly would be hard for anyone to accept that they were the first inheritor not to be up to the role. But that didn't in any way excuse his affairs, his betrayal, his abandonment of his family.

Another photo flashed up, this time a family photo of the four of them all linking arms in front of his father's beloved Citroën Traction Avant. He glanced in the direction of his parents, who, like all of the other guests, were standing in the darkness on the lawn to watch the projection show. His mother smiled at something his father said and then they both looked in his direction. Thrown by the affection in their expressions, he studied them, his brain trying to process the easy love in the pictures being displayed on the wall and this new, calmer and contented version of his parents in comparison to the chaotic and angry people they had been when he was a teenager. His mother's smile faded.

He became aware of someone moving beside him. 'You were a beautiful family.'

He jerked at Hannah's softly spoken comment. Her attention remained on the wall, her head tilting when a video played of himself and François running through a forest, shouting to one another and then disappearing. Then there was the sound of his father's voice, playfully calling out to them, but then Laurent could hear the panic growing as he called and searched for them to no avail. The crowd tensed, as his father's panic grew. His voice became more desperate. The dense forest took on a sinister air. Laurent held his breath. Unease rippled through the guests. And then, as one, the entire crowd started when Laurent and François burst out of a heavy growth of ferns and then relieved laughter ran around the startled guests.

The video cut to one of Lara and Stella playing in the snow as toddlers.

Hannah shifted closer to him. She glanced at him, her eyes twinkling. 'Of course, you're still a beautiful family.'

He smiled at that, but then, glancing in his parents' direction, he said, 'I'm not sure you could call us a family.'

Hannah came even closer, spoke softly so only he could hear. 'I saw how upset you were when your dad was ill. How keen you were to get back here to support your mother. I know they hurt you in the past, but I also know that in your own way you love them greatly.'

Laurent gazed past Hannah to the wall, smiling automatically when Lara fell against the snowman she and Stella had been building, demolishing it completely. Stella's crying rang out while Lara lay in the snow, looking horrified at first but then rolling around in the snow chuckling to herself.

He glanced in his father's direction. Then back at Hannah. She was waiting for him to respond. He shrugged but did not look away from her. Her gaze held such a tenderness, an understanding, that he felt his heart crack open. He wanted to place his arm around her shoulders, pull her to him. Take refuge in the warmth of her body, for even a minute feel the full force of how grounded, how real he felt in her presence.

New sounds had them both look towards the château wall. Lara, aged seven or eight, dressed in pink shorts and a rainbow-coloured tee shirt, was chatting to the camera, excitedly exclaiming that they were panning for gold. The camera moved beyond Lara towards the small stream behind her, to a girl standing in the water. Hidden behind a mass of dark hair, the girl lifted a household colander out of the water. Her arms were thin, her denim shorts hanging loose on her waist. Her quietness was in stark contrast to the excitement of Lara, who was now wading into the stream with her yellow wellington boots, oblivious to the fact that she was splashing the other girl, who didn't even flinch. From behind the camera, Lara's father called, 'Any luck yet?'

The dark-haired child turned to the camera. With a start Laurent realised it was Hannah. Solemn brown eyes, much too pronounced cheekbones faced the camera and with a single shake of her head she returned to her job of sifting through the gravel in the colander.

He leant down and whispered against her ear, 'Did you find any gold?'

Her gaze held a distant haunted expression and for a moment she looked at him blankly before finally answering, 'A fake gold ring, but I saw Lara's mum plant it in the water.' She stopped and gave a faint smile. 'To this day Lara thinks we unearthed it.'

Dieu! He so badly wanted to pull her into a hug, to comfort her. A desire that became even more intense when photos of Lara and Hannah a few years older flashed on the wall, Hannah's gaze more open, her thinness no more, then them as teenagers, dressed for a night out, their make-up too extreme, their skirts much too short, but the happiness and joy in their expressions quickening his heart.

His respect, pride, admiration for her soared. She'd survived her childhood, moved beyond it, to become a warm and loving and compassionate person with a huge strength of character.

Next, photos of Lara's and then François's graduation appeared. In Lara's she was surrounded by her family and friends, including Hannah. In François's photo, however, it was just him and François. At the time, neither of them were in contact with their parents. A few years later, François had begun to have regular contact with them again, but Laurent had kept up minimal contact with them until his father's stroke.

He glanced over at his parents. Was Hannah right? Should he talk to his father? Would it backfire on him? He swallowed. The slow realisation hitting him that he was scared. Was that even the right word...? Scared seemed wrong for a grown man to use, but, yes, he was scared of once again confronting his father's disapproval and dismissive attitude to his ability to run the business. An attitude he'd been facing since the age of sixteen. He could never do well enough in his father's eyes and it tore strips off his heart.

The slideshow came to an end with a selfie picture of Lara and François on the evening François had spontaneously asked her to marry him, sitting together in the gardens of Villa Marchand, Lara flashing her makeshift engagement ring of bound grass as proudly as she would a diamond.

Around them the guests began to move back towards the terrace and ballroom. For long seconds his and Hannah's gazes met. Something fundamental passed between them. A silent understanding. He touched his hand against hers. Skin against skin. A brief connection. He smiled at her and was rewarded with a tender smile in response.

Then he spotted François and Lara unhappily looking in their direction. Guiding Hannah towards them, he excused himself, saying he needed to play host, intending to go and speak to an old friend from Paris but instead finding himself move towards his father, who was walking back towards the ballroom alone.

The band had long stopped playing and Lara and François had left for Villa Marchand hours earlier, but Laurent and Hannah still had to encourage the small but determined group of guests intent on partying through the night into their awaiting taxis as the sun slowly rose in the August sky.

Hannah laughed when one of Lara's friends leant out of the window as his taxi pulled away and shouted merrily, '*À bientôt*, we'll see you later… I want a rematch, Laurent, and my ten euro back.'

'Remind me to lock the gates when we go inside,' Laurent said wryly.

Hannah folded her arms and gave him a pretend look of chastisement. 'That'll teach you for taking on drunk opponents when you're completely sober.'

Laurent raised his hands in exasperation. 'For the last time, I didn't take his money. Anyway, it was his idea to challenge me to a game.'

As she remembered the sight of Laurent, jacket removed, shirtsleeves rolled up with a table tennis bat in his hand, taking on opponent after opponent, his reflexes lightning sharp as he cleared the ball easily time and time again over the net, then his quiet pride at winning that was so infectious, a slow warmth spread throughout Hannah.

Arching his back as though to stretch the long night out of his spine, Laurent said, 'Time for bed, I think.'

Hannah nodded, trying not to react to the tenderness in his voice, how it added to the giddy sense of anticipation that had been slowly building inside her all night.

The dancing had taken place in the ballroom, but the wedding guests had also partied out on the terrace, where the impromptu table tennis tournament had sprung up, Laurent being crowned the overall winner as the caterers had finally taken their leave at four in the morning. It had been at that point, when she and Laurent had thought that the party was finally coming to a close, that some of the younger guests had dive-bombed into the swimming pool. She and Laurent had stood by the pool and tried to encourage them to get out, laughing between themselves at their good-natured high jinks.

Inside the hallway, Laurent closed the main door, turning the key in the lock.

'It was a great night, really fun,' she said.

He turned and studied her for a moment, his eyes holding hers fondly. 'Thanks for your help. I'm not sure how I'd have managed if you weren't here.'

It would have been so easy for Laurent to have ended the party hours ago, but seeing what fun everyone was having, François and Lara in particular, he'd asked for Hannah's assistance in extending the celebrations.

'I didn't do much.'

'You arranged for the caterers to remain here after their planned finish time to look after the guests, drove my parents home and on your return had to act as a life-guard and fish out some guests from the swimming pool and organise for them to dry off inside.'

All night they had easily fallen into a way of managing and communicating over everything that had needed to be taken care of as the party had evolved, and for a moment Hannah was on the verge of pointing out what a good team they made, but thankfully good sense kicked in and instead she said, 'Your mum looked exhausted. I was happy to drop them both home.' Pausing, she asked, 'I saw you talking to your dad earlier. Did it go okay?'

He grinned and Hannah almost melted at the playfulness sparkling in his eyes. 'I asked him why he accepts your help and not mine.'

'And what did he say?'

Laurent crossed his arms on his chest, the teasing smile intensifying. 'That you're a whole lot prettier.'

Hannah could not help but giggle. 'I guess it was a start at least in you two talking.'

Pointing down the corridor, Laurent moved away. 'Come on, I think we both deserve a drink.'

He led her in the direction of the kitchen. Daylight was starting to flood the downstairs rooms, light bird-song filtering in from outside. As she walked by his side, lazy, happy tiredness washed over her.

'I mentioned Nicolas Couilloud's threatened price increase to him.'

Entering the kitchen, she asked, 'What did he say?'

'At first he asked me what I had done to cause the increase.'

Hannah winced. 'Oh.'

'Precisely.' He moved away from her and opened a cupboard teeming with drinking glasses. 'What would you like to drink—wine, spirits or a soda?'

Hannah shifted towards the countertop and, lifting the electric kettle, popped it under the tap to fill it. 'This time of the morning I can only face tea.'

Laurent closed the cupboard door. 'I'll join you.' Taking some teacups from a cupboard, he placed them on the countertop before leaning back against it. 'My father eventually accepted that Nicolas's increases were unwarranted. He's pretty incensed about it all.'

'So you don't think he was involved?'

'No.'

Pouring hot water into the white china teapot Laurent had placed on the countertop, Hannah asked, 'Had he any ideas on how to resolve it all?'

'He offered to talk to Nicolas. I was tempted to say no but, seeing how important it was to him to take it on, against my better judgement I agreed.'

'And his affairs, did you speak to him about those?'

'No. I'm not sure what there is to be gained.'

'I think you deserve to have your father understand what impact those years had on you.'

He just shrugged at her comment and brought the teacups over to stand beside the teapot. Hannah expected him to back away but instead he stood looking down at her. 'I never got to dance with you tonight.'

Heat exploded in her belly at his nearness and shot

all the way up onto her cheeks. She looked towards the kitchen door. 'I should really go to bed. I have a busy week ahead. I need to fly to Edinburgh first thing Monday morning.'

He backed away a fraction, studied her for a moment, then, reaching for the teapot, he poured tea into the cups before passing one of them to her. 'Before you do go to bed, tell me something—the hope you spoke about yesterday during the ceremony, was that what got you through your early years?'

Thrown by his question, Hannah ran a finger around the rim of her cup before answering. 'I guess. I was very young, my memories are hazy, but I remember hoping for small things, that they wouldn't leave me alone in the house, that one day I'd be able to bring my friends from school home with me…but then I stopped going to school.'

'It kills me to hear what you went through.'

By the anguish reflected in his eyes, Hannah could see that he really meant what he'd said. She reached out, touched his forearm, her breath catching at the warmth of his skin. 'Those years were tough but then I was taken in by the most amazing parents anyone could ever wish for. I'm so grateful I had them and Cora and Emily. They taught me so much about love, about trusting in others, about being honest about my feelings and owning them.' She paused, the sudden realisation that she'd never been honest about how she felt about Laurent mocking her. But that was an act of self-preservation; surely she was right to keep those feelings to herself.

She looked out of the window over the sink and nodded towards the ceremony chairs that were stacked by the walled garden and ready to be collected later today. 'You'll be glad to get back to normal after the chaos of the past few days.' The thought of leaving pinched her heart. 'And poor Bleu must want to get home. I still feel so guilty that you had to send him away.'

'Bleu regularly stays with Phillippe when I'm travelling and he loves spending time with Phillippe's spaniels. You have no reason to feel guilty.' Pausing, he considered her for a moment before asking, 'Your fear of dogs— did something happen when you were with your birth parents?'

Her head snapped up at the perceptiveness of his question. She arched her neck and lifted her shoulders to ease out a kink, only now realising that her whole body was aching with tiredness. She wanted to go to bed. She glanced out again at the ever increasingly bright morning sky, grimacing at the realisation that she wanted to go to bed with Laurent. She wanted to lie next to him. Have him hold her. Hear his breath as he slept. She shook herself. That type of thinking was crazy.

'I don't remember exactly what happened, I just vaguely remember a man and a woman coming to the house with a dog. He was huge, dark coated. I must have gone to bed because the next thing I remember is waking to find him next to my bed growling. Every time I went to move, he growled even more, baring his teeth.' She brought her cup to the sink and rinsed it, thrown by how upset she felt. 'I have no idea how long it took for my mum to come in and find him. I tried calling but there was music playing too loudly downstairs. I tried not to cry. I thought that would only make him angrier. I remember pushing myself against the wall and pulling my duvet against myself, hoping that would protect me if he attacked.'

When Laurent came to stand beside her she gestured that she would wash his cup too. But, shaking his head, he placed the cup out of her reach and, laying his hands on her shoulders, he gently turned her around to face him.

'I wish I'd been there to protect you.'

Her heart tumbled at the intense care in his voice, emotion welled in her throat, and she blinked rapidly, trying to hold back the threatening tears. He pulled her into him, his long arms tightly wrapping around her. His body enclosed hers as though he were trying to protect her from shellfire, his shoulder tilting to form a sheltering hollow for her forehead to rest on. His hand ran along her spine, light movements that had her fall even harder against the strength and shelter of his body. She didn't fight him. Her need to have his care right now was far greater than her need to protect herself.

Fully aware of what she was doing, she pulled back, and even though her heart was racing, her voice was surprisingly calm and assured. 'I don't want to be on my own when we go upstairs.'

He studied her for a moment, as though trying to decide if he'd heard right. Then in a tender voice that had her want to cry all over again, he said, 'You know why that's not a good idea.'

'Just hold me. I want to be with you.' There was so much more she was desperate to say, to explain why she wanted to be with him—her confusing mix of elation and loneliness at seeing Lara so happy, her dread at leaving later today, all the bittersweet memories this weekend had unearthed. But she couldn't tell him any of that because to do so would expose what he meant to her.

Laurent took a step back. Dizzying disappointment crashed over her.

But then his fingers trailed softly against her cheek, his gaze moving from concern to understanding acceptance. Taking her hand in his, he led her upstairs to his bedroom. He left her staring at his king-sized antique bed, the imposing headboard and curved footboard made of wood and cane, ornate roses carved into the pale painted wood, the crisp white linen and mountain of pillows making her sway with tiredness…and the dizzying anticipation of lying there with him.

Her gaze shot to the adjoining bathroom. What if he was about to change his mind? She heard the sound of running water and then he was back out in the room with her, opening a drawer in the three-door armoire that matched his bed with the same carved roses along the woodwork and garlands on the cane. Lifting out a grey tee shirt, he handed it to her. 'The shower is running for you.'

For a moment she hesitated. Suddenly having second thoughts.

'I'm going to hold you, Hannah, be there for you. No more. I'll keep you safe, but if you want to go back to your bedroom then I'll walk you there.'

No. That was not what she wanted. She shook her head firmly and on a shaky breath turned for the bathroom. Knotting her hair up into a bun, she allowed the warm water to ease the tension in her body and wash away her racing thoughts.

When she emerged from the bathroom, he was standing in front of the bed wearing only bed shorts, running a towel through his damp hair.

'I didn't mean to throw you out of your own bathroom.'

Walking past her, he threw his towel into a linen basket. 'I used the bathroom in the guest room next door.'

She tugged unconsciously on his tee shirt she was wearing, wishing it smelled of him rather than some unfamiliar fabric conditioner. His expression tense, he went and closed the shutters of the room, plunging them into darkness. It took a few moments for her eyes to adjust enough to be able to see him remove some pillows from the bed before he came and released her hair from the band holding it up and, leading her to the bed, gestured for her to lie down. When she curled on her side, he curled in behind her, his thighs skimming against the backs of hers, his arm lying on her waist.

He whispered, *'Dors bien.* Sleep now. I'll be here.' His hand shifted up, first to skim over her arm, and then over her hair, the soft reassuring pressure, the comfort of his huge body lying next to her having her eyes droop with tiredness.

CHAPTER SEVEN

LAURENT SIGHED, DROWNING in a sea of happy confusion. He shifted his body, an unwelcome ray of awareness intruding on his dreams, telling him to fight against the bone-tired contentment that was dragging him back towards sleep and oblivion.

A deep shiver ran the length of his body as a warm weight passed over his chest. His abs contracted as the weight continued moving downwards over the band of his shorts. Adrenaline surged through his body. And then he was awake, leaping up in the bed and pulling away from Hannah.

She was awake. Just about. She considered him through drowsy eyes, her sensual smile slowly fading away.

Had she even been conscious of what she'd been doing? Of where her hand had been travelling towards? He closed his eyes for a second, trying to control the need drumming through him, trying to get his body under control. Which was nigh on impossible with Hannah lying there, looking sexy and cute and irresistible, with her huge soft brown eyes holding the same need that was pulsing through him. He tried not to stare at her pale pink lace underwear where her tee shirt had ridden up, or at the outline of her breast, a hardened nipple visible beneath the grey cotton.

He collapsed back down onto the bed, keeping a safe distance between them. He knew he should get out of the bed. But it felt as if he'd had only an hour's sleep, and in truth he wanted to lie here with her.

For long minutes they stared at one another, the quietness of the early morning, the low light in the room casting an intimate, dreamlike air to the moment.

He longed to reach out and touch his finger to her lips, plump with sleep, touch the warm silkiness of her flushed cheeks. She shifted her hips to turn fully onto her side, the tee shirt riding even further up so that the inch of lace on her hip was exposed along with the soft wave of her hip bone.

He pulled in a long deep breath as blood pounded in his ears. A year of sleeping alone, of dreaming about her, was catching up with him.

Her hand moved out, rested on the expanse of sheet between them. Her gaze met his. 'I want to be with you.'

He sucked in some air at the soft surety of her voice. 'We can't.'

She tipped her head, her skin flushing even more. 'Are you saying you don't want me?'

He gave a disbelieving laugh, shifting fully onto his back, running a hand through his hair as he stared at the ceiling before turning his gaze back to her. He'd known when he'd taken her to his bedroom that this was the most likely outcome, but he also had wanted to lie down with her and simply hold her, have her forget all the things that she'd told him about her past. 'Nothing has changed, Hannah. I don't want to hurt you again.'

'I know all of that. But last night, when I told you that my parents taught me to be honest, I realised that I'm not being truthful with you.' She paused, bit her lip, her hand pulling down the tee shirt over her hip, covering the deli-

cious curve of her bottom. 'I'm deeply attracted to you...
I need you physically. I have no expectations or wishes
or hopes other than to have sex with you.' She smiled, a
beguiling smile that was both sexy and shy all at once.
'We were always great in bed together.'

He could not help but smile back. 'On that point I can't
argue with you.' Taking hold of her hand, he threaded
his fingers through hers. 'Are you certain this is what
you want?'

'I want sex with you. Is that clear enough?'

He laughed at her teasing tone that also held a hint
of frustration. 'You were never patient when it came to
sex, were you?'

Her eyes lit with mischief. 'I never thought I'd complain about having too much foreplay.'

He lifted her hand and one by one kissed each finger
before flipping her hand over to kiss the palm. 'You need
to slow down when lovemaking, cherish every single
moment.' His tongue ran a circular path around the soft
skin of her palm.

With a groan she shifted onto her back, her hips wrig-
gling against the mattress. 'But it feels like torture.'

He trailed kisses up the inside of her arm, his cheek
brushing against the side of her breast, and then his
mouth found her neck, her back arching as his tongue
licked against the soft skin behind her ear. He moved
along her jawbone and at her mouth he hovered over her
parted lips, his heart tripping over at the wonder and
passion and need in her gaze. 'Are you certain this is
what you want?'

She made a noise of annoyance. 'Will you quit asking
me that?' And then to cement her answer she wrapped her
arms around his neck and pulled him down to her mouth.

His pulse rocketed, his body tightened, all thought left

him as her mouth explored his with a frenzy he understood and responded to, her legs wrapping around his,
her entire body moving upwards to press into his.

For a brief intoxicating moment, as he moved towards
where she lay in his bed asleep, Laurent saw the long
seductive length of Hannah's back, but then, as though
she'd sensed his approach, she twisted from her side onto
her back, pulling the sheet up. For a moment he considered giving in to the temptation of lying back down beside her and losing himself again in the cocoon of her
warmth and musky scent.

He placed a teacup and a plate with a freshly baked
croissant and an apple on the nightstand, smiling when
she gave a faint snore. He'd never told her that she snored.
For some reason he'd wanted to keep that a secret to himself. Just as he'd never told her how he'd watched her
every morning before he'd left for work as she'd slept,
her contented form grounding him for the day ahead, her
warmth and beauty making the world a whole lot brighter
before he'd even stepped out into the day.

He sat on the side of the bed, his eyes trailing over
her dark arched eyebrows, her nose twitching ever so
slightly in her sleep, her cheeks still flushed from their
lovemaking. He buried his head into his hands. How was
he going to manage the next few hours before she left
for London? When she woke, despite her insistence that
she'd wanted to be with him, would she be upset, angry,
regretful over their lovemaking? Would she look at him
with the same hurt and bewilderment as she had in London before he'd left for France?

He inhaled a deep breath. Feeling more rattled than
he'd ever been in his life. Their lovemaking earlier had
been intense—a year of absence and regrets and affec-

tion all spilling out into a confusing but beautiful act of passion, connection and tenderness.

Making love with her, having spent the weekend together, the intimacy of what they had shared with one another about their pasts, all added up to the inescapable fact that today was going to be even harder than London. He needed to tread carefully, make saying goodbye as painless as possible for them both. His gaze moved back to her. Tonight he would lie here in this bed without her. He closed his eyes. Hannah leaving for London was for the best. But somehow, and he was still not sure how, he wanted to show her before she left that he cared for her even though he would never be able to give her the love and commitment she deserved.

He bowed his head for a moment, recalling his mother's shouting, his father's silence. Recalling the night he'd watched his father dump suitcase after suitcase into his car and drive away. The awkward telephone conversations in the months that had followed when he'd been at first too confused and then too angry to speak to his father, who had demanded to know if his mother was poisoning Laurent against him. And then, months later, when his father had returned to the château, his foolish, excited, naïve relief that it was all over. Only to have to endure it all again when his mother had left the following year. And then his father's frequent absences in the years that had followed when he'd left to continue his affairs. He'd stopped trusting in others, stopped allowing himself to be vulnerable by loving them. He cared for Hannah. But he could never love her.

He laid his hand on the warmth of her shoulder, his thumb stroking the oval birthmark below her collarbone. The first time they had gone sailing together, he'd seen it when she'd changed into her red swimsuit. Dumbstruck by the gorgeousness of her curvy body, he'd wanted to maraud his way down the boat to where she was sitting chatting with Lara, and throw all the other males on board who had also been staring in her direction overboard. Instead he'd bided his time, waited for Lara to invariably be drawn back to François, before he'd gone and spoken to her. Spotting her birthmark, he'd told her that it was a kiss from the gods. She'd folded her arms and looked at him suspiciously, rightly knowing that he was trying to charm her, but as she'd turned away to stare out to sea, he'd seen a smile lift on her mouth.

'Hannah, it's time to wake up.'

Her eyes drowsily opened. For a moment she gave him a contented smile, her eyes sparkling with a sexy affection that had him lower his hand from her shoulder for fear of lowering his mouth to her soft lips.

Her smile faded at his movement and she bolted upright in the bed, clasping the sheet to herself. 'What time is it?'

'It's close to ten o'clock.'

Her eyes widened. 'I didn't mean to sleep in for so long.'

'Yesterday was a long day.' He paused, cleared his throat, the remembrance of their disturbed sleep adding a husky note to his voice. 'You needed to rest.'

She dipped her head for a moment, biting her lip, and then looked back at him, the heat in her eyes having him shift on the mattress as desire surged through him.

In need of a distraction, he lifted the teacup and handed it to her. She yanked the sheet even higher against her chest and considered the cup of tea before her gaze shifted back to him. He winced at the sadness in her eyes.

But then her expression hardened. He cursed himself for wincing. He was about to make an excuse but, with a firm shake of her head, Hannah refused the tea and, yanking the sheet further up against herself, she said, 'I should go for a shower and get dressed.'

Placing the teacup back on the nightstand, thrown by the coolness in her voice, her desire to get away, he cleared his throat and said, 'About earlier—'

She interrupted him with a shove against his back, forcing him to stand. Swinging herself out of the bed, she wrapped the sheet around herself. Waddling awkwardly across the room, she said, 'There's really no need for us to talk about earlier, is there?' and gathered up her dress and shoes from where she'd placed them on a bedroom chair last night.

He watched her shuffle towards the door, yanking up the falling sheet time and time again. Her urgency, her insistence on acting all cool and calm, irrationally irritated him. And then that irritation disappeared to be replaced with an uneasy thought that maybe their lovemaking really didn't mean as much to her as he'd thought it did. Her words on Thursday night sounded in his brain. *'I'm over you, Laurent. I've moved on. Don't overinflate your importance in my life.'*

Following her, he called out, 'You forgot these.'

He tried to hide his amusement at her horrified expression when she spotted her lace knickers hanging from his index finger. She grabbed them from him and in the process the sheet dropped to expose a gorgeously erect dusky pink nipple. She tugged up the sheet furiously.

Dieu! He wanted to pull that bloody sheet away. Make love to her. Thick, dangerous desire was pumping through him. He stepped back. 'Wait, I'll give you my bathrobe to wear.' Seeing her reach for the door handle, he added, 'I don't want you giving my housekeeper,

Marion, a heart attack by having your sheet fall down as you walk back to your room. Her heart gives her enough trouble as it is.'

In the bathroom he removed his bathrobe from the hook. Back out in the bedroom he held it out for her to put on. She dumped the items in her hands onto the floor, turning her back to him as she placed her hands into the robe sleeves. The sheet fell slowly and seductively to the floor. She tied the belt of the robe with a yank and, turning around, she lifted her own items and the sheet, which she threw in his direction. 'Yours, I believe.'

He caught the sheet, feeling more in control now that her initial icy coolness had been replaced by an air of defiance. Gesturing to the bathrobe, the arms hanging well below her fingertips, the white material swamping her frame, he shook his head. 'It's much too big for you, and I'm detecting a certain lack of gratitude in me gifting it to you.'

She eyed him cautiously. In London, they used to tease each other this way. Spring surprises on one another.

He stepped closer. 'In fact I'm having second thoughts about letting you wear it.'

Her eyebrows shot upwards. And then she was making a dash for the door.

He chased after her and wrapped his arm around her waist and lifted her off the ground.

'Laurent Bonneval, you put me down, you brute.'

He laughed and could feel her body jerk with silent laughter too.

And then rather primly she said, 'Yesterday you said you needed to work today. Please don't delay heading into the office on my account.'

He lowered her down and turned her around to face

him. 'My father was right when he said as your host I should ensure that you are looked after. I've decided not to go into work today.'

She looked at him with surprise. 'Oh.'

He opened the bedroom door. 'Downstairs is in chaos thanks to the clean-up after yesterday. I have a beach house in Royan—we can go there to escape the noise. Marion is packing a picnic for us to take.'

'But my flight is at seven this evening. Do we have time?'

He nodded. 'I'll drop you straight to the airport from Royan. So bring your suitcase.'

She eyed him curiously for a moment and then with a shrug she went to pass him, but out in the corridor she turned to him. 'I want to go and see Lara before we leave for Royan. I'd like to say goodbye to her.'

'I'll ring ahead and let them know we'll call in.'

'You said yesterday that you were going to collect Bleu from Phillippe today on your way into work.'

'I'll also ring Phillippe and ask him to keep Bleu until this evening.'

She shook her head. 'No. He has been away from you for too long already. Let's collect him on the way to Royan. We can take him for a walk on the beach.'

Bleu adored the beach. And Laurent couldn't wait to see him again. But despite the determined tilt of Hannah's chin as she waited for his response the quiver in her voice told him how much of an effort it would all take. 'I'll collect him later this evening.'

Tugging the belt of the robe tighter, she grimaced and said quietly, 'I need to get over my fear of dogs. It's gone on for far too long.' Her bare feet on the marble floor of the hallway shifted and her gaze moved to a point beyond

his shoulder. 'I'd like to try to spend time with Bleu…
knowing that you are there.'

Without stopping to think, Laurent moved to her.
Touched his hand against the soft white cotton of her
bathrobe. 'In his size Bleu is intimidating, but he really
is a marshmallow. My vet believes he was mistreated by
his previous owner. Bleu and I have spent a lot of time
with a dog trainer, training him to respond to my commands. All he wants is love and affection.'

She gave a wry chuckle. 'That sounds familiar.'

An awkward silence settled between them. Hannah's
cheeks reddened. She cleared her throat, gave him a hesitant but teasing smile. 'I'll blame you, though, if Bleu
tries to eat me.'

Walking back to the nightstand, he picked up the teacup and plate of food and handed them to her. 'Have
something to eat and drink. We'll leave to collect Bleu
as soon as you are ready so that we can make the most
of the day at Royan.' He laughed lightly and added, 'And
don't worry, if Bleu strays too close to you, I'll do my
best musketeer impression and will protect you.'

She laughed at that. 'I'd give anything to see you wearing tights and a floppy hat while wielding a sword.' Then,
sobering, she looked him directly in the eye. 'But I can
protect myself. I don't need you.'

And walked away.

CHAPTER EIGHT

SHUTTING THE DOOR to her bedroom, Lara leant against it with a sigh and asked, 'What's up?'

Taking in Lara's wedding gown, hanging perfectly on a white satin clothes hanger on the door of the wardrobe, Hannah said, 'I'm guessing that you didn't drag me upstairs after all in order to hang your dress properly.'

Dropping down onto the bed, Lara answered, 'Obviously. You're jumpy and clearly upset. What's up?'

Running her hand over the delicate lace of Lara's wedding dress, Hannah shrugged, swallowing down the temptation to tell Lara the awful truth that in sleeping with Laurent she'd realised that she was still in love with him. 'I guess it's post-wedding blues. I hate the thought of going back to work tomorrow.' Turning, she gave Lara a smile. 'And I'm going to miss you while you are away on honeymoon.'

Lara shook her head and sighed. 'Guess what? I'm not buying any of that.'

Hannah rolled her eyes, trying to act nonplussed when in truth an ache was gripping her throat. Why did Lara have to be so perceptive?

For a moment she considered changing the subject but knew that Lara deserved the truth, even if she was going to go crazy about it. 'I spent the night with Laurent.'

'Hannah!'

Hannah held her hands up in admission. 'I know. But don't freak out about it. We both know that it was straightforward, uncomplicated sex.'

Lara covered her face with her hands, shaking her head in despair before saying, 'Oh, Hannah, why? Why allow yourself to get hurt again?'

Hating Lara's disappointment in her, hating just how vulnerable she felt, Hannah bit back. 'Why don't you believe me when I say I'm over him? That I have my own plans and dreams to follow?'

Anger flared in Lara's eyes. 'Because I see the way that you look at him.'

Trying not to blush or give in to the frustrated tears threatening at the backs of her eyes, Hannah snorted. 'He's a good-looking man. Of course I look at him.'

Lara stood. For long seconds she looked at Hannah sadly. 'You're still in love with him, aren't you?'

'Do we really need to talk about this now? We should be talking about yesterday.' Forcing herself to give Lara a cheeky smile, she asked, 'So how's married life, Mrs Bonneval?'

Lara inhaled an impatient breath. 'Are you going to tell him about how you feel?'

'He doesn't want a relationship. I'm cool with that.'

Moving to the bedroom window, Lara looked out of it. Joining her, Hannah saw that she was studying Laurent and François, who were sitting at the garden table next to the river. Lara shook her head. 'I want to go down and throttle him. He shouldn't have slept with you.'

'Don't blame him. It was me who initiated it—you could say that I slept with him.'

Eyes wide, Lara turned and asked in an appalled voice, 'Why on earth did you do that?'

Hannah searched for some glib reply, but as she began to speak her voice cracked and to her horror a fat tear spilled down her cheek. Knowing her pretence was now of no use, she answered, 'Because I'm lonely…because I miss him.'

With a sigh, Lara pulled her into a hug. Then, grabbing a tissue from the dressing table, she wiped Hannah's tears and asked quietly, 'What are you going to do?'

With a wry laugh, Hannah answered, 'Get through today. Continue to pretend I have no feelings for him other than that he's a friend of sorts. And after today, go and forge a new life for myself.'

Later that morning, above the hum of the air conditioning, Bleu's snoring reverberated around Laurent's four-by-four like low rumbling thunder.

'Does he always snore like that?'

Slowing at a junction, Laurent glanced over at her. 'I think snoring is cute.'

Hannah stared at him, confused by the amusement playing out in his expression as he signalled to the right and pulled out into the heavy traffic when a gap became available. Conscious that Lara had so easily seen through her pretence, and determined not to allow Laurent to see that her heart was a mangled mess, she attempted to adopt a congenial tone. 'He certainly was happy to see you.' Folding her arms, she added, 'But I thought you said that he was well trained.'

Laurent gave a guilty chuckle. 'Usually he follows my commands.'

Reaching forward to lower the air conditioning, Hannah threw him a teasing look. 'I was just glad I was in the safety of the car when he bounded towards you. I was certain he was going to knock you over.'

He grimaced at that. 'He'll be calmer when we get to the beach house, I promise.' Then, his gaze meeting hers for a moment, he added, 'You seem to be coping with having him in the car. That's an incredible step forward for you.'

Her heart melted at the admiration and care in his voice. But she knew that she needed to maintain the nonchalance and teasing banter she had been hiding behind all day in a bid to harden herself against his effect, his ability to tear out her heart and leave her confused and vulnerable and so incredibly lonely for him even though he was sitting right next to her. How could they be so close, both physically and on a surface emotional level, but yet be so distant from one another? She hated all of this pretence and dishonesty. It wasn't who she was. Or at least trying to be. But what other option did she have? She could hardly casually drop into their conversation that she was in love with him.

Instead she turned and eyed the rear of the car where Bleu was lying in the back compartment and, thanks to her frayed nerves, gave an almost hysterical laugh. 'Coping. Are you kidding me? I'm a bag of nerves. The only reason I'm not tempted to jump out of the car is because there's a metal grid separating him from me.'

She jumped when Laurent's hand came to rest on the side of the seat, his fingers almost touching her thigh. His gaze remaining fixed on the heavy flow of traffic ahead of them, he said quietly, 'We're almost at the beach house. When we get there I'll show you into the house and then take Bleu out. You don't have to spend time with him.'

A lump formed in her throat at the understanding in his voice. She swallowed hard, knowing that she needed to toughen up, not only with Bleu but also in how she allowed his master to get to her. 'No, I meant it when I said I wanted to spend time with him.'

Laurent glanced at her. 'Are you sure?'

'I'm tired of having mini panic attacks every time I jog through Richmond Park and a dog comes near me. Last week, I actually screamed when I almost tripped over a dog no bigger than a hamster who came flying out of the high grass. He was being walked by two teenage girls who clearly thought I was crazy and ended up doubled over laughing at me.'

Laurent cleared his throat, clearly trying not to laugh at the image she'd painted. 'Okay, I can see why you want to deal with your fear.'

Turning her attention back to the passing scenery, she smiled when a golden beach and glistening sea appeared on the horizon. 'What an incredible beach. How long is it?'

'About two kilometres. *Sirocco* is moored here in Royan.' Pointing towards the far end of the beach, he added, 'You can see the marina in the distance.'

Hannah blinked away all the threatening memories that came at the mention of his yacht and the days they had spent on the Solent. 'Do you get out on *Sirocco* often?'

'Not as often as I'd like to. Work has been crazy since I got back here.'

'What about the beach house?'

He glanced at her and shrugged. 'Even less.'

'Maybe if your dad had a role in the business, even for a few hours every week, it might take the pressure off you.' Thinking about Lara's pregnancy, she added, 'Perhaps in time François might be interested in joining the business too. I'm guessing his environmental background could be of huge benefit.'

Laurent slowed and pulled off the main road into a residential street. Halfway down the street he pulled into a driveway and used a remote control to open grey panelled wooden gates. 'It's a possibility…about François. Up until now he hasn't been interested in working in the company, but his circumstances are changing.' Driving through the gates, he added wryly, 'However, I'm really not convinced about my father permanently getting involved in the business again.'

A tall cypress tree towered over the front lawn of the Malibu-style, single-storey beach house. Beyond the house Hannah caught a glimpse of the vast expanse of the beach. 'What a location.' Turning as Laurent switched off the engine, she asked, 'Did you inherit this house too?'

'No. I bought it a few years back.'

She tried to hide her surprise and hurt and said with a forced smile, 'You never mentioned that you owned a property here when we were together.'

From the rear of the vehicle, Bleu stirred, his movements rocking the car. Hannah glanced back to see him looking with adoration in Laurent's direction.

Opening the door of the car, Laurent answered, 'It didn't seem important at the time.'

'No, I don't suppose it did.'

About to get out of the car, he paused and turned back in her direction. 'This is my first time visiting the house in over five years. Only the second time since I bought it.'

Her mouth dropped open. 'Seriously?'

'It was once my family's summer home. My parents sold it over fifteen years ago. I bought it back from the family who bought it from them.'

'But why have you never used it?'

'We spent our summers here as children. Both I and François were disappointed when my parents sold it.

They said at the time that they sold it because we were insisting on spending our summers in Paris. I always felt guilty about that. Five years ago, when I told my mother that I had purchased the beach house, she told me the truth about why they had sold it.'

Given the anger and pain in his expression, Hannah asked quietly, 'Which was?'

'Apparently it was here that my father lived with his mistress when he left home.'

Hannah winced. 'Oh.'

'Exactly.'

Following Laurent's lead, Hannah climbed out of the vehicle. The white walls of the house sparkled in the midday sun, the lush, well-maintained planting in the garden swaying in the light breeze. 'It doesn't look like you haven't been here in years,' she said, joining him as he walked up the gravelled path to the front door, glass panels at the side showing an open-plan living space with a huge sea-blue sofa and an off-white painted kitchen to the side, enormous windows running the length of the back wall with views over the bay.

'I've paid for it to be maintained.'

As Laurent placed a key in the lock she asked, 'Weren't you tempted to sell it?'

Laurent ran a hand against the base of his neck. She longed to reach there as she'd done countless times in London, laughing when he groaned in pleasure, the tight knot which he frequently arrived home from work with loosening under her touch. 'I thought about selling several times over the past few years but couldn't bring myself to. But if business doesn't improve I might be forced to.'

'I didn't realise things were that serious.'

He shrugged and gestured for her to enter the house

and said, 'I'll let Bleu out of the car. You can wait inside here or come out and join us if you decide it's what you want to do.'

As he walked away she asked, 'Why did you decide we should come here today?'

Stopping, he turned. His dark skin glowed in contrast to the whiteness of his button-down shirt. His hair caught in the breeze and he had to smooth it down. 'I thought visiting here might be easier with you at my side.'

She stared after him when he turned away, wondering if she'd heard his gently spoken answer correctly.

For a few seconds indecision rooted her to the spot but then, seeing Laurent about to open the back door of the car, she called out and ran towards him.

Coming to a stop, she smiled at him, her heart lifting as he returned her smile even though his held an element of puzzlement. 'Thanks.'

Despite her promises to harden herself to him, the power of their earlier lovemaking, the connection, the synchronicity between them that felt so instinctive and right made what followed inevitable.

He reached for her, one hand on her waist, the other touching her cheek. He kissed her with an aching tenderness and her heart kicked both in fear and delight.

Even with his blood pounding in his ears Laurent could not ignore Bleu's barking. With a groan he pulled away from Hannah and gave her a regretful smile.

Her lips were swollen from their kiss, a deep blush on her skin.

He backed away, away from the temptation of resuming their kiss, his need for Hannah more intense now than it had ever been before.

Placing a hand on the rear door, he asked, 'Are you certain you don't want to stay inside?'

Hannah shook her head. But then stepped to the side of the vehicle as though searching for cover.

Opening the door, Laurent patted Bleu and spoke to him in a low comforting voice. Bleu's barking ceased, to be replaced with a delighted wagging of his tail.

Turning to Hannah, he gave her a triumphant smile. 'See. I told you he responds to me. You have nothing to be concerned about.'

But no sooner had he said those words than Bleu bounded out of the car, ran down the driveway and, turning in a wide arc, leapt over low hedging, before racing back towards them. Hannah yelped and ran behind him, her forehead digging into his back, her fingers coiling around the belt loops of his waistband.

A wave of protectiveness for Hannah had him shout at Bleu as he neared them. *'Non! Couche.'*

At his command Bleu came to an immediate stop, his head tilting to the side at his master's never-before-heard yell.

Reaching behind him, he took hold of Hannah's hand and, pulling her around to stand at his side, he gave Bleu a further command. *'Assieds.'*

Immediately Bleu sat.

Hannah was shaking. Placing his arm around her, he pulled her into a hug. 'Are you okay?' She nodded yes, but still she shook. He ran a hand against her hair. His own heart was pounding, the strength of his instinctive need to protect her taking him aback. Against the lemon scent of her hair he whispered, 'Wait here. I'll lead Bleu inside.'

She backed away from his hug, gave him a grateful

smile that liquefied his heart and, glancing in Bleu's direction, said, 'No. I want to get closer to him.'

Admiration swelled in his chest at the determination in her voice. And then the image of Hannah as a young child curled up in bed, shaking and terrified by the snarls of a dog, had him clasp his hands tightly in rage.

He gulped down that rage and went to Bleu, whose tail swept across the driveway in large arcs of happiness when he approached, his head falling back in adoration, anticipating a rub, his brown eyes tracking every movement as though it were precious.

The rage inside him flowed away as he rubbed Bleu, his love for this animal, who had been so weak and accepting of his fate when he had found him starved and dying in the woods, rooting him to the spot. Sudden, unexpected emotion stuffed the backs of his eyes. A vulnerability, a loneliness, a bewilderment that he couldn't comprehend. Disconcerted, he tried to blink it away.

Behind him, surprisingly close, he heard Hannah's soft laugh. 'Bleu reminds me of François when he looks at Lara—complete infatuation.'

Turning, he grinned up at her. 'And I adore him.' Rubbing Bleu along the long length of his spine, he added, 'Don't I, boy? Aren't you the bravest, most lovely dog ever?'

Panting hard with happiness, Bleu rolled over onto his back, wanting his belly rubbed. Four giant legs and paws reached skywards like mini skyscrapers.

Once again Hannah giggled. 'That is the most ridiculous thing I've ever seen. You're right. He is a complete marshmallow…albeit a donkey-sized marshmallow.'

He held out his hand to her. 'Come and crouch beside me. Rub him too if you feel like it.'

With a worried look in Bleu's direction, she tentatively took Laurent's hand. She was still trembling. He gave it a little squeeze. For a moment she paused in her tentative steps towards Bleu. He inhaled a breath at the question in her gaze—can I trust in you? Instinctively he wanted to pull his hand away, tell her not to trust in him, not to invest any emotion in him, but shame and annoyance at that reaction had him smile and nod encouragingly instead.

When she was crouched at his side, she reached slowly for Bleu's belly and rubbed him with short jerky movements. Taking her hand once again in his, Laurent guided her to make longer, more soothing movements. He heard her gasp in, but then as her hand moved against Bleu time and time again and Bleu gave a comical yawn of contentment, she exhaled a long breath of relief.

'Good job.'

She smiled proudly at his praise. His heart tumbled at how her eyes were sparkling with relief and joy.

'It's hot out here.' He stood and added, 'Let's go inside. Bleu should be in the shade.'

Positioning Hannah to one side and Bleu to his other, he led them into the house. Taking Bleu immediately into the storage room to the rear of the kitchen, he plucked some beach towels out of a cupboard and made a temporary bed for Bleu while asking Hannah to find a suitable bowl in the kitchen for him to drink from.

When she appeared at the door with the bowl he nodded for her to place it by Bleu's bed. Lowering it down, she tentatively moved her hand towards Bleu's head, placing it a short distance away from where he was lying on his side curled up, ready for yet another sleep. Bleu slowly, instinctively, as though sensing Hannah's fear, nudged his nose towards her hand and sniffed it. Then withdrawing, he tucked his head down towards his chest and closed his eyes.

Hannah stood and smiled down at Bleu. 'I think I could actually fall in love with him.'

Laurent could understand the wonder in her voice. 'There's something special about him, isn't there?'

Hannah nodded and then gave him a teasing smile. 'I thought Bleu was lucky that you found him when he was so ill, but maybe you're the lucky one to find him.'

Laurent gave a low disbelieving laugh. 'I was just thinking that. These simultaneous thoughts are getting out of control.'

Hannah placed her fingertips to her temples. 'Okay, let me guess what you're now thinking.' She scrunched her face, as though deep in thought. 'You're going to suggest we go for a swim.'

'How did you know that?'

'It could be telepathy…or the fact that you're standing there holding beach towels.' Grinning, she walked out of the room. 'I'll go and fetch my bikini from my suitcase.'

Laurent knew Bleu would be comfortable in the shade of the room and, with one final pat for him, closed the door to the room gently.

After showing Hannah to a guest bedroom where she could change, he threw on swimming trunks he'd brought to the house five years ago, fetched the picnic basket from the car and then, going back into the living room, he opened the doors that led out onto the decked terrace. Stepping out, he inhaled a deep breath of sea air and turned and regarded the house. The previous owners had modernised both the interior and exterior, but the overall house structure and the sweeping views had remained the same.

The last time he'd visited the house, five years ago,

he'd only stayed long enough to unpack. Unable to handle the sickening thought of his father spending all those months here when he should have been at home.

He'd driven back to the airport, not bothering to even pack his luggage, and taken the first flight back to London.

He walked to the pool, stared down at the tiled dolphin at the base, which he and François had spent endless hours racing to.

At the sound of footsteps behind him, he turned and smiled as Hannah tugged down her blue-and-white striped dress, the yellow straps of her bikini visible. She came and stood beside him. 'This view is amazing.' Then with concern she asked, 'What are you thinking about?'

He led her towards the steps down to the beach. 'I thought you were telepathic.'

From behind him, her flip-flops slapping on the concrete steps, she asked gently, 'Are you remembering your childhood here?'

He waited until they reached the beach, his bare feet sinking into the soft sand, to answer. 'Our time here was idyllic. I lost all of that when I found out about my father… He had always refused to answer my question as to where he was staying when he called home. For the past few years I've been incredibly angry with him for sullying my memories, but maybe it's time that I create new ones for this place.'

She nodded but there was a sadness to her expression that punched him in the gut. He smiled, wanting to lighten the mood, and headed in the direction of the sea. 'Starting today.'

He went further down the beach, dropped the picnic basket and blanket onto the sand.

She was still at the steps eyeing him dubiously but then

walked towards him with a mischievous expression. 'So what memories will you have of today?'

He waited until she came to a stop in front of him before he answered. 'You rubbing Bleu's belly, being brave and determined.'

Something low and carnal throbbed in him when she pulled off her dress to reveal her yellow bikini. An inch of the soft flesh of her high breasts was exposed, the strings of the bottoms tied into a bow on the swell of her hips. He tucked her hair that was lifting in the breeze behind her ear. 'I'll remember also how incredibly beautiful you looked.' He lowered his head, whispered against her ear, 'I'll remember how I was woken this morning… and what followed.'

She leant into him, her breasts skimming against his chest for a much too brief second. And then she was stepping back from him, giving him a look full of bravado that didn't match the heat in her cheeks. She called to him when she was well out of his reach, pointing towards the sea. 'You can also remember how I beat you in a race to the swimming platform.'

Enjoying the sight of her running to the breaking surf, he allowed her to gain a considerable lead on him. Then, breaking into a light jog, he followed her, diving into the sea, gasping at the coldness. Out on the sea platform, he waited for her by the ladder.

When she arrived, she looked dumbfounded when he reached down to help her out. 'How on earth did you get here before me?'

He laughed and pulled her up. 'You really need to learn to swim in a straight line.'

For a while they lay in silence on the platform, staring up at the wisps of clouds that were passing overhead.

Then with a loud exhalation, Hannah admitted with a laugh, 'I'm so out of breath.'

Her chest heaved up and down and he fought the temptation to place his hand on her wet skin. 'I'll have to teach you how to sea-swim properly some time.'

'You've promised me that numerous times.' Her gaze darted away from his but he saw the disquiet that flickered there. Shielding her eyes, she added, 'Anyway, my sea-swimming is better than your tennis.'

'You beat me once.'

She grinned. 'Just saying. What height advantage do you have over me?'

'You well know that it's eight inches.'

Her eyes twinkled. 'A whole eight inches.'

And suddenly their conversation was taking on a whole different meaning. He leaned over her, deliberately being provocative, his mouth close to hers, his gaze playing with hers. 'It's what you do with those eight inches that counts.'

Her eyelids fluttered. 'Care to remind me again?'

He raised an eyebrow. 'I'm not sure that I do.'

She wriggled, her hip bumping against his belly. Her fingertips trailed over the valley between her breasts. 'Are you really certain about that?'

'I've never been able to resist you, have I?' And then his mouth was on hers, elation spreading through him at her softness, at her warmth, at her groan. His hand ran over her ribs, down over her stomach and over her hips. Her hands gripped his neck, her thumbs stroking the indent at the top of his spine.

Her body pressed upwards against his. Knowing he was about to lose control, he broke away from her mouth, groaned against her ear. 'If we don't stop we'll be arrested.'

Lying down next to her, he took hold of her hand. He could suggest that they go back to the house. Finish this off in private. But the need to do right by Hannah had him lie there beside her instead.

'Lara's so happy with Villa Marchand. It was such a thoughtful and generous present.'

He turned his head, considered her. 'I would almost swear that Lara deliberately pinched me when I hugged her goodbye earlier. Does she know about us?'

Hannah gave him a panicked and guilty look but then, with a shrug, she regained some of her composure and said, 'I told her I seduced you.'

He laughed at that. And then realised she was being serious. 'Please tell me that you didn't.'

Her answer was a smug smile.

He shook his head and something lodged in his throat when he remembered François's earlier delight when-ever he looked at Lara, his buoyant mood and excite-ment for their honeymoon in the Galapagos Islands, how at home they both had seemed in their new house. 'Villa Marchand will be a great family home.'

Taking her hand from his, Hannah propped herself up onto her elbow. 'François told you?'

He feigned confusion. 'Told me what?'

Clearly thrown, she shrugged. 'Nothing. Forget about it.'

He frowned and asked, 'Is there something I should know?' but then, unable to stop himself, he laughed and added, 'You're so atrocious at lying.'

She gave him a playful slap on his arm. 'My parents brought me up to be honest.'

He was sorely tempted to kiss her again, run his hands over her body, but instead he admitted, 'I didn't realise how excited I'd be at the prospect of being an uncle.'

CHAPTER NINE

HANNAH COULD FEEL her pretence that she was in control and wasn't about to spew out all the thoughts and emotions crowding her brain and making her heart crumble at Laurent's words. She wanted to say that based on his love for Bleu he would make for a brilliant uncle. She wanted to point out to him that, not only would he be an incredible uncle, but, if he allowed himself, he would be an amazing father too. She turned onto her back. Closed her eyes.

She couldn't look at him today without her pulse soaring. But as her pulse soared, her heart felt as though it were slowly melting into nothing. It felt as though two beings were inhabiting her body: a physical self who was hyperaware of the chemistry spinning between them, and an emotional self, whose soul was aching with the need to connect fully with him.

Opening her eyes to the brilliant blue sky overhead, she said, 'I spoke to my parents before we left the château. They were asking about you.'

'In a good or bad way?'

'Good, of course. Why would you think otherwise?'

'I thought your parents, your family in general, might not be too happy with me.'

Despite her having invited him to visit her parents on

several occasions, Laurent had always had an excuse as to why he couldn't. But six months into their relationship she'd finally persuaded him to go with her. The weekend had been a disaster. Laurent had been disengaged, his reluctance and caution around her parents totally throwing her. 'They liked you but would admit that they never really got to know you.' Pausing, she added, 'The weekend you visited them with me, you seemed uncomfortable.' She swallowed and added, 'Didn't you like them?'

He sat up and stared at her. '*Dieu!* Of course I liked them.'

Hurt and bewilderment surged inside her, some of it months old, some fresh from the past twenty-four hours. Sitting too, she asked, 'Did you think I was trying to put pressure on you by inviting you to visit my parents? Because that wasn't the case. I wanted you to get to know them because they're fantastic people…and I love them to bits.'

Closing his eyes, Laurent inhaled a breath while running his hand tiredly down over his face. 'Being with your family, seeing how you all love one another, reminded me of how fractured my own family are. Your parents are wonderful, Hannah. I just didn't want to raise their expectations in terms of where our relationship was going.'

A swell of emotion grabbed her heart. He would never really know her parents, her sisters. She breathed against the loneliness that was threatening to drown her. 'They're good people.' She shot him a meaningful look. 'They deserved better from you.'

He grimaced and then with a nod said, 'You're right. Will you pass on my apologies?'

She wanted to say that he could do so himself. But,

of course, he would never see them again. Instead she asked, 'Have things improved with your family at all?'

He looked back towards the beach house. 'Not really.'

'Do you want a good relationship with them?'

'I'm not sure.'

'I think you do. I think you love them despite everything that happened.'

At that Laurent gave a disbelieving laugh. He glanced in her direction and then away. 'I don't understand love.'

Despite the heat of the day, Hannah shivered at the quiet certainty in his voice. 'You show love all of the time with your family. You've cared for and protected François since you were both teenagers. And when your parents were in crisis last year, you responded. Caring, protecting, responding to the other person, that's all love.'

He shook his head. 'You're forgetting that it was my opportunity to take over Bonneval Cognac.'

'I saw how upset you were the night your mother called to say how ill your father was. Getting to him and your mother was your priority. I bet the business didn't even enter your mind. Am I right?'

He gave a non-committal shrug. 'Perhaps.'

It felt as if an invisible wall had suddenly sprung up between them; she could feel Laurent distancing himself from her. Panic was curling inside her. She shifted around to face him directly, desperate to try to connect with him. 'There's time for you to develop a good relationship with them again.' She paused, trying to gather her breath against the hard thumping of her heart. It felt as though her body was sensing something that was about to come.

Frowning, he studied her for a long while, as though trying to understand her. An intense pain squeezed her heart at the coolness of his gaze. 'How do you manage to be so trusting of others despite everything you have gone through?' he asked.

'It's not easy. But my parents always told me that I need to be honest, to respect and own my feelings.' She stopped and gave an involuntary smile as his expression softened, but inside she was increasingly feeling vulnerable and desperate. She wanted him to understand her fully. She was so tired of pretence and hiding her true self. 'It was an important part of me coping with everything that had happened.'

His hand reached for her bent knee, his fingertip running over the faint scar there she got when she tripped over a tractor tyre in the barn one day. 'Your parents are very wise.'

'Yes, they are. But unfortunately I don't always follow their advice. Before you I was very cautious around guys. I was worried about getting things wrong. With my family, with friendships, I was okay...' she paused, not sure if she should continue, but something deep inside her was telling her to be honest with him '...but I've always been afraid of falling in love.'

A guarded expression formed in his eyes. She knew she should stop. She was only going to embarrass herself. She had worked so hard to get over him and was now about to throw all of that away. She was about to compromise all the plans she had made for an independent future. She was going to make herself vulnerable all over again. But she couldn't put a brake on the words that insisted on being spoken, how her heart wanted to have its say after months of being kept in check. 'I really, really care for you, Laurent.'

She smiled at him in hope, in embarrassment. Waited for him to say something. But instead he looked away from her, frowning. She wanted to cry. She wanted to yell at him. She twisted away from him. Willing him to say something. But they sat in silence, the happy cries from children on the beach washing over them; a swirl of embarrassed anger rose up from her very core and her heart shattered with the pain of feeling so utterly alone and disconnected from the man she was in love with.

Trying to quell the panic growing inside him, Laurent pulled in one long breath after another. He bunched his hands, self-loathing vying with his panic. 'This morning was a mistake.'

Hannah's gaze shot to his. 'That's wonderful to hear.'

He exhaled a breath at the sarcasm in her voice, his stomach churning to know he was to blame for all of this. He caught her gaze, gave her a smile of appeasement. 'You know I didn't mean it that way.'

She folded her arms. 'Do I?'

'After yesterday, we were both feeling emotional. Weddings do that type of thing to people.'

She shifted away from him, towards the edge of the platform, and gave a bitter chuckle. 'You make it sound like it was sympathy sex.'

He shook his head furiously. 'When did I say that?'

'Well, you're clearly regretting it.'

Taking in the defiant tilt of her head, the heavy emotion in her voice, the hurt in her eyes, he asked gently, his heart heavy with fear, 'Aren't you?'

For a moment her expression softened, and her gaze caught his as though pleading with him to understand. But to respond to her, to take her in his arms as he wanted to, would be cruel. He knew what Hannah was trying to say to him. She wanted more from him, from their relationship, than he could ever give.

Her expression hardened again. 'Well, I'm certainly regretting it now.'

He flinched at her hurt, her anger.

He tried to think straight, to find something to say, but his heart was pounding too hard, his brain a too-confused mess of panicked thoughts. He'd numbed his heart, his expectations, his need for love, for closeness, for trust, for comfort, so long ago, he didn't know how to open himself up to it all again...or if he ever wanted to.

'Things are never going to be right between us, are they?'

He barely heard her question, she'd spoken it so quietly. He grimaced and shook his head. Standing, she threw him an infuriated look before diving into the sea.

Hannah flicked off the shower. Towelled herself dry furiously. Yanked on her underwear and dress. She knew she needed to calm down. The anger inside her frightened her. But as hard as she tried she couldn't hold it back. It felt as though years and years of repressing herself were spilling out in Laurent's cold indifference to her telling him what he meant to her. Had he any idea how exposed, how hurt, how embarrassed she felt? Couldn't he have at least tried to meet her halfway, say something of comfort?

He was out in the living room, showered and changed, when she went there on the way out of the house.

She pulled her suitcase even closer to herself, tightening her grip on the handle. 'I've called a taxi to take me back to my car at the château. There's no need for you to take me to the airport.'

He gave her a disappointed, almost impatient look.

She gritted her teeth, telling herself to leave here with some dignity, but that pledge lasted all of five seconds because suddenly words were tumbling out of her, words that made her cringe at their neediness and bitterness, words that reminded her that she was her birth parents' child. She gestured around the room, out towards the beach. 'Why the hell did you bring me here? What was the point of all this?'

She didn't wait for him to respond but instead she paced the marble floor and continued, her hands rising to hold her head in disbelief. 'You know, you make me want to pull my hair out. You're…you're the most infuriating man.'

She came to a stop, suddenly breathless, her anger gone in those sharp words to be replaced by a tiredness, a confusion that physically hurt in her chest. 'What we have is good. Isn't it? Or is it just me being delusional?' She waited for him to respond. When he didn't she considered walking out of the door, but something was pushing her to speak from her heart, to explain her feelings and not be ashamed of them. For so long she'd been ashamed of her background, had felt sullied by it, ashamed that her classmates had known her when she had been withdrawn and terrified, ashamed of loving her parents more than her birth parents, ashamed that she was so terrified of so many things in life: dogs, loud knocks on the door, unexplained noises during the night. 'This morning, when we had sex… I saw how you looked at me. And anyway, it wasn't sex, was it? We made love, Laurent. I don't know why I'm saying all of this. I know I'm humiliating myself but I can't go around pretending that my heart isn't breaking.'

He buried his head in his hands, rubbing at his skin. When he looked back at her his expression was bewildered. 'What do you want from me, Hannah?'

Her throat closed over, her legs suddenly weak. 'For you to be honest with me.'

He walked across the room, came to a stop a few feet away. 'I'm happy with my life as it is. I can't offer you any commitment, a long-term relationship. I've always told you that.'

His voice was pained, his eyes brimming with confusion. Stupidly she wanted to cry at how alone he seemed. 'Yes, but why?'

'I don't seem to have the capacity for it.'

She laughed at that. 'That's such rubbish.'

'Okay, so we stay together. Maybe even marry, have kids. And then one day one of us grows bored, becomes disappointed in the other person. And we hurt one another.'

'Not necessarily.'

He turned from her, walked to the doors out to the terrace, stared out towards the beach before turning and asked, 'Doesn't it worry you that *both* of my parents had affairs?'

'Have you ever been unfaithful before?'

'No.'

She moved towards him, stepping onto the sea-green rug at the centre of the room, her bare calf touching against the wooden coffee table. 'Then why do you think that you'll be unfaithful in the future?'

He threw his head back and inhaled deeply. 'I've never been tested in a relationship, have I? I never dated anyone as long as I dated you. I always ended other relationships within a few months, before they got too serious.'

Thrown, she said, 'I never knew that.' Then with another disbelieving laugh she added, 'You're even more messed up than me.'

'Exactly.'

She moved towards him again and asked, 'Why are you so scared of love? What are you scared of, Laurent?'

He moved away from her, towards the kitchen counter. He opened up the picnic basket and answered, 'Nothing.'

She followed him and stood beside him. 'Not being able to love, how cynical you are over marriage because of what your parents did...it all feels like a front for something else you're hiding.'

He turned and looked at her, bewildered. 'I'm not hiding anything.'

'Maybe you're hiding it even from yourself.'

His eyes narrowed at that. 'I'm not following what—'

They both jumped at the sound of the intercom ringing.

She looked towards the front door. 'That will be my taxi.'

He pulled baguettes and cheese and ripe peaches from the basket. 'Stay. Have something to eat. I'll drive you to the airport.'

She walked away, grabbed hold of her suitcase.

He stopped her at the doorway. 'I don't want us to part like this.'

She stared into the brilliant blue eyes of the man she loved. And answered from her heart. 'I've told you my feelings...you've made it clear once again that there's no future for us.' She opened the door and, about to step into the bright light of the overhead sun, she turned and said, 'I hope you find happiness in the future. You deserve it. You just don't accept that right now.'

CHAPTER TEN

NOT FOR THE first time, Hannah looked blankly at another sales clerk in the airport duty-free who was waving a bottle of perfume and asking if she wanted to try a sample. The woman's smile faded when Hannah didn't respond. Realising how rude she must appear, Hannah took hold of the thin strip of sample paper, sniffed, made some appreciative noises before backing away. She felt numb, dumb and empty. And with hours to go before her flight, unable to read, unable to sit still, unable to bear being out in the packed waiting lounge near laughing families and excited couples, she felt as if the duty-free store and its bright colours and promises of contentment via cosmetics and alcohol and chocolate was the only place she could find refuge in.

She moved into a hidden corner that seemed forgotten by both staff and customers and vacantly inspected the stacked rows of lipsticks. She tried to read the improbable names—Moroccan Magic, Cupid's Bow, All-Nighter—but her brain soon zoned out and she stared at them vacantly.

What she wanted more than anything in the world was to be somehow magically transported back to her apartment. Back to her bedroom with the blinds pulled down.

She picked up a silver eyeshadow. Her mum would

love it. Recently her mum and dad had taken up ballroom dancing and her mum liked to wear dramatic make-up for their competitions. Hannah gave a faint smile, a fresh weight of heaviness clogging her throat when she remembered the time she was home visiting for the weekend and they'd arrived back from their first ever dancing competition, proudly announcing that they had come sixth. Hannah had clapped in delight. And then her parents had laughed and admitted that there had only been six couples in their category. They hadn't cared that they had come last. For them, taking part, dancing together, was all that mattered. They had been so animated in recalling the night and some of the extremes some of the couples had gone to to psych out their competition, finishing off each other's stories and sentences without even realising it. They loved each other so much. And never took that love for granted.

Hannah popped the eyeshadow in the small net shopping basket she'd picked up at the entrance, and realised it wasn't her apartment she'd choose to be transported to should a genie appear and grant her one wish. It was in fact her parents' house. There she might shake off the awful emptiness inside her through their calm and undemanding warmth and love. She wanted to be loved.

But she couldn't go home. Her parents, her mum especially, would notice her upset. And the last thing she wanted to do was worry her parents even more than they already were about her. They tried to hide it but even as a child she'd been aware of them studying her closer than they did Emily and Cora, more easily forgiving when she did something wrong. Now they worried over her lack of a relationship. They had never said anything but their delight and obvious relief when she'd told them that she was bringing Laurent home to meet them had said it all.

She wandered into the aftershave section. Was there something wrong with her? Was that why he couldn't love her? Was she too needy, too clingy, not pretty enough? Was it her background? Was the truth behind all his reasons for not wanting commitment the fact that he was waiting to meet someone from his own privileged background?

She eyed a familiar-shaped bottle of aftershave. Told herself to move away. But like an addict needing a hit, she lifted the lid and sprayed some onto her wrist. Closing her eyes, she inhaled the woody, musky scent. Laurent's aftershave. He never wore anything else. She blinked hard, a dense lump forming in her throat.

She didn't know what Laurent found lacking in her, but she could certainly identify one area of weakness— her judgement. How could she have allowed herself to get so tangled up with him again? She'd walked through this airport only three days ago determined that she was over him and was going to be nothing but professional and emotionally detached around him.

She'd made a complete mess of things. She moved into the alcohol section but even looking at the bottles made her queasy. Especially when she spotted the distinct blue-and-gold labels of Bonneval Cognac. She snatched her gaze away, a fresh wave of disbelief washing over her.

Had today really happened? First she'd asked him to sleep with her. Then to make love to her. Then later she'd more or less told him she loved him. Yip. Her judgement sucked.

She lingered by the confectionery section waiting for the embarrassment radiating from her cheeks to subside and trying not to give in to the temptation to buy a super-sized bar of chocolate, before approaching the checkout.

Showing her boarding card to the cashier, she bought the silver eyeshadow.

She had a choice. Feel numb and dumb for the foreseeable future or try to pretend this weekend never happened. For her own sanity, she knew she needed to do the latter.

Finding a seat amongst a group of pensioners sitting at a gate displaying a Rome departure destination, she pulled out her phone and deleted Laurent's number and then, as quickly as her fingers allowed, every image of him in her picture gallery. Then, logging into the airport Wi-Fi, she began to research wedding celebrants in the Granada area of Spain.

Sitting in the boardroom of Bonneval Cognac, his father to one side, Nicolas Couilloud on the other, Laurent tried and failed to focus on the conversation of the two other men, who were arguing over the details of a five-year-old contract, which both were aggrieved about. He closed his eyes to the migraine lurking behind there.

'Laurent, is everything okay?'

He opened his eyes to Nicolas's terse question.

Nicolas sat back in his chair, a gleam entering his grey calculating eyes. 'You don't seem well. Perhaps you should leave these negotiations to your father and myself.'

He was about to answer but his father got there before him. 'Laurent is CEO now. It's he who has to finalise the contract. I'm only here to facilitate the negotiations.'

Laurent blinked, startled by his father's admission. He gave a brief nod of agreement and, for the first time in a very long time, they shared eye contact that wasn't more than a fleeting glance.

Nicolas cleared his throat. 'Has Mademoiselle Mc-

Ginley returned to England? You seemed particularly close at the wedding.'

'She left two weeks ago, immediately after the wedding.'

Nicolas shrugged, gave a knowing smile. 'There's plenty more attractive women out there keen to date you.'

Though he was tempted to stand, Laurent remained seated and, folding over his notepad and shutting down his laptop, he said to Nicolas, 'Considering that you are an old family *friend*, and our businesses have worked together for the past twenty years, you will get a two per cent contract increase.'

'We need at least eight per cent,' Nicolas spluttered.

Laurent stood. 'Two per cent.'

'Antoine, you can see that Laurent's offer is unreasonable,' Nicolas said, looking in appeal towards his father.

For a moment his father hesitated, his gaze shifting between Nicolas and him, but then with a shrug towards Nicolas he said, 'Laurent is CEO.'

His migraine worsening, and wanting these negotiations over and done with once and for all, Laurent stepped forward, thrown by his anger towards Nicolas for so casually dismissing Hannah, thrown by how suddenly he didn't give a damn about the business. All he could think about was Hannah. It felt as though he were living in a cloud of guilt and panic since she'd left.

He held out his hand, forcing himself to give Nicolas a conciliatory smile. 'I look forward to continuing our good working relationship that is so mutually beneficial.'

Nicolas's jaw tightened. After a long pause, he reluctantly reached out and shook his hand.

Leaving his father and Nicolas in the boardroom to discuss a vintage car that Nicolas was trying to persuade his father to sell to him, Laurent returned to his office.

He was irritably ploughing through his emails when his father appeared a while later.

'You look as tired as I feel.'

Laurent took in his father, his lopsided smile, the walking stick he was leaning on.

'I'm glad that you're finally listening to your physio's advice and using your walking stick.'

His father made a grumbling noise. 'I've decided I must look after myself now that you need my help with the business.'

Taken aback, Laurent studied his father and then had to bite back a smile at the teasing gleam in his father's eye.

He stood and pulled his visitor chair away from his desk so that his father could easily sit, before returning to his side of the desk.

'Well negotiated,' his father said.

'If you call giving an ultimatum negotiating.'

'Sometimes people need to have things spelt out loud and clear with no ambiguity.'

Laurent chuckled at that and his heart lifted when his father joined in. He cleared his throat. 'Thanks for the support in there.'

His father's attention shifted to something outside Laurent's office window. 'You're doing a good job.' Pausing, he tipped his walking stick against the floor a couple of times. 'You were born for the role.'

Laurent stared at his father, who cleared his throat noisily. 'Your mother said that you were asking about our...hmm...about our...about how we both left home.'

'Your affairs, you mean?'

His father nodded, and shifted his gaze to a point on the opposite wall, the colour in his cheeks rising. 'I was very unhappy back then.'

Laurent was about to interject and say that he didn't want to hear his excuses, but his father's guilt-ridden and anguished gaze met his and Laurent remembered Hannah's advice that he needed to listen to and try to understand his father.

'I couldn't cope in the role of CEO. I was out of my depth. I felt deeply ashamed and a failure. I met a woman who distracted me from all of that but it was a short-lived affair.'

With an impatient exhalation, Laurent interrupted, 'Hardly. It went on for years.'

His father's cheeks darkened even further and he swallowed hard. 'The times you thought that I was away continuing my affair, I was actually in hospital being treated for depression.'

For a long while Laurent stared at his father incredulously, wondering if he had heard right. 'Why didn't you tell me?'

His father bowed his head. When he eventually looked back up he grimaced. 'I'd like to say it was only because I didn't want to worry you, but I had seen your disgust when I returned after my affair—I couldn't bear to think of you having an even lower opinion of me, so I begged your mother not to tell you.'

Laurent gave an angry laugh. 'That makes no sense. You preferred for me to think that you were having an affair rather than tell me that you were unwell?'

'I didn't want you to think that I was weak.'

'Mental illness has nothing to do with weakness. I can't believe you kept it from me, robbed me of the chance of helping you. I could have helped. I would have wanted to support you.'

His father looked at him, perplexed. 'You would?'

'Of course I would. You're my father.'

'I thought I had lost my right to expect anything of you. I had let you and François down so badly.'

Laurent nodded. 'Yes, you did...but if I had understood how much you were struggling, I would have been there for you.'

Laurent swallowed when he spotted his father quickly wiping at his eyes and, looking down, studied the wood of his desk where generations of Bonneval had worked. He stared at a long paper-thin scratch in the wood. Hannah had been right. He did need to speak to his father. He lifted his gaze to see that his father, with bowed head, was looking towards the floor, his forehead creased, and wondered at his suffering and the extremes he must have gone to, to hide his illness from François and himself. All because he had feared their reaction.

His father lifted his head and, when their gazes met, in a flash Laurent realised just how deeply he had missed his father for the past twenty years.

He rolled his neck, trying to make sense of the fact that his parents' affairs were only part of the story. It was the feeling of being abandoned and shut out that had done the real damage. They'd never spoken to him before they'd left, explained what was going on, had been vague and distant in their sparse calls home. And when they had returned, they had always been preoccupied, never there for him.

His father slid a card across the desk to him, a pastel drawing of London Bridge on the front. 'I received this card in the post yesterday morning. It's from Hannah, thanking me for taking her on a tour of the House and apologising that she didn't get to say goodbye.'

Laurent picked up the card and studied her neat handwriting. She knew all about his parents but still showed them respect. At the wedding she'd slotted into the role of co-host, seeing that he needed support. Time and time again she'd shown her care for him. *'I really, really care for you.'* He'd panicked at her words, at the time thinking it was because he was averse to any form of commitment, but in truth it was because he was so scared of loving someone, and for them to leave him one day. He wanted to avoid at all costs having to ever face again the same grinding emptiness, the torrent of zero self-worth, the confusion, the self-blame, the panic of his teenage years.

His gaze shot back to his father when he shifted in his seat and attempted to stand while saying, 'I'd like to go home now if that's okay with you.'

Laurent went to his side but his father insisted on standing by himself. He escorted his father down to Reception, where the company car was waiting to bring him home.

At the car, his father once again refused his assistance, but as Laurent went to close the car door, his father leant forward and held out his hand.

Laurent took hold of it, his heart pulling when his father said, 'Thank you.'

On the way back to his office, bewildered, disappointed and exhausted by his conversation with his father, Laurent wondered what had it taken Hannah, given her background, their relationship history, to be so open and forthright with him? And he'd given her nothing in response. He inhaled a long breath, remembering her last words before she'd left, wishing him happiness in the future. He'd closed down on her but she'd still found it in herself to say those words to him.

Nothing about Hannah said she'd ever hurt him.

All along he'd thought he wasn't capable of giving love when in truth it really was about him not being able to accept love.

Back in his office he realised his father had forgotten Hannah's card to him. He looked at the handwriting again, loving its precision but also the quiet flourishes at the edges of the letters that spoke of Hannah's personality. He studied the words again too, that were thoughtful and kind and generous.

He loved her.

He'd loved her for such a long time but had hidden his fears behind denial. But twice he'd rejected her. What would that have done to her? Guilt and fury towards himself twisted in his gut. And then a fresh wave of panic had him pull at his tie, open his top button. Would she ever want to talk to him again?

Given the late hour and the fact that it was the school holidays, Hannah's Friday night train ride home from work to Richmond was for once almost pleasant. She'd found a seat and the man who had come to sit next to her was absorbed by his book, no loud headphones on, no shouting down the phone.

It was the perfect space for her to daydream about her future. To weigh up the pros and cons of staying in London or moving to Singapore or Granada.

For close to two weeks now she'd been trying to focus on making a decision, but her concentration was shot and her thoughts kept wandering off into a reel of flashing memories—how Laurent had silently contemplated her as he'd rowed them to the restaurant on her first night in Cognac, him fisting his hand in the air when he'd won the table tennis tournament before running over and high-fiving her, the wonder in his voice when he'd spoken of becoming an uncle, how closed he'd been when she'd tried to tell him what he meant to her.

The train rattled past row upon row of red-brick

houses, most with lights on in the downstairs rooms, given the gloom of the evening due to the low grey clouds hovering over the city.

Work were looking for an answer from her about the Singapore transfer. She had asked for a week's extension to consider it further and she needed to give them an answer on Monday. But she was finding it impossible to think straight. The hollowness, the aimlessness, the embarrassment inside her were too overwhelming.

She stared at the light drops of rain that were starting to splatter onto the window of the carriage, her cheeks reddening with not just humiliation, but the crushing memory of trying to reach out to Laurent and be honest about her feelings for him and then the humiliating realisation that he wasn't going to respond.

She pulled her gaze away from the window and studied the page of her notebook she'd divided into three columns—her two possible new lives along with her current position.

Her current life had so many pros. She liked her team. She liked her apartment. She was well paid and respected in her profession. London was a great place to meet new men. She grimaced at that. She wasn't going near another man for a very long time. She drew a definite X through London. It was time she moved on. Widened her horizons. Followed a life that felt true and meaningful.

She stood as the train pulled into Richmond station. And not for the first time scanned the platform for Laurent. Which she knew was crazy but she couldn't help herself. Or help how her heart went from being positioned in her throat with keen anticipation and sank faster than a pebble in water down to her stomach when she saw that he wasn't there.

It had been their thing. The first time she'd agreed to

go out for a drink with him, they had arranged to meet at seven the following Friday outside Richmond station when she would be arriving on her regular train home. But on the Thursday he'd been waiting for her, standing on the platform holding the most amazing bunch of pastel-pink-and-lemon tea roses he'd brought all of the way from his supposedly week-long trip to Paris.

He'd explained with an irresistible smile that he'd cut his trip short because he'd wanted to see her. And for the following ten months that they had dated, Hannah had never known when he would be there waiting for her, invariably with another gorgeous bunch of tea roses. And that unknown anticipation had given her days a sparkle that had had her practically bounce with good cheer through every meeting, every phone call, every mundane task of her job.

Outside the station she walked along the streets that took her home, a leaden weariness having her walk slowly despite the now persistent rain.

Stepping out onto the road to cross over to her street, she gasped at the blare of a horn and stepped back onto the footpath as a car whizzed by her, the young female driver and passenger laughing in her direction.

She stared after the car, her heart hammering, tears springing to her eyes. An elderly man stopped and asked her if she was okay and began to mutter about young troublemakers driving too fast.

She opened the communal front door to her apartment building with shaking hands. Closing it behind her, she rested against the wooden panels and resolved that, once and for all, she'd consign Laurent to the past.

Over the weekend she would make her decision on her future. And start mending her heart. She'd done it once before and could do it again.

CHAPTER ELEVEN

SLOWING TO A JOG, Laurent came alongside Bleu, who had run ahead of him and was now lying flat on the ground outside the chicken coop, staring forlornly in the direction of the hen and her chicks.

Perhaps he was being foolish but he would almost swear Bleu only wanted to hang out with them. Reaching down, he stroked his coat. 'Maybe I need to get you a companion.'

Bleu twisted his head, his gaze as ever trusting and loyal, his tail now wagging over the grass.

'Time for bed, Bleu.'

Bleu stood and, after receiving his nightly rub that included having his ears scratched, ambled off in the direction of the stables.

Inside the château Laurent eyed his phone where he had left it on the hallway table. He'd texted Hannah before he'd left work for the weekend and again an hour ago before he'd gone for his run with Bleu.

He picked up the phone, willing her to have responded to his message saying he would like to talk with her. But there was only a single message from François.

In the oppressive silence of the château he tried to control his worry and frustration. He wanted to speak to her. Now. Tell her that he was sorry, that he loved her.

But he knew he needed to slow down. He had no idea of Hannah's feelings for him now. In all probability she would never want to see him again.

He should wait until the morning. Give her the night to think about his message. Some time and space would probably do him good too; he knew he loved Hannah but it felt as if part of him was still trying to play catch-up with that. For so long he'd refused to believe he'd ever allow himself to fall in love, and accepting he'd done just that wasn't proving easy to reconcile with.

He walked towards the stairs and lifted his gaze up to the domed stained-glass roof that had so entranced Hannah. Depending on the time of the day and the level of sunshine, different shades and patterns of light were reflected on the walls and the white marble treads of the stairs.

He turned back to the hall table. Picked up the phone. Found her number. Squared his shoulders and pressed the dial button.

It rang out to her voicemail. His heart pulled to hear her voice, clear with precise instructions on what details the caller should leave but also with a warmth that said you were welcome into her world.

He cleared his throat when the beep sounded, suddenly lost for words. 'Ah... *Oui...?* I left you some messages. I think we should talk. Call me back. Any time.' He was about to hang up but then blurted out, 'I'm coming to London tomorrow. I'd like to see you.'

He hung up. Travelling to London had never been his intention. He caught a glimpse of himself in the hallway mirror and was thrown by the aloneness of his reflection.

He climbed the stairs and wondered if she would respond.

Her answer was there when he got out of the shower, in a succinct text message.

I don't want to see you. There's nothing else to be said.

He rubbed a towel over his damp hair, his gaze on his bed. Hannah had been so right when she'd said that they had made love there. In truth, their intimacy had always been way more than just a physical act. It had always held a tenderness, an honesty. They had always exposed their true selves to one another during their lovemaking, but he'd been too blinkered by fear and a conviction that he was following the right path in life to recognise that.

He picked up his phone and called the executive travel agency employed by Bonneval Cognac and arranged his flights. Whether she wanted it or not, he was going to London.

Sunday morning, and Laurent's taxicab passed by the early morning joggers as he made his way towards Richmond. Once there, he rang Hannah's intercom, just as he had done endless times Saturday afternoon and evening. He held his breath, the knot of tension in his stomach tightening, willing her to answer.

But when she did answer with a hesitant, 'Hello,' he was so surprised after the frustration of yesterday that he jerked back and stared at the silver mouthpiece.

'Hello,' Hannah repeated.

'It's me.'

A long silence followed. He began to speak. 'Can I—' But the buzz of the front door opening interrupted him.

He walked past the bicycles belonging to the other tenants, stored in the hallway, and up the stairs to her first-floor apartment, remembering the time he'd carried her up to her apartment when she'd twisted her ankle one evening when stepping off a pavement wearing impossibly high heels.

She was standing at her door dressed in black yoga pants and a loose white top, a black and white sports bra visible underneath, her hair tied up in a bun, her expression and crossed arms screaming impatience and annoyance.

He paused a few feet from her, thrown at seeing her again, realising how much he'd missed her, not just during the past two weeks but for all the past year since they had split up. Yet another thing he'd deliberately blinded himself to in a bid to protect himself from ever exposing his heart to the world.

He clenched his hands, hating what an idiot he'd been.

Hannah shifted away from the doorframe she'd been leaning on, her expression growing ever more irritated.

Had he read too much into what she'd said about caring for him? What if that was all that she'd meant, that she cared for him, but she had not meant that she loved him as he'd assumed?

'Why so early?'

He tried not to recoil from her icy tone and answered, 'I called several times yesterday. I wanted to catch you before you left today.'

She didn't even try to argue that she hadn't planned on escaping from her apartment for the day in a bid to avoid him and said instead, 'I know I could spend the next ten minutes arguing with you about why I don't want you to come in, why there's no point in us talking, but I know how stubborn you can be.' Turning, she walked into the apartment, adding, 'You can have five minutes. After that I want to get back to my yoga.'

He nodded towards the yoga mat set on the floor beneath the opened sash window, the laptop on the kitchen table, the screen on pause showing a woman reaching her arms skywards, a foot pressed against the opposite thigh. 'Is that the yoga teacher you follow?'

'Yes, Kim Ackerman.' She went and sat on the piano stool in front of her upright piano, the farthest point from him in the combined kitchen and living space. 'What do you want to talk about?'

'I'm here to apologise.'

Her jaw tightened; her eyes took on a cold glint.

When he realised she wasn't going to say anything in response, he added, 'I've missed you...and I've come to realise how much you mean to me.'

She exhaled a disbelieving breath at that.

Uncomfortable, anxiety-induced heat flamed at the back of his neck. He wasn't sure of what to say, how to get across how he was feeling, trying to articulate it in his second language making it particularly difficult, and Hannah's cool scepticism wasn't helping either.

Thoughts rattled through his brain. In the end he decided to try to speak from his heart even though he felt like choking on the words that were so alien to him. 'You asked me at the beach house what I was so scared about. I had no idea what you were talking about. But since you left, my relationship with my father has changed, things aren't quite as tense.' He paused, gave her a wry smile. 'I listened to what you said about giving him a role in the company. He now works in an advisory position.'

Hannah's expression remained unmoved.

'We spoke about his affairs—he admitted to his first affair but I was wrong when I thought he was away having other affairs in the years that followed.'

'Where was he?'

'In hospital, receiving treatment for depression.'

Hannah gave a swift inhalation of surprise before saying, 'The poor man. That's terrible.'

'He said he didn't tell myself and François because he was ashamed. Which is bloody stupid.'

Hannah grimaced but then she regarded him with sad compassion. 'I'm guessing that he thought he was protecting you.'

A sizeable lump of emotion lodged in his throat when he saw tears in Hannah's eyes. He swallowed hard to dislodge it before adding, 'After he told me, I realised that it wasn't just his supposed affairs that devastated me but how abandoned I felt. When François and I were younger, our family was a happy one—a normal family. But then, when my father took over the business, it all unravelled. He became short-tempered, my mother preoccupied. We stopped being a family. And then the affair happened. And François and I were left in the dark from that point forward.'

He moved towards the window, suddenly feeling extremely restless. Outside a man was pushing a lawnmower along the footpath. He turned back to Hannah, rolling his shoulders against the ache in his shoulder blades. 'I wish they had told us that he was in hospital. Things could have been so different. I'd like to think I would have understood and been supportive—between my grandfather and me we could have helped him. As a teenager I felt responsible for François. I had no one I could speak to. I hated how alone I felt, how insecure, how out of control everything around me felt. I hated that lack of stability, feeling so vulnerable. And the constant roller coaster of my father coming and going only added to that. In truth I'm angry with both of my parents for robbing the rest of the family of the opportunity to support them, for not trusting us to care. But I can't change the past, I can only influence the present and hope for a better future for us as a family.'

Exhausted, he stopped. For long moments they stared at one another.

'Does any of this make any sense?' Then he exhaled. 'I must sound self-indulgent in everything I'm saying. I know I should have coped better in everything that happened, especially in comparison to everything that you went through.'

'Both of our backgrounds were pretty horrible. There's no point in comparing them. I'm so sorry that you were so alone back then.'

A jittery sensation ran through his legs at the compassion in her voice. 'And I'm sorry I reacted so poorly to what you said in Royan.'

Her gaze turned away from him towards her laptop screen. 'It hurt, but that's life, I guess.'

He moved across the room, coming to a stop by a low coffee table. Some pens and glue were piled neatly in a row on a dark wooden tray lying on top. 'Now, I can see how much it must have taken you to open up like that to me, given how I ended our relationship before, what you went through as a child.'

Hannah blinked. Her jaw working. 'Where's this conversation going?'

He pressed his leg against the coffee table, trying to gather his rambling thoughts and words. If any of his ex-banking colleagues who had always commended his negotiation skills saw him now they would scoff at his incompetence. He reeled back everything he'd said in his mind and then tried to answer her question as truthfully as he could, regardless of how uncomfortable it felt.

'I now realise why I was so set against relationships,

against ever falling in love. It isn't because I'm cynical, or have no interest in commitment. It's because I'm terrified of loving someone and for them to leave me. Up until now I haven't wanted to give another person that power over me.'

'I'm glad you've come to that understanding.'

He looked at her blankly for a moment. '*Dieu!* I'm really messing this up.' He cleared his throat. 'What I'm trying to say...' He moved around the coffee table and sat down on the nearest chair to her. 'The reason why I am here...' He stood back up. His heart felt as if it was going into arrhythmia. He circled back to the other side of the table. 'The reason we need to talk...' He closed his eyes and blurted out, 'We need to talk because I want you to know that I love you.'

Shooting off the stool, Hannah dodged around the sofa rather than having to pass Laurent, her heart hammering. At the kitchen table she flipped down the laptop screen where Kim Ackerman, the London-based online yoga superstar, had been instructing her audience in 'inhale love, exhale love.' It seemed to be a travesty to have Kim's image in the same room as her right now, because her blood was boiling with rage. And she was scared.

Scared of believing Laurent.

She swallowed down the temptation to laugh hysterically.

He was saying what she had longed for, that he loved her. But it felt wrong. It was too late. She was moving on from him. She glanced over to the mood board she'd spent yesterday creating in a café close to Richmond Park, where she'd hidden away from Laurent having guessed rightly that he would call at her apartment even though she'd said she didn't want to talk.

She'd also guessed he would turn up today. Just not this early.

'Hannah?'

She turned to him.

'Did you hear what I said? That I love you.'

She was almost taken in by the nervousness in his voice, how drawn and pale he suddenly looked.

Not that it made him in the slightest bit unattractive. That made her even crosser. Here she was standing in some tatty old gymwear, overheating from too many down dogs and warrior poses, and he looked as if he'd stepped out of a photo shoot for how Europe's top ten eligible CEOs dressed when off-duty.

Wearing dark jeans, a white open-neck heavy cotton shirt and a zipped navy bomber jacket, he was carrying himself with his usual understated sophistication. His hair had been recently cut and she hated how it emphasised the beautiful shape of his skull, the sharpness of his jawline, the brilliance of his blue eyes.

She went and yanked up the already open sash window to its maximum opening. Turning and trying to project a semblance of calmness, she said, 'I heard you, Laurent. But quite frankly I really don't understand what you mean when you say that you love me.'

He went to answer but the anger and fear inside her had her add, 'And can I point out that you seemed to find it hard to actually tell me that—to say those words? It seemed like you were having to force yourself, so please forgive me if I don't believe you.'

He stepped back, almost losing his balance when he banged against the coffee table.

Hannah turned away and went into the kitchen. She'd been sipping on green tea before he'd arrived but now she needed coffee. And not her usual instant, but strong percolated coffee.

She bent and searched the corner cupboard for her rarely used coffee maker, refusing to speak to Laurent. He clearly thought he could waltz in here and tell her he loved her and, hey presto, all would be rosy in the garden.

No way. Not by a long shot.

Eventually she found the machine at the furthest reaches of the cupboard and, dragging it out, cursed to herself when the cord and plug dropped to the floor, the plug whacking against her bare toes.

Her mood didn't improve when Laurent came and stood beside her. He said nothing but instead watched her wash out the jug and the water reservoir and then search her freezer compartment for some ground coffee.

When she couldn't take another minute of silence she turned to him and said, 'You're welcome to leave, you know.'

'Not until I tell you why I love you.'

She tried desperately to hold on to her anger, but the softness in his voice, the sincerity in his eyes was a much too strong opponent.

Backing against the counter, she eyed him sceptically, telling herself not to fall for his easy words, not to lose herself to her lousy judgement again. She needed to protect herself.

'When we first met, I was instantly attracted to you. You're the most beautiful and beguiling woman I have ever met. You project a cool calmness, a wariness, but behind that you're gentle, kind and forgiving. At times I wanted you to dislike my parents, I wanted to feel justified in my pain, but instead, while you understood my feelings towards them, you were also non-judgemental about them. Your openness to them, and especially now that I know about my father's depression, has made me stop and realise that I need to be more understanding, to realise that I haven't walked in their shoes.' He came closer. 'There's so much more I love about you—how in tune we seem to be with one another...' he smiled '...the synchronicity of our thoughts, our shared sense of humour. With you I feel complete, whole. Without you, I feel incredibly alone and lost. The past two weeks have been horrible.'

Hannah's heart felt as though it were a lead weight in her chest—the loneliness in his voice was so real. 'What has changed, Laurent? Why are you telling me now that you love me? Why not before?'

His gaze shifted to her fridge where there were numerous photos of her holding Diana, as a newborn, in her christening gown and at her dad's birthday party last month. Something altered in his expression and when he looked back at her it was with almost a pleading look.

'When we were together in London I was still carrying the emptiness and fear that had been in me for years.' As though anticipating how she was about to argue that he'd always seemed so confident, he added, 'My confidence, my self-esteem, despite outward appearances, was terrible. I hid that fact from myself as much as everyone around me. But being back home in Cognac, knowing that I'm making a difference to the business's future, understanding my parents a little better, have all helped restore how I feel about myself. All along I thought I wasn't capable of loving other people, when in reality the issue was that I couldn't accept love. I didn't think I was worthy of it and I worried about leaving myself open to pain. But your honesty at the beach house, knowing the courage it must have taken you to tell me that you cared for me, I now appreciate how much you must have meant those words.' His hand reached out as though to touch her but then, bowing his head, he pulled it back. 'I've messed you around, Hannah. I've hurt you. I'm truly sorry that I did. You said you wanted to be honest with me and I want to reciprocate that truthfulness. The honest truth is that I love you and want to spend my life with you.'

Hannah sank against the countertop, her legs shaking. It would be so easy to tell him that she loved him too. For a moment she felt dizzy with the wonder of what would happen if she did.

But just as quickly she dismissed that thought. 'Spend your life with me—what does that mean?'

'I've been thinking about how we could make this work. I know you want to change the direction of your career. Why not come to Cognac? You could run your wedding celebrant business from there. Or even join the House—your financial expertise would be of great benefit.' He stopped and gave her a hopeful grin. 'I'd get to take you out to lunch that way, commute to work together even.'

Hannah shook her head, trying to cling to the fragile excitement she'd felt yesterday when she'd finally come to a decision on her future.

She edged past Laurent and went and grabbed the poster-sized piece of cardboard that formed her mood board for her future.

She turned it to him, propping it on the kitchen table. 'I'm moving to Spain.'

'Why Spain?'

'I contacted an established marriage celebrant business in Granada and they're looking for a business partner. It's a husband-and-wife team at the moment, and they are struggling with demand. I've found an apartment in the city to rent.'

Running a hand over the image on the mood board of the one-bedroom apartment in an old Moorish building she'd found on the internet, she added in a low voice, 'I need a new start. Put the past behind me.'

'What about us?'

She held his gaze for the longest time, seeing bewilderment and hurt and pride all play out in his expression.

She looked away, trying to control a thousand different voices and emotions flooding her brain and body and soul, and spoke straight from her heart, being honest as he'd asked her to. 'I can't trust you. I don't want my heart broken again.'

Standing outside Hannah's door, Laurent felt as if he'd stepped into a vortex about half an hour ago and had just been spat back out again. Dazed, he wondered where he would go. What he would do.

A woman approached him, the straining Labrador on a leash making a beeline for him. The woman apologised as the Labrador's paws skidded on the pavement in his attempt to get close to Laurent. Crouching down, Laurent stroked the dog, who instantly calmed. Emotion caught him in the throat. He missed Bleu. He missed Cognac. He wanted to go back there. He'd never thought he would feel this way about his birthplace.

With one final hug for the Labrador, he waved him and his owner off.

He stepped out onto the road. Looked up to the first floor, the sound of Kim Ackerman's encouraging instructions just about audible.

He closed his eyes. He'd blown it. He'd waited too long in recognising what he felt for Hannah.

He breathed against the panic churning in his stomach. What if this was it? That there was no way back from this?

Part of him wanted to walk away, the part that always believed that relationships would be toxic and painful.

But the need to have Hannah in his life was too great. The need to prove to her what she meant to him pushed him towards the train station and then into a café in central London where he plotted for the next few hours how he would get her back. He was not going home without her.

CHAPTER TWELVE

MONDAY MORNING, AND with the dawn light creeping beneath her blinds Hannah knew she should get up, do something useful, but her body felt as if it belonged to a worn-out rag doll while her mind was spinning around and around, trying to make sense of yesterday, and unfortunately she was making very little progress.

He'd said he loved her. Had even thought through a future for them together. But it had all felt too easy for her to say she believed him, say that she loved him too and attempt to live happily ever after.

As much as Hannah wished it were, life simply wasn't like that.

She'd been honest yesterday when she'd said she didn't trust him. She didn't trust him not to change his mind, to realise that in fact he'd been right all along and love and commitment weren't for him.

Her birth parents, who instinctively should have loved and cared for her, had put their addictions and needs above hers. What if Laurent's love was equally fragile and no match for what life would throw at them?

She pushed herself up and off the bed and wobbled with light-headedness. She had a presentation to give to the board of a client company today and had no idea how she was going to pull it off.

She changed into her yoga pants and top, hoping that Kim Ackerman would once again help her focus on the day ahead.

Out in the living room she flicked through Kim's on-line videos and with a droll sigh picked one that was called, 'Yoga for a sore heart.'

She rolled out her mat and pressed play. Five minutes into the video, her mind still refusing to calm, she jumped when the intercom rang.

It had to be Laurent. Who else would be at her door this early? She refused to answer it but after three buzzes that had her startle each time, ruining Kim's guidance to 'free your mind of all that is troubling you,' she picked up the intercom hand piece and said curtly, 'There's no point in us talking.'

A soft, familiar-sounding female voice said, 'He said you'd say something like that.'

'Who's this?'

'Hannah, it's Kim, Kim Ackerman.'

Hannah swivelled around to stare at her laptop screen where Kim was frozen in a cat pose, wondering if her mind was playing tricks on her. Running to her win-dow, she yanked it open and stared down towards the front door.

Standing there with her sleek black hair tied back into a ponytail, a yoga mat under her arm, was Kim Acker-man.

Stunned, Hannah went back to the intercom. 'Kim... hello!' She grimaced at her overexcited fan-girl reaction that hadn't dimmed despite having spent a whole week in Kim's company in India, before asking, 'What are you doing here?'

'Laurent contacted me yesterday via my website. I don't usually do private visits but he was very persuasive.' She stopped and after a light chuckle she added in a serious tone, 'He asked me to tell you that he wants to prove how much he understands you, how sorry he is that it has taken him so long to realise how much he loves you and the pain that has caused. He wants to prove to you that you can trust him.'

Hannah shook her head and dryly responded, 'Most men send flowers.'

Kim laughed. 'I'm guessing he has a lot of apologising to do.'

And his apologising didn't stop there. No sooner had Kim left after an hour of soul-reviving yoga, when her intercom rang again. This time it was a delivery from the French bakery in Putney Heath that had been her and Laurent's favourite in London. Even with her stomach in a knot, Hannah had been unable to resist the delivery of still-warm croissants and freshly brewed coffee.

After a quick shower she'd spent the entire journey to work looking over her shoulder, wondering if Laurent was about to appear at any moment.

But later in the day, when her dad phoned her at work, she realised she need not have worried because when she had been waiting at the station for her train, Laurent had been pulling into her parents' farm in a rental car.

Apparently he'd apologised for how he'd behaved on his previous visit. And confessed that he had hurt Hannah and wanted to make amends. Her dad chuckled down the phone at that point and told her he hadn't been prepared just to take Laurent's word on this and had presented him with a pair of wellington boots and tasked him with carrying out the hardest jobs on the farm for the morning—mucking out the yard outside the milking parlour, washing down the mud-encrusted tractor, carrying endless bales of hay from the trailer into the barn.

And all the while her dad had interrogated him, wanting to know how they could be sure he wouldn't hurt Hannah again, why he loved her and what his intentions were towards her with regards to marriage and children.

At this point Hannah closed her office door and pleaded down the phone, 'Oh, Dad, please tell me that you didn't ask him that.'

She could hear her dad's pride on the other side of the phone when he answered, 'I did. I saw how upset you were when you visited after he broke it off with you last year. I didn't say anything. I know your mother tried to ask you why you were so down but that you said that you didn't want to talk about it. And that's fair enough. Sometimes we all need space. But I tell you this, I wasn't going to let Laurent off lightly today.'

Hannah sat heavily onto her chair, glad she'd given her presentation before this bombshell had landed. 'I don't know...' She paused, feeling so lost and confused. 'I don't know what to do. I don't know if he really loves me. I love him, but I know I can't have my heart broken again.'

She heard a rustling on the line and imagined her father running his hand back and forth over the crown of his head, as was his habit when thinking things through. 'Your mother and I—' He broke away and spoke to her mother, who was obviously standing right next to him. 'Isn't that right, Jan?' Hannah could hear her mum murmur in assent. 'Your mother and I have spent the last hour since Laurent left discussing whether we should tell you that he visited us. He didn't ask us to. He said he just wanted to apologise to us and let us know how much he loves you.'

A sizeable lump formed in Hannah's throat to hear her dad say that Laurent loved her. She could hear the emotion in his voice, his concern. She squeezed her eyes shut and tried to concentrate on what her father was saying. 'I think we are good judges of character and believe he was being sincere.'

There was a shuffling on the other side of the phone and then her mum spoke. 'Follow your heart, Hannah. You'll know deep down if you can trust him. If you can love him with all your heart. Listen to your instinct. Be honest with yourself, both why you want to be with him, but also if you decide not to be with him. Is it Laurent or something inside you holding you back?'

Hannah ended the call wishing she could tap into that instinct her mother spoke about but it seemed to be encased in an ice pack of fear and doubt.

Leaving work that evening, Hannah was once again on high alert, looking out for Laurent. Which wasn't easy considering she had to peep over the biggest bunch of pastel-pink-and-lemon tea roses she'd ever seen. She had attempted leaving them in her office but as she'd walked to the lift, Amy, one of the juniors on her team, had run after her carrying them, exclaiming with an amused laugh that she couldn't believe that Hannah had forgotten them.

Hannah had been on the verge of telling Amy to keep the flowers but their arrival had caused enough consternation; Hannah didn't need the added speculation from her team as to why she didn't want to keep them.

Taking the escalator down to the underground platforms at Liverpool Street station, Hannah stumbled as she tried to get her footing and cursed Laurent.

He wasn't going away easily.

And in the crowded tunnels she cursed him again when she was thrown endless irritable looks from her fellow commuters, who clearly weren't impressed with being whacked by a bunch of flowers.

Then beyond a group of chattering and jostling visiting students she spotted a handmade sign posted onto the tunnel wall. Written on the plain white paper in thick black marker was one word.

HANNAH

Odd.
A few feet further on, she glimpsed another sign.

I

The writing was familiar and sent a shiver of apprehension down her spine. She wanted to stop and study it but the tide of commuters carried her on to another sign.

LOVE

And then another.

YOU

And at the entrance to the platform, where the crowd thinned out, there was yet another sign.

IT'S YOU WHO BRINGS ME HAPPINESS

Popping the flowers under her arm, not caring if they got squashed, Hannah pulled down the sign and then ran back and pulled down all the others, garnering strange looks as she did so, praying all the while that none of her colleagues had seen the signs.

She was shaking when she ran back to the platform in time to squeeze onto a carriage before the doors shut.

There were no seats available so she tucked herself into a corner and studied Laurent's handwriting.

At Waterloo station, she caught her train in a daze. And when she got to Richmond she braced herself to find him standing on the platform.

But she swallowed down a gulp of disappointment with each step she took towards the exit, realising that he wasn't there.

She wanted to see him.

His signs that she'd folded and placed inside her handbag, her disappointment that he was nowhere to be seen, were thawing her numbness.

Turning into her street, she braced herself again, her gaze shooting towards the front door of her house. But there was no sign of him.

Inside her apartment she crowded the tea roses into the three vases she owned and had no choice but to place the remaining flowers into a drinking glass.

She changed into her black jeans and a sleeveless white lace top and waited for him to ring her intercom.

An hour later she was angry and cross. What was he playing at?

By nine o'clock she was a bundle of nerves. Had something happened to him? She pictured him lying on a hospital trolley.

She picked up her phone. She needed to call him, make sure he was okay. She yelped when her intercom rang.

She picked up the hand piece. 'What the hell are you playing at, Laurent?'

A young hesitant male voice answered, 'Is that Hannah McGinley? I've a package for you.'

Hannah ran down the stairs and apologised to the startled-looking delivery driver, who handed her a poster-sized package and legged it back to his van.

Upstairs Hannah pulled off the plain brown paper wrapping to find a mood board beneath. She stared at the images on it, trying to understand what they all meant, a giddiness, a disbelief fizzing through her bloodstream. She gave a little cry when she spotted at the centre of the board a photograph of herself and Laurent high-fiving each other at Lara's wedding. Her breath caught at the shared affection and familiarity in which they were smiling at one another, at how unbearably handsome Laurent looked with his shirtsleeves rolled up, evening shadow adding to his dark looks.

She stared at the board, guessing what each photo and carefully written word might mean, desperate to hear Laurent's explanation.

She picked up her phone, realising he was going to wait for her to contact him.

He was waiting to see if she would trust and believe him when he said he loved her.

A hand resting on her stomach, she closed her eyes and listened to her instinct.

Then she rang his number. When he answered she struggled to speak, completely overwhelmed by how tenderly, how nervously he said her name.

Eventually she managed to ask, 'Where are you?'

'I can be with you within half an hour.'

Hannah sighed out her answer—'Good!'—and hung up.

Laurent willed the taxi driver to drive faster but knew that they were already at the upper speed limits.

Hannah had sounded upset on the phone.

What was he facing?

He lowered his window, needing some air.

When he arrived at her apartment she buzzed him up without him even having to press the intercom button.

He took the stairs slowly, dreading what might come.

She was at her door waiting for him and with an uncertain smile turned and led him inside.

It was only when she lifted the mood board he had delivered to her, and he saw how her hands were shaking, that he realised that she was as nervous as he was.

'Will you explain what all these images mean?'

He gave her a self-deprecatory smile. 'Given how poorly I managed to explain myself verbally yesterday, I decided to follow your lead and show you in images the future I dream of for us both.'

Taking hold of the board, he pointed to the various travel images on the top right-hand corner. 'These are the places I want to visit with you. Costa Rica, Whistler, St Petersburg...' Pausing to point to one image in particular, he added, 'The Soap Museum in Antwerp.'

He was gifted with an amused smile from Hannah and, taking courage from it, pointed to the image of four children on a beach, all looking cute but mutinous, their dark hair ruffled, clearly not impressed to have been forced to stop digging an enormous hole in the sand. 'These four represent the children I want us to have, strong, independent, spirited children.'

With trembling fingers she tucked a strand of her loose hair behind her ear and nodded for him to continue, her eyes bright, her cheeks flushed.

'And this couple, celebrating their fifth wedding anniversary with friends and family, I want that to be us. But of course we will be having champagne and brandy cocktails.'

Touching the photo of the children, Hannah said, 'Kim Ackerman, the croissants, the flowers, the signs, this board...are all incredible, but what means the most to me is that you went and visited my parents.'

He swallowed at the raw vulnerable emotion in her voice, felt his heart about give way with the tension of it all. 'Your parents deserved my apology. And I needed to show you how much I love you.'

She took the mood board from his grasp and placed it down on the table. Then, coming in front of him, she stared up into his eyes, as though she was trying to fully know him. 'You do love me, don't you?'

It wasn't a question but more a statement of wonder.

He wanted to reach out and touch her. But he stayed where he was, instinctively knowing he needed to give her space. 'I realised I loved you one evening when waiting for you at Richmond station. Your smile when you got off your train and saw me lit a fire of happiness in me that was extraordinary in its power but also terrifying.' He heard his voice crack and paused in a bid to gather himself before admitting, 'I was terrified of loving you and being hurt.'

She stepped towards him, her bare toes curling over the tops of his shoes. Her hand reached for his cheek; he closed his eyes at how tender her touch was. 'I will never hurt you.'

He opened his eyes and said the most honest words he'd ever spoken. 'I know you won't.'

He touched her cheek, their gazes holding, holding, holding, silently communicating the wonder, the beauty, the hope of this moment. Then he gently kissed her, his heart aching with the honesty between them, his bones dissolving at the sensation of being in the place where you belonged, where you could be the true version of yourself.

Reluctantly he pulled back, knowing they still had things to discuss.

Taking her by the hand, he led her over to the sofa. When they were both seated, angled into one another, he asked, 'Have you decided what you are going to do work-wise in the future?'

Hannah nodded. 'I told my senior partner that I'm leaving today.'

Laurent flinched. 'Are you still going to Granada?'

She dipped her head for a moment. He braced himself. She hadn't actually told him her feelings for him yet. She had never said that she loved him. When she looked back up, she tilted her head, gave him a shy smile. 'There's a château in Cognac that sounds more appealing.'

He grinned at that but then, shuffling on the sofa, he said quietly, 'I love you…but I still don't know how you feel about me.'

Hannah stared at him, perplexed, and then she started giggling. 'I love you, of course! How could you not know that?' Lifting a pillow, she hit him with it playfully. 'I love you, Laurent Bonneval. I love your loyalty to François, to your parents, to your family business. I love your kindness, your ability to read my mind, I love how sexy you look twenty-four-seven and I love the future you have mapped out for us. I love everything about you and will even tolerate the smelliest of cheeses in our fridge.'

Laurent grinned and grinned and then, placing a tender kiss on her forehead, he knelt before her.

Hannah paled.

He cleared his throat, suddenly really nervous again. 'I want to ask you something but I'm not sure if it's too early.'

Her eyes were glistening with tears. 'I'm not going to change my mind about anything. I love you and want to move to be with you in Cognac.'

'I spoke to your dad today, got his permission.'

At that a tear dropped onto Hannah's cheek. 'You did?'

'And when I got back to London this afternoon I went shopping.'

Hannah gasped when he took a pale blue box from his blazer jacket. Holding it out towards her, he said with the honesty that he wanted to be the trademark of their marriage, 'I'm still not sure I fully understand love, but I'm going to stop trying to understand it and just believe in it instead.' Opening up the ring box, he held his breath as Hannah stared at the five-stone diamond ring.

'It's so beautiful.'

He grinned at her softly spoken awe and, taking the ring out of the box, he took hold of her hand and asked, 'Hannah, will you be my wife?'

Hannah nodded, laughed, wiped away a tear from her cheek, laughed again, made a funny exclamation noise when he placed the ring on her finger and then grinned and grinned at him, her hands flapping in excitement.

And when she calmed, she edged forward on the sofa, her hands capturing his face, her nose touching his. 'I will love you for ever and ever, Laurent.'

EPILOGUE

IT WAS A tricky manoeuvre, getting the full skirt of her wedding gown down the narrow steps of the farmhouse while carrying a heavy train. Hannah knew she could call for help but preferred to let her family and Lara chat and lark about in the kitchen instead.

At the bottom of the stairs, she paused to gather her breath and smiled at the consternation coming from the kitchen. Her mum and dad were arguing over how he should correctly knot his bow tie, Cora was pleading with her husband to stop Diana, who was now an adventurous fifteen-month-old, from crawling along the floor and Lara was cooing to her three-month-old daughter, Ruth.

Laurent had been right after all when he'd insisted that their wedding blessing take place on her parents' farm. At first Hannah had said no, that the château was a more suitable venue. Not only because of its size and facilities but also because it was the place where day by day they were becoming ever closer, where laughter rang out during their long weekend lunches with family and friends, where Hannah got to study Laurent and wonder at the security, the grounding, the absolute peace his love brought to her.

Now, though, she could see that the farm was the perfect place for them to marry. This house, so full of warmth and love, had been integral in nursing the terrified child she once had been.

They had officially married earlier in the week at a low-key but deeply intimate civil ceremony in Cognac Town Hall before making the journey to England.

She listened to all the voices in the kitchen, all the people she loved so dearly, tears filling her eyes at the knowledge that their marriage was soon going to be blessed in their presence.

She was excited, nervous and ever so slightly dazed.

But most of all she was grateful. Grateful that both she and Laurent had been able to deal with their pasts and focus on the future. Grateful that they had found one another. Grateful that they were surrounded by so much love and positivity and hope. She was grateful for Laurent's love, his daily kindness and unwavering support as she established her celebrant business, his loyalty, his determination to create and maintain a strong and honest marriage.

Hannah smiled when Lara opened the kitchen door. Ruth, wearing a lilac dress in the same shade as her mum's, was asleep in her arms. Lara along with Emily and Cora were her bridesmaids today, Diana her flower girl.

Lara gave a gasp. 'Oh, Hannah, I'm going to cry. You look so beautiful.'

A rush from the kitchen ensued and Hannah giggled at all the excited exclamations.

Coming towards her, tears in his eyes, her father passed her bouquet of irises to her. The flowers of hope.

And then they were all on the way out through the front walled garden, passing by the meadow with views out to the green valley beyond, and around to the terraced garden to the side of the house, her mum's pride and joy, the borders surrounding the cricket-pitch-worthy lawn abundant with clematises, pastel tea roses, lilies and alliums.

Her heart kicked hard when she saw Laurent standing in front of the seated guests.

Gripping her dad's arm even tighter, she walked towards him, her heart brimming with love and hope.

When Cora and Diana reached him, Laurent scooped Diana up and pecked her affectionately on the cheek. Diana's giggles ran across the entire terrace and the guests laughed in response and suddenly the suspenseful tension of the day was gone.

And when Lara arrived at the top of the aisle, Laurent gently touched his hand against one of Ruth's tiny lilac socks and smiled in delight and pride at his niece.

And then it was her turn.

His brilliant blue gaze enveloped her.

She moved towards him, the momentous significance of declaring their love publicly causing a tear to float down her cheek.

Laurent hugged her father.

And then he was smiling down at her, his eyes reflecting her own nervousness and amazement, and then he pulled her into him.

'Don't cry,' he whispered against her ear.

She pulled back a fraction. Gave a little hiccup. 'It's my hormones.'

Laurent frowned and then his mouth dropped open. 'Are you...?'

Nodding, she whispered against his ear, her heart kicking at the security, the sense of peace that she found standing so close to him. 'Pregnant. Yes.'

His eyes dancing with wonder, he captured her face between his hands, was about to kiss her until Jamie, their wedding celebrant and a friend of Hannah's, cleared his throat loudly and said cheerfully, 'That's for later, folks.'

They grinned at one another and turned towards Jamie, Laurent lacing his fingers through hers.

Hannah turned for a moment to her family. She smiled at her dad and then looked at her mum, who gave her a knowing smile and nod that said that now Hannah was living life as it should be—trusting and hoping and loving and being honest with yourself.

She turned back to Laurent.

He dipped his head and said softly, 'I will treasure you, our baby, and every day of our marriage.'

* * * * *

IT STARTED WITH
A PREGNANCY

CHRISTY JEFFRIES

To Patty Kawano Barberio. Thank you for taking a young and sometimes smart-mouthed girl under your wing and being a bonus role model. You showed me how to shop for jewellery, how to play blackjack, how to travel independently and how to love dogs again. Most importantly, you showed me how to be kind to others. You are the heart of my hearts.

Chapter One

Rebekah Taylor stared at the pregnancy test in her hand. How could it be positive? They'd used protection, one of the condoms she'd gotten as a gag gift from a friend's bachelorette party a couple of years ago. Sure, the thing had been an embarrassing shade of glittery pink, but it should have worked in the heat of the moment.

Except it hadn't.

Had the condom expired? Rebekah glanced at the reflection of her wide, panic-filled eyes in the mirrored medicine cabinet. Every six months she methodically went through all her kitchen and bathroom cupboards and threw out everything that was even close to its expiration date.

How had she missed something as important as this? Sighing, she slouched lower on the toilet seat. Probably because she'd hidden the little heart-shaped box in a back corner of her nightstand drawer, where it was out of sight and out of mind. It probably would've stayed in its hiding spot indefinitely if she hadn't been so desperate.

And so lonely.

Although, at least she'd had a condom to start with, unlike the carefree Grant Whitaker, who'd come to her house unprepared for a one-night stand eight weeks ago. Not that either one of them had been expecting things to get physical that night.

In fact, Rebekah hadn't been able to stand the guy the first few times he'd visited Spring Forest, North Carolina. Flying in from Florida in his board shorts and T-shirts and flip-flops every couple of months, he looked more like a surf instructor than any kind of business professional.

And the weird thing was, for such a relaxed-looking guy, he'd always watched Rebekah like a hawk. She was the director of Furever Paws, his elderly aunts' nonprofit organization, yet he constantly kept his eye on her—as though he expected she would stuff her pockets full of dog biscuits and sneak them into the puppy kennels if his back was turned. Of course, he was pretty much like that with everyone who worked at the shelter. Everyone who wasn't family, at least. The guy was undoubtedly protective of his relatives.

"Nobody would mistake you for being a part of the Whitaker family," she told her reflection. As a biracial woman with an African American mother and an Irish American father, Rebekah's deep bronze skin and black, springy curls were a stark contrast to Grant's lighter, sun-kissed complexion and wavy blond hair. Would their baby favor one of them over the other? Or would their child be blessed with the best of both gene sets. "Stop it!" she commanded herself. She'd barely known about the pregnancy for three minutes and already she was letting her emotions overrule her logic.

Maybe that first test was just a dud. Rebekah frantically tore open another package, this time from the manufacturer that promised a plus sign instead of two striped lines. Ten minutes later, though, the result was the same.

She would've sunk to her knees right there in her brand-new townhome and curled herself into a little ball if she'd thought it would help. But grown women with mortgages and MBAs and lead positions at nonprofits didn't break down and cry every time something went wrong.

They examined the problem, researched solutions and made lists of what to do next. Taking out a pad of paper she wrote down, *1. Make doctor appointment*. She got as far as writing the number *2* on her to-do list, but then couldn't think of what she should do next.

Tell Grant?

A tremor shook through her at the thought of how that conversation might go. The man would probably react in one of two ways. He might say, "Right on," and then eventually forget about her and their kid because they didn't fit with his bachelor lifestyle. Or he might accuse her of getting pregnant on purpose to trap him—just like Trey once had.

There really wasn't any sense in doing anything until she'd confirmed things with the doctor. Crumpling the list in her hand, she tossed it into the wastebasket, right on top of the pink-and-blue boxes.

Walking to the kitchen, she flipped on her coffee machine out of habit before remembering that pregnant women were supposed to limit their caffeine intake. A tic started at her temple and Rebekah wondered how she could possibly give up coffee for nine whole months.

Wait. Longer if she decided to breastfeed.

Her cell phone pinged behind her and she turned and swiped the screen, looking at the text message her mom had just sent.

Did we book my class's field trip for the first or second Tuesday of September?

Rebekah pinched the bridge of her nose. Her mother was a first-grade teacher and had been begging Rebekah to set up a tour of the pet rescue for a bunch of six-year-olds. Thank goodness she didn't have to deal with that headache today.

Mom, it's scheduled for the eighth. I put it in the online calendar I set up for you last week.

Dimples, you know I'm never going to use that calendar thingy. It's too complicated. Plus, your dad accidentally deleted the app off my phone when he was trying to reset our wi-fi password.

Before Rebekah could respond, another message popped up on her screen. This time from her dad.

Hey there, Dimples. Your mom screwed up our wi-fi password again and I can't find the paper where you wrote down all our log-in codes. Any chance you can come up this weekend and reset things for us?

Rebekah was convinced that her parents purposely remained technologically challenged because it gave them the perfect excuse to summon their dutiful daughter home for long weekend visits. Normally, she didn't mind the thirty-minute trips to Raleigh, but Rebekah wasn't quite ready to face them yet.

After typing a detailed response to her father, including a description of where she'd filed their log-in information and an online link to a video giving them a step-by-step tutorial on how to change their password, Rebekah found the number for a local obstetrician with excellent ratings and took a deep breath before placing her call.

A male receptionist answered and Rebekah had to clear her throat several times before finally getting the words out. "I think I might be pregnant and I'd like to schedule an appointment with Dr. Singh."

"Congratulations," the deep masculine voice replied and Rebekah took solace in the fact that at least there was one man in this world who was happy about her revelation. "How far along are you?"

"Um, I'm thinking eight weeks," she offered, going off the app on her phone that tracked her cycle. She could organize everything else in her life to a T, but much to her frustration, she'd never been very regular when it came to her periods.

"And do you know the date of conception?"

Embarrassment threaded through the lower half of her torso, squeezing around her stomach. Of course she knew the exact date of conception. She even remembered the spicy lettuce wraps and the blackberry mojitos that had been on special during that fateful happy hour. It had only been one night of weakness. Yet apparently, one night was all it took. Instead of admitting as much to the receptionist, she simply told him the date.

"Usually Dr. Singh doesn't see her patients until they're closer to twelve weeks. I can put you on the books for October."

Rebekah clenched her jaw so tightly, her back molars vibrated. It was currently the end of August and there was no way she could wait that long without knowing for sure. She hated to even think about the last time she'd found herself in a similar situation, let alone use it as an excuse to garner special treatment. However, she needed to take action, she needed to be in control of the situation this time. "Actually, I have a history of ectopic pregnancy, so I'm sure the doctor will want to see me sooner."

"Of course," he replied, and she heard him tapping on a keyboard. "In that case, the soonest we can get you in will be next Thursday."

He listed the appointment openings, and after finding one that worked for her schedule, Rebekah wrote down the time in her day planner. Then she mumbled her thanks and disconnected the call so she could also program the appointment into the calendar app on her smartphone.

Getting into the shower, she made a firm decision to put the whole thing out of her mind until next week.

That vow lasted a whole forty-five minutes—when her teal blue Fiat was idling at the intersection near a large chain drugstore. She glanced at the clock on her dashboard and wasn't surprised to see she had plenty of time to swing inside, grab some prenatal vitamins and still get to work half an hour early.

When she came out of the pharmacy, she walked over to Great American Bakery, because she couldn't very well take the vitamin on an empty stomach. Besides, if she couldn't have coffee, then a warm chocolate croissant would be the next best thing to settle her nerves. No, not her nerves. She refused to be nervous. This uneasy feeling in her tummy was simply due to hunger. Or the pregnancy cravings she'd only heard about but never experienced.

Climbing back into her car, she realized that she'd surely get crumbs and chocolate all over her brand-new silk blouse. Many of the people employed at Furever Paws wore much more functional clothes for working with animals, but Rebekah had a lunch with a potential donor this afternoon and then a city council meeting tonight. Her bosses, Bunny and Birdie Whitaker, were going to request a zoning ordinance to allow for a cell tower on their farm, which adjoined the pet rescue's learning center. The tower would provide the sisters some much-needed financial revenue, and it would provide the town's new development of Kingdom Creek some better wireless service.

Not everyone in the suburban town was happy with how quickly their little city was blossoming, though, so she was expecting to confront some annoyed townspeople tonight.

By the time she pulled into her parking spot at work, her stomach was growling and her temples were pounding from the beginnings of a headache—probably due to a lack of caffeine. Grabbing the bags containing the vitamins and the croissant, she tried to shove both in her already full tote.

It wasn't like her to pick up a breakfast treat and not bring in a box to share with everyone else at work. However, she didn't necessarily feel very social this morning and just wanted to sneak into her private office and hide behind a mountain of paperwork and a closed door.

Many of Rebekah's coworkers were more focused on the rescue center's animals than on the humans who worked there. So hopefully nobody would notice that her entire world was threatening to topple off its axis. She checked her reflection in the rearview mirror, assuring herself that there was no sign of a pregnancy glow or anything else that might give away her secret before she was ready to disclose it.

Thankfully, it would be easy enough to avoid Grant until she was able to confirm that her pregnancy was real—and had worked out the best way to tell him. She'd already managed to avoid him since their night together, although it helped that he lived in another state. The last contact she'd had from him was the note with his cell number that he'd left the morning he sneaked out of her townhouse.

Not wanting the temptation, she'd immediately thrown the number away without programming it into her own phone. As amazing as he'd made her feel that night, there was no way she could allow a repeat performance of their one-night stand. And even now, there still might not be a reason for her to call him. Her pregnancy wasn't confirmed yet—not officially. Her father had made his career on giving people advice and was especially fond of the phrase, *Don't borrow tomorrow's problems today.* Rebekah repeated those words in her mind.

Balancing her purse and tote bag on one shoulder, Rebekah grabbed her other two bags and used the thick wedge heel of her espadrille sandal to close the car door behind her.

She took a deep breath before heading toward the entrance and then froze at the sound of the unmistakable deep voice coming from behind her. "Looks like the early bird definitely gets the worm all to himself this morning."

Grant Whitaker was unfolding his long, athletic frame from some nondescript rental car she hadn't even noticed in the parking lot. Right this second, he didn't look so much like an early bird as he did a hawk. Wait. That meant that she would be the worm in this scenario. Although, she couldn't deny that she was currently trying to slink on by without drawing his deep blue gaze and giving herself away.

The second he gave her that knowing smile, though,

her mouth went dry and her tummy went completely topsy-turvy.

Or maybe that feeling was actually her first bout of morning sickness.

Grant Whitaker's elderly aunts, Birdie and Bunny, loved it whenever he found the time to fly in from Jacksonville to visit them and help out at Furever Paws. Apparently, though, they had kept the details of this visit to themselves. Judging by Rebekah Taylor's wide-eyed stare and dropped jaw, she had no clue that his aunts had asked him to review the latest marketing plans in order to get more people at their adoption events.

Even if his aunts hadn't asked for his help, he probably would've found another reason to get back to Spring Forest to see Rebekah before long. He hadn't talked to the no-nonsense director of the animal shelter in more than a month. He'd thought they'd finally turned a corner after sharing a couple of drinks—and much more—that night. She'd been sound asleep when he'd had to leave to catch his flight back to Florida, so he'd left his number in a place where he knew she wouldn't miss it. And while he hadn't expected a call the first few days after they'd spent the night together, Grant had been hoping for at least a "see you next time you're in town" text.

Rebekah Taylor was as straitlaced as they came and had a reputation around the pet shelter for running a tight ship. Or as tight a ship as one could run with the elderly Whitaker sisters in charge. The director was wound so tightly, she reminded Grant of one of those coils that launched like a bouncing spring the second someone released some of the pressure. Several weeks ago, when he'd run into her and her friends at happy hour, he'd ended up being the lucky one who'd helped her unwind.

He'd had a good time that night—better than good, if he was being honest with himself—and he'd thought she'd enjoyed herself, as well. In fact, right this second, his fingers twitched instinctively, as if they were also remembering the way her muscles had clenched against them when he'd brought her to...

Grant's already sunburned neck grew warm and he had to give his head a quick shake to clear it while Rebekah fumbled with her keys as she tried to unlock the front door.

"Here, can I give you a hand?" he asked as he reached out to take the keys from her. The second his thumb grazed her palm, an electrical current shot through him. As she jerked her arm back, he realized that she must've felt it, too.

So the attraction was definitely still there, even if Rebekah was holding her giant tote bag between them like a shield, blocking his view of her full, round breasts. As though he hadn't already committed to memory the sight of the dark bronze skin framing deep-brown nipples.

She had a death grip on the two white bags in her other hand and blew a curly strand of black hair out of her face. While she didn't look angry, she also didn't look very pleased to see him. In fact, the smooth skin at the base of her neck revealed a jumping pulse, making him think the overly controlling office director wasn't feeling all that in control right this second.

Grant tried to hide his grin at this sudden revelation. Just because she'd let her guard down around him once didn't mean she'd be willing to do it again. Rebekah was a tough woman to read, but he remembered her slightly tipsy words that night as she'd finished her third mojito after her friends left the bar. "We can't let anyone know about us drinking together like this. It would be extremely unprofessional for me to socialize with a member of my bosses' family."

"Then we probably shouldn't tell anyone that I'm going to come over to your place when we leave the bar," he'd replied just before signaling for the check. Her thick lashes had lowered seductively and one corner of her full lips had lifted in invitation. It'd been a bold pickup line from a guy who normally didn't have to resort to lines to get women, and Grant hadn't expected it to work with someone as reserved as Rebekah. It turned out that his taking charge that night had worked out extremely well for both of them.

However, something in her hazel eyes—possibly panic—told Grant that he shouldn't re-create the same take-charge strategy at her workplace. Or in the light of day. He cleared his throat and turned back to the door, jamming the first key he saw into the lock. It only went halfway.

"It's the third one," she said, using her chin to nod toward the key ring that had suddenly become slippery in his damp hands. It took another two tries, and when he finally pulled the glass door open, she rushed by him in a cloud of the plumeria scent she always wore—he'd noticed the bottle of expensive lotion on her bathroom counter that night—and headed straight past the empty reception desk and down the hallway leading toward the business offices.

Grant stood there for a few seconds, letting the air-conditioning from inside filter past him to the humid summer heat outside. She hadn't even thanked him for getting the door, let alone said goodbye. It was one thing to want to keep their personal business on the down low, it was another to completely brush him off. Some of the animal handlers were probably on duty in the back, but since the shelter wouldn't be open to the public until ten o'clock, there wasn't anyone in the newly refinished reception area to see them. It was almost as though she wanted to pretend he wasn't even there.

Grant wasn't in the habit of having one-night stands with his aunts' employees—or anyone else, for that matter—so a part of him understood her desire to try to forget the whole thing had ever happened. He'd felt the same way the past few weeks when it had become apparent that she wasn't going to call him. By avoiding any sort of conversation, Rebekah was actually providing him with the perfect escape, the perfect excuse to avoid any sort of messy emotions or awkward conversations about how things could never work between them.

But the memory of Rebekah's curves pressed against him and the sound of her throaty moans were too fresh in his mind.

Plus, he still had her keys.

Grant's flip-flops slapped against the lacquered finish of the concrete floor as he took long strides toward the biggest office. The door was already closed so he gave a brisk knock before twisting the handle and letting himself inside.

Rebekah stood behind her desk, both hands braced on the tidy surface and her chest puffed out, as though she'd been in the middle of some deep breathing exercise before he'd barged in.

Grant didn't do tension or uncomfortable silences. So when his eyes landed on one of the bags in front of her, he shifted gears to a neutral topic.

"Sutter's Pharmacy, huh?" He hooked his thumbs into the waistband of his favorite board shorts and tried to appear as casual as possible. "Are you feeling out of sorts?"

"I'm fine!" Rebekah's words came out in a squeak and her round eyes grew even larger as they filled with alarm. Whoa. He'd just been trying to lighten the mood. He hadn't meant to make her uncomfortable.

"If you say so. Anyway, I came in here because you forgot your keys," he said, dangling them in front of his chest. His father had raised him to be a gentleman and he knew the proper thing to do would be to place the key ring with the silver softball charm on her desk. But he couldn't stop himself from testing to see if the sensation he'd felt from their earlier physical contact had just been a fluke.

Rebekah was a tall woman and easily reached one arm across her desk. When her fingers met his, another flare of heat shot through him. She yanked her hand back so quickly, it knocked one of the white sacks off her tote bag.

There was a rattling sound as something rolled out of the bag and fell to the floor right by his feet.

Rebekah must've raced around the desk because she was suddenly diving at the container in front of him. But she wasn't fast enough. The words on the label flashed in his brain as though they were blinking in neon lights, even after she clutched the bottle to her chest.

Something in his gut twisted, and the air in his lungs suspended. It took him several times to get the words out and his voice sounded far way when he finally asked, "Why are you taking prenatal vitamins?"

Chapter Two

Rebekah bit her lip, trying to resist the urge to hide the bottle behind her back. She'd already flung herself on the ground in front of him as though she were a combat soldier jumping onto a live grenade. At this point, there was no way to pretend the emotional explosion hadn't already detonated around them.

Still.

How had he read the label so quickly?

She didn't realize she'd spoken the question out loud until Grant replied, "I won the national speed-reading championships for my high school four years in a row."

"You're a speed reader?" she asked as she rose to her feet, seizing on the opportunity to redirect the conversation.

"I was also the Duval County Spelling Bee champion

in eighth grade," he added. "But I don't especially feel a need to discuss my academic accomplishments right this second. Is there something you want to tell me, Rebekah?"

She watched his soft lips move, yet his question sounded so formal, as did the way he said her name. Her parents were the only ones who called her Dimples, and she hated it when people used the common nicknames Becky or Bekah, or even Beck. So it wasn't as though Grant should be calling her anything other than Rebekah. Still, his question felt like a chastisement all the same.

Straightening her spine, she forced herself to look him directly in those ocean-blue eyes and said, "I might be pregnant."

"Whoa." He sank into the paisley upholstered chair right in front of her, swiping the sun-bleached blond hair off his forehead. "I mean...whoa."

Yep, *that* was the response she'd been anticipating.

And now that he was acting as she'd initially expected, Rebekah felt her own role fall back into place as she took charge of the situation. "I took a test this morning, but I'm waiting for the doctor to confirm it."

"How..." he started, then scrubbed a hand over the golden stubble on his jaw. "I mean..."

"How did this happen?" she offered. "I'm sure the usual way."

"I was actually going to ask how far along you are." He used his tan forearms to push himself up a little straighter and Rebekah wondered if he was already calculating the date in his mind.

"I'm four weeks late, so that would put me at eight weeks." She held up a warning finger. "*If* I am, in fact, pregnant. Like I said, there's no need to get all worked up over a store-bought test."

Or two tests, if anyone was counting.

Grant sucked in a deep breath, his nostrils flaring slightly as he exhaled. "So when do we go to the doctor to confirm it?"

We. The skin on the back of her neck tingled. "Well, *I* have an appointment next week. If you want, I can send you a text afterward and let you know if there's any news."

There was no point in mentioning that she'd need to ask for his cell phone number again.

"A text? If there's any news?" When his eyes finally focused on hers, Rebekah swallowed a tiny lump of guilt. There was accusation practically shooting from their blue depths. "Were you even planning to tell me?"

"Of course I planned to tell you." Eventually. After she'd figured out what she was going to do. She twisted her lower lip between her teeth.

She waited for the next question to come—the one about whether the baby was his—but he only studied her intently before slowly nodding.

Grant slid his smartphone out of his pocket and she remembered when the device had been sitting out on the table that evening while they were closing down happy hour. She'd commented on the battered cover and the cracked screen and he'd told her the story of how he'd been testing out one of his company's waterproof cases when he'd wiped out near a coral reef and cracked his surfboard in half. The still-functional phone was one of his biggest marketing tools when it came to selling his company's tech products. Not that she had a very clear picture of exactly what it was he did for the company.

This wasn't good, she thought, giving her head a quick shake to clear it. She might be having this man's baby, yet she didn't even know what he did for a living.

"What day is the appointment?" he asked as he swiped at an app on his phone. It was the same online calendar she'd unsuccessfully tried to get her parents to use.

"Um…" Rebekah tilted her head, unsure if she wanted him to know. Unfortunately, he'd practically accused her of keeping the pregnancy from him already and she didn't want to give him any reason to think that she had something to hide. Besides, it wasn't like he'd actually stay in town long enough to go with her. Or that he'd even want to go. "It's next Thursday."

"Uh-huh," he said as he tapped something else. "What time?"

"Grant, you aren't actually planning to go to the doctor's office with me, are you?"

At this, he lifted his eyes to hers again and she could see that the full force of his earlier suspicion had returned. "Of course I'm planning to be there. You didn't think I'd leave you to go through this alone, did you?"

There was no polite way to answer that question. Frankly, there wasn't even an honest way of answering without admitting that not only had she been thinking that exact thing, she was hoping for it. Instead, she opted to remind him of the logistics involved. "But don't you have to be back in Jacksonville for work or…something?"

His fingers flew over his cracked phone screen, typing as he spoke. "Actually, I'm flying to a digital marketing conference in San Francisco tonight after I check in on my aunts. I'll just change my return flight so I can swing by here on the way home next week."

Rebekah heard him speaking, but the only word her brain seized on was *aunts*. A rush of unease shot to her stomach. "You can't tell your aunts about this."

"About what?" he asked, his attention seemingly focused fully on the electronic device in his hands and—luckily—not on the beads of sweat breaking out across Rebekah's forehead. She resisted the urge to grab one of the vet reports off her desk and fan her heated face.

"About me. About us." Her finger pointed back and forth at each of them, before her hand dropped to her still-flat belly. "And especially not about the baby."

He lifted his head finally, his eyes zeroing in on her. Not in the suspicious way that she was accustomed to from him, but in a sexy, hungry sort of way. All that tension in her tummy doubled and a sudden warmth spread under her skin.

Lord help her, but even as she faced the very man who now had the power to redirect her entire future, she was still hopelessly attracted to him.

Stiffening her shoulders, Rebekah commanded her body to get itself together. This reaction must be some sort of pregnancy-induced hormonal imbalance.

Not that she was exactly mother material herself, but Grant was the complete opposite of the type of guy she would choose to father her baby. What made things even more unbearable was the way his elderly aunts doted on him and acted as if he'd hung the moon, making his job down in Jacksonville sound like the most important career in the world. In reality, he worked for a tech company that encouraged beach days and flexible hours and spontaneous yoga sessions in their cubicle-free environment. While some might describe him as easygoing and charming, to Rebekah, Grant seemed like one of those men who'd never really grown up. Maybe it was because she'd yet to see him dressed in a shirt with a collar.

Or a shirt that didn't highlight his strong, broad shoulders.

As she stared at the faded logo on the soft cotton tee stretched across his muscular chest, she ignored the desire curling inside her and wondered for the hundredth time this morning how she'd ended up in this situation with this man, of all people.

Because he was sexy as hell. That's how.

"Rebekah." Grant finally rose to his feet before walking over to stand in front of her. When she ducked her head to avoid those piercing eyes, he softly placed a finger under her chin and lifted her face to meet his gaze. "I won't say a word to anyone until we get the green light from the doctor."

All she could manage was a slight nod and a slow release of air from her too-tight lungs. She didn't want to talk about green lights or anything else with him until she had a concrete plan in place.

A plan that most likely wouldn't involve her spending any more time with Grant Whitaker.

Standing face-to-face, Grant didn't immediately remove his hand from the curve of Rebekah's cheek as he studied her resigned expression.

It wasn't that he didn't trust her. Despite the fact that he doubted she would've told him about the pregnancy quite so soon if she hadn't nervously knocked over that bag, he did believe she was honest and honorable. But there was something about the woman that always threw him off-balance. Something that she kept locked up tight behind the professional clothes and the detailed financial reports and the organized meeting notes she always passed off to his aunts, who would inadvertently leave the meticulously typed documents behind in the kennel of a sick Labrador or under a pallet of kitty-litter bags. In fact, while he'd been waiting for Rebekah in the parking lot this morning, he'd wandered over to the stables and found one of the llamas eating the cell tower proposal that Rebekah had drafted for a city council meeting.

Rebekah was nothing if not thorough. Which made it difficult for him to believe that she hadn't already formulated a specific course of action.

Eventually, she took a step back, forcing his hand to drop as she pivoted to rearrange some papers on her desk. Without making eye contact, she began to speak. "Well, I appreciate you stopping by and…you know…"

"Bringing you your keys?" he suggested, not about to let her simply dismiss him without some sort of confirmation that she would be in contact with him soon. "Oh, and for offering my unflagging support at the doctor's appointment as well as with any decisions that need to be made?"

"Are you hoping for a certain decision, Grant?" Even from this side view, he could see her shoulders square off as though she was preparing for battle. So it was no surprise when she fully faced him with the dimples in her cheeks completely hidden as she forced out a heavy breath. "Perhaps one that lets you off the hook?"

For the first time in his life, he felt completely unequipped to handle the situation before him. Grant was the problem solver in his family, the one who dropped everything to help those who needed him. However, the determined line of Rebekah's clenched jaw suggested that she didn't want his assistance in solving this problem.

Not that her being pregnant was a problem, he corrected himself as he rolled his shoulders backward to loosen the tense muscles.

He carefully thought about his next words. "Actually, if the decision were up to me, I'd have a house full of kids."

Her perfectly arched brows shot nearly to her hairline, and before she could open her mouth, he already knew what she was thinking.

"Not that I would have purposely gotten you pregnant!" The words tumbled out of his mouth defensively and his right hand lifted as though he were swearing a solemn oath.

"Shhh!" Her eyes darted right past him and toward the reception desk. From outside the office, he could hear a door opening and what sounded like a couple of volunteers discussing last night's episode of *Top Chef.*

He lowered his voice. "I'm just stating for the record that none of this was my intent. In fact, I even used that hot-pink condom that left glitter all over my..."

She immediately clapped her hand to his mouth.

He mumbled more words behind her palm, but she didn't remove it. So he did what any man would do when presented with a beautiful woman's skin so close to his lips. He kissed the sensitive spot right between her thumb and forefinger.

Rebekah yanked her palm back and her eyes narrowed into a warning glance. Her voice came out in a fierce whisper. "Well, at least *I* had...protection."

Her implication hung in the air between them.

"Listen, I'm sorry for not being better prepared." It was an odd feeling, being on the defensive like this, and for a moment it was difficult for him to get the words out. "As much as you might want to think otherwise, I usually don't go home with—"

"Grant," Aunt Bunny interrupted as she swept into the office. Rebekah jumped away from him so quickly, he heard a *thunk* against her desk. The sweet older woman glanced down at his preferred beach attire. "I wasn't expecting you this early. Were the waves too small to hold your interest this morning?"

"You know me too well, Aunt Bunny." Grant lifted his arms and shrugged his shoulders. "When I saw that the surf was under two feet, I caught an earlier flight into Raleigh–Durham and figured I'd rent a car and swing by to go over the marketing plans for the upcoming adoption events."

Bunny's attention turned to Rebekah, who was holding herself so rigidly she could've been one of his surfboards. Except with many more curves. Did it make him a bad person to want to pull the sexy and stiff woman close to him and run his hands along her waist and over her full hips until she relaxed and melted in his arms?

His normally absentminded aunt might tend to pay

more attention to animals of the four-legged variety than she did to humans, but her eyes were uncharacteristically sharp as her glance bounced back and forth between Grant and Rebekah. Finally, Bunny asked, "Where are they?"

"Where are what?" Grant sidestepped around the upholstered chair, pivoting his body in the hopes of blocking Bunny's view of the empty pharmacy bag threatening to fall off Rebekah's desk again. He had to command his own eyes not to scan the room for the prenatal vitamins.

"Your marketing plans?" His aunt lifted a thin gray brow.

"Oh. On my laptop," Grant replied, hoping she wouldn't ask why he'd left his computer in the rental car. He didn't want to admit that he'd been in such a hurry to follow Rebekah inside the building this morning, he hadn't given his initial excuse for flying into town a second thought.

"All that will have to wait." Bunny waved a work-roughened hand at him. "Since I have both of you together, come outside and see our new sign. The old one was destroyed with all that tornado damage, and we wanted to install an extra one at the edge of the parking lot so people can now see it from the road."

"Oh, they're early." Rebekah jumped at the excuse to get out of the office and away from the conversation they'd been having. Literally. Her knee-length skirt fluttered open at the slit as she made a little hop to skip past him.

As he followed her and Bunny past the reception

desk and through the lobby, Grant had to restrain himself from hurrying to catch up with them. Now that Rebekah was no longer watching him so intently, waiting to see if he'd give the wrong reaction, he could take a moment to let her words sink in.

She was possibly pregnant. With his child.

What he'd told her about wanting a house full of children was true. However, he hadn't expected to become a father quite so soon. Rebekah's earlier revelation had landed like a sucker punch to the gut. The blow had been swift and unexpected and heavy, dropping him into the chair as he attempted to wrap his mind around what had just happened. Then, just as quickly, Rebekah had pulled back emotionally, that initial hit leaving a hollow, empty feeling in his stomach.

He was used to being needed and usually relished his role as the guy who came in and solved things. It was what made him so good at his job. It was why his mom and his sisters often relied on him to keep his family's surf shop on top of the latest trends. It was why he was currently in Spring Forest to oversee his elderly aunts' troubled financial situation.

But Rebekah didn't seem to want *anything* from him. At least, not yet. Maybe she would change her mind after the appointment next week.

Either way, the woman would need to get used to Grant being around. If she was, in fact, having his child, she would soon learn that he always put his family first.

Chapter Three

Rebekah had never been so relieved to see someone as when Bunny Whitaker had walked into her office five minutes ago. Sure, she'd had to paste a calm smile on her face while awkwardly reaching behind her blindly in order to shove the bottle of prenatal vitamins into the tote bag sitting on top of her desk.

Still, the older woman's fortunate arrival got Rebekah away from facing more of Grant's potential follow-up questions. Questions Rebekah didn't have all the answers for yet.

Speaking of the man, his flip-flops smacked against the flat gravel as he caught up with them in the parking lot. Rebekah's jaw clenched as he approached behind her. She had to swallow several times and take deep breaths in through her nose—not so much from annoyance at the man for always appearing at the worst times, but from the fact that her stomach was still doing somersaults and she was afraid that the morning-sickness fairy was currently paying her a visit.

"Hey, Aunt Bunny, what happened to the logo that my graphic designer sent you?" Grant asked from behind Rebekah's shoulder. Rebekah's eyes shot to the five-foot piece of painted aluminum tilted between two men wearing Signs 4 Less T-shirts.

Oh, no. Rebekah ignored the tiny rocks flicking between her toes and the soles of her wedge sandals as she strode across the parking lot to make sure she wasn't reading the sign wrong. She could hear her boss's voice as Bunny and Grant caught up to her.

"Well, the owner of Signs 4 Less felt real bad about not taking our advice to get his dog spayed, so when we found foster homes for all of her puppies, he offered to give us a great price if we just used standard lettering with no artwork."

"But I'd already negotiated a deal with the sign company out of Raleigh," Rebekah said. "I left the contract on your desk last week so you could approve it and sign it."

"I know, honey, but poor Marv had really bonded with those sweet pups and he was just an absolute wreck when he had to say goodbye to them. He started crying right there in the foster intake area and told me that his wife was moving out and his company wasn't doing so hot." Bunny shrugged her shoulders. "Plus, he gave us a nice discount if we cut out the logo and used fewer letters. I meant to tell you, but it must've slipped my mind."

Rebekah knew the woman and her sister were incredibly smart when it came to animal care, but when it came to business matters, they tended to follow their hearts instead of their heads. It was why they'd hired a director in the first place. It was also why they'd hired an attorney earlier this year to look into quite a bit of money that had gone missing. Unfortunately, they didn't always follow Rebekah's or the attorney's recommendations.

Worse than that, they tended to rely on the wrong people. They'd entrusted their money to their brother Gator—Grant's uncle—and it looked like he might have embezzled from them. And they'd entrusted this sign to Marv and...well...

Rebekah shot a pleading look at Grant and once she caught his attention, she pointed her chin first at the sign and then at his aunt. She wanted to tell him that this wasn't her fault, but first she needed to make sure he was seeing the same thing she was.

"Poor Marv, huh?" Grant nodded toward the sign that the workers were trying to hang between the wooden posts. "Let's just hope his return policy is better than his screen-printing skills."

In bright red letters were the words F-EVER PAWS, however the hyphen between the F and the E was so minuscule, that from far away it appeared to say, FEVER PAWS.

"I'm not sure if he has a return policy." Bunny pushed a strand of white hair back into her messy bun. "I think we should just leave it for a few days. I'm sure it'll grow on us."

Grant groaned and Rebekah experienced an unfamiliar tug of solidarity at his frustration. "Aunt Bunny, it says Fever Paws. Customers are going to think all the animals here are sick."

"Grant, we don't have *customers*." Bunny waved another hand at him. "We have prospective adopters looking for family companions."

"Well, your prospective adopters are going to drive right by when they see that sign," Grant replied.

"I guess you're right." His aunt sighed. "Well, we'll just have to call it a loss. I don't want Marv to be out any expense."

"Aunt Bunny." Grant gently rested his hand on the older woman's shoulder. "Your heart is bigger than your current bank account. The shelter really can't afford to take a loss like this. I'm going to tell the guys to take the sign back and re-do it."

Rebekah's heart softened at the way he gently, yet effectively steered his aunt back to reality. Really, it was *her* job to keep Furever Paws on a budget and, as the director, she should've been the one talking to the Signs 4 Less guys, not Grant. But she had plenty of other headaches to look forward to today, and if it got the man out of her hair for a few more minutes, she'd take whatever breaks she could get at this point.

Turning on her heel, she headed toward the shelter's entrance and thought about the cool air-conditioning and chocolate croissant waiting for her in her office. But a movement in the oak trees near the street caught her eye.

Bunny must've seen the streak of gray fur, too, because her boss let out a squeak before announcing, "Everyone stay completely still."

Rebekah knew that most of the staff at the shelter, as well as a few people in downtown Spring Forest, had reported sightings of the elusive gray dog that always seemed to outsmart them. She held her breath as Bunny slowly walked toward the stray, one of the treats she always carried in the front pocket of her faded overalls now outstretched in the palm of her hand.

Unfortunately, before Bunny could get within ten feet of the animal, one of the installation guys dropped his end of the FEVER PAWS sign and the sound of the aluminum clanking against the gravel burst out with a gong-like echo. The scruffy dog took off on its short legs, running directly toward the oncoming cars traveling in both directions on Little Creek Road.

Without looking, Bunny took off after the creature and only stopped when the horn of a big rig blasted through the air seconds before its huge chrome bumper nearly clipped the older woman. Grant caught up to his aunt first, and when Rebekah made it to the shoulder of the road, she could hear his admonishment about Bunny getting herself killed. His words fell on deaf ears as the woman craned her neck, watching the dog dart into the copse of trees on the other side of the street.

"I can't believe he got away again." Bunny shook her head as a mail delivery truck drove past, leaving a heavy gust of wind in its wake.

"Come on, Aunt Bunny," Grant said as he led his aunt toward the building. "If that dog wants to be caught, he'll come back."

"What do you mean *if* it wants to be caught? He's a stray, running from place to place. Why wouldn't he want a real home?" Rebekah heard the words coming out of her mouth and tried not to flinch at her accusatory tone.

Grant shrugged. "I mean not every animal should be domesticated. Some things are meant to be wild and untamed."

Some things? Or some *people*? Rebekah bit the inside of her cheek to keep from asking Grant if he was referring to himself. He'd better not be implying that her getting pregnant was any sort of attempt to domesticate him. Not that she'd ever want to, but even if she'd been willing to try, she knew she'd have better luck taming a tidal wave than taming the unpredictable force that was Grant Whitaker.

She took several calming breaths and commanded her legs to walk confidently back inside the building despite the tiny pieces of gravel that were now digging into the arches of her feet.

She refused to give him a second glance as she stormed ahead of him. The man had absolutely nothing to worry about. She wasn't about to force anyone to be anything they weren't.

The following Thursday, Grant was still kicking himself for not getting the address of Rebekah's doctor before he drove into Spring Forest. He'd had to take a red-eye flight from San Francisco with a layover in Chicago to make it to Raleigh before ten this morning. After landing, he'd barely had time to splash some water on his face and brush his teeth in the airport bathroom before racing to Furever Paws. If she'd called him, or offered her own phone number, he could've driven straight to the appointment and met her there with nobody being the wiser.

As it stood, they now risked having his aunts and everyone who worked at the shelter see them leave together. But at least he was pretty sure she'd be spending the morning at work since she'd scheduled the doctor's appointment during her lunch hour.

Grant checked the clock on the dash of his rental car right before pulling into the parking lot at the animal shelter, then felt his chest ease the second he spied Rebekah's blue car. She hadn't left yet.

Just as he turned off the engine, one of the double glass doors opened and a very beautiful Rebekah strode out wearing a sleeveless dress that hugged her waist before floating down to her knees. Again, she was wearing heels and the sight of her long, shapely legs made his lungs constrict.

By the time he'd exited his rental, she already had the back of her sporty little European car open and was wrestling the giant tote bag she always carried off her shoulder.

There were several other vehicles in the lot, but nobody else was outside. Still, Grant kept his voice low when he strode over to her. "Hey, looks like I'm just in time."

Rebekah jumped back, hitting her head on the corner of the rear hatch. Grant winced at the impact and sympathetically reached out to cradle her scalp in his palm. But her own hand had already beaten him to it and he ended up resting his fingers over hers. "Are you okay?" he asked.

She nodded then took a step back, her eyes darting around the lot as though she was making sure there weren't any witnesses to their interaction.

"Nobody's outside," he said as he followed her around to the driver's side of the vehicle.

Rebekah cleared her throat, but her gaze was firmly fixed on the glass double doors when she asked, "What are you doing here?"

Grant tilted his head. "You're seeing the doctor today, remember?"

"Of course I remember my appointment. I just didn't really expect you to show up."

The implication stung, but Grant forced himself to shrug it off. "I would've met you there, but I wasn't sure if your doctor's office is here in town or if you have a practitioner in Raleigh."

Back when he was a kid, visiting his aunts along with his family, there'd only been a few established doctors in Spring Forest. They hadn't needed medical services much during their trips, but he recalled one summer when his aunt Birdie had driven him to a small clinic in the older part of town for rabies shots after he'd gotten too close to a protective mother raccoon who didn't appreciate a nine-year-old Grant wanting to hold one of her babies. He knew there was now a new medical practice located in a building off Spring Forest Boulevard, but he doubted that Rebekah would use a local obstetrician and risk running into someone from town.

The muscles in her neck moved as she gulped. "Like

I said last week, you don't need to go to the actual appointment with me. I can meet you at Whole Bean Coffee afterward and fill you in."

She must've thought Grant was an idiot if she believed he would fall for that. Rebekah didn't even want to be seen in the parking lot of Furever Paws with him. No way was she going to share a coffee in public with him where anyone they knew could walk by and overhear them discussing her pregnancy. If she was going to try and outplay him, then he'd just double down on his challenge.

"Lunch sounds great. We can grab a bite to eat after we go to your appointment. Together." He held up his keys. "Should we take your car or mine?"

She did that sexy thing where she lowered her chin and tugged a corner of her lip between her teeth. Her hand gripped the driver's door handle, looking as if she was ready to yank it open and jump inside to speed away. "Why don't you just follow me?"

"And risk having you ditch me at one of the intersections?" He gave her a wink before shaking his head. "No way."

"Fine." She sighed then clicked a button on her keyless remote, electronically shutting the rear hatch of her car. "But get in quick and duck down so nobody can see you."

Grant tried not to smirk as he jogged around the front of the car to the passenger side. It was impossible for his six-foot-two frame to sink very low without jamming his knees into the glove box. Not that he would've actually hidden anyway. He understood that she didn't want anyone knowing her personal business, but he'd be damned if he was going to continue playing the role of her dirty little secret. He said as much when she tore out of the parking lot, shooting up gravel as she fishtailed onto Little Creek Road.

Rebekah made a slight chuckling sound. "That'd be a first."

"What would be?" Grant asked, finally getting his seat belt locked in.

"*You* being *my* dirty little secret," Rebekah said, the engine revving as she gained speed. "I would've thought it would be the other way around."

Something tingled along the edges of Grant's nostrils and he tried not to sniff. "Why would you be the secret?"

"Oh, come on, Grant. You're the golden boy of the Whitaker family. I just work here."

Well, the fact that she worked for his aunts wasn't the real problem bothering her right now. No, Grant heard what she wasn't saying aloud—that he might not feel comfortable going public with their…fling? Relationship? He wasn't really sure what to call their situation, but that wasn't the issue. His only concern was her feelings and assuring her that he heard her. It didn't matter how beautiful, intelligent or accomplished Rebekah was. There were always going to be some people who thought they shouldn't be together because they were different. While he couldn't deny that Rebekah's feelings were likely the result of her own experiences, he also wanted her to know that he'd always been proud to be with her. "For the record, I have never thought of you as the hired help. In fact, I'm not the one who's embarrassed to have people finding out about us."

"It's not that I'm embarrassed about you." Rebekah flicked her eyes at him before turning on her signal and pulling onto Spring Forest Boulevard. "It's that I've worked really hard to become the director of an organization that does amazing things in the community. As a nonprofit, we're governed by a different set of rules than regular corporations. That makes my job fall under more scrutiny when it comes to ensuring that everything stays aboveboard."

"So you're saying dating me wouldn't be aboveboard?"

"First of all, we're not dating." Rebekah turned to him as her car idled at an intersection. Grant tried to ignore the pang of disappointment at her words, despite the fact that he'd been telling himself exactly the same thing these past several weeks, ever since their night together. "Second of all, as you know, there's currently an attorney looking into some of your family's past investments and I don't want to risk any appearance of impropriety or otherwise suggest that there might be any conflicts of interest."

Ouch. He especially didn't like the reminder that there were potentially some financial issues going on right now with his uncle Gator.

The man had always been a financial whiz. That was why Birdie and Bunny had trusted him to manage the investments used to support their living expenses and the shelter's overhead. Gator always seemed to know just how to deal with every shift in the market, using his intelligence and intuition to help his sisters and also to build his own personal fortune. But then something had gone wrong. Suddenly money wasn't where it was supposed to be. When the storm hit Spring Forest and the shelter took heavy damage, the aunts discovered that Gator had let their insurance lapse and couldn't provide a good explanation for where the money for the premiums had gone.

The situation had seemed to get more tangled by the day, until the aunts had had no choice but to hire people to look into it. Now, Gator was nowhere to be found and some people in town were suggesting that Grant's favorite uncle had gone missing to avoid being questioned about his alleged mismanagement.

"Okay, obviously we're not dating," he readily agreed, trying to ignore the fact that there was a sour, mildew-type odor in this car that easily overpowered the scent of Rebekah's flowery lotion. "I think we both made it pretty clear that night that we weren't in the market for a serious relationship."

He certainly wasn't—especially with someone who lived a two-hour flight away. The light turned green and Rebekah barely got out a nod before pulling forward, allowing Grant to continue.

"However, with circumstances being what they are…" he glanced down to her still-flat stomach behind the seat belt "…don't you think people are going to eventually find out that you're pregnant?"

She held up a finger. "*If* I am, in fact, pregnant. Remember, the doctor hasn't officially confirmed it."

"Is there any reason to think you're not?"

The muscles in Rebekah's toned arms stiffened as

she gripped the wheel tighter. She opened her mouth as though to say something, then made a sniffing sound. "I'm not the only one who smells that, right?"

The stench that had been slowly building inside the car was becoming unbearable, and Grant finally gave in and cracked a window. "Yes, I've been smelling it for the past five minutes but was hoping it was coming from outside."

She hit a switch and both of their windows whirred all the way down. Grant inhaled the fresh, warm air filtering in as Rebekah's corkscrew curls whipped around her face. While lowering the windows improved things slightly, the scent still lingered.

"It's definitely coming from inside the car," Rebekah said, pinching her nose as she slowed for a four-way stop. "What could it be?"

"It reminds me of the time one of Aunt Birdie's goats got into the henhouse and stomped on all the eggs before rolling around in chicken poop."

"But twenty times worse," Rebekah said right before making a gagging sound.

Just then a loud yip came from somewhere in the back of the car. Grant and Rebekah nearly butted foreheads as they whipped their necks around. A mangy animal with long gray fur covering its eyes poked its head up from the storage area in the very rear of the car. The thing growled low and deep, revealing tiny yellowed teeth, and its front legs were perched on the back seat as if it was about to leap over and attack. Grant held himself perfectly still and lowered his voice. "What in the hell kind of animal is that?"

"I think it's that stray dog that everyone has been

trying to catch. Remember the one from last week that your aunt chased into the street? I've never seen it this close up, though, so I can't be sure."

"What's it doing in your car?" Grant asked.

"How should I know? It must've jumped in when I left the back hatch open to argue with you in the parking lot."

"Okay, where is your extra leash?"

Rebekah was also holding herself very still, which made her raised eyebrow even more prominent. "My extra what?"

"My aunts always keep an extra leash and a few lengths of rope in their pickup truck for this exact reason. They say they never know when they're going to come across an animal that needs help."

"Grant, just because I work at a pet rescue doesn't mean I go driving around town looking for actual pets to rescue."

The dog growled again and made a snapping motion, as if it was about to lunge at them. "Well, we probably shouldn't stay in here with him. Or her. Let's get out slowly and then I'll call an animal control officer to come take him."

Rebekah nodded. "On the count of three, we'll both get out at the same time."

Grant began the count. "One, two—" He didn't make it to three because Rebekah was already out her door.

"Oh, hell," Grant said, following suit.

Unfortunately, neither one of them realized that they'd left the windows down until the scruffy mutt launched himself over the back seat and leaped through the driver's-side window. It made a strangled yelp as it landed awkwardly on its left hind leg before it began limping across the street.

"Oh, no," Rebekah took off after the dog, calling out over her shoulder. "The poor thing is hurt."

The animal must've been more afraid than injured because when it realized Rebekah was following, it hobbled even faster, past an iron gate that had been propped open and into the yard of one of the older stately homes on Second Street.

Well, the home might've been stately at one time. It currently needed quite a bit of work involving a weed whacker, a few gallons of fresh paint and, Grant noted as he got closer, a new roof. Just as Rebekah was closing in on the scruffy pup, it found a hole in the base of the rotting porch and scurried underneath.

Grant dropped to his knees in the dried-out hydrangea bush near the hole, but it was too dark to see how far back the crawl space went. He brushed the dirt off his hands as he looked up to Rebekah. "Do you have anything we can use to bribe him out?"

Her eyes opened wider and she jogged back to the car without so much of a hint as to what she had planned.

Grant swallowed his groan. The woman certainly had a habit of doing whatever she wanted and then filling him in on the details later.

Chapter Four

Rebekah stared at the shredded bakery bag in the rear of her car. Now she knew what had lured the stray dog into becoming a stowaway. She carried the empty muffin wrapper back to the porch where Grant remained on his knees, keeping watch.

"I used to have an apple spice muffin in my tote bag, but I guess the dog already found it and had himself a picnic in the back of my car."

"Well, I'm more of a chocolate croissant kinda guy, but I can't blame the mutt for getting his baked good fixes wherever he can find them."

Something wobbled inside of Rebekah's knees. Sure, plenty of people liked chocolate croissants, but as far as she could tell, it was the first thing she and Grant had in common. In fact, she'd already had three croissants in the past week, but the bakery had been out of them this morning when she'd gone in to place her order. "I guess it's a good thing that it wasn't anything chocolate. I hear that it can make dogs really sick."

"You *hear*?" Grant lifted a brow at her.

"I've never actually owned a dog," Rebekah admitted, causing Grant to rock back onto his haunches so that he could stare at her in disbelief. "Don't look at me like that. My dad is severely allergic to them. And to cats. I wasn't able to have either growing up."

"But you work at an animal shelter."

"It's not that I don't like them or anything," Rebekah defended herself, placing her hands on her hips. "I'm just not much of a pet person."

Grant's lips lifted into a smirk. "I'm guessing this is another thing that you don't want my aunts to know about."

"Well, I'm not walking around advertising that particular fact," she said, trying to ignore his calculating gaze. Why did he always watch her as though he suspected she was hiding something? "Besides, your aunts didn't hire me to be hands-on with the animals so my experience with them isn't exactly a job requirement."

There was another growl from underneath the porch and Rebekah suddenly remembered why they were there in the first place. She held up the empty wrapper. "There's a few crumbs still stuck on here, but he pretty much licked the thing clean."

Grant stood up. "Maybe we should knock on the door and ask the owner for a treat of some kind."

Rebekah glanced at the brick house that she drove by every time she came into downtown Spring Forest. There was a smashed window on the second floor and the front screen door hung crookedly on only one hinge. "I'm pretty sure the owner no longer lives here."

"That's a shame. But it explains how the place has gotten so run-down." Grant ran a hand through his blond hair. "I've driven by a few times and always thought that it was an eyesore on this block."

Rebekah gasped. "It's not an eyesore. I mean, it could use a little bit of love and some elbow grease, but it has a ton of character. See the matching turrets that round off the front corners? None of the other mansions on this street have them. And the lot size is huge. Imagine if it had a new porch that extended all the way to here." She took several steps back and spread her arms so he could better see her vision. "Then, if I tore that rotted iron fence down, I could add a few comfy benches and make a whole seating section out here and be able to talk to my neighbors and watch kids ride their bikes and…"

Her face heated as she trailed off, mortified that she was practically admitting she'd dreamed about this particular home more than a few times—before she'd made the more practical decision to buy a smaller, more affordable townhome.

"No, don't stop," Grant said, walking closer to her. His encouraging smile and broad shoulders beneath his faded T-shirt made Rebekah grow even warmer. "Would you keep the shutters and the door the same color?"

She gulped. "I'd go with black for the shutters, but the front door I would paint a bold blue. Not quite royal blue, but not powder blue, either. Somewhere in between."

As he studied her, she realized she was describing

the exact shade of his eyes. She shivered and tried to cover it with a shrug. "But none of that matters because it's not like I'll ever own this house."

"Why not?" Grant asked. There was genuine puzzlement etched into the lines on his brow and Rebekah wondered if the guy was ever told no. Ever told that he couldn't have something he wanted.

"For one..." She held up a forefinger and tried not to notice that she was overdue for a manicure. She'd read in an online pregnancy forum that the folic acid in prenatal vitamins caused the hair and nails to grow like crazy. "Even with the house in this condition, I probably can't afford it on my salary. Second of all, if I'm having a baby, all of my money will be going for diapers and daycare and whatever else babies need. I won't have anything left over for home improvement projects."

His arms crossed in front of his chest and his entire face shifted into a frown. "You realize I'm going to help support both you and the baby, right? That means not only emotionally but financially, too."

Grant was at least wearing a pair of sneakers today instead of his normal flip-flops. But she didn't want to point out the fact that, judging by his wardrobe, she probably made more money than he did. A ring sounded from his back pocket, yet he ignored the beat-up cell phone and remained rooted in place as if he was waiting for her to respond to what he'd said.

But Rebekah didn't know what to say besides, "We should probably get to the doctor's office."

Really, there was no point in discussing any of this before they knew if she actually was pregnant. And even if she was... Grant sounded like he seriously wanted to be a part of the child's life, but Rebekah had a hard time believing it.

If a man who had been with her for six years didn't want to raise a child with her, then how could this man— who had only known her a few months—want to?

While Grant wasn't anything like her ex-boyfriend, Rebekah was also no longer like her young and naive self. She wasn't about to wait around for him to get scared and leave first—especially when her body couldn't be trusted to not react every time he smiled at her.

"Okay." He nodded, dropping his arms to his sides. "But just so you know, we will be having a conversation afterward. And maybe we can pick up another muffin or a double cheeseburger or something on our way back to lure the dog out from his hiding spot."

Rebekah's rib cage felt as if it were squeezing in on her. She cursed herself for going into work this morning to finish that grant proposal and for not taking an early lunch break. If only she'd slipped out of the office a few minutes before Grant had arrived, she could be doing this on her own, without his heavy stares and his weighty statements about taking care of her and the baby.

Grant's phone rang again when they got back into her car but he must've let the call go to voice mail because he didn't so much as glance at the thing while Rebekah drove the next couple of blocks to Dr. Singh's office.

She pretended not to be paying attention, but clearly he was making a point of proving that he was completely focused on her and not on whoever was on the other end of that phone call. Unfortunately, the short ride would've been much more bearable if he'd been distracted.

Dr. Singh's office was housed in another brick mansion on Second Avenue and the waiting room was decorated to resemble an old-fashioned parlor from the Victorian era. When Rebekah handed her insurance card over to the male receptionist, he smiled at Grant and asked, "This is Daddy, I presume?"

Rebekah's neck snapped to the velvet upholstered chaises and sofas in the small waiting room to see if the only other patient present had overheard. But the woman was struggling to keep a piece of fabric draped over her shoulder and finally threw the thing in the stroller beside her. When she met Rebekah's gaze, the lady said, "Sorry for the show, but these nursing covers are a lot more trouble than they're worth."

"No problem." Rebekah tried to smile at the breastfeeding mom, but all she could focus on were the dark circles under the woman's eyes. Rebekah's mother's eyes had often appeared equally tired after being up all night with one of the many newborns her parents had fostered over the years. Being around one crying baby after the next had easily convinced a teenaged Rebekah that motherhood wasn't for her.

So then, how had she wound up here? And with Grant, of all people? At least he'd found a seat in the corner and was politely avoiding looking at anything besides the parenting magazine he must've picked up from one of the side tables.

Thankfully, she'd saved time by completing all the

new patient forms online. How awkward would that have been to fill out her medical history chart with Grant hovering nearby?

Taking several deep breaths, she slowly trudged to where he sat and had no more than settled into a plush, emerald-green velvet chair when a woman wearing floral printed scrubs called from a doorway, "Rebekah Taylor?"

Rebekah grimaced at the use of her full name, and thereby the loss of her anonymity, then forced another fake smile as she stood up and walked toward the door.

The nurse pointed out the bathroom, then held up a small plastic cup with a lid and said, "While you give us a sample, I'll take Daddy here to the exam room."

Rebekah's head pivoted and she gasped at seeing Grant now standing behind her. When she'd told him he could come to the doctor's, she'd meant to the parking lot. Maybe as far as the lobby. Nobody had ever mentioned anything about him actually being inside the exam room with her. He must've seen the daggers her eyes were shooting because he took a step back.

"Or would you rather I wait out here?" Grant asked, and Rebekah wanted to retort that she'd prefer he waited in Jacksonville, Florida. Instead, her mouth opened and closed several times because she wasn't quite sure how to say this in front of the nurse without revealing that she'd been comfortable enough to have the man in her bed, but was not quite comfortable having him present in any other aspect of her life. When she didn't reply, Grant faced the nurse. "Is it normal for fathers to go in the exam room?"

"Very normal." The nurse nodded a bit too eagerly. "We like the daddies to be involved whenever possible. In fact, we have one patient whose husband is on deployment right now and she brings in her laptop and a webcam so he can watch via video chat. It's really the sweetest thing."

Oh, great. Rebekah should've spoken up when she had the chance. It was bad enough that the nurse was encouraging Grant to come back there with her. Now he'd think that she should broadcast all of her future appointments when he couldn't be there in person. At least he still had the courtesy to lift a questioning brow at her before barging through the door behind her.

"Fine," she sighed, then lowered her voice as they walked along the hall. "But don't you dare look when I get on the scale."

Rebekah stepped into the restroom to give her urine sample and then made her way into the exam room where Grant was staring wide-eyed at a colorful poster showing each stage of the cervix during the dilation process. She would've laughed at how pale his face had gone if the nurse hadn't pointed to a hospital-style gown and instructed Rebecca to change out of her clothes.

Grant gave a discreet cough before telling nobody in particular, "I'm just going to step down the hall and grab a drink from the water cooler."

When she was finally left alone to change, she hurriedly unzipped her dress and attempted to toss it over a nearby chair, but the thing—along with what was left of Rebekah's pride—slithered to the floor. Actually, Grant would probably need to sit in that chair anyway, since the doctor would likely use the stool. So she hung her dress on the hook behind the door, then quickly peeled off her bra and panties and wadded them into a ball to hide in her purse. She was still tying the gown closed when there was a knock on the door.

"Hi, I'm Dr. Singh," a very young woman said as she breezed into the room. "I already met Daddy outside in the hallway and he told me you guys think you're nearly nine weeks along."

Grant followed the doctor inside and Rebekah wanted to scream that there was no "you guys." There was only her. And why in the hell did everyone who worked here keep calling Grant "Daddy?" The back of her neck prickled every time she heard the presumptuous word.

But at least he'd gotten the timeline accurate.

She gulped before answering. "That's correct."

"Okay, let me pull your record up here and take a look before we get down to business." Dr. Singh logged on to a computer that was mounted on a retractable arm attached to the wall. Rebekah was relieved to note that, despite the Victorian-era waiting room, there were other modern technological advancements—such as an ultrasound machine—back here. "So on the medical history form you completed online, it says you experienced a loss of pregnancy five years ago. Tell me about that."

Rebekah's whole body went numb, as though she was frozen in a state of shock. Her eyes focused straight ahead, yet saw nothing, while her ears picked up every single sound. Including Grant's sudden indrawn breath. The wheels on the doctor's stool squeaked as Dr. Singh rolled toward her. "Rebekah? Are you not comfortable talking about this?"

She drew in a ragged gulp of air and tried not to glance at Grant to see his reaction to what she was about to admit. The paper covering the exam table shifted and crackled underneath her as she attempted to sit up straighter. "I…uh…had an ectopic pregnancy five years ago. The dose of methotrexate they gave me didn't help…dissolve, uh, anything. So they had to go in laparoscopically to remove the egg from my fallopian tube."

"I'm sorry that you went through that." Dr. Singh laid a small hand over hers and Rebekah stared at it as the initial numbness was pushed away by all the emotions now filling her. The procedure had been significantly less painful physically than it had been emotionally. At the time it happened, she'd told herself that losing the baby was for the best. That she hadn't been ready to be a mother and didn't know if she ever would be. It wasn't until right this second, surrounded by the memories of that past pregnancy, when she realized that she'd never really allowed herself to mourn that loss.

Using the sleeve of her borrowed cotton gown, she dabbed at the corner of her eye before a tear could spill out. When she finally braved a peek in Grant's direction, she saw that he was studying the pictures of the dilating cervixes with great interest.

"Well." The doctor rose to her feet. "After your past experience, I'm sure you're eager for me to check you out and give you some good news."

Dr. Singh asked routine questions as she performed a pelvic exam and took measurements of Rebekah's stomach. Grant would occasionally glance over, but mostly he stared at the wall or at the floor as he shifted in his chair and alternated which knee to bounce rapidly. It looked like the guy was seriously regretting his decision to come with her. And it served him right. Had there ever been a less interested father in this situation?

The doctor pulled a heartbeat monitor out of her pocket and squirted a blob of cold gel onto Rebekah's stomach. With the handheld machine running over her exposed skin, back and forth, Rebekah squeezed her knees together and her eyes shut, praying that if Grant *did* decide to finally show some interest, he'd keep his gaze averted to the upper half of her torso.

Not that he hadn't seen her without panties before. But this time, it was different. Not only were they currently in a clinical setting with very unflattering lights overhead, there was also a lack of lime-flavored rum to lower her inhibitions.

The machine whizzed and whirred and the doctor made some murmurs. At one point, a crease formed between the woman's dark eyebrows. "Hmm. I'm going to use the ultrasound for a better read."

Rebekah reminded herself to breathe in through her nose, out through her mouth, as more cold gel was applied to her belly. The doctor was gentle as she pushed and rotated the probe against Rebekah's stomach, which was now feeling queasy and doubly nervous.

Grant must've sensed something was wrong, as well, because he had stood up and was silently studying the screen on the ultrasound machine as though he had the training to understand what all those white squiggly lines were against the black background.

The doctor finally cleared her throat. "Excuse me for a second while I call the nurse."

* * *

Grant had seen the panic written all over Rebekah's face as the doctor took forever to perform the ultrasound. When Dr. Singh stood up to push an intercom button on the wall, he immediately reached for Rebekah's hand. She squeezed it tightly, but kept her eyes closed as she continued to take long, steady breaths.

Spending summers on his aunts' farm was the closest Grant had ever come to witnessing a birthing experience. He'd thought of picking up a book at the airport bookstore, then told himself to wait until they had more answers. But nothing he'd learned so far had prepared him for hearing about Rebekah's previous pregnancy. While she'd talked about it, her words were matter-of-fact, but her voice was shaky and he'd glanced away as soon as he saw that first tear well up. He didn't know if he should offer comfort or if he should pretend he didn't understand English. It suddenly occurred to him that the reason she'd been reluctant to discuss the pregnancy in the first place was because she wasn't sure whether or not this one would have the same result.

He stroked a thumb over her knuckle and when her eyes cracked open, he leaned closer to her ear and whispered, "I'm here for you no matter what."

The doctor resumed her place near the ultrasound machine and just when he was about to demand some answers, Dr. Singh smiled and announced, "Congratulations. You're having twins. Both of the—"

Grant didn't hear anything else except a loud bang before he crumpled to the ground.

Chapter Five

When Grant came to, Dr. Singh was kneeling beside him and the nurse was checking his pulse. Rebekah was still lying on the exam table, but was now leaning over the side and frowning at him. "So much for being here for me no matter what."

He blinked a couple more times before sitting up and rubbing at the bump forming on the back of his skull. "Did I hit my head?"

"You stepped back so quickly, you knocked into the lamp." The nurse extended her hand to help him up. "Don't worry. You're not the first dad that's happened to. Come on, big guy."

"That's why I called for the nurse." Dr. Singh took his other hand as the two medical professionals helped him to his feet. "Once I had a father faint when I told him they were having triplets."

"Did you ever have a mother pass out?" Rebekah waved her hand to get their attention. "Because it's just as startling for the half-dressed person up here on the table with cold, gooey gel everywhere."

"Sorry about that." Dr. Singh smiled as she returned to her actual patient. "So there are two strong heartbeats, both on my monitor and on the ultrasound machine."

"And they're both where they're supposed to be?" Rebekah asked hesitantly, and Grant made a mental note to research ectopic pregnancy when they left. Right after he researched twins.

Wow.

Dr. Singh nodded. "Yes. Your uterus looks great and is measuring a little bigger than what it would be for nine weeks gestation if this was a single embryo, so you're right on target for twins. Still, I'd like to do some blood work to get an idea of your hormone levels and make sure everything else checks out as normal."

Grant's head throbbed as he tried to keep up with the conversation. "So...you're sure there are *two* of them?"

"Positive. We'll be able to run more tests later in your pregnancy to determine if they're fraternal or identical. In about five or six weeks, we may even be able to determine the sex of the babies, if you're interested in finding out ahead of time."

Rebekah's eyes immediately shot to him and they were filled with shock and possibly even fear. Suddenly they'd gone from having nothing to talk about when it came to this pregnancy to having everything to talk about. Grant gently laid his hand on her shoulder, wanting to ease as much of her stress as he could. "It'll be okay," he whispered to her before turning to Dr. Singh. "I think we're going to need time to let everything sink in."

"Of course. I'm sure both of you are feeling overwhelmed right about now and nobody has to make any decisions today. But I'm going to have the nurse put together some reading material for you, and I'd like to schedule a follow-up appointment four weeks from now."

Both the doctor and nurse left the room and he and Rebekah sat there with the heavy weight of silence settling between them. Eventually it became apparent that the woman carrying his child—he shook his head, make that *children*—wasn't in any hurry to climb down from the exam table.

Finally he let the air rush out of his lungs in a deep exhaling breath that sounded like a deflating balloon. "So, twins, huh? I bet neither one of us were expecting *that*."

Rebekah shrugged, causing one side of the hospital gown to slip down and expose the very sexy curve of her shoulder. "I wasn't expecting *any* of this."

"What do you want to do?" he asked, his chest filling with an uncomfortable tension as he awaited her response.

She looked at the clock on the wall. "I guess I should go back to work."

He'd meant what did she want to do about the babies.

But she was probably still too shell-shocked to come to any sort of decision right this second.

"Well, I meant what I said about being here for you. Tell me what you need."

"I don't know what I need just yet."

"Fair enough. We'll take it one step at a time." He passed her the dress hanging on the back of the door. "Why don't you get back into your clothes and I'll wait outside."

When she met him in the hallway, she let him lead her to the front desk and even allowed him to schedule the next appointment with Dr. Singh. He asked for her car keys and she passed them to him without protest.

"Should I drive you back to your place?"

She shook her head. "No. I think I'll feel better once I get to the office and throw myself into work. Besides, you need to pick up your car."

Grant had grown up surrounded by strong women and his gut told him that Rebekah was only holding herself together because she didn't want him to witness her inability to stay in control. If he tried to push her right now, she would only close herself up more.

"Okay, I'll drive you back to the office, but only on the condition that we stop somewhere along the way and get you something to eat."

She didn't agree so much as she just didn't protest. In fact, she didn't say a word after they got into the car and he had a feeling that if she couldn't manage a conversation in the private confines of her vehicle, there was no way she'd want to step foot in a public restaurant with him. So he went to a drive-through burger place, and when he asked her what she wanted, she stared out the opposite window instead of looking at the menu board. "Whatever is fine."

He ordered for them, but she only managed a couple of French fries and a sip of sweet tea as he drove her back to work.

"Are you sure you don't want me to come inside?" he asked when he pulled into the lot at Furever Paws.

"I'm sure." Rebekah was normally so capable, so in control. Seeing her like this made Grant nervous, made him want to take a step back. Having worked as a beach lifeguard during college, Grant was accustomed to diving in headfirst at the first sign of danger.

So when he climbed into his rental car, defeat settled around him because, for the first time in his life, it felt as if he were running away from a challenge.

But how did he help someone who didn't want to be helped?

Twins.

The word replayed on a constant loop in Rebekah's head for the next hour. Despite what she'd told Grant about returning to work to clear her head, she'd been staring at the same rabies vaccine invoice since she'd gotten back to her desk.

There was no way she'd get a single bit of work done this afternoon with her mind and her nerves in such disarray. So far, she'd been able to avoid Bunny and Birdie, but she doubted that she could finish out her work day without running into Grant's aunts at least once.

A chorus of barking came from outside her office

window and she looked out to see Mollie McFadden, one of their trainers, working with two of their newest arrivals. Salt and Pepper were a bonded pair of Maltipoos that had been surrendered after their owner lost her job and couldn't afford to take them when she left to move in with her sister, who lived across the country. Seeing them suddenly reminded Rebekah of the scruffy gray dog that had jumped out of her car earlier that morning.

Standing up, she grabbed her tote bag, along with the grease-stained paper sack that still contained the now-cold burger Grant had insisted on buying for her.

"I have to go see about an animal," she told Nancy Frye, the foster coordinator who was covering at the reception desk.

Nancy was kind enough not to point out that Rebekah rarely interacted with the animals herself. Or maybe Rebekah had just raced by so quickly, Nancy hadn't gotten the chance to say anything.

In the parking lot, Richard Jackson, the veterinarian who volunteered at the shelter, lifted his arm in greeting. She managed a quick wave to the older man known as Doc J, but she didn't have the brainpower to wonder why he was stopping by when the vet clinic was already closed for the afternoon.

Rebekah started her car, the air-conditioning vents immediately blasting out the lingering scent of stale French fries and unbathed dog, and drove straight toward that old brick house on Second Avenue. She was already unwrapping the burger as she walked up to the weathered front porch.

"Here, boy," she said, awkwardly kneeling down in

her dress and heels, the cold beef patty pinched between her thumb and finger as she held it out. "Or girl. Not that it matters what I call you. You're probably just happy to have some food."

But the gray dog didn't so much as growl.

"You know, every single person at Furever Paws and probably half of the residents in this city have seen you running around on the streets. Do you know how many people have been trying to snatch you up and find you a good home? Are you still under there or did you go out on the town to scavenge your own lunch?"

Still no response.

Rebekah craned her neck toward the street to make sure some passerby wasn't watching her as she attempted to negotiate with some stray animal who probably couldn't understand a single word she was saying—and who might not even be there at all.

"Look, I didn't forget about coming back to feed you. It just took me a little longer to get here because I was in a complete daze." Rebekah groaned impatiently. "I mean, if you had any idea what kind of shock I've just been through, you'd understand why I'm standing outside some abandoned house during the hottest part of the day blabbering on and on to a stinky dog that probably isn't even under there anyway."

The muscles in her thighs began to protest her kneeling position, so she shifted until she could sit down on one of the porch steps. As much as she wanted to lure the dog out of hiding, she also didn't want it to attack her. But there was no way to get the animal to trust her unless she let down her guard slightly.

"I'm just gonna keep this yummy, all-beef patty right here next to me in case you wanna come out and have a little taste." She wrinkled her nose at the plain, cold meat that didn't look so appetizing to her without its bun or condiments. "I probably should've ordered the bacon cheeseburger. I bet you would've preferred that. But Grant was doing the ordering and I just sat there like a big dummy, too stunned to say a damn thing. I know, I know. You're probably thinking that Grant was in just as much shock as I was about the twins. But at least *he* had his escape plan already in place, conveniently having to fly back to Jacksonville this afternoon for some important meeting tonight. I mean, I guess I should be glad the man is gainfully employed. After all, everything is going to cost twice as much now that we're having twins."

The breeze picked up and she caught the now-familiar odor of stinky, wet dog, which meant the little pup must be close by. From what she'd heard, nobody had been able to get this close to the stray. Maybe if she kept talking, he or she would realize that Rebekah wasn't much of a threat.

"So, yeah. Grant took off. Just like he did the morning after we slept together. I'm not saying that he doesn't have other responsibilities. It just seems like more than a coincidence that anytime things get too heavy, he always has an easy out and can pick up and leave whenever he wants. You should've seen him today in the doctor's office. The second she told us it was twins, he stepped back from me so fast that he hit his head on a lamp and all but collapsed. It actually would've been hilarious if I wasn't so damn scared myself, let me tell you.

"I don't care how hot the guy is. Or how my insides turn all gooey every time I see him. This attraction will wear off eventually." Rebekah dug around inside the carry-out bag for a cold French fry. All this talking was finally bringing back her appetite. "But it certainly doesn't bode well for our children if their father can't even handle the first surprise of the pregnancy. Not that I handled it all that well myself." She bit into the top half of the soggy fry. "Bleh."

She tossed the remainder to the dirt near the hole under the porch where she'd seen the dog scurry earlier today. She could've sworn she heard something rustling around down there, but it could've just as easily been a squirrel. Or a rat. Or a snake. Before Rebekah could think about what other critters might've burrowed their way under there, she heard the Bluetooth ringing from her car.

She had no idea how long she'd been sitting here, but her mom had been calling her every day this week after school let out to make sure everything was ready for her class's field trip to the animal rescue next Tuesday. At this point, it was almost like a regularly scheduled alarm, letting her know that it was close to four o'clock.

Rebekah stood up and brushed the dirt off her rear end. She set the burger down near her discarded French fry and grabbed her trash. "You win," she told the little gray dog, or whichever other animal was under the porch. "I've gotta go call my mom back and tell her the news. Wish me luck."

There wasn't even a yip in thanks as she made her way across the potholed driveway and toward her car. But as Rebekah pulled away from the curb, she caught a glimpse of gray fur darting out of the hole and then back under the porch.

Apparently, the scruffy little mutt had been listening to her the whole time.

The following week, as the flight attendant made her safety presentation over the loudspeaker of the plane, Grant paid very close attention despite the fact that he could probably give the exact speech by heart. He'd flown so much recently, and the constant traveling was beginning to take its toll on him. Or maybe it was the added stress of knowing that he was going to be a father that had him feeling so shaky.

As the plane accelerated down the runway, he performed the same ritual he always did at the beginning of a flight. He closed his eyes, rotated his neck, pushed back his shoulders, adjusted his arms, stretched out his fingers. Deep breath. Then he extended his legs as far as they would go in the business class row and rolled his ankles in counter-clockwise circles before finishing with the wiggling of his toes. Another deep breath.

Repeat.

It wasn't that he was superstitious, but the familiar routine helped him to relax. He'd been a nervous flyer ever since he was eight years old. That had been the first summer he'd flown all by himself to visit his dad's sisters in North Carolina and his plane had hit major turbulence. Then there was the summer he was ten and an unexpected hurricane diverted his flight and he'd been stuck at the airport in Nashville with only a handful of airline employees. He hadn't confided his fears to anyone, mostly because he'd had such an amazing time on his aunts' farm those years and knew that if anyone thought he couldn't brave another flight as an unaccompanied minor, he might not get to visit again. Then his younger sisters began accompanying him and he'd been forced to become the brave knowledgeable brother.

But he still didn't like planes.

So while he loved his marketing job and his amazing company, there were definitely days when he wished he could travel a lot less. When they finally reached cruising altitude, he powered on his tablet and read his downloaded copy of *What to Expect When You're Expecting*.

"Is that book still around?" the passenger next to him asked.

Grant had to blink a few times before he figured out what the middle-aged gentleman in the loud Hawaiian-print shirt had said.

The guy nodded toward Grant's iPad and said, "My wife made me read the same book way back when."

"Any advice you can give me?"

"Yeah. No matter how well you plan, there's always going to be something that comes up to throw you for a loop." The man chuckled before adding, "After having twenty-eight newborns, I still get a curveball thrown my way every once in a while."

"You have twenty-eight kids?" Grant hoped his eyes weren't completely bugging out of his head.

"Well, technically, we just have one. A daughter.

Smart as a whip and pretty as a peach. But my wife and I were foster parents and we used to get all the calls for the newborns. So we've had a lot of babies in and out of our house over the years."

"By any chance, were any of them twins?"

"Oh, boy. Is that what you and your wife are having?" the man asked, then glanced down at Grant's bare ring finger.

"My girlfriend," Grant clarified. Okay, so technically, Rebekah wasn't exactly his girlfriend, either. But some stranger on a plane didn't necessarily need those kinds of specifics.

Just then, a baby a few rows back began fussing and the man looked behind them. "Poor thing. Probably has plugged ears from the altitude. So, how far along is your girlfriend?"

"Almost ten weeks. Here's the ultrasound picture from our first appointment." Grant swiped his finger across his tablet to go to his stored photos. He'd taken a screenshot of the printout Dr. Singh had given them, but since Rebekah hadn't wanted to tell anyone yet, Grant hadn't said a word to his family or to anyone at work.

He didn't realize how eager he'd been to finally show the picture to someone until the older man said, "Yep. There's two of them, all right."

The baby's cries picked up volume and a whiny toddler joined in. Several passengers near them adjusted their earphones or sent the mother of the fussy children pointed looks.

"Excuse me," the man said, unsnapping his seat belt and standing up. Grant had to rise to let the man pass.

Since Grant hated the views from window seats, he always asked to be assigned to the aisle. He remained on his feet, observing Hawaiian Shirt Guy speak quietly to the young mother before gently taking the baby into his arms. The crying immediately ceased and the young mom was able to focus her attention on the toddler next to her.

Grant sat back down, then watched in awe the rest of the flight as this miracle stranger did a bouncing/rocking motion while pacing up and down the aisle until the baby rested its chubby cheek against the man's shoulder and fell soundly asleep. When it was time to begin their descent, the mom worried that transferring the finally calmed child might wake her up so Grant slid over to the window seat—after shutting the shade—allowing the man to take the aisle seat closer to the mom. Hawaiian Shirt Guy made it all seem so effortless as he gently shifted the baby to his other shoulder, then sat down and got his seat belt back on without so much as an eye flutter from the tiny girl now drooling all over the palm tree fronds printed on his shirt.

"Have you thought of writing a book of your own?" Grant asked his seatmate when the plane touched down.

The older guy just laughed. "The thought has crossed my mind a time or two."

"Or you could give private lessons," Grant suggested. "I'd pay anything to learn how to do that."

"You'll figure it out on your own, son. Just the fact that you *want* to get it right already speaks volumes about the kind of father you'll be."

As the rest of the passengers raced each other to reach the overhead compartments and line up for the exit, the tiny girl with black curls and a lopsided pink headband finally opened her eyes. Grant prepared his ears for a sudden shriek that was sure to come when the baby realized that neither the man in front of her nor the one holding her was her mother. But the baby quickly smiled at him, revealing one tiny white tooth in her otherwise gummy grin, and Grant felt his heart turn into a puddle.

Would his own children ever smile at him that way? Would their mother?

The man beside him stood up and passed the baby off to a very grateful mom, but Grant remained in place, a million thoughts running through his head. What would being a father really be like? His own dad had set the bar pretty high when it came to being an amazing parent, but Moose Whitaker had passed away right after Grant graduated high school and was no longer around to offer that sound advice he'd always happily dished out. Whether it was an intimidating wave or a midterm exam in calculus, Moose had always known the right thing to say to inspire Grant to conquer his biggest challenges.

He was so lost in thoughts about parenthood, he didn't realize the plane had emptied and the flight attendants were letting the cleaning crew aboard. He yanked his carry-on suitcase from the overhead bin and made his way to the rental car desk. The clerk on duty greeted him by name and Grant realized that his visits to North Carolina were coming with increasing frequency.

During the forty-five-minute drive to Spring Forest, he made several work-related calls and told himself that as long as he still handled his job duties, it didn't matter how much time he spent out of the office. Which was a good thing since, with all of Rebekah's upcoming doctor's appointments and birthing classes and whatever else people did to prepare for a baby, he'd be racking up even more frequent flyer miles.

Speaking of which, he should probably come up with another excuse to give his aunts for why he was in town again so soon. The truth was that he wanted to check on Rebekah, but he couldn't very well tell them that. Hell, he couldn't even tell Rebekah that.

When he turned into the parking lot at Furever Paws, his eyes immediately landed on the same Hawaiian-print shirt that he'd sat next to on the plane. Certainly, it couldn't be the same guy, he told the knot of tension forming in his belly.

But, sure enough, as Grant exited his car, he recognized the man who was now standing near an older-model Subaru Outback and tearing into a pack of Claritin. His former seatmate swallowed some pills and then grabbed a floppy hat out of his back seat before waving at Grant. "I hope you didn't follow me all the way out here to ask for more baby advice."

Grant's lips tightened as he looked around to see if anyone had heard the man's words. "No, actually, my aunts own this place."

Please don't ask about the woman I told you was my girlfriend.

"Oh, Bunny and Birdie are your aunts? My daughter thinks the world of them. In fact, I'm meeting her and my wife here for lunch." The man jerked a thumb at the big yellow school bus lumbering into the driveway. "And there's my wife now. Our daughter arranged for this field trip for my wife's first-grade class and neither one of them thought I'd make it back from my book tour in time to help chaperone. Good thing our plane landed early, huh?"

The man walked over to the bus that was idling on the edge of the property before Grant could ask him who his daughter was. But he didn't have to.

Because, just then, Rebekah came walking up from the side of the building, her wide smile indicating she hadn't yet seen Grant frozen between the two cars. The bus's engine shut off right as she began speaking.

"I didn't know you were coming." She threw her arms around the man's shoulders, nearly knocking off his floppy hat. "I hope you brought some extra-strength allergy medicine with you, Daddy."

Chapter Six

"I need to talk to you," Grant whispered to Rebekah as she passed out clipboards to the parent chaperones who were herding the schoolchildren into groups named after animals.

Thankfully, she had on her sunglasses and nobody could see her squeeze her eyes shut at the sound of his voice. His breath was so close to her ear, she nearly shuddered. "What are you doing here, Grant?"

"I wanted to get some pictures of the new picnic area so I could add it to the brochures I'm creating."

"What brochures?" Rebekah's smile fell. "I never authorized the money for any new brochures."

"We can talk about that later." His voice was still low and laced with an edge of desperation. "Right now, I really need to speak to you about…*you know.*"

"Here you go." She handed a clipboard to another parent chaperone and forced a smile, trying to pretend that the father of her babies wasn't standing directly behind her while her own parents were only a few feet away. "Your group will be called the Ducks and your tour guide is going to be Hans, the silver-haired gentleman over there wearing the purple shirt."

As the Duck group headed off, Rebekah looked anywhere but at Grant and spoke through clenched teeth. "Now is not a good time to talk about...*you know.* Not only am I working, but it just so happens that those are my parents over there."

"That's exactly why we need to talk about—"

"Here you go." She cut Grant off again as she reached out to hand another clipboard to a man who had lost all control over six girls, who were now running in circles and trying to play tag. "Your group will be called the Frogs and your tour guide is going to be—"

"I don't want to be a frog," a little girl with box braids said.

"Why can't we be called the unicorns?" another little girl with a blond ponytail right above her forehead asked. "See? I already have a unicorn horn and everything."

"I'd rather be a Tyrannosaurus rex," a third girl said, pushing a pair of blue-framed glasses up on her nose. "A T. rex could probably eat a unicorn, you know."

"Could not," the blonde retorted, putting her hands on her hips.

The remaining three girls stopped their impromptu game of tag to join in the argument of dinosaurs versus mythical creatures and Rebekah decided right then and there that she would never organize another field trip again. She tried to wave her mom over, hoping the experienced Mrs. Taylor would be able to get her students to stop their bickering. But her mother was several yards away, introducing the other two teachers to Doc J, who would be giving the classes a tour of the vet clinic.

"Technically…" Grant raised his voice, stepping directly into the center of the fray "…T. rexes are carnivores, which means they only eat meat. And unicorns are made out of rainbows and fairy glitter and wouldn't be at all tasty to a meat-loving T. rex. Fairy glitter is way too sweet. Bleh." Grant made a shuddering sound and all the girls laughed. He winked at Rebekah before continuing. "Since there were no such things as dinosaur dentists back then and a T. rex's arms were obviously too short to get a toothbrush into those hard to reach spots, eating a unicorn wouldn't have been at all worth the risk of so many cavities."

"Are you sure?" The little girl with glasses was also wearing a T-shirt displaying the periodic table on it and didn't quite looked convinced.

"Of course I'm sure." Grant nodded and pulled out his cracked smartphone. "In fact, I'm pretty sure that an archaeologist once found some cave drawings showing a dinosaur and a unicorn being friends. I'll look for pictures of them while you guys start your field trip."

"I still don't want to be a frog, though," the original little girl said, crossing her arms in front of her.

Grant grabbed the clipboard from Rebecca and took the pen that was attached to the metal clasp. He scribbled something out and then wrote something else before handing the clipboard over to the dad whose skeptical facial expression probably mirrored Rebekah's.

"Now you guys are the Uni-rexes." Grant wiggled his eyebrows at them. The girls all squealed in delight and ran off toward the volunteer tour guides stationed near the picnic tables.

"Very well done." The sudden sound of her mother's voice behind them caused Rebekah to startle. "My husband tells me that you're Bunny and Birdie's nephew."

Grant's Adam's apple bobbed up and down as he gulped, his wide eyes darting between Sheila and Mike Taylor. Was he surprised to see that her parents were polar opposites—at least in terms of appearance? Her father's graying red hair and light complexion were protected from the harsh effects of the sun by his dorky hat. Her mother's hair was black and had a natural curl—not a single gray hair to be seen—while her smooth skin was a dark umber, set off by the bright colors of her cotton tunic. It clashed horribly with the Hawaiian-print shirt her dad always wore when he was traveling to promote one of the many books he'd written about his adventures in fatherhood.

Growing up as a biracial child, Rebekah became accustomed to people doing double takes at her parents, trying to figure out which one she resembled more. She resisted the urge to put a protective hand over her belly as she wondered whether her own children would face that same experience. Perhaps Grant was wondering the exact same thing. She could see the beads of perspiration forming on his brow and, despite the fact that it was still warm in mid-September, she had a feeling his discomfort was due to this unexpected meeting.

No doubt he was wishing he could be anywhere but here. Again.

He cleared his throat as he answered Rebekah's mother. "That's correct, ma'am. I'm Grant Whitaker."

He held out his hand and her mother grasped it with both of hers. "So, do you work with Rebekah?"

He opened his mouth then closed it. Then he glanced at his rental car before turning to Rebekah and allowing his gaze to dart down toward her waist.

"Sort of," he said, causing her stomach to sink under his pointed gaze. Her lips remained in a firm line as her eyes pleaded with him not to say anything more. Where was the calm, laid-back Grant who'd scheduled her next doctor's appointment when Rebekah was in a daze, or the take-charge and creative one who invented Uni-rexes for arguing little girls? She could certainly use some of that creativity to spin a story right now.

Because her parents were now staring at both of them while she and Grant stared at each other, Rebekah had to jump in and say something. "Grant works in Jacksonville."

He immediately nodded. "That's right. I work in Jacksonville. And I live there. I live *and* work in Jacksonville. Florida."

"Then that explains why you were on my flight," her dad replied. He turned to his wife. "Grant and I sat together on the plane."

"We hadn't officially met, though." Grant rocked

back on his heels and took a deep breath. His blue eyes had gone a shade darker and his normally tan face had gone a shade paler. "So I had no idea that he was your dad, Rebekah."

What did that mean? Was he trying to apologize for something? It didn't seem like he'd been rude to her father—in fact, they seemed to be getting along well. So what was the problem? A knot formed in her chest as she looked between Grant and her dad, who was now smiling.

"When I saw him reading the *What to Expect When You're Expecting* book, I struck up a conversation and gave him some advice about fatherhood." Her dad put a hand on Grant's shoulder. When he turned to his wife, Rebekah tried not to bite all the way through her lip as he continued. "Grant's girlfriend is pregnant with twins. Isn't that exciting?"

And that was when her own forehead broke out in a cold sweat.

Grant knew by her wide eyes filled with remorse that Rebekah hadn't told her parents yet about the pregnancy.

As they stood in the parking lot of the animal shelter with the midmorning sun beating down on them and the excited voices of about fifty first graders echoing all around, Mrs. Taylor took one look at her daughter and her smile dropped. Guilt was written all over Rebekah's face—and if Grant could read it that clearly after only knowing her for a short time, it must be completely obvious to her parents. Grant couldn't help but think all of this could've been avoided if only she'd told them.

Or if he hadn't gotten antsy waiting around for her to call and hopped on that flight this morning.

"Are you…" Sheila Taylor began to ask her daughter, her dark eyes darting down to Rebekah's midsection.

Rebekah sighed and put her forehead in her palm. She didn't look at either parent when she answered, "I was going to tell you both this weekend."

"Tell us what?" Mike Taylor asked, and his wife used her elbow to nudge him in the ribs. He squinted one eye at where Sheila was staring and then his head pivoted to Grant.

"My *daughter's* your girlfriend?"

Rebekah gasped. "Well, technically, we're not—"

"It's complicated," Grant interrupted and put a protective arm over Rebekah's shoulders. "But we're working things out."

"Oh, my gosh." Sheila covered her mouth and her eyes grew damp. "So we're going to be grandparents?"

"And it's twins." Mike clapped his hands together. "That means double the fun."

"Twins!" His wife gripped his upper arm. "I'm going to need to get the bassinet back out of the garage."

"And the baby swing." Mike giggled as he lifted his wife up in a quick hug. Then he locked Rebekah into a bear hug before releasing her to pivot back to Sheila. "Or did we get rid of it a few years ago? If so, we're gonna need to get another one."

"Two," Grant said holding up two fingers. He immediately felt Rebekah's elbow against his rib cage.

Like mother, like daughter, apparently. "What? I'm just pointing out that we're going to need two of everything."

One of the parent chaperones yelled for Mrs. Taylor and she waved back. "Okay. I have to go supervise the field trip. But, oh, my gosh. We're going to have so much to do. This is so exciting." Then the woman pointed at Grant. "Don't go anywhere. We'll have dinner tonight to celebrate."

"Yes, ma'am," he told her and braced himself for another tight-lipped frown from Rebekah.

But she was being swept up in another hug by her father. "I can't believe my little Dimples is gonna be a mom. This is so exciting."

"We'll talk more about it later, Dad." Rebekah seemed as if she was trying to smile, but Grant could see the expression didn't quite reach her eyes. "You better go help Mom and that poor parent who got stuck chaperoning the Frog group."

It was actually the Uni-rex group now, but Grant didn't think Rebekah would appreciate the correction right that second. When her parents walked away, she lowered her face into her palms. Grant placed a hand on her lower back and rubbed slow circles. "Are you feeling okay? Do you need to throw up?"

"I'm too busy to throw up." Rebekah finally lifted her eyes to him. "I have to oversee a field trip for fifty kids, I have a tour group from the city council's office coming this afternoon to see our plans for where we plan to place the cell tower and I have a budget meeting with your aunts at five. Oh, and now my parents want to have dinner with us and probably quiz me about the status of our nonexistent relationship."

"Nonexistent? Ouch."

"You know what I mean, Grant. You yourself called it complicated." Rebekah used her fingers to massage the deep crease forming right above her nose. If she hadn't looked like she was about to hyperventilate, her reaction might've actually been considered cute. Oh, who was he kidding? Even overwhelmed and frustrated, Rebekah Taylor was still a mighty attractive woman. Too bad all of that frustration was currently directed at him. "This was *not* the way I wanted them to find out."

"I tried to tell you that we needed to talk," he reminded her. "Once I realized who your father was, I wanted to warn you."

"You could've just waited for me in my office," she suggested.

"Your dad had already seen me in the parking lot. Then, when they came over, I was trying to think of a fast way to throw them off the topic while simultaneously hoping your dad would have forgotten what I'd said on the plane."

"Is that what you were doing? You went all pale and looked so nervous, I thought you were going to faint again like you did in Dr. Singh's office."

"I didn't faint," he defended himself. "I knocked myself out. By accident." Okay, so even he knew that was lame.

She rolled her eyes. "Whatever. The only thing I've asked from you through all of this is to keep it under wraps until I was ready to tell people. And you couldn't even handle that."

The hurt in her tone hung between them and his heart hammered as he schooled his features and woodenly returned Mike Taylor's thumbs-up gesture from across the parking lot.

She had a point. Sure, he'd talked to a stranger—uh, sort of—on a plane, and not the editor of the *Spring Forest Gazette*. But he had made her a promise, and he could see why she felt betrayed. Now he needed to make things right. To show her that she could trust and depend on him.

"Again, I didn't know the stranger sitting next to me on the plane was your father."

Grant watched Rebekah cross her arms over her chest, which only served to thrust her attractive breasts up higher. "Besides, you said you were planning to tell them last weekend. I had no way of knowing that you hadn't gone through with it. But now they've found out, and while I obviously don't know them as well as you do, they seemed to take it well enough."

"The fact remains that I wasn't ready for the whole world to know I was pregnant just yet. And I especially wasn't ready for them to know that you're the father."

"What's wrong with me being the father?"

"Can we not do this here?" Rebekah wouldn't meet his gaze and the sting from her earlier comment about him not being able to handle his side of the bargain intensified. "There's your Aunt Birdie. I know she and Bunny will figure things out eventually, but I would like to keep my personal life and my work life separate for as long as possible. Let me deal with my parents and you keep your aunts occupied today so they don't find out from my dad, who is probably already on the phone with his publicist trying to score free samples of all the latest baby gear."

Rebekah walked away, her desire to keep their relationship a secret leaving a bad taste in his mouth. Wait, she'd specifically told him that they didn't have a relationship—secret or otherwise. And while he knew she was upset, that was still a little more than he was willing to stomach. It wasn't as if he was feeling the urge to settle down and get married, himself. But they were going to be in each other's lives for at least the next eighteen-plus years, so she'd better figure out pretty quickly how to explain his presence to people. And not blame him for every single thing that she couldn't control.

Screw it. If she didn't want anything to do with him, then he'd give her exactly what she wanted. She could keep her secret and protect her precious reputation and go at it alone.

Grant was about to walk back to his car and drive to the airport when Aunt Birdie interrupted his thoughts. "She's a wonder, isn't she?"

"She's something, all right," Grant replied, not taking his eyes off Rebekah.

"The girl has been a blessing to the shelter. Not only does she keep us organized, but she's full of all these big ideas for bringing awareness to our adoption program. This field trip was her idea and if today goes well, we're gonna partner up with some of the local schools and get more kids out here for a hands-on learning experience about animals."

"Hmm" was all he could manage in response. He wasn't really in the mood to hear every single one of Rebekah's praiseworthy attributes when was currently trying to pretend that he didn't exist.

"I heard you two went out for drinks together a couple months back." Birdie was more direct than her sister, and her eyes narrowed behind her glasses. "I've been hoping that meant you were getting along better now."

"What makes you think we don't get along, Aunt Birdie?"

His aunt answered by rolling her eyes and using a bobby pin to adjust the already tidy gray bun on top of her head. "So, what brings you to Spring Forest today, son?"

Grant couldn't very well admit that he'd flown out here purposely to see Rebekah. And after her comment about his fainting in the doctor's office and the accusation that he hadn't kept her pregnancy a secret, he decided that this was the perfect opportunity to prove to her that he could handle anything she threw his way. Besides, he had an excuse prepared—the same one he'd given Rebekah earlier. "I was actually going to take some pictures of that new picnic area for a brochure I'm working on."

Birdie's smile lit up her face and she put a wrinkled and work-roughened hand on his biceps. "A brochure would be fantastic. We could hand them out at adoption events or when we do our booth at the annual street fair. Why are you always so good to your old aunties, Grant?"

See, Rebekah wasn't the only one who could come up with innovative ideas. And it wasn't just a cover story— he really did want to do all he could for his aunts and for the shelter that meant so much to them.

It was no secret that when his Whitaker grandparents had died, they'd left all their property to their four children in equal shares. His father had sold off his first, while his Uncle Gator had held on to his and then reaped a financial windfall by selling when the market was at its peak. Birdie and Bunny were the last two to own parcels of Whitaker Acres, yet their money had been so mismanaged recently, they'd hired an attorney to look into the possibility of recouping some of their losses. In the meantime, he'd been the one to suggest the possibility of leasing land to some of his contacts in the wireless industry for a cell tower, as well as any other money-producing ventures he could think of to keep his aunts' rescue shelter afloat.

Grant slipped Birdie's hand into the crook of his arm and led her to the building's entrance. "I also wanted to pick your and Bunny's brains on the possibility of doing a big gala here as a fund-raiser."

"Like a fancy dress-up party?"

"Well, not too fancy. But we could have dinner and dancing and maybe a silent auction. And people can bring their pets in dress-up costumes. When I was at my conference in San Francisco, the hotel where I stayed was hosting something similar. They called it a Fur Ball."

"A Fur Ball!" Birdie clapped her hands. "Wait until I tell Rebekah."

"Let's not bother her right now while she has her hands full with the field trip kids. I'll take you and Aunt Bunny to the Main Street Grille and we can talk about it. If Amanda Sylvester is there, we can ask her about catering the event. Maybe we can add on to the picnic area and create an outdoor party space."

Grant had no idea where any of this was coming from, but he kept talking about any innovation he could think of as he steered the older woman toward the office. Hopefully, he could grab his other aunt and then get them far away before the field trip ended. He shuddered to think of what Rebekah's reaction would be if her parents ran into the aunts and completely blew their secret.

Rebekah didn't know where Grant had gone, but she didn't take an easy breath until her dad's old Subaru was long gone and the school bus had rumbled out of the parking lot after lunch. Her mom was only twenty minutes down the road when she sent a text asking where they should make a reservation for dinner tonight with Grant.

She shot back a quick reply saying she'd talk to Grant. Rebekah would let him be the one to come up with an excuse about why they couldn't come to Raleigh tonight for dinner.

When she finally finished her tour with the city council members later that afternoon and they'd driven off, she realized there weren't any cars left in the parking lot that she didn't recognize. That was weird, considering Grant always rented one when he came to town.

She went to her office and gobbled down one of the banana-nut muffins she'd been too busy—and nervous—to eat earlier. It was a little stale from sitting on her desk all day, but her stomach was growling in protest. She took a few quick bites as she made printouts of the budget reports she'd prepared for her bosses. However, when Bunny and Birdie arrived at her office, they barely glanced at their pages of detailed line item numbers, since they were too busy talking about all of Grant's latest ideas for something called a Fur Ball.

"And if the gala goes well, we could possibly start hosting bigger events," Birdie told her.

"Like weddings," Bunny added. "That could really bring in some much needed revenue."

"But we're a nonprofit animal shelter," Rebekah tried to remind them. "I think there might be tax ramifications if we turn the place into some sort of party venue."

"That's why we have you to look into all this for us. Grant said you'd know who to talk to about stuff like that."

Oh, had he now? Rebekah felt her unappeased hunger give way to annoyance.

"Um, speaking of your nephew," Rebekah sneaked a peek at her phone screen, which had two new text notifications from her dad. "Is he still around?"

The two sisters looked at each other quickly before turning their faces to Rebekah.

"Did you want to talk to him about something?" Bunny asked. She was the more absentminded of the

Whitaker sisters. Very sweet, but usually had her head in the clouds. There was no way the woman would have reason to think something was up.

"Um… I only wanted to talk to him about the pictures he was going to use for the brochures."

"Oh, he got some great ones of the kiddos sitting on the new wooden bleachers Bobby Doyle built. Doc J had the llamas out and half the class was raising their hands wanting to ask questions. He said he'd email the photos to us when he gets back to Jacksonville tonight."

Rebekah's head jerked back. "He went home already?"

The sisters shared another look and she realized she needed to get her emotions under lock and key. She certainly didn't want them knowing that their precious nephew was supposed to be having dinner tonight with her parents so they could all talk about the pregnancy nobody was supposed to know about yet.

"I mean, I figured he was leaving, but I wanted to make sure none of his shots showed the children's faces. We would need signed release waivers to publish their images and…uh…we'd probably rather not have to deal with that entire legal headache."

"Well, why don't you call him?" Birdie, the more sensible and pragmatic sister, asked. "His plane should've landed by now."

Her bosses stared at her expectantly and Rebekah was relieved that her answer was completely honest when she sank back in her seat and said, "I don't have his number."

Birdie rattled off the digits and then they both sat

there as though they had no intention of leaving until Rebekah actually called the man. There was no way she was going to have a conversation with Grant in front of the women. Who knew what the guy might say? Or what her own facial expressions might give away?

"Why don't I just send a text? That way, I'm not bothering him if he's still at the airport and he can respond whenever it's convenient for him."

The ladies still didn't budge, so Rebekah somehow managed to keep her fingers from trembling as she typed in the number and then wrote a quick message asking about the pictures for the brochures. She pressed Send and the whooshing sound echoed in the office.

She used her thumb to discreetly set her device to vibrate and then shoved it deep in her purse, just in case Grant responded and his aunts wanted to know what he'd said. "So, I'd better be off. I've got to drive to Raleigh tonight and have dinner with my parents."

"Oh, no." Bunny scratched at a loose gray curl near her temple. "We didn't get to talk to your mom while she was here. Grant kept us out and about all day. He even took us by that old house on Second Street where he thinks the little gray dog might be hiding."

Rebekah was already on her feet and shoving her laptop into her tote bag when her ears perked. "Did you guys see him?"

"How do you know it's a him?" Birdie asked.

"Or her." Rebekah quickly corrected. She actually had no idea what gender the thing was but she'd been leaving little treats near that same porch every day and, with the exception of the soy bacon she'd accidentally ordered last Sunday at brunch, all of the food was gone the next day. So the dog—or whatever other wild creature lived under there—definitely had a healthy appetite.

"Nope." Bunny shook her head. "No sign of the little dear."

It wasn't until Rebekah was out in her car that she realized Grant had actually followed through with something besides showing up for her doctor's appointment. He'd kept his aunts occupied all day so that her parents didn't see them and accidentally reveal anything about her pregnancy.

Maybe the guy could be useful, after all.

Chapter Seven

As soon as the plane landed and he powered on his phone, Grant saw a text from an unknown number. When he realized it was from Rebekah, he smiled as triumph coursed through his body. She might be talking about business stuff and legal releases, but at least he now had her number.

Taking whatever minor victories he could get at this point, he typed in a reply.

Don't worry. All of the pictures I took showed the kids facing away from me. I may not know much about babies, but I know all about marketing and licensing agreements.

Not expecting a response, he was surprised when he got to the long-term parking garage and felt his phone vibrate in his pocket.

Thanks for keeping your aunts busy today. You filled their heads with lots of crazy talk about Fur Balls and animal-themed weddings, but at least they don't suspect anything about us.

He wanted to tell her that she couldn't keep the babies a secret forever. Instead, he wrote,

Sorry for bailing out before dinner with your parents tonight. I figured you'd prefer me not being there to make things even more awkward, but I still hope you'll make my apologies to Mike and Sheila.

A few dots appeared, indicating she was typing something, then they disappeared. When he got to a stoplight, he saw a new text from her.

Yeah. Awkward is one word for it.

Now that he finally had her texting him, he wanted to keep the conversation going. But a horn sounded behind him and he had to drive.

When he pulled into the underground parking garage at his condo complex, he saw that she'd sent a follow-up message.

To be honest, I also bailed out on dinner. It's been a long day and I need more time to prepare myself for all their questions.

The reception down here was nonexistent (like their relationship), so Grant waited until he'd let himself into his condo to respond. He stood in front of the floor-to-ceiling sliding glass doors that looked out over the Atlantic Ocean, but he didn't notice the view because he was too busy staring at the electronic keyboard on his screen. Finally he typed, If you want, I can fly back this weekend and face them with you.

Thanks for the offer, but I think having you there would only make me more flustered.

So I fluster you. He added the winking emoji then pressed Send.

Of course. Her reply caused a burst of satisfaction to swell through his chest. His pulse sped up. Then a second bubble appeared right after. The whole situation has me all out of sorts.

Grant knew that her addendum was an understatement. He'd also been thrown for a loop when he'd found out they were having twins. While they'd both been active participants that night and had taken steps to prevent this exact thing, he only had to deal with the mental and emotional aspects of her pregnancy. Rebekah had the added physical and hormonal burden.

I was reading that stress isn't good for the babies. Is there anything I can do to make things easier?

He expected her to tell him to stay as far away from her as possible. Instead, she answered, Go to dinner with my parents on my behalf.

He was about to tell her that he'd book a flight right then, but she immediately added, I'm only kidding. I'm sure once I get through their interrogation this week-end, it'll get easier telling everyone else.

Then let me help prep you for all their questions.

What do you mean?

I'll pretend I'm your parents and ask you whatever par-ents would ask in a situation like this.

Grant collapsed on his leather sofa while he waited for her reply. He could almost imagine the sound of her breathless sigh as she wrote, Fine.

Okay. First question. What's your due date?

Easy. March 1. But sometimes twins come early.

They do?

Is this a question from you, Grant? Because I'm pretty sure my parents know everything there is to know about babies. Even twins. My mom has a master's in early childhood development and my dad has pub-lished several books on newborns and being a fos-ter father.

Grant stood up to retrieve his iPad out of the back-pack he'd left near his carry-on suitcase. He opened the internet search engine and typed in the name Mike Taylor. Her dad's picture popped up along with links to several of his bestselling books. No wonder the guy had laughed at Grant's suggestion on the flight.

Sorry. I've only had time to scan through some of the reading material Dr. Singh had suggested and I must've missed that part.

He started to type that he wished her dad had clued him in when they'd been on the airplane together, but it was probably best not to remind her about his accidental information leak in the first place.

All right, back to THEIR questions. Are you going to find out the genders?

I think I'm going to want to know the closer it gets to the due date. You know I'm a planner and like to be prepared for everything ahead of time.

Grant let out a whoosh of air. That was good to know. Personally, he was dying to find out if they were going to have girls or boys. Or one of each. Since they hadn't really had the chance to open up with each other and discuss it, this role-playing-via-text thing was actually working out in his favor. But it would only succeed if he legitimately sounded as though he was channeling her parents and asking questions they would ask their daughter. Which was difficult because the only thing he knew about the Taylors was that they lived in Raleigh and they were apparently experts when it came to babies.

He returned to his internet search on his iPad and typed, *biggest issues for new parents*. An article enti-

tled "Breastfeeding versus Bottle" popped up and Grant
quickly turned the device off. Nope. There was no way
he was going to ask Rebekah anything about her breasts.
At least, not yet. Although, he did like to think about
them often. "No, focus," he told himself.

We can't wait to hold our grandbabies. If you move
back home, we can help take care of them.

He pressed Send, then wondered if that sounded too
over the top. But surely her parents would want to be
close to their new grandchildren.

I would love for you guys to help out on the weekends,
but I'm happy at my job and my home is in Spring Forest.

Her townhome was nice, but it was one of the smaller
units with only two bedrooms. And if Grant remembered correctly, one of those bedrooms was set up as
her office.

You'll probably need more space when the babies get
older. Maybe a place with a yard.

He remembered the way she'd looked when she was
talking about the old brick house on Second Avenue and
he wondered if she was thinking about that exact yard.
Finally, she replied,

Well, I'll have to see what I can afford when the time
comes.

Speaking of money, what about the father? What's his name again? Greg?

Grant. Her response could've been keeping to their roles, or it could have been her rolling her pretty hazel eyes at him—meaning *knock it off and be serious*.

So he quickly added,

Well, we're sure this Grant guy is going to help you out financially. He seems like a responsible and dependable sort who wants to be active in his children's lives. And he's incredibly handsome.

She didn't respond for a few minutes and Grant walked over to his kitchen to grab a beer. His fridge contained three Coronas, two expired containers of yogurt his sister had dropped off when she'd delivered some groceries over a month ago and a nearly black banana from one of the boxed lunches he usually brought home from his work cafeteria.

He bet Rebekah's fridge was full of healthy meals she'd already prepared earlier in the week and then labeled in containers with color-coded lids. He opened the beer and was swallowing the first frothy gulp when his phone lit up with her response.

He's kind of handsome.

Kind of. Kicking off his sneakers, he took another drink and opened the doors leading out to his twelfth-floor balcony. He could get her to do better than that.

Kind of incredibly handsome. Your kids are going to be gorgeous. Hopefully with your dimples and his surfing skills. Plus, they'll be smart.

Surfing, questionable (and only if it's in shallow water). Dimples, maybe. Smart, probably. But that'll also be from me.

Obviously, he wrote. So do you and this kind of incredibly handsome Grant with the amazing surfing skills plan to raise your children together?

I'm not sure how that'll work. Hopefully, my parents aren't going to ask for those kind of details.

Well, the role-playing gig had been good while it lasted.

Don't you think they'll have questions about our relationship, Rebekah? Like how long we've known each other. Whether we plan to get married. Things like that?

Again, she didn't reply right away and Grant ran a hand through his hair and looked at the waves crashing on the beach below. His phone finally buzzed. But this time, it wasn't a text. She was actually calling him. He nearly dropped the phone as he scrambled to slide his thumb across the screen and answer. "Hello?"

"I honestly don't know what to tell them," she admitted, not bothering with a greeting.

"There's always the truth."

"Grant, I can't tell my parents that I had a one-night stand with my bosses' nephew."

"Do you think they'd disown you or something? Your parents seemed pretty reasonable and progressive to me."

"Obviously, I *can* tell them. I just don't *want* to. I'm their only child, the apple of their eye. High school valedictorian and top of my class at Duke's School of Business. I love my parents and they love me, but you know how they used to foster all those babies? Well, that took up a lot of their time and energy when I was a child. They've always counted on me to be responsible and self-reliant and, well, now they're used to me always doing things right. I'm not the type of person who makes mistakes."

Ouch. Was she calling him the mistake? Or their children the mistake? He pinched the bridge of his nose and said, "So then don't tell them it was a one-night stand. I mean, you heard your dad earlier today. He already referred to you as my girlfriend."

"Because that's what you told him on the plane." The reminder still held a trace of accusation and Grant could feel the defensiveness building in his throat.

"Yet again, I had no idea that was your father. Besides, you weren't exactly blowing up my phone with conversations and I had to talk to someone about it."

She made a huffing sound, then grumbled through the receiver. "Well, I'm talking to you about it now."

"So going back to my suggestion earlier. Why not just let people think we're dating each other? Or do I embarrass you?" He wasn't exactly a player, but he'd never really had to work too hard at attracting women. At least, he hadn't until he met Rebekah. He held his breath as he awaited her response.

"Fine." This time he heard her actual sigh and a current of electricity shot through him. "We can pretend we're dating each other."

"Can I pretend to take you out to dinner when I come into town next week?" he asked.

"It depends on what your definition of *pretend* is."

"Oh, you know, the usual. I pick you up at your place and hold the doors open for you. Maybe you smile at me and laugh at my jokes as though you enjoy my company."

"I've smiled at you before, Grant."

"Only when you've had a couple of cocktails, which are now apparently off-limits according to my baby book."

"I know. So is coffee, unfortunately."

"So you'll have to be sober and uncaffeinated and smile at me anyway," he added. "Possibly even hold my hand. I'd also be more than willing to engage in some public kissing displays, if you think it'll make us seem more legitimate."

"And you're hoping that people will actually see us? That a dinner with some hand-holding—no public kissing displays—will convince them that we're boyfriend and girlfriend?"

"They will if we go somewhere romantic. Not, like, too romantic because that would seem like we're trying too hard. But maybe a nice place that requires you to wear the green, silky top you had on that night at happy hour. The one with the V-neck that showed off the magnificent view of your—"

"Grant." Her voice came out in a squeak and she cleared her throat. "I don't know if this kind of pretending is such a good idea."

"Trust me. I'm in marketing and can make anything look believable. Besides, what could go wrong?"

"I should've told him that a million things could go wrong," Rebekah said to the hole under the front porch of the old brick house the following Thursday. She still had no idea whether the scruffy gray dog was currently hiding under there, but every day she'd been stopping by on her way to work and *something* had been eating the specialty canine cookies she'd been adding to her usual order at the bakery.

"Grant Whitaker is like this flaky, buttery croissant right here. I know he'll end up being bad for me, but I can't seem to resist him." She bit down, letting the layers of pastry melt into her mouth as she tried not to think about all the extra calories. Swallowing, she added, "It's just that he'd been talking about my dimples and my cleavage and saying all these other flirty things that kept distracting me. My brain was flashing the warning lights, but my heart was bouncing around inside my chest and my hormones were going crazy, which is supposedly normal according to the research I've been doing. So, yeah, I guess that's how Grant convinced me that we should pretend we're boyfriend and girlfriend."

A truck drove by slowly and Rebekah prayed the driver didn't notice the crazy pregnant woman sitting outside of a house that didn't belong to her and talking to an elusive stray animal that probably wished she'd just shut up and leave it alone. Or maybe find a human to whine to, instead.

Sure, Rebekah had several girlfriends who lived in town, but most of them either volunteered at the animal shelter or were somehow connected to someone who worked there. So it wasn't like she could talk to them about what was going on between herself and Grant. At least, not yet.

"So I finally bit the bullet and called my parents last night," Rebekah continued after a few more cars passed. "They pretty much asked me every question that Grant and I had already practiced. But I felt like the biggest fraud on the planet when I told them that Grant and I had been seeing each other for a while. Anyone who knows me will realize that he's totally not my type. He's all laid-back and I'm more of a type A personality. He has all these big, bold pie-in-the-sky ideas and I'm a realist. Everyone'll see through this whole stupid fake relationship idea that he thinks is foolproof. And you know who's going to look like the biggest fool in all of this?"

Not that Rebekah expected the dog to answer, but the question gave her time to take a sip of her decaf latte. "Me. I'm going to get swept up in all his flirty banter and his sexy smiles, and before you know it, even *I'll* start believing that our relationship is legit. Do you know what he told me when we were on the phone? He said he was in marketing and could make anything look believable. I mean, the guy might as well have said that

he tells lies for a living. And this is the man I'm supposed to trust? Who I'm supposed to raise kids with?"

A rustling sound came from under the porch and Rebekah held herself perfectly still as her excitement spiked.
She had to remain calm and keep talking if she wanted
the dog to feel safe enough to come out from its hiding
spot. Staring intently at the hole as though she could will
the mutt to do her bidding, she dropped a small piece of
the canine cookie. "You and I are a lot alike, you know.
We both have trust issues, obviously, and prefer to keep
to ourselves. We both like baked goods and bacon on our
cheeseburgers and hanging around old front porches of
houses that don't belong to us."

"You smell a whole helluva lot better than that dog,
though," Grant said as he walked up the rutted driveway.

Rebekah scrambled to her feet, heat radiating from
her cheeks. "What are you doing here?"

"I always stop by here when I'm in town to check
on our friend." Grant held up a fast-food bag. "I was
hoping a sausage biscuit might do the trick to lure him
out today."

Just when Rebekah had herself convinced that Grant
was all kinds of wrong for her, he showed up out of nowhere, doing something sweet and thoughtful to make
her completely rethink her entire opinion of the man.
Like feeding a stray dog, or refereeing a schoolgirl argument about unicorns and dinosaurs, or asking a stranger
on an airplane for tips on the best way to soothe a crying baby—her dad hadn't stopped talking about Grant's
earnest commitment to being a good father.

She commanded her nerve endings to settle down

and pushed a few curls behind her ear. "I meant why are you in town? I thought you weren't coming until this weekend."

Their plan had been to go out in public together a few times here and there, then maybe next month he could stop by her office and take her out to lunch. Once people were used to seeing them together, then they'd tell everyone about the babies. But his showing up out of the blue like this wasn't sticking to the plan. Even if it was only a day ahead of schedule.

"Oh, Aunt Bunny has it her head that we should build some sort of aviary on the premises and wants me to go with her to check out this bird sanctuary near the Outer Banks. I'm going to use the drive to try to convince her that they're not running an actual zoo here in Spring Forest."

"Oh. Okay. Well, I guess I'd better get to the office." She grabbed her bag and her decaf latte off the porch steps.

Grant's gaze traveled the length of her body and every inch of her skin zapped with electricity as his eyes passed over her. Finally, he lifted his face to hers and asked, "What? No kiss hello for your boyfriend?"

Rebekah's mouth went dry and her knees gave a little wobble. "Um...here? There's no one around to even see us. It'd be like putting on a show with no audience."

"Yeah, but when it's curtain time, we're going to want our performance to look as real as possible." Grant lifted one of his broad shoulders in a shrug. "We can consider it a dress rehearsal."

He moved in closer and Rebekah's breath caught in her throat. Her tummy did a little cartwheel and she immediately moved her hand to her midsection. "Don't you think we've already had enough practice?"

His head lowered to the slight rounding just below her waist. It was probably only noticeable to her, but she'd purposely worn an A-line skirt this morning to make it less apparent and to buy herself a little more time before everyone noticed.

Instead of looking suitably chastised, the man lifted one side of his mouth into a satisfied smile. He took another step closer. His fingers reached up to a curl that had blown into her face, gently toying with it before pushing it behind her ear to join the others. "In that case, I'll follow you to the animal shelter and then we can actually get the show on the road."

Rebekah's knees gave more than a wobble as she hurried to her car. If he kept looking at her with those steamy blue eyes, nobody was going to think her physical reaction to Grant was just an act.

Chapter Eight

It wasn't until Rebekah was a mile down the road that she realized she'd forgotten to leave the rest of the canine cookie for the gray dog.

"Our friend," Grant had called it. She could turn around and go back, but that might make it seem to Grant as though she was stalling for time to avoid being seen with her pretend boyfriend, who was also the very real father of her children.

Seeing his rental car in her rearview mirror, she realized that she probably should've taken him up on his offer of a dress rehearsal. If they'd just kissed and gotten it over with, then she wouldn't have all this awkward anticipation rioting around inside of her right this second.

When they did pull into the parking lot at Furever Paws, there was so much activity going on Rebekah wanted to keep driving. But everyone had probably already seen her unmistakable car and Grant's plain white rental sedan.

The sign guys were back and installing the newly reworded sign with the shelter's full name. Bobby Doyle, the mechanic who'd built the small bleachers for what was now being called the Learning Center, was under the hood of the older van they used to transport animals. Plus, there was a small bus from the Senior Center unloading volunteers who called themselves the Snuggle Crew.

The only blessing was that Bunny and Birdie were nowhere in sight when Grant exited his car and walked over to her driver's-side door. Rebekah knew that this might be her only chance to have the upper hand and so she rose to her full five feet nine inches and tried to sound as casual as possible when she said, "Oh, hey, Grant. What a surprise to see you here."

Without checking to see if their audience was even paying attention, Rebekah gave him a quick peck on his cheek. He must not have been anticipating it, because he stood there rooted to the spot, despite the fact that her tote bag accidentally bounced off his hip as she tried to hustle past, pretending her lips weren't still tingling from where they'd pressed against his golden stubble.

When he caught up to her near the front entrance, he pulled open one of the glass doors and said under his breath, "I think our kisses hello could definitely use more practice, Taylor."

With the way he'd used her last name, as if they were some sort of teammates, she was half expecting him to give her a smack on the butt like they were coming out of a football huddle. Instead of being offended, though, a tiny thrill shot through her. They *were* on the same team and, for the first time, it wasn't based solely on their mutual attraction. She and Grant were actually partners in something that was bigger than both of them.

Her eyes dropped to his lips and her heartbeat pounded in her chest. "I guess a little more practice wouldn't hurt."

"There you are," Nancy said from behind the reception desk and Rebekah felt the heat rise to her cheeks. She'd been about to kiss Grant, right here in front of everyone at work. What had she been thinking?

Walking on unsteady legs, Rebekah realized Claire Asher was also standing near the reception desk.

"Hey, Claire," Rebekah greeted her friend, hoping the woman didn't notice that her voice was still a bit breathless. "Isn't it a school day?"

"It is, but most of my English students are on a field trip with their eighth-grade science teachers." Claire smiled and pointed to her fiancé, Matt Fielding, who was standing nearby in the lobby and talking to one of the senior citizen volunteers. This particular man was wearing a blue cap embroidered with the words Vietnam Veteran. "Matt convinced me to call in a substitute so we could get a jump start on the wedding planning."

"Have you guys set a date yet?" Rebekah was happy for the engaged couple who were also renovating a fixer-upper they'd recently purchased, but she wasn't sure why they'd come to an animal rescue when they should be out sampling cake flavors.

"We're thinking around Christmastime. In fact, I was talking to Nancy the other day about taking on a couple more fosters now that we've got our yard finished and she mentioned that Furever Paws was going to be throwing some sort of fund-raiser gala soon. She said we should come by and check out the new party pavilion you guys were working on. So here we are."

"What party pavilion?" Rebekah tilted her head as she looked at Nancy.

"Isn't that what you called it in your brochures, Grant?" the middle-aged foster coordinator asked, reminding Rebekah that her supposed boyfriend was right behind her.

"Everyone kept referring to it as the picnic area," he said, placing his hand on Rebekah's lower back. The heat from his palm was immediately noticeable and caused an unexpected shiver as he slid it to the opposite side of her waist. "But I figured that once we get the freestanding roof built, it'll be well suited to hosting parties and should have a catchier name. It's also technically on Whitaker Acres, which is private land, so it shouldn't affect the nonprofit's tax exemption status."

Of course Grant had come up with yet another solution to an issue Rebekah had tried not to think about. She should be grateful, but instead she saw the boundaries between them growing even fuzzier.

A phone rang down the hall and she shifted her tote bag to her other shoulder, thereby dislodging Grant's arm from around her waist. "I really need to get to my office and take that call. Grant, why don't you show

Matt and Claire your so-called party pavilion for their upcoming wedding?"

Let her friend Claire be the one to point out to the guy from Florida that it often snowed in Spring Forest during December. How practical would his fancified outdoor picnic area be then?

"Well, I'm not exactly a wedding planner..." he started and Rebekah raised one eyebrow as though to say, *you're not exactly my boyfriend, either, but you have no problem using your marketing skills to play pretend when it suits you.* He must've understood her look because he finished with, "But I'm happy to show you guys around."

She rolled her eyes and was halfway down the hall when Grant's voice stopped her. "Hey, Rebekah, let me know what time you want to go grab lunch."

Grant had never wanted to kiss a woman more than he had when he'd seen Rebekah sitting outside that old mansion this morning, talking to a stray animal that refused to come out of its hiding spot.

He'd surprised her by showing up today instead of tomorrow like they'd planned. He'd also surprised her by putting his arm around her when she was standing in the middle of the lobby for all the shelter volunteers to see. The thin, silky material of her top wasn't much of a barrier between his palm and her heated skin underneath, and he'd ended up being the one surprised by his physical reaction to her.

Which was why he'd made that parting shot in front of everyone about taking her out to lunch. He'd needed to feel as though he hadn't totally lost control where she was concerned. In fact, when the poised and proper Rebekah Taylor was thrown off her game, it provided Grant the opportunity to come in and save the day.

And he'd always been good at saving the day.

"You ready?" he asked as he walked into Rebekah's office at noon.

She kept her eyes on her computer screen and her fingers on her keyboard as she spoke. "Ready for what?"

"For lunch. I was thinking Main Street Grille, but we can go somewhere more romantic if you really want to put on a show."

Her head slowly swiveled toward where he stood, and despite the fact that she was still in her desk chair, she appeared to be looking down at him. "Fine. Main Street Grille, but for lunch only. No show."

He lifted his right palm as though he was taking an oath. "I promise to keep my hands to myself. Unless you beg me to put them on you. Like you did that night—"

"Grant!" she yelped, which made him laugh. The only thing better than surprising Rebekah was shocking her.

Several heads turned in their direction as Grant kept pace with her long-legged stride toward the exit. After their near kiss on the way in earlier, everyone would be talking about them before they even made it out of the parking lot. His chest instinctively expanded as he held the door for her.

Yep, their fake relationship was off and running.

Speaking of running, they were halfway to his rental car when he saw a gray flash in the distance.

"Hold on." He grabbed her elbow and she shot him a frown before giving a pointed look at where he was touching her.

"Is this your way of keeping your hands to yourself?" she asked.

"No, look over there." The gray dog was under one of the bushes near her little blue Fiat, its beady black eyes watching them. He felt Rebekah's muscles tense under his fingers.

"I have a treat for him in my car," she whispered to him. "I'm going to slowly walk over there and open the passenger door. Stay here and don't make eye contact."

The Furever Paws van was still in its parking spot where Bobby had been working on it, which meant Grant could turn his head in the other direction and watch Rebekah in the reflection of the rear window. His pulse thrummed in his ears as her high heels crunched against the gravel. After at least a million seconds, the door handle finally made a clicking sound.

As Rebekah slowly retreated from the car, her eyes met his in the reflection from the van window and she paused a few feet away from her Fiat, her back to the dog.

They held their positions for what felt like forever but was probably only a few minutes. Grant could smell the dog well before he saw it approach the car. The scruffy mutt hopped up on the passenger seat and, when its nose was buried in the white paper bakery bag, Rebekah ran the few feet and slammed the door closed.

Without a backward glance, she raced toward the front entrance of the building.

She was already inside when the gray dog pressed its paws against her passenger window and began barking for all it was worth. The animal's frightened eyes narrowed as Grant walked closer to the car, trying to murmur words that would calm the poor thing down.

"You're okay, buddy. We just want to help, that's all."

The dog's barking subsided for a second and Grant thought he was making progress, but then Davis Mc-Intyre, the on-duty vet tech, came outside with a lead pole and a small metal kennel. Lauren Jackson, the veterinarian who had taken over her father's veterinary practice, followed. Judging by the way the small dog was growling and baring its teeth, Grant wanted to call out the suggestion that they bring a tranquilizer gun, too.

One of the volunteer dog handlers emerged from the shelter's doors wearing long, thick gloves made out of suede and it was then that he caught a glimpse of Rebekah standing behind the door of the building. Was she afraid of the dog? Or maybe she was worried about getting bitten by a feral animal and she wanted to protect the babies.

There was lots of barking and growling and *whoa theres* but they finally got the poor little beast out of the car and into the crate. That was when Rebekah flew through the doors and grabbed Grant's arm. "Is he okay?"

"Judging by all the commotion he's making, I'd say he's mad as hell. But they've got him."

Rebekah's palm slid down his arm and into his hand, her fingers lacing with his as they followed everyone inside to the exam area in the rear of the building. When they set the crate on a stainless steel table, the dog's barking picked up speed, a scared animal who knew there was no getting away but wasn't going down without a fight.

"I'm going to have to sedate him so I can perform the examination," Dr. Lauren said, opening a package that contained a syringe. There was more growling and the crate shuddered but the vet and vet tech blocked their view.

Gradually the barking grew intermittent and that's when Rebekah finally approached. "It's okay, buddy. You're going to be okay."

She held out her fingers and the overgrown gray muzzle nuzzled against the metal bars as though it wanted to rub up against her hand. "That's a good boy." Rebekah looked toward Dr. Lauren. "He's a boy, right?"

"I only got a quick glance, but it looked that way to me," the vet said as she laid out supplies on the tray near the table.

"You remember me, don't you?" Rebekah asked the animal who was now lying on his side, his barking subdued but his eyes still very wary. "I'm the one bringing you all those good treats all the time."

A little pink tongue poked out of the mass of gray fur and licked Rebekah's fingers. "That's a good boy. Now, these nice people just want to check you out and make sure you don't have any ouchies. Then when you feel better, I'll have another treat for you."

"Ouchies?" Grant asked when Rebekah finally backed away from the now-peaceful dog and let the vet go to work.

"Sorry. It's something my parents used to say when I was little. With all the stress, I guess it slipped out."

"Is that why you stayed inside when they were trying to get the dog out of your car?" Wanting to check her heart rate, he used his thumb to trace the pulse point on her wrist. "Was it too much stress?"

"No, I was hiding because I didn't want him to see me and think I was the one who trapped him."

"So you were leaving me out there to be the bad guy and take the fall?"

"As if anyone could ever think that Grant Whitaker is the bad guy."

"What's that supposed to mean?" he asked, but then Davis appeared in the doorway holding an extra chair.

"Since both of you don't seem to want to go anywhere, you can just sit over here where you'll be out of the way." Davis was great with animals but had never seemed especially fond of humans.

"Is April Oliver around?" Dr. Lauren asked, referring to the professional groomer who often volunteered at the shelter. "The hair around his ears is so matted, I can't even lift them. We might need her to groom him before I can get in there and really examine him."

"I have a feeling this might take a while," Grant told Rebekah. "Are you hungry?"

"I don't think I should leave. When I was talking to him a few minutes ago, it seemed like he knew my voice and it helped relax him."

Or it could be the sedation doing the relaxing, but Grant admired her for wanting to stay by the dog's side. She might not be excited about her pregnancy but judging by the concern etched all over her face for some stray animal, she was going to make one hell of a mother.

"Despite being on the thin side, he's relatively healthy," Dr. Lauren told Rebekah over an hour later. "Poor guy was probably in a ton of pain, though, with all that matted hair pulling on his skin and the flea bites underneath. The hair inside his ears was so bad, it had grown into these waxy dreadlock things that were harder to remove than a cork out of a champagne bottle. There's an infection in both canals, but I was able to flush them out and we'll get him started on some antibiotics."

"He already looks like a completely different animal," Rebekah said, stroking her hand against the soft gray fur that had been shaved down to half an inch of fuzz. April had been able to carefully bathe him earlier and he smelled like a whole new dog, as well.

"Be cautious, though. When he wakes up, he might be just as grouchy as he was before we sedated him."

Grant had gone to get sandwiches for them and Rebekah had only been able to get down a few bites. She'd been on the edge of her seat the whole time the groomer and then the vet had been working on the dog.

"We got a hit on his microchip." Birdie waved a piece of paper in the air as she came into the exam room with Doc J behind her. "Two-and-a-half-year-old schnauzer and terrier mix named Angus. He belonged to Rupert MacKenzie, who used to live at 436 Second Avenue. But Rupert went into a skilled nursing facility after he had a stroke over a year ago. He passed away after a few months with no known relatives and the house is now tied up in probate."

"That explains why the little guy was hiding under the porch over there," Grant said, his large, tan hand following Rebekah's as he petted the still-sleeping animal. "You were looking for your owner, huh, Angus MacKenzie? Wow, that's a proud Scottish name if I ever heard one."

"He's probably got some Scottie in him," Doc J added, as he looked over his daughter's patient. The man was supposed to be retired, but he sure stopped by an awful lot to check on things. "They can be pretty independent and stubborn, so that's why he was so determined to stay close to home."

The dog let out a big breath and his eyelids fluttered open. His gray bangs had been cut back, allowing him to see better. Although now they stood up straight, as though his brow was lifted in a permanent state of annoyance. Rebekah felt the vibration in his chest as he started to growl. "You're okay. Take it easy. As soon as Dr. Lauren says it's okay, I'll get you something to eat."

His freshly trimmed ears lifted in surprise and his little nub of a tail began to wag in earnest. An encouraging smile spread across Rebekah's face. "Do you recognize the sound of my voice, Angus?"

The dog's tail wagged even more and he sniffed Rebekah's hand before licking it. "He's probably just excited to hear anyone's voice at this point," Dr. Lauren said as she put the oxygen mask away. "As bad as his ears were, he probably couldn't hear a lot for the past few months. It certainly explains why he was so afraid of everyone and kept running off."

That might be true, but despite all the people in the room, Angus's round black eyes were focused on Rebekah. Sure, she'd been having in-depth conversations with the animal for over a week now, as though he was her personal therapist. However, there was something else pulling at Rebekah's heart as she slowly stroked the area between his ears and down his neck. Some unexplainable connection that drew her to this dog.

"I'm going to try and take the lead off," Dr. Lauren advised them. "April found this green plaid collar that looks pretty fitting for our little chieftain here."

Rebekah took a step back to give the vet room to work, but Angus made a whining sound.

"He seems to prefer you," Grant told her. "Maybe you should put the collar on."

Dr. Lauren passed her the collar and Rebekah slowly put it around Angus's neck. The last thing she wanted to do was startle the poor guy and get him agitated again. As soon as the plastic clasp clicked into place, the dog rose onto his four legs and used his nose to nuzzle into her hands.

"Look at that tail." Grant gave her a smile of encouragement before chuckling. "It's wagging so hard, his whole rear end is shaking along with it."

"So how long do we need to keep him under observation?" Birdie asked the younger vet. "We're pretty full right now and I'd really hate to put him in one of our temporary kennels after all the earlier trauma he endured this morning. They might remind him of a cage and stress him out again."

"I'd keep an eye on him for another hour or so, but he should be good to go if you can line up a foster home tonight."

"Do you hear that, Angus?" Rebekah murmured as the dog cuddled against her, burrowing himself into her arms until she was practically carrying him like a baby. "You get to go to a foster home tonight where someone will love on you and take care of you and feed you yummy treats…"

Her voice trailed off as she realized that every eye in the room was on her.

"What?" Rebekah narrowed her eyes at Grant, because his knowing grin was the most unsettling.

"I'm pretty sure that the only home Angus is going to be happy with is yours."

"But I don't foster dogs. Or any pets." Rebekah could see that her protests were falling on deaf ears. Which reminded her that while the little gray bundle of fur had recently been partially deaf, he could probably hear her *now* as she was telling everyone that she didn't want him. "It's just that my place isn't really set up for a pet. I don't even have a food dish or any supplies."

"Honey, we're an animal shelter." Birdie shook her head. "We have everything you could possibly need. I'll even let you pick out some new stuff from the gift shop out front."

Angus's soul-searching black eyes didn't so much as blink as he stared at her adoringly.

"That's it, Angus." Grant scratched the dog's lower

back and Rebekah could've sworn she felt the thing purr along with the man's playful tone. "Keep giving her that sad puppy-dog look and guilt her into taking you home with her."

But Angus didn't need any coaching. He was already as good as Grant when it came to wearing down her sense of logic.

Rebekah's heart hammered. This was all happening way too fast. She needed to think of a way to get out of it. "What if that sad look is really just the aftereffects of the sedation? What if I get him home and he gets all worked up again?"

"That's a good point." Grant kept his eyes on her when he told the others in the room, "We really wouldn't want to put Rebekah in a situation that could risk the... could risk her health."

She lowered her lids at him in warning, but he only lifted his brows and shrugged at her in response. If she hadn't been so busy trying to silently communicate with him, she might've seen his aunt studying their interaction.

That's why Rebekah choked back a gasp when Birdie suggested, "Why don't you take Grant with you and Angus back to your place? That way, if the dog seems like he's going to turn on you, you won't be on your own."

Damn it. Rebekah was supposed to be getting herself *out* of this foster-dog commitment, not digging herself in deeper. Now she was supposed to be taking both the dog *and* Grant to her house?

"But what do I do with him tomorrow?" she countered. "I work all day and wouldn't really be able to watch him."

"I was actually going to talk to you about your schedule." Her boss shifted forward and Rebekah saw something in the older woman's eyes. "Bunny was supposed to go to the bird sanctuary with Grant today, but then you guys got busy with Angus here. Since she's busy tomorrow, I'm going to need you to go with Grant to the bird place. You can take Angus here with you and see how he does with cars rides and leashes. If that goes well, maybe take him to a park to socialize him with other people and animals. We need to know if he'll need some training classes with Mollie before we can officially adopt him out."

She opened her mouth to attempt one last stand. But Birdie and Doc J were already walking away. Besides, at this point, any further arguments would clearly only result in Rebekah landing herself in an even deeper hole she would not be able to dig her way out of.

"Fine," she mumbled, then patted the dog's chest. "But you two had better not get me into any trouble."

Angus made a contented sigh and Grant was looking anywhere but at Rebekah. Although she couldn't help but note his lips were twitching at the corners.

Chapter Nine

"Sorry for throwing off your plans with your aunt today," Rebekah said to Grant as he drove her and Angus to her townhome. She'd left her car back at the shelter so she could hold Angus in case he needed to be soothed during the ride. "I didn't intend for you to miss out on your trip to the Outer Banks with Bunny."

Now that the chaos of the afternoon had receded, he could sense her slipping back into her perfectly composed self. Or, at least, she was making a brave effort. But Grant could still feel the imprint of her fingers from where she'd clung to his hand while the animal was being examined.

"I figured you and Angus needed me more." Grant smiled across the center console, reaching to pet the dog who was currently balanced on Rebekah's lap and had his snout halfway out the window. "Isn't that right, big guy?"

Angus turned his face toward Grant, giving him a cautious appraisal before looking back out the window. He sure was a cute little thing now that he'd been cleaned up.

"To be honest, this kind of works out better anyway," he offered.

"How so?" Rebekah changed her grip on the plaid leash that matched the dog's collar, probably because she was worried the pup was going to make another break for it through the open window.

Grant held back a chuckle. As much as she'd argued against fostering the abandoned animal, everyone in that room could see the connection between her and the dog. It was going to be interesting to watch how she and Angus interacted once he got them back to her place.

"Now we have even more reason to spend time together and get people thinking that things are serious between us." He felt the corners of his mouth lift in a smug grin.

"Serious between us? I thought we were just pretending to be boyfriend and girlfriend, remember? Why do you always have to take things to the next level?"

"Always?" he repeated, his bold wink hidden behind the dark lens of his sunglasses. If Rebekah was arguing with him, it meant she was back to feeling like herself. Since his current goal was keeping her as stress-free as possible, he'd gladly engage in a spirited debate to distract her from worrying about her new foster dog. "What else do I take to the next level?"

Her curls were blowing around in the wind from the open window and she groaned as she tried to use her free hand to hold them back. "How about that party pavilion, for starters?"

"So I took a few liberties with the name. But you have to admit that it has a nice ring to it."

"The problem is that we're running an animal shelter, Grant. Not an events venue."

"But it's an animal shelter that's barely making ends meet. I would think that with your business background, you'd see my aunts desperately need to be bringing in more revenue."

"They wouldn't need to bring in more revenue if…" Rebekah's words trailed off.

"If what?"

She sighed. "It's no secret that there's an investigation right now into what happened to their investment money."

Sure, he was hoping that the attorney investigating the matter would get to the bottom of the matter, but he was also hoping that Uncle Gator would be cleared of any wrongdoing in the process.

"Have you been updated on that investigation lately?" she asked.

"No, because I don't want to deal with theories or what-ifs. I want hard, concrete proof of whoever could possibly be behind their current money mismanagement."

Rebekah lifted a finger. "Nope. Not *current* mismanagement. As their office director, who is solely responsible for the budget, I can assure you that that all their financial issues happened well before I was ever hired. So you can quit giving me the side-eye."

"What side-eye?" He lifted his sunglasses to the top of his head and squinted in her direction.

"The one you're giving me right now." She reached up to the rearview mirror and lowered it to reflect his suspicious expression. "You've been looking at me like that for the past year, as though you think I'm hiding something."

"I don't necessarily think you're hiding something. I just have a feeling that there's another side to you. One that I've only gotten glimpses of so far. Plus, I'm trying to stay focused and resist the urge to stare at your long, pretty legs."

He could hear her intake of breath and tried not to laugh as she attempted to tug the hem of her dress down past her knees. Too bad she couldn't move it past Angus's squirmy hind end.

"Why do you do that?" he asked.

"Do what?"

"Get all embarrassed whenever I pay you a compliment."

"I'm not embarrassed." Rebekah defended herself even as she shifted in her seat and seemed fixated on the billboard advertising the new Kingdom Creek development. The same billboard she probably passed every single day on her way home from work. "It's just weird, that's all."

"Me being attracted to you is weird?" He had to say it out loud to make sure he understood her.

"No, you being attracted to your aunts' employee is weird."

"It has nothing to do with you working for my family. Even if you were the employee of an entire herd of feral Uni-rexes trying to take over the planet, I'd still be attracted to you."

Rebekah pointed at the road ahead. "Go right at the next light."

"I know it's been a couple of months, but I remember how to get to your townhouse." He saw her cheeks suck in as she inhaled and it stirred his blood. He added, "In fact, I remember a lot of things about that night."

Angus again yipped in excitement and she covered the dog's floppy ears. "Don't talk about...*you know*... in front of the dog."

"I doubt he can understand what we're saying." Grant nodded at the animal who was currently using his open mouth and tongue to try and catch the air rushing by the open window.

Rebekah frowned. "I know it sounds crazy, but I'm pretty sure he knows *exactly* what's being said."

"Well, then, he's going to find out sooner or later that his new mommy is going to be a mommy to some humans pretty soon."

"I wish you wouldn't call me that."

Grant cocked his head at her while they waited at the stop sign in front of her complex. "You don't want our kids to call you mommy?"

"No, I don't want the d-o-g to start thinking of me that way." She'd lowered her voice to spell the word. "This is only a temporary fostering situation."

Ten minutes later, after Angus had left his mark on every shrub and patch of grass along the walk from the parking lot to her unit, the so-called d-o-g was curled up in the center of her white leather sofa as though it was his throne. Grant chuckled as he filled up the new water dish. "Looks like our Scottish warrior has laid claim to the castle and has no intention of this being a temporary situation."

"But I don't really want the responsibility of a pet," Rebekah whispered as she filled the equally new ceramic bone-shaped storage canister with dog treats. "Especially right now with everything else going on."

"Sometimes we don't get to pick our pets." Grant shrugged. "Sometimes our pets pick us."

"Do you have any pets back home?" Rebekah leaned against the kitchen counter across from him. It was one of those questions that would've come up already if they'd gone on any proper dates. Or had been in an actual relationship and not just pretending.

"I always had a dog growing up, but now I travel too much to take care of one." He put his hands on the counter behind him and rolled back his shoulders in an attempt to stretch his upper torso. "My mom has a corgi, though, and I get my animal fix whenever I visit her surf shop. Or, obviously, when I come see my aunts."

"Which you've been doing with increased frequency lately." Her eyes lowered to his chest, which he knew was on full display under the very thin cotton of his T-shirt. Her tongue darted out of her mouth to lick her lips and then her gaze jumped back up to his face. "Not that I've noticed or anything."

Too late, he thought, flexing his pec muscles. Rebekah's earlier admission, as well as the unresolved sexual tension, hung in the air between them.

"Well, you'd better get used to it, because now that I'm going to be a father, I'll be here an awful lot more." Okay, so Grant hadn't really thought much about the logistics of living so far away while still being there to support Rebekah through the pregnancy and parenthood, but as soon as he'd said the words, he realized that he couldn't keep up with the back-and-forth travel indefinitely. Something would have to give.

"What about your job?" Rebekah turned to open the refrigerator and pulled out two bottles of water, handing him one. His fingers grazed hers and he was reminded of how her hand had clung to his most of this afternoon while Angus had been under sedation.

Despite her attempt to avoid his gaze, Grant was willing to wager that she'd just remembered the same thing. In fact, he saw her fingers twitch slightly before she drew them back, gripping the counter behind her as though she were holding herself in place. She shook her head and he caught a whiff of her plumeria scent and inhaled deeply.

"One nice thing about my job is that I can work from pretty much anywhere." He twisted off the water bottle's cap and took a long drink. When he lowered his head, he caught her staring at his neck.

A current of electricity shot through him and when she licked her lips a second time, Grant took a step closer. He didn't know if it was desire or courage currently flooding his body, but he'd grown extremely warm and he needed Rebekah to understand that he could only take so much heat before he needed to get out of this kitchen.

"Rebekah?" Her name came out in a near groan.

"Huh?" she said, giving her head another little shake before lifting it to face him.

"You know how you told me in the car that I'm always looking at you with a side-eye?" He took another step closer.

"Uh-huh," she managed as her eyes darted down to his mouth.

"And I told you that I stare at you because I'm attracted to you?"

She sucked in her cheeks and gave a brief nod.

"Well, you have a tendency to watch me in the exact same way." She was still wearing her heels, making her nearly the same height as him. Which meant that his face was within inches of hers.

"What do you mean?" Her whisper-soft answer was so close, he could feel the ice-water coolness of her breath against his mouth.

"It means that if you keep looking at me like that, we're going to end up in your bedroom again."

One minute Rebekah had been in the kitchen guzzling cold water in an attempt to cool down the throbbing of awareness heating her blood. And the next she was kicking off her wedged heels as Grant led her backward toward her bed. His lips were just as warm and as fierce as she remembered and his mouth consumed hers while she lifted up his T-shirt to stroke the golden skin underneath.

"Are you sure?" he asked when they were nearly to her bed.

Lately, it seemed as if everything was being decided for her—unexpected twins, foster dogs, party pavilions. But her body was still the one thing she controlled. And she was absolutely sure that she wanted just one more night with Grant—one night to really get it right.

Not that alcohol had totally impaired them last time, but she was more than sober right this second and needed to prove to herself, and maybe even to him, that whatever it was between them wasn't really a big deal.

However, when she finally got his shirt over his head and those perfectly broad shoulders were in full view, all she could think was, *This is a very big, very muscular deal.*

How could one man be this incredibly handsome? Or smell this good? She knew he'd been on a plane and then at the animal shelter all day, yet his skin still held traces of coconut-scented sunscreen. Rebekah would've used her tongue to taste him; however, her mouth was currently occupied by his deep, exploring kisses.

She slid her palms over the wall that was his chest, then over the smooth ridges of his abdomen until she got to the muscular lines that dipped into his board shorts. Her heart sped up when she got to his waistband, yet her hands slowed down. If this was going to be the last time she allowed herself to sleep with the man, then she was going to take her time.

Grant, though, must've mistaken her pause as a request for assistance because his hands encircled hers at his waist and then she heard Velcro rip as he released the fastening. Rebekah was about to have sex with a man for a second time and she didn't even know if he owned a proper pair of pants.

When he stood before her completely naked, his casual clothing preferences suddenly didn't matter. Rebekah gulped, unable to take her hands off him.

Or her eyes.

She didn't want to ruin the moment with logical thoughts about him eventually flying out of her life for good. So she looked her fill, instead, memorizing every perfect muscle forged by years of swimming and surfing.

"Now my turn," he said, his fingers making their way to the zipper on the back of her dress. As the coolness from her air-conditioning unit hit the bare skin along her lower spine, Rebekah suddenly had the urge to pull her dress closed. She'd always been on the curvier side, but her stomach was even less flat than it had been a couple of months ago. Or even a couple of weeks ago.

Then his hands were on her breasts and Rebekah forgot every single thing she'd been thinking up until that point. Throwing her head back, she let out a moan and Grant pressed his lips to her jawline and then trailed kisses down her neck and along her shoulder blades.

She whimpered when he removed his hands from the sharpened peaks of her nipples, which were now aching for more. "Be patient, sweetheart," he murmured in her ear. "As sexy as this purple silky bra is, I need it out of my way so I can feel all of you."

When she was finally standing bare in front of him, it was Grant who groaned as he reached out and gently stroked her breasts. "I've been thinking about your body for months, thinking about all the ways I'd like to touch you and make you feel—"

He wasn't able to finish because she captured his face between her hands and pulled his mouth back to hers. Months, he'd said. Knowing that all this time Grant had been thinking about her body the way she'd been thinking about his made Rebekah nearly drunk with power.

He tilted his head and deepened the kiss while maneuvering the matching panties over her hips. After she kicked them free, he hooked his right wrist under her left knee and she could easily feel his arousal at her opening. The hard length of him slid against her and Rebekah wondered if Grant planned to take her right there, standing up. She arched her hips toward him and he drew back. "I brought protection along this time, but it's in my carry-on bag. Which is outside in my car."

"At the risk of killing the mood," Rebekah replied, her voice sounding raspy to her own ears. "Unless you have some test results you need to share with me, I think we're past the point of needing protection."

"Good point." Grant slanted his mouth over hers while hooking his left arm under her right leg. The next thing she knew, the bed was underneath her and Grant was above her, sliding the tip of his shaft against her damp heat.

"Please," Rebekah begged, sliding her hands down his muscular back and pulling him toward her.

Grant threw back his head and let out a deep moan when he buried himself inside of her. He was raised on his elbows, his chest grazing hers as he searched her eyes. "Sweetheart, I'm trying to hold myself back but if you keep rocking your hips like that, I won't be able to."

Again, she felt that thrilling sensation that her body had this much control over his. She locked her legs behind him and said, "The last thing I want to do right now is hold back."

Chapter Ten

Grant had planned to take things slowly, to savor each moment, but Rebekah was so eager and so encouraging. When she started making those little hiccuping sounds in his ear and then shuddered in his arms, he lost all control.

She gave another small shudder when he eased onto his side and he kept his hand curled around her waist as he asked, "Are you okay?"

Her eyes remained closed, with her silky lashes fanning her cheeks, but she was able to manage a slight nod and a very satisfied smile.

The past few weeks, he'd rarely seen Rebekah do much more than offer a pleasant grin—and that had usually been directed at someone else. Pride swirled around him at the realization that he'd been the one responsible for this particular smile. He pulled her closer against him, absorbing every inch of her satisfaction through her relaxed muscles.

The sound of tinkling metal filtered in from outside the bedroom, followed by the echo of little claws on the hardwood floors. Rebekah jerked up into a sitting position, taking the top sheet with her and covering that beautiful view. "What's that noise?"

"That's right. You aren't familiar with the pitter-patter of little doggy feet yet." Grant smiled at her embarrassed expression when Angus appeared in the doorway. "Look who's up from his nap."

"He probably needs to go outside for a walk." Rebekah's eyes searched frantically around the room until they landed on the crumpled dress that had landed in a heap a few yards from the bed. "Can you distract him for a second so that he doesn't see me getting dressed?"

Grant smothered a chuckle. "Are you afraid he'll know what we were doing?"

"Don't wiggle your eyebrows at me. This dog is a lot smarter than he looks and he understands way more than he lets on."

"Come on, boy," Grant said, rising to his feet. "Mommy doesn't want you to see her naked and know that we were doing very sexy grown-up things in her bed."

She made a squeaking sound and pointed at Grant. "Now he's seeing you naked."

"Rebekah, I hate to be the one to break it to you, but Angus isn't exactly dressed, either. I don't think he cares what we wear so long as we feed him and take him on walks."

Grant was easily able to dodge the pillow she sent sailing in his direction.

Not bothering to cover his laughter this time, he found his board shorts on the floor and pulled them on right before the second pillow hit him straight in the forehead.

"Mommy's got a good arm." He scooped up Angus so that the little dog didn't have to keep jumping to see what was going on in the bed eighteen inches above him. The dog gave a happy yip when he saw Rebekah, so Grant placed him right on her lap.

"That's because Mommy went to Duke on a softball scholarship," she told the dog as she scratched him behind the ears. The motion caused the cotton sheet to drop and Rebekah quickly yanked it up over her breasts again. Angus, on the other hand, mistook her quest for modesty as an invitation to play tug-of-war with her bed linens.

"Attaboy, Angus." Grant cheered on the scrappy mutt, who was now growling and yanking for all he was worth. "Get those covers away from her. Don't let her hide that perfect body from me anymore."

Rebekah let the dog win so that she could launch a third pillow in Grant's direction. This time he caught it and enjoyed the view.

"Okay, boy, we won," he said after Angus got himself so tangled up in the sheet, he rolled off the bed and landed in a pile of bedding. Grant picked up the happy dog in one arm and scooped his T-shirt off the ground with the other as he walked toward the bedroom door.

"How about I take you for a walk while Mommy recovers from Daddy's skilled lovemaking?"

A fourth pillow hit the doorjamb as Rebekah yelled out, "Stop talking to him about that!"

Angus took his time as Grant walked him around the property, sniffing every tree, flower and curb along the way. He kept expecting the dog to try and make a run for it, or to at least pull against his leash, but Angus seemed content sticking close to Grant's side.

The poor mutt must still have been groggy from the sedative and the trauma of the day's big adventure because as soon as they returned to the townhome, Angus crashed out again on the sofa. Rebekah had taken a shower while they were gone, and when Grant saw her emerge from the bedroom in a pair of dark blue lounge pants and an oversize Duke softball sweatshirt, he realized that he preferred this casual outfit to the formal clothes she tended to wear all the time.

"I didn't order dinner yet because I wasn't sure what kind of food you liked," she said as she pulled her hair up into a ponytail. It should've sounded weird—the fact that he was having children with a woman and neither of them knew whether the other preferred Italian or Chinese for takeout.

However, the neckline of her sweatshirt dropped to the side and exposed a bare shoulder and suddenly Grant didn't care about food at all.

He leaned over to kiss her gently, and she gazed at him, then took his hand to lead him back to her bedroom—this time closing the door softly behind them to make sure Angus wouldn't distract them.

After another round of lovemaking they agreed on pizza, which was delivered while Grant used Rebekah's shower.

"I guess eating on the sofa is out of the question since Angus has established that as his new bed," Grant said after he emerged from the bathroom. The dog gave him a dismissive glance before burrowing deeper into the throw pillows. "That's a pretty big improvement from the dank porch you slept under last night, huh, big guy?"

"Actually, I was hoping you wouldn't mind me working through dinner. I need to go over a draft for the latest grant proposal I'm putting together for the animal shelter." Rebekah had her back to him and was pulling plates out of a kitchen cabinet. "I was supposed to do it today at the office, but then…"

She trailed off as she stared at the pup relaxing on her furniture. The zesty smell of pepperoni and tomato sauce surrounded them and Grant tugged at the neck of the clean T-shirt he'd found in his carry-on bag. It would've been quite the homey scene if he'd actually felt at home here in her living room. Or even in her presence.

Rebekah was looking everywhere but at him and he suddenly had the feeling that maybe he'd been too presumptuous in bringing his overnight bag upstairs. Sure, he'd spent the night here a couple of months ago, but that had been a one-off. Grant didn't usually play house with the women he dated.

Not that he and Rebekah were actually dating. They were just sleeping together. And having kids together. And pretending to be in a relationship so that everyone else around them would think they were...together.

Hell. Grant scratched at his damp head. He was supposed to be the guy who usually got people out of sticky situations. So how, exactly, had he ended up in this situation with no exit strategy in sight?

He cleared his throat. "That's cool. I actually have a presentation I need to work on. We're setting up a product launch for my company's latest design of waterproof cases for video equipment."

They sat down on opposites sides of the table and hid behind their respective laptops as they ate. Despite the fact that there were so many things that needed to be said between them, so many decisions that needed to be made, neither one of them spoke while they worked.

She would yawn. He would ask if she was tired—according to the pregnancy book he'd just finished, she should be—and she would insist that she was fine and continue clicking away at her keyboard. Yep. She was definitely avoiding something. Grant glanced down the hall to her open bedroom door. So far, the bed was the one place where things weren't awkward between them.

After an hour, Angus roused himself enough to jump to the floor and sniff his way to the front door. Rebekah finally looked up from her screen. "Do you think he needs to go outside again?"

"I'll take him." Grant didn't know about Angus, but he was dying to go out and take a break from this tense silence. He slammed his laptop closed and sprang up to get the dog's leash.

"Thank you," Rebekah said around another yawn. She'd resumed her typing before he and Angus were even out the front door.

"Any suggestions on how I can get her to open up?" Grant asked the dog a few minutes later as they followed their earlier route around the perimeter of the property. In response, Angus lifted his leg against one of the decorative lampposts.

"It's not like she can avoid the topic of...*you know*... forever," Grant continued, more to himself than to the canine who kept on walking. "The woman can't even say the word *pregnancy*. She just calls it *you know* all the time. So how am I supposed to figure out what she wants when she won't tell me?"

Angus tilted his head and gave him a lopsided look. "You're right, I shouldn't be out here talking to a dog about this. I need to go back in there and have a conversation with her."

As they made their way back to her door, Grant made a mental outline of everything he wanted to say to Rebekah. Unfortunately, when he got inside, he found her with her head slumped onto the table near the keyboard of her laptop. Sound asleep.

Rebekah sneaked a peek at Grant's sleeping form next to her and then squeezed her eyes shut as she buried her face deeper in the pillow. She had a hazy recollection of him carrying her from the table to her room last night, and she supposed that after everything else they'd done in this bed together, it was probably only natural for him to assume that they should sleep there together, as well.

However, waking up next to the man felt as though she was going in the opposite direction of where she needed to be. She was supposed to be getting him out of her life. Or, at least, not building up her expectations for having him in it on a permanent basis.

Her hands fisted in frustration at how easy it had been to fall under his spell again. When her ex-boyfriend had found out she was pregnant a few years ago, it had led to a swift breakup. Sure, it had been heartbreaking at the time, but at least Trey hadn't lingered, making promises that he knew he never truly intended to keep.

Logically, Rebekah knew she shouldn't be comparing the two men, especially while one of them was still in her bed. And really, Trey and Grant were as different as night and day. Her ex had been focused, steady; she'd always known what to expect with him, even down to his unbending intentions to never be a father. But Grant was so…was so…she lifted her arms to cover her head in frustration. She didn't even know what Grant was, or more important, what to expect from him.

All she knew was that, against her better judgment, she was attracted to him and she could easily be swayed into believing his promises if she let her guard down around him. She also knew that she wasn't about to waste another six years of her life on a man who wouldn't stay by her side no matter what.

She attempted to scoot her body toward the side of

the bed, but Grant immediately rolled with her, stretching an arm across her waist. As the sheets shifted, a growl sounded from between their two bodies.

Grant's eyes were closed as he tousled the dog's ears. "Is Mommy stealing your sheets again, Angus?"

"What happened to his spot on the sofa?" Rebekah sat up gently. She'd recently learned that moving too quickly in the morning could bring on an extra bout of queasiness.

"He came in here in the middle of night and was whimpering on your side of the bed. I didn't want him to wake you, so I just pulled him up here with us."

With us. Rebekah had always slept alone, and suddenly she was sharing her bed with both a man and a dog. How had things gone from pretend dating to this?

Her phone vibrated on the bedside table. She'd had it beside her when she was working last night, so Grant must've carried it in here, too. She saw the name on the screen and gasped. "It's your Aunt Bunny."

"Tell her I said good-morning." Grant stretched, the bare muscles of his shoulders and chest on prominent display. Her eyes immediately went downward, her mind straying toward thoughts of what was under the sheet. Apparently, he was perfectly comfortable making himself at home in her bed.

"I'm not answering it." Rebekah sent the call to voice mail. "And I'm definitely not telling her you said hello or anything else that might make her think that you're here with me."

"I'm sure Birdie told her yesterday that I was staying the night to help keep an eye on Angus. Plus, your car is still in the parking lot at Furever Paws. She's probably calling to give you last-minute instructions about our visit to the bird sanctuary."

"Oh, no, I forgot about the bird sanctuary." She looked at Grant. "Do we really have to go there today?"

"Have you met Aunt Bunny? I know she's the more forgetful aunt, but when it comes to animals, she can be pretty focused and determined."

Rebekah's phone immediately rang again and Grant said, "Which means she's not going to stop calling you until she knows we're on the road."

He gave her a wink, then stood up and practically strutted to the bathroom.

Yep. He'd been totally, comfortably nude under that sheet.

Why hadn't Rebekah insisted on setting some boundaries between them last night? She asked herself that question for the eight hundredth time as they drove down Route 64 along the Albemarle Sound.

Instead, she'd had sex with him—twice—then pretended to work during dinner before falling asleep and waking up with Grant in her bed. Never in her life had Rebekah been so reluctant to face a challenge or make hard decisions. She squeezed her eyes shut behind her dark sunglasses.

This whole pregnancy must be doing something strange to her emotions. That was the only explanation that made any sense.

Hell, she'd even agreed to foster a dog yesterday.

She glanced behind her at Angus, who'd taken over the

back seat of Grant's rental car the same way he'd taken over her sofa. Grant wasn't doing anything to rein him in…but to be fair, neither was she—and that was totally unlike her. Clearly, she wasn't making logical decisions.

Which was why she'd been even more determined to go to this bird sanctuary at her boss's request to gather as much information as she could for a full report and recommendation. If Rebekah kept her mind focused on work, she wouldn't have to worry about her thoughts slipping to how perfectly she'd fit in Grant's arms last night. Or how perfectly formed his body had looked this morning as he'd walked around her townhome half-dressed.

Despite the fact that her morning sickness was now flirting with possible car sickness, she mostly kept her eyes glued to the tablet on her lap as she researched the bird sanctuary and made notes about their business model.

"Go ahead and email me the notes from those focus group discussions." Grant spoke into his wireless Bluetooth, the one he'd been using for the entire two hours that they'd been on the road. "I'll take a look at them before the video conference call with the retail suppliers this afternoon."

Rebekah didn't feel so bad about avoiding conversation with the guy when he clearly had his own business matters to handle. Of course, it also made her question why a busy man like Grant was spending so much time in North Carolina lately—helping out his aunts with things that Rebekah or other members of the Furever Paws staff could probably be doing.

Before she could ask as much, Angus's ears perked up as the car slowed to take the highway exit and he lifted his paws onto one windowsill before marching along the back seat to observe the scenery out of the other window.

Grant lifted his eyes to the rearview mirror. "Laird Angus looks like he's standing sentry along the castle keep, going from one watchtower to the next."

Just like her, the animal seemed much more apprehensive than excited about arriving at their destination.

"Maybe I should've left him at home," Rebekah said. What she really meant was perhaps both she *and* the dog should've stayed home.

"Remember, Birdie thought it'd be a good idea to get Angus out and try to socialize him a bit more. See how he interacts with other people and animals."

It turned out that Angus did fine interacting with the office staff. In fact, he was so quiet and so low to the ground, Rebekah had to wonder if anyone behind the counters had even seen him. It was the socializing with other animals that soon became a problem. Angus went nuts at the sight of the flamingos near the entrance and barked his little furry head off, straining at his leash in his attempts to try and round up the birds as though they were a flock of sheep.

"We usually only allow service animals," the director explained as Grant laughed at Angus's antics while Rebekah tried to shush the dog and get him under control.

Rebekah had a sudden glimpse into what raising children with Grant would be like. He'd be the playful one, the parent who would indulge their children in sugar and wrestling matches and get them all amped up before bedtime. And Rebekah would be the rule enforcer, the parent who made them eat their vegetables and wash their hands.

Her gaze narrowed and Grant must've picked up on her annoyance because he cleared his throat and said, "Why don't I take Angus out front to the park and let him run around while you take the tour?"

To the park? To have fun while Rebekah did all the work? Not that taking a tour was necessarily work but taking thorough notes so she could report back to Bunny and Birdie afterward would require quite an effort. Especially when Rebekah already knew that she'd have to inform them that there was no way Furever Paws could accommodate birds with their limited budget. There was no way to save all the animals all the time.

"Actually," Rebekah responded. "Since this was *your* trip initially, why don't *you* go on the tour and *I'll* take Angus out and play?"

She didn't wait for a response, but scooped the still-barking dog into her arms and carried him toward the exit. Maybe it was childish and petty, but the sooner she set a precedent of Grant taking on his fair share of the menial, less playful tasks, the sooner she could prove that he wasn't cut out for long-term fatherhood.

Not that she didn't think her kids needed a father in their lives, but if she kept her expectations of Grant lower, then she wouldn't be setting herself—or their children—up for disappointment when Grant took off at the first sign of trouble.

It hadn't even been a full hour when he came to

find Rebekah and Angus in the park, proving her right. Smugness coursed through her, but there was also a tinge of disappointment. "I see you couldn't last the full two hours for the entire tour."

"No need to." Grant smiled and held up two bottles of water he must've bought in the gift shop. "I'd already researched the place last week when Bunny mentioned it to me, and the director had answered most of my questions in an email a few days ago. If my aunt was here, she'd want to see each and every bird, but I'm more of a dog guy myself, right Angus?"

Grant handed Rebekah one of the bottles and then knelt down next to the dog and poured some water into a cupped hand. Angus eagerly lapped it up and Rebekah sizzled with guilt for not thinking about the fact that the dog might be thirsty. It had to be eighty degrees in the shade, and she was gulping her water just as greedily as he was.

She wiped her mouth on the back of her wrist, trying to make the action as ladylike as possible. "So if you'd already done the research, and you didn't plan to see the birds, why'd we drive all the way here?"

He could've at least mentioned something before she'd made herself carsick staring at her tablet for over two hours of the ride, learning everything she possibly could about the bird sanctuary.

"Because my aunt asked me to." He rose to his feet as if that explained a perfectly logical waste of Rebekah's entire day. "The director told me there's a great restaurant a couple of miles down the sound. It has outdoor seating and is dog friendly. You wanna grab some lunch, boy?"

Angus yipped and tugged on his leash as he led the humans toward the car.

"Or we could head back to Spring Forest and I could get some actual work done today," Rebekah suggested.

"You know," Grant said as he opened her passenger door, "it's okay to take the day off every once in a while."

Rebekah felt her eyes narrow and it took every ounce of control not to unleash her annoyance at him. She still wasn't exactly sure what Grant did at his job—besides make things sound better than they were. But he apparently did it well.

Maybe she could use their lunch detour as an opportunity to find out something more about the guy who'd fathered her children. At this point, the only things she knew with any degree of certainty were that he was infuriating...and good in bed.

Chapter Eleven

Good thing Grant wasn't trying to impress anyone at lunch with their pretend relationship because this fish-and-chips stand was far from romantic. But at least it was outdoors and airy, which hopefully meant the smell of seafood was less likely to make Rebekah queasy. The place was packed, and they ended up having to share one of the wooden patio tables with a family of five. The crab cakes were amazing, though, and the tartar sauce was the best he'd ever tasted.

He couldn't really have anything resembling a private conversation with Rebekah because they were stuck next to a toddler who kept stealing French fries off of her mom's plate and giving them to Angus under the table. The five-year-old boy wanted to know who Grant's third favorite superhero was, the preteen was watching music videos on her phone at full blast, and the parents kept apologizing to Grant and Rebekah for the chaos.

An older couple with an overweight dachshund sat down at the table next to them and suddenly Angus had some competition for the French fries that were now being stolen off Rebekah's plate, as well.

Because the dog had been living on the streets for so long, Grant wasn't sure how well Angus would do sharing food with the plump, sausage-shaped dog.

"Come on, boy." Grant took the leash from where Rebekah had looped it up to her elbow. Then he picked up his used plate and the used napkins closest to him and told the dog, "Let's go down to the beach and take a little walk before we get back in the car."

Rebekah caught up to him near the trash cans. "Why do you always do that?"

"Do what?"

"Take off for the fun walks and leave me with the work."

"What work?" he wanted to know.

"Well, earlier, it was the tour at the bird sanctuary. And just now it was…" She paused as she looked down at the plastic tray with the remainder of their trash. He took it out of her hands and disposed of it just before a seagull landed on the trash can and squawked at them.

"Listen, I would've taken your plate for you, but Angus was already straining on the leash and you didn't look as though you were quite done with your food."

"I was done as soon as the little girl started swiping my fries with fingers covered in dog saliva." Rebekah pulled a bottle of antibacterial gel out of her enormous tote bag and squirted a stream onto her hands. "Where are you going?"

"I was going to take Angus down to the beach for a walk. Remember?"

"I thought you were just saying that as an excuse to get away from all the kids and that mean wiener dog who kept growling at him."

"Well, it was partly an excuse, but I also thought it would be fun to let him play near the water."

"Are you sure dogs are allowed down here?" she asked as they walked along the wooden planks toward the sand below. There weren't many people out here since it was a weekday afternoon.

"I didn't see a sign forbidding it." Grant bent over to unhook Angus's leash.

"What are you doing?" Rebekah placed a hand on his shoulder. "What if he runs away?"

"Let's give him a little freedom and see what he does," Grant suggested. Noting her response, he then added, "What was that for?"

"What?" she asked.

"You just rolled your eyes at me. And now you're doing that huffy breath thing. If you're mad about something, you can just tell me."

"Let's just say I'm starting to get a glimpse of how it's going to be if we decide to coparent. You'll always be the fun one, giving the kids all kinds of freedom and letting them get away with everything. And I'm going to be the rule enforcer that they never want to be with."

"What do you mean, *if* we decide to coparent?" Something twisted in his gut and he didn't think it was just the fried food from lunch. "I told you already that I plan to be in our children's lives. So it's not a matter of *if* we coparent but *how* we coparent that we need to discuss."

Rebekah's eyes were clear and calculating as she studied him. But she didn't offer a rebuttal. Or anything else that would constitute an actual discussion of the very topic she'd been avoiding for the past couple of weeks. Grant put his hands on his hips, ready to get the battle of words out of the way once and for all.

Rebekah sighed. "Fine, you can let him off the leash. But if he takes off, I'm not going to be able to chase after him in these heels."

It wasn't the concession he wanted to hear from her, but he had the sense that it was the best he'd be getting right now. Grant shrugged. "Then take your shoes off and experience the relaxing feeling of being the fun parent. Let me worry about Angus."

She swallowed a groan, then braced herself against him as she removed her strappy sandals. He flexed his biceps under her hand as she balanced herself on one foot and then the other.

"Now your turn, boy," he told the dog as he bent again to unhook the leash. Luckily, Angus didn't run away. But he did run to the edge of the water and then back again. In fact, he did several laps, and when Grant found a piece of driftwood, he gave it a little toss to see what the dog would do.

Angus proudly retrieved the driftwood and carried it back, dropping it at Rebekah's feet. She laughed and threw it again for him, and Grant decided he could stand here all day, watching her laughing and playing with the dog. Eventually, the stick ended up in the water and Angus barked at it, as though he could order the wood to return to the shore.

Grant slipped out of his flip-flops and walked into the water. When he was up to his knees Angus let out a series of happy yips and came crashing into the water near him.

"No!" Rebekah yelled. "Grab him before he drowns."

But the dog's short legs began paddling and Angus deftly motored his little body to the stick and retrieved it before easily making his way back to the sand.

"Look who's a natural at swimming," Grant said excitedly. He threw the stick back in the water over and over again, and Angus eagerly retrieved it every time.

"I think I'm going to need to take you out on the waves with me one day," he told the dog, who was now panting lazily at Rebekah's feet.

"No way," Rebekah said. "He's too little to go surfing." Angus's response was to shake water all over her.

Grant knew that Rebekah cared way more about the dog than she was letting on. In fact, he had a feeling that she cared far too much about a lot of things, and that's why she wasn't allowing Grant to get too close to her. To test his theory, he bent down to clip the leash to Angus's collar and said, "Is that your way of telling Mommy that you want to go surfing with Daddy? Maybe we'll teach your brothers or sisters how to surf, too."

Rebekah didn't roll her eyes this time. Instead she looked at the clock on her phone screen. "We should probably get going before we end up stuck in rush-hour traffic."

Apparently, playtime was over.

* * *

Grant figured the rental car company would be adding a cleaning charge to his bill to get rid of the wet, salty dog smell from the back seat. But seeing Angus enjoy the water so much made the extra expense well worth it.

"So what are you going to tell your aunts about the bird sanctuary?" Rebekah asked when they finally pulled out of the parking lot. It was nice to have her full attention, where her head wasn't buried behind a laptop or an electronic tablet.

"I'm going to tell them that it's a great program, but the licensing requirements they operate under are way too narrow to be a fit for what they want to accomplish. Furever Paws has too many species for something like this to make sense on my aunts' property. With their finances being so strained, it just isn't feasible in the foreseeable future."

"I agree. You know, I see how close you are to your aunts, and it makes me wonder why you haven't spoken to your Uncle Gator on their behalf."

The skin along the back of Grant's neck prickled. "Spoken to my uncle about what, exactly?"

"Oh, you know. You could use your smooth-talking marketing skills and put in a strong word to him and suggest that he repay that missing money."

Grant was glad that the light to the highway on-ramp had turned red and he didn't have to pull over to the side of the road so he could pivot and face Rebekah. "You actually think my uncle has something to do with their investments going bad?"

"It doesn't appear to be as simple as just some failed investments."

"Are you saying they suspect it was embezzlement? That my aunts believe this, too?" A heavy weight settled in the pit of Grant's stomach and he wanted to have this out, convince her she was wrong, but a horn sounded behind them and he had to resume driving.

"I'm not sure what exactly your aunts believe at this point. But I think it's a little odd that you are always in town to help boost their revenue, but you've never really questioned why there was a need to boost it in the first place."

"It's not odd," Grant said.

"Is burying your head in the sand a better way to put it?"

"Is that what you think I'm doing, Rebekah?" It was on the tip of Grant's tongue to suggest that she should be familiar enough with the concept, seeing as how they walked on eggshells every time the subject of her pregnancy came up. But he decided to come at it from a different angle. "I prefer to believe that people are innocent until proven guilty."

They both knew that Rebekah kept expecting the worst where he was concerned, but he couldn't tell if his words had hit their mark because Rebekah didn't take the bait. She simply held herself stiffly, her eyes fixed on a spot outside the windshield.

The outside sounds of traffic filtered in and the urge to say something else pressed against the back of his throat. Eventually she would come to see that Grant was serious about being a father. Eventually, he'd prove himself to her. But it wasn't going to happen today. And in the meantime, his uncle wasn't there to speak for himself and needed defending more.

After at least ten minutes had gone by, he finally spoke. "Listen, there's no way Uncle Gator would do that to his own sisters. At least, not intentionally. I mean, he can be a little arrogant, but that's because he really is good at what he does. It's how he made his fortune. That doesn't make him a crook—especially not when it comes to his family. Whitakers look out for each other. You don't know him, so you don't trust him. Fine, that's understandable. But even if you don't believe me when I say that that's something he just wouldn't do, there's also the fact that it doesn't make sense. It's just not logical. With all the money he has, he doesn't need to steal from Bunny and Birdie."

"It wasn't my place to bring it up." She shifted her legs to the side, so that her body was angled toward the door, as though she were dismissing him. "Forget I said anything."

Emotionally, he wanted to say that she was right and it really wasn't her place to discuss his family's issues. However, logically, he knew that she oversaw the finances for the animal shelter and was merely repeating what she'd heard from the people who'd been hired to look directly into the matter.

Still.

"Obviously, there was some mismanagement of finances going on, and obviously it happened under Gator's watch. But that doesn't mean it was intentional." At this point, Grant didn't know if he was trying to convince her or himself. There was no way his uncle was capable of something so underhanded. The whole thing had to be an accident or a misunderstanding. "It's just that you don't know Uncle Gator like we do."

"You're right. I probably don't really know any of you Whitakers. I just work for your family."

Grant felt frustration vibrating against the back of his throat, but he held the groan back, not wanting to insult her any further. "I'm not saying you don't know any of us. You're around Aunt Bunny and Aunt Birdie every day and they're pretty much an open book. Obviously, you know me better than anyone else who works there…"

He trailed off when she tilted her head his way and cocked an eyebrow at him. Okay, so she was probably right to question that statement. They knew each other physically, but did either of them really know the other that well? That was a whole other conversation, though.

"My point is that my family dynamics—especially where Uncle Gator is concerned—are kind of complex."

She leaned her elbow against the door so she could prop her head on her hand. "If you say so."

"Hear me out," Grant said, even as he was thinking she probably would've preferred to take a nap. "My dad was the first of the Whitaker siblings to sell their property. He made a modest amount, but when he moved to Florida, he funneled all that money into the surf shop originally owned by my mom's parents. Gator always gave my dad a hard time about choosing his wife's family over the Whitakers. Anytime I came to visit over the summer, my uncle would immediately welcome me into the fold and would often remind me that family should always take care of each other."

"So that explains why you're often in town helping out your aunts," Rebekah said.

"It also explains why Gator couldn't have possibly embezzled that money. At least, not intentionally. He has always been adamant about looking out for his sisters."

"You said not intentionally," Rebekah pointed out. "So isn't it possible that Gator took the money thinking that he could eventually pay it back? Which is still, by definition, embezzlement."

"I know the definition of embezzlement." Grant gripped the steering wheel defensively. "You're not the only one who took business courses in college."

"I guess your constant beach attire threw me off," she replied, confirming his suspicion that she never took him seriously. She yawned. "Look, I don't want to argue with you about your uncle or your family's finances."

"Then what do you want to argue with me about?" he asked. "Because you sure as hell don't seem to want to talk to me about our children."

He'd made that layered comment earlier about being innocent until proven guilty and it had taken every fiber of strength she possessed not to remind him that, with two children on the way, her first duty was to protect them. If that meant holding reserving judgment until Grant proved himself, then so be it.

Rebekah knew she should now take the opening, to explain to him all of her fears about becoming a mother. But she also just wanted to close her eyes and nap. Unfortunately, her phone rang and she wasn't able to do either.

She looked down at the screen resting in the center console cupholder. "It's my mom."

"I figured that, based on the word MOM across the top and the big picture of Sheila Taylor underneath." Grant's voice held a sarcastic edge and she couldn't really blame him for being frustrated at the interruption.

"I'll let it go to voice mail," Rebekah offered.

"No, go ahead and take it. Our conversation has waited this long. It can certainly wait another few minutes."

Rebekah slid her finger across the screen. "Hi, Mom."

"Hey, Dimples. Your dad and I are running late. We won't get to the restaurant until after six."

"What restaurant?" Rebekah glanced at Grant as though he could tell her that she wasn't crazy.

"Aren't we supposed to meet you and Grant for dinner tonight?" her mom asked. "I have it in the calendar app you set up for me."

"That was last Tuesday, Mom. Did you set it up as a repeat event again?"

Her mom said something, but her voice was muffled, probably because she'd pulled the phone away from her ear and was tapping at her screen. Finally, she came back on. "Yep. It looks like we're having dinner with you two every Tuesday and Friday for the next five years."

Rebekah's phone pinged with a message. She glanced down, then sighed. "Dad's texting me. He wants me to know that you guys will be running late tonight. So I guess his calendar got scheduled wrong, too."

Grant gave her a side-eye and she lowered her phone and said, "My parents are wonderful with kids, not so great with technology. They thought we were supposed to have dinner tonight."

"Who are you talking to?" her mom asked, and Rebekah realized she should've covered the receiver.

"I'm in the car with Grant. We had to go to a bird sanctuary near the Outer Banks. We're on our way home now."

"Oh, that's perfect, then. If you're on Highway 64, we can just meet you in Raleigh and nobody will be late."

"But, Mom, we didn't actually have dinner scheduled." Rebekah squeezed her eyes shut.

"We can stop and meet them for dinner," Grant offered a little too loudly.

"Actually, we can't." Rebekah saw a spot of gray fur on the back seat and her heart lunged with hope. "We have Angus with us."

Upon hearing his name, the dog lifted his head and let out a half-hearted yip.

"Who's Angus?" Sheila asked. "Is that a dog?"

"He's one of the dogs from the shelter. I'm fostering him. Temporarily."

"Since when did you become a dog person, Dimples?"

"Long story," Rebekah grumbled.

"Good thing we'll have time for you to tell us over dinner."

"But, Mom, I just said we can't meet for dinner because we have a dog with us."

"I'm sure we could find a pet-friendly restaurant in Raleigh," Grant offered a little too cheerfully, considering the fact that he'd just gotten done telling her to stay out of *his* family's business. So why wasn't he staying out of hers?

Rebekah could feel her eyes widening in horror as she shook her head at him while simultaneously putting a finger to her lips. But she was too late.

"I'll start looking for a place now," Sheila said happily. "I'll call you back."

Over the next hour, her mom called three more times with questions about what time they would arrive—five o'clock; Grant's favorite type of food—Mexican; and Grant's second-favorite type of food since Via Rancheros only allowed service animals. In between those calls were her dad's texts with screenshots of his calendar app settings and follow-up questions about how to reset the year.

Really, it wasn't Rebekah's fault that she and Grant never got the opportunity to talk about her pregnancy again before they arrived at the restaurant. If Grant had kept quiet when her mom called, they wouldn't be going to dinner with her parents in the first place.

Ever since she'd first slept with the man, nothing had gone as planned. It was as though they were reading the same instructional manual, but they were always on different steps in the assembly process.

If they couldn't get on the same page and have an actual conversation, then how would they ever manage to truly parent their babies together?

Chapter Twelve

When they arrived at the restaurant, Rebekah went straight to the restroom. She'd gone before they left the beach, but her bladder seemed to be holding less, while her stomach was trying to hold more.

Although, currently she had no appetite whatsoever. She wanted to blame it on the fact that they'd had a late lunch, but really it was because her tummy was a bundle of nerves. Grant had met her parents before, but this would be the first time they had the chance to ask him all those questions Rebekah hadn't been able to answer herself last Tuesday.

You can do this, she told herself in the mirror over the sink. But the reflection staring back at her didn't look too convinced. Taking a deep breath, she steeled her spine and headed back to the restaurant lobby. She only hesitated when she saw that her parents had already spotted Grant and Angus.

"Nice to see you again, Mrs. Taylor." He held out his hand in greeting, but her mom pulled him into a tight hug instead.

Angus, of course, loved her dad. It was like an animal instinctively knew when a person was trying to avoid it because they then centered all their attention on that one individual.

"I hope you took your allergy medicine, Mike," her mom said as the dog sniffed away at her father's freckled legs below his cargo shorts.

"I did, but I'll sit on the other side of the table, just in case." Her father gave her a quick peck on the forehead. "Looking healthy, Dimples."

Her dad must have been lying because two minutes ago in the bathroom mirror she'd looked anything but healthy. At least, mentally. But she appreciated the sentiment all the same.

"So tell me how you ended up a dog mom," her mother said when everyone finally took their seats on the patio.

The server brought a small dog dish with water and took their drink orders while Rebekah told them the story about Angus, leaving out the parts where she'd sat on the porch of an abandoned house talking to the stray dog. "There wasn't any room at the shelter to house him last night, so we took him home."

"We?" Her dad wiggled his eyebrows before giving her mom a knowing look. Oh, great. She hadn't meant to let that part slip. But it did kind of add to this whole pretense that she and Grant were actually together.

"Here, boy, don't lick that," Grant said to Angus, who was going to town on a spot of spilled barbecue sauce under the table. At least, Rebekah hoped it was just sauce.

"Sounds like you and Grant are getting a test run at being parents." Her mother smiled. "How's it going?"

Rebekah opened her mouth to argue that it wasn't like that, but Grant spoke up first. "So far, so good. I have a feeling that twins are going to be a little bit more work—although this guy eats enough for two."

Her parents laughed and Rebekah felt her molars grinding at the fact that Grant could so easily make jokes about their situation. That he could be so casual and unaffected about the amount of stress that they'd be under less than a year from now. But that was Grant, always making things sound better than they were. The guy currently had his charm level turned up to the lay-it-on-thick setting.

"It's actually taken some adjusting," Rebekah said. "I was away from my office today and now I'm behind on everything."

"You'll get to it, sweetheart," Grant said, placing his hand along the back of her neck. Rebekah practically shot out of her chair before she remembered that they were supposed to be pretending to be in a loving relationship. "Those budget reports will still be there when you get back on Monday."

He used his thumb to massage the knot forming between her shoulder blades and it felt so amazing, she wanted to arch her neck and moan in delight. But they were sitting across from her parents and his words only brought on more anxiety. "Yeah, they'll still be there when I get back, along with all the work I'm supposed to do on Monday, as well."

Her mom leaned forward to grab a piece of corn-bread from the basket, then offered the mini crock of honey butter to Grant. "Our daughter has always been very orderly. Never liked leaving anything to the last minute. But you've probably already picked up on that."

"I got that impression the first time I met her." Grant nodded before taking a big gulp of his sweet tea. "And then it was reaffirmed when I saw that her townhome was set up like one of those model homes. Not so much as a dish in the sink or a throw pillow out of place."

"Sorry to break it to you, Dimples," her father chuck-led. "But as soon as those babies start walking, you can kiss that fancy white sofa and all those breakable knick-knacks goodbye."

Rebekah gulped. She loved that sofa. It had been her first major purchase after college and it made her feel like an adult who was in complete control of her life. The thought of changing her whole living room just to accommodate children had her tapping her feet under the table.

"You should've seen her watching Angus last night when he got up on that couch." Grant teased. "She kept glancing over at his paws for any sign of dirt."

"That sounds like Rebekah, all right," her mother agreed. "No time for messes in her schedule."

The server came to take their order and Grant kept

his hand casually draped along her shoulders as he whispered to her. "I'm not very hungry. Do you want to share something?"

In an effort to seem less controlling than everyone at the table was making her appear, she gave a stiff nod and said, "Sure. I'll just have a couple of bites of whatever you get."

"We'll take the sampler platter and the rib combo plate." Grant handed the menu to the server.

"I'd rather have the chicken," she said, then snapped her mouth closed because she'd just proved them all right. "But the ribs are good."

"Apparently, we'll take the chicken and rib platter instead," Grant said to the waiter.

"And what would you like for your three sides?" the man asked.

"How about the barbecue beans," Grant started but Rebekah couldn't keep from scrunching her nose. "Make that the macaroni and cheese." He looked at her. "Do you like coleslaw?"

"I'd rather have the wedge salad. And their onion rings are really great. Maybe some more French fries since Angus ate all of mine earlier?"

"Are you sure you don't want to get two meals, after all?" the server asked.

Rebekah realized she hadn't been sure of anything for a long time.

Grant knew that Rebekah was anxious as hell, because he could feel her leg nervously fidgeting beside his all through the meal. But he was actually enjoying his dinner with Mike and Sheila Taylor. They were full of stories about their daughter and they asked all the hard questions that Rebekah had been avoiding until now.

"So do you plan to stay home from work for a while after the twins get here? Or are you looking into child-care and nannies?" Mike Taylor asked as he slipped a piece of brisket to Angus under the table.

The dog's manners were going to be atrocious after all the dining excursions today, but Grant wasn't about to say anything that would distract Rebekah from her father's question.

"We haven't decided that yet," she said before polishing off a piece of cornbread. If Grant had a dollar for every time she'd given that same response, he could pay the nanny's first week's salary. If they decided to go with a nanny.

"Grant, are you okay with Rebekah going back to work full-time?" Sheila asked and Grant gave Rebekah a sideways glance.

"Obviously, I'm okay with whatever makes Rebekah happy."

"Good. That was a trick question." Sheila nodded at him before turning to her daughter. "Although, if you can take some time off to bond with the twins at first, that would be ideal."

"Mom, you know I'm not very good with babies," Rebekah admitted. Grant leaned back in his chair to carefully listen to this new revelation that explained at least some of why Rebekah had been so uneasy discussing the pregnancy.

"That's crazy," her dad said. "Anybody can handle a baby."

"Really?" Rebekah drew back her chin in disbelief. "You know all those babies you guys fostered? Did I ever interact with any of them?"

Her mom folded her hands together, giving Grant the impression that the woman was ready to get down to business. "You did with Janelle."

"Who?" Rebekah asked, a frown line forming above her nose.

"You might not remember her because you were so young when she left," Mike said, then exchanged a glance with Sheila, who gave him a nod of encouragement. "Dimples, when you were two years old, you started asking for a little brother or sister. That's all you wanted for Christmas, for your birthday, for Valentine's Day. Your mom and I tried to conceive, but no luck. I mean, we really, really tried. Every morning and night we were at it. Babe, remember that lovemaking schedule—"

Rebekah covered her ears. "Gross, Dad. Nobody wants to hear about you guys and your schedule."

"Anyway, when we realized that we couldn't conceive, we started seriously talking about all the other options. We researched adoption and filled out questionnaires and talked to attorneys and social workers and decided fostering was the way to go. Janelle was the first baby we brought home from the hospital. You were four years old and you loved her like crazy. You thought she was your own baby. We had her for six months and then got the call that the court was going to start the reunification process with her biological family. When she left, you were absolutely inconsolable."

Sheila reached across the table to pat Rebekah's hand. "Initially, we were planning to give you time to get over Janelle's leaving, but the agency called us the next week and needed an emergency foster for just a few days. When we brought *that* baby home, you wanted absolutely nothing to do with it. In fact, after Janelle left, you stopped playing with your dolls and even your stuffed animals altogether."

"I don't remember any of this," Rebekah said, her forehead creased in confusion. Grant's hand returned to the back of her neck and he stroked the tight muscles underneath the skin, finally understanding why Rebekah had been so apprehensive about motherhood.

"You were very young," Sheila reminded her. "But ever since then, you've always stayed away from babies and smaller kids. You even stayed away from animals, which was why we were so happy to find out that you'd taken the job at Furever Paws. We were hoping you were coming around."

Mike clapped his palms together. "And now here you are, pregnant and fostering a dog of your own. When it rains, it pours."

Rebekah sat at the table, numbly nodding her head at her parents as Grant paid the check and then made plans to see them again in a couple of weeks. She was sure there'd been some talk of double strollers and ultrasound appointments, but she'd been lost in her own memories, Grant's reassuring hand along her spine the only thing that kept her grounded in the present.

"Are you feeling okay?" Grant asked as he climbed into the driver's seat ten minutes later. When he'd opened the passenger door for Rebekah, Angus had decided to jump up onto her lap instead of claiming the back seat. "It's like the dog senses something's wrong and he's trying to console you."

"He probably has a bellyache from all that brisket my dad was feeding him under the table," Rebekah reasoned, even though Angus's black eyes were studying her intently, as though he was looking for some sort of sign that everything would be okay. She stroked the dog's back. "Let's get you home, boy."

"Rebekah, I'm not starting the car until you tell me what's bugging you. You mentally checked out toward the end of dinner and I can't make it better if I don't know what's wrong."

"Who says you need to make me feel better? I don't need fixing."

"I'm a fixer. A saver. It's what I do. Now, I've learned to tell when you're mad, when you're annoyed and when you're legitimately busy with work." Grant's chest expanded with his deep breath. "As opposed to when you're just faking being busy with work to get out of talking to me."

She opened her mouth to protest, but he held up his palm. "Hold on. I've also learned when you're flustered, and I've learned when you're overwhelmed and scared about something. Right now, you're clearly scared. So let me help."

"It's not something you can help with. You heard my parents. I'm not a baby person. Yet, here I am, having two of them."

"I believe *you* were the one who claimed you aren't a baby person and your *father* said that was crazy."

"But then they told that story about how I wanted nothing to do with the other babies. What if the twins get here and I feel the same way?"

"Rebekah." Grant lifted her chin, forcing her eyes to meet his. "You were a child when that happened. It was a defense mechanism because you'd already lost someone close to you and didn't want to go through that heartache again. But our kids aren't going anywhere."

"What if something happens to them, though?" She could feel the wetness at the corners of her eyes and tried to blink back the tears.

"Is this about the pregnancy you lost?" He traced his hand along her jaw and up to her ear so he could gently smooth the curls away from her face.

"Yes. I mean, no." She couldn't decide. "Maybe. When I got pregnant back then, it couldn't have come at a worse time. I was still in business school and my boyfriend was adamant that he didn't want kids. I'd been on the pill and never missed a day. But then I'd gotten strep throat and the antibiotics made the birth control ineffective. Trey accused me of getting pregnant on purpose, but I told him that I didn't want a baby any more than he did. We had a huge fight and broke up. A few days later, I found out that the pregnancy wasn't viable and, I know this sounds crazy, but all I could think before the laparoscopic procedure was that my baby had heard me say that I didn't want it. And that's why I…why I…" She couldn't hold back any longer.

"Aww, sweetheart. You can't blame yourself. Not for any of it." He used the back of his hand to wipe the tears trailing down her cheeks and leaned his forehead against hers. "Is that why you keep referring to this pregnancy as *you know*? Because you don't want the twins to hear us talking about them?"

"I guess. But also because I really *am* afraid that I won't be the kind of mom they deserve."

He pulled back and met her gaze. "Look at you with Angus. You're going to be a great mom. You just need to get out of your own head."

"I've only had Angus for twenty-four hours. And you've done half the work with him. What happens when it's just me on my own?"

His hands moved to either side of her face, forcing her to look squarely at him. "That's what I keep trying to tell you. It won't be just you on your own. I'm not going anywhere, Rebekah."

He kissed her damp cheeks, stopping one of the tears from going any farther. She almost believed him.

But then his cell phone rang.

Chapter Thirteen

Rebekah knew that if Bunny or Birdie had called Grant to come fix a leak in their roof, he would've been out the door in an instant. So when his mom had called him the previous evening about the leak in the surf shop, it was no surprise that he'd asked if he could drop off her and Angus so that he could get to the airport and catch a flight home that night.

She appreciated his dedication to his family, but didn't they have roofers and plumbers in Jacksonville? Certainly Grant wasn't the only one who could save the day.

"All I'm saying is that anytime things start getting too intense, he always has to fly back to Florida," she told Angus as he whimpered by the front door as though he was waiting for Grant to walk through any minute. "I know. I'd probably run off, too, if my pregnant fake girl-friend was having an emotional breakdown in my car."

Walking into her bedroom, she stubbed her toe on the corner of his carry-on suitcase, which was still open on her rug. She muffled a curse under her breath.

Angus made a low growl as his triangular ears perked up into points.

"You didn't hear that," she told the dog.

She wanted to pitch the whole suitcase and its contents out her front door, but then she'd have to look at the mess when she left tomorrow. Instead, she threw everything inside—trying not to inhale the scent of Grant on his clothing or remember how his bare skin smelled even better—and zipped it closed before shoving it into the hallway closet.

The guy had only spent a total of two nights here in the past few months, but already his absence was noticeable. As she climbed under the covers that evening, her bed suddenly felt way too huge, way too empty. How could she already miss something she'd never really had?

The following morning, she stared longingly at her coffee machine through half-lidded eyes rimmed with dark circles. A chocolate croissant would come in pretty handy right about now, but her car was still parked at Furever Paws. While she didn't normally work on Saturdays, it was often one of the busiest days of the week for the shelter since that's when they usually had families coming in for adoption events.

So she could either call an Uber to go get her car and possibly catch up on some of the work she'd missed yesterday, or she could sit around her townhome thinking about all those tear-filled emotions she'd unloaded on Grant last night.

She pulled up the Uber app on her phone and grabbed Angus's leash off the entry table. "Looks like we're going to work today, big guy."

The dog was all tail wags and panting out the window for the ride to the shelter. But as soon as the driver pulled away, Angus was glued to her leg, cowering behind her. "Don't be scared," she told him. "I know you don't have great memories of this parking lot, but I'm not going to leave you."

He plopped himself on the gravel, and not wanting to drag him behind her, she scooped him up into her arms and carried him into the lobby.

"I thought I saw your car outside this morning," Birdie said as she came from behind the reception desk. "Did Daddy drop you guys off?"

Rebekah stumbled in surprise and it wasn't until Angus was licking at something in Birdie's hand that she realized the older woman had been talking to the dog, not her.

She wanted to correct her boss and explain that Grant wasn't the dog's daddy. She wasn't even the mommy, for that matter. But arguing at this point would only draw more attention. "No. Grant flew back to Florida last night."

"That boy is always on the go. He's a hard one to pin down." Birdie didn't need to tell Rebekah that. The woman made a *tsking* sound then continued, "You look exhausted, dear. Did the road trip to the bird sanctuary tire you out?"

Crap. With Grant taking off like that last night, it again fell to Rebekah to be the bearer of bad news and tell his aunts that their plans for saving birds wouldn't work. "No. I just didn't get much sleep last night."

"Having a new bundle of joy will do that to you," Birdie said and Rebekah tried to suck in her stomach. "Did you keep Mommy up last night?" she asked, and Rebekah realized that the woman was again talking to the dog.

"He sure did." Rebekah didn't add that Angus had been up half the night whimpering at the door and then pacing the house looking for Grant. Sometime around midnight, she'd heard him wrestle something out from under the bed and saw that he'd found one of Grant's T-shirts. He wouldn't go to sleep until she pulled him—and the shirt—onto the bed with her. "Hopefully, he'll nap in my office so that I can get some work done."

"Is that the little gray dog?" Emma Alvarez asked as she walked through the lobby with her fiancé, Daniel Sutton, and their three girls. "He looks so much better."

"Rebekah is fostering him," Birdie explained.

"We had fosters," Penny, the middle girl, said. "But they were kittens."

"Four of them." Pippa, the youngest girl, held up four fingers. "But now they're gone."

Something tugged at Rebekah's heart. "You must miss them very much."

"Kind of. But they have forever homes now." Paris,

the oldest daughter, sounded as though she was reminding her younger sisters of the positive outcome.

Pippa's smile revealed a missing top tooth. "Emma and Daddy said we could come see the new cat room and maybe pick out some more foster kittens that need us."

"Come on, guys," Penny said, pulling on her father's hand. When the family walked away, Rebekah stood there staring at them.

"Sweet family, huh?" Birdie said and Rebekah nearly jumped because she hadn't realized she'd been caught gawking.

"Very sweet. But I was just thinking that it must be very difficult for kids to foster—to bring a pet into their family and then later have to let go of something they love so much."

"It isn't exactly easy for the adults, either." The older woman patted her shoulder. "You just take a little piece of that animal along with you. It's amazing how much love your heart can accommodate once you decide to open it up."

Birdie walked away, probably intending to leave Rebekah thinking about that cryptic statement all day. Instead, all her mind could focus on was the older woman's earlier words about Grant being a hard one to pin down.

"Can I ask you a question, Mom?" Grant dumped the last bucket of collected rainwater into the industrial sink in the board-shaping room. A crew of workers was on the surf shop's roof above them, pounding new shingles into place.

His mother leaned against the push broom she'd been using to sweep up the wet plaster from last night's leak. "What's up, kiddo?"

Lana Whitaker was a slight five foot two, and in her denim cutoffs, Costa Rica Surf Tours T-shirt and bleached-blond hair pulled into low pigtails, she didn't look old enough to be calling anyone kiddo.

"What are your thoughts on Uncle Gator?"

"Your dad's brother?" she asked. "He means well, I guess, but he can come off a little condescending at times."

"Do you think he might be the one responsible for Aunt Bunny and Aunt Birdie having financial issues?"

"Oh, no. I'm staying out of that mess. I learned long ago not to get involved in anything that has to do with Whitaker Acres. I love your aunts like they're my own sisters, but when it comes to that property and what everyone did with their shares, I'm keeping my mouth shut."

"Oh, come on, Mom. Can't you just give me a little insight about your early years with dad's side of the family? I'm sure he'd tell me himself if he were still alive."

"My sweet Moose." His mom lowered her eyes and Grant immediately felt remorse wash through him.

"Sorry, I didn't mean to make you feel sad."

"No, you're right. Your dad's heart was the biggest thing about him." That was certainly saying something, since Moose had been six foot three and required a custom longboard to accommodate his 250-pound frame. But Grant knew his mom was right. She continued, "He hated it that Gator never seemed to get over Moose's choice to sell off his shares of the family property to move to Florida."

Grant pointed his finger in the air. "That's exactly what I told Rebekah."

"And Rebekah is the very beautiful and very smart director of Furever Paws that you keep flying to North Carolina to visit?" His mom's knowing smile lit up her face.

"I haven't been flying up there *just* to visit her," Grant said. He wanted to tell his mom about the babies. But he'd made a promise to wait a few more weeks. "How did you know about me and Rebekah, anyway?"

"Because there're only two things that would keep my son from work."

"Oh, yeah?" He lifted himself into a sitting position on the counter near the sink. "What are those?"

"Either a sweet set breaking off the south shore or a sweet someone needing him."

Grant rolled his shoulders. "How do you know that it's Rebekah that needs me?"

His mother studied him the way she used to when he'd been a kid and would promise to reapply his sunscreen, but then inevitably returned home with a sunburned face. "You're so much like your father, always the first one in line to help out with no thought as to what it might cost you in the long run. It kept me up a lot of nights when you volunteered for the lifeguarding deep sea rescue team. But you can't always save everyone, Grant."

"Who am I trying to save?" he asked. Rebekah certainly wasn't the kind of person who needed rescuing. She was far too strong, too controlled, to need anyone.

"Um, how about me, for one?" His mom gestured at the water stain on the ceiling. "You didn't have to rush here to deal with this, you know."

"You told me that there was a major leak at the surf shop."

"Yeah, but only because I wanted to know if your sister and I could store some of the merchandise at that fancy condo you hardly ever seem to use anymore. Not because I needed you to fly home and help me dump out buckets. And do you really think that Bunny and Birdie need you swinging by North Carolina every week or so to oversee the pet shelter that they've been running on their own for how many years?"

Okay, so his mom had a good point. He would've told her as much; however, she continued talking.

"Rushing in to rescue people is your way of having a little adventure. First you wanted to be a lifeguard. But then you saw that the surf shop had been hit by the recession, so you decided that a better-paying job would provide you with more income to send our way. The next step was getting into the business of saving companies by rebranding their products. Now you're this marketing genius who makes more money than you know what to do with, and yet you're still restless. Have you ever thought that maybe you need to take a step back and figure out what's missing in your *own* life that makes you want to become so involved in everyone else's?"

"Geez, Mom." Grant felt the weight of his mother's

knowing stare. "You make it sound like I'm a solution in search of a problem."

"Kiddo, how easily could you cut a check to Bunny and Birdie to get them back on their feet after that tornado?"

"You know they won't take money from me."

"Exactly. So you found other ways to help them. Whether they want that help or not."

"Of course they want my help. You should see how happy they are every time I come out."

His mom lifted her brows and he recognized her playful smirk because it was the same one he made when he was holding back his own laughter. "It just so happens that by helping them, you also get to help yourself to more time with their director."

There was a puddle of water on the counter next to him and he used his fingers to flick some her way. "Are you done teasing me now?"

His mom's squeal of laughter brought one of Grant's sisters to the doorway between the shop and the shaping room. "Some of us are trying to make phone calls to our vendors and order replacements for all the merchandise that got ruined last night. You think you guys could keep it down back here while you discuss Grant's new girlfriend?"

Clearly, his family had already heard about her, which meant the news of their fake relationship had already made its way down here.

"You know, I was going to help you clean up this mess and then buy you guys lunch." Grant said with a dismissive shrug. "But I wouldn't want to make myself too helpful."

His sister's reply was to stick her tongue out at him, making his mom laugh even harder.

After his conversation with his mom and then a question-fueled lunch with his little sister, Grant's head was swirling with thoughts of Rebekah. He found himself checking his phone for missed texts every fifteen minutes while he finished clearing wet debris and soggy cardboard boxes from the storage room of his family's surf shop.

He wasn't sure if he should give Rebekah space or if he should try to reach out and apologize for leaving so soon after promising to stick by her side.

They hadn't exactly parted on the best of terms. She'd brought up all that stuff about Gator, and then she'd cried in his arms about her previous pregnancy. The woman had finally let down her guard in front of him and he'd taken off.

Although, in his defense, he'd thought his mom actually needed him.

But Rebekah had needed him, too.

Or maybe not.

The sex had been incredible and at first, that had been enough of a reason to fly up to see her. But soon, he found that he couldn't stop thinking about her—and now that he had a chance at a real relationship and future with her, the fact that she might not want the same hurt more than he expected. There were too many emotions swirling around in his head and not a single clear thought. He stretched, and his eyes landed on his dad's old longboard hanging on the wall in the rear of the store. Moose Whitaker used to always say that the ocean washed away the world's problems.

Had there ever been a better time to hit the waves?

Rebekah didn't hear from Grant that entire Saturday. On Sunday evening, she got a text from him asking her how Angus was doing. But there was no reference to her pregnancy or her emotional breakdown in his rental car a couple of nights ago. In response, Rebekah sent a picture of Angus chomping away at his food bowl. Then asked, How are things going at your family's surf shop?

Grant wrote, It was a mess, but my mom has it under control.

Rebekah frowned at her screen. So, now that the leak situation had been taken care of, was he planning to return to Spring Forest anytime soon? To pick up where they'd left off?

Angus hopped up onto the sofa beside her, that stupid T-shirt of Grant's hanging from his little mouth. "I know you miss him, boy." She stroked the spiky hair that made the dog look as though he had serious eyebrows. "But who knows when he'll come back. He lives in Florida."

She sighed and leaned her head against the white leather, watching the rain falling outside her window. This would probably be the same conversation she'd be having with her kids a couple of years from now. *I know you miss Daddy, kids. But he has a life somewhere else. Who knows when we'll see him again?*

Just thinking about the hurt on her unborn children's

faces made Rebekah want to forget Grant's phone number all over again.

On Monday, she threw herself back into her job. Not that Rebekah didn't always fully commit to her work, but she'd made a promise to herself the previous night that she could only control what she did with her life. She couldn't control Grant.

Angus had a little bed in the corner of her office, but if she got up to get something out of a filing cabinet or to head to the reception desk to scan the latest adoption report, the dog trotted along behind her.

"All that time alone on the streets and now the little guy won't leave your side," Bunny said, bending down in her work overalls to give Angus one of the small treats she always carried in her pockets for the animals.

"I know." Rebekah's shoulders dropped. "Hopefully, it's a good family that eventually adopts him."

"Families don't always pick the animals they're going to adopt." Bunny rose to her feet and stared at her through clear blue eyes. "Sometimes, it's the animals who pick the families."

Grant had told her something similar, but she didn't want to hear it any more now than she had last week. Rebekah pivoted toward the reception desk, looking for some papers or folders or anything else that needed her attention so that she wouldn't have to face the older woman and pretend that she didn't know exactly what Bunny meant.

"How about all that rain we got yesterday?" Bunny said, thankfully changing the subject. "The storm also hit Florida pretty badly before coming up here to us."

Was the mention of Florida supposed to be an opening for bringing up Grant? If so, she wasn't going to fall for it. Rebekah managed a murmur as she arranged the clipboards holding blank adoption applications.

"I called Grant last night to tell him that we're having some drainage issues with the creek that runs through the farm." Yep, Bunny had purposely steered the conversation in the direction of her perfect nephew, the Whitaker golden boy.

Rebekah's spine straightened. "Let me guess. He's on his way to save the day?"

"That's the weird thing." The woman's head tilted so far to the side, the messy white bun on top was in danger of tumbling down. "Lately, he's come running at the slightest mention of a problem on the farm or with the shelter. But this time all he did was offer to call an excavation company to come out and take a look."

"Well, he might be pretty busy with his job in Jacksonville. He *has* been out of his office a lot lately."

"But that's because he has someone special now in Spring Forest."

"No, he comes to see you and Birdie, too."

Rebekah realized her slip as soon as the corner of Bunny's mouth lifted slightly. Damn. The woman had gotten her to admit that not only had she observed Grant's comings and goings, but also that she knew it had something to do with their relationship. The relationship that was supposed to only be pretend.

"Well, when you talk to him today, let him know that Megan Jennings is going to want to meet with all of us soon." Bunny gave Angus another treat before walking away.

If Megan—the lawyer investigating the Whitakers' financial problems—wanted to meet, that probably meant there had been a break in the case. Grant would want to know…but it wasn't as if Rebekah was going to bring up the subject of his aunts' missing money, let alone the findings of the attorney's investigation. Let Megan be the one to tell Grant that his Uncle Gator was clearly behind the whole thing.

When she left work that afternoon, Rebekah saw the yellow backhoe chugging along the creek on the farm's property. She half expected to see Grant in the driver's seat, trying to dig the new drainage trench himself. The guy came to town to take pictures for brochures or to take forty-five minute tours of bird sanctuaries that he'd already researched online. But suddenly he couldn't be bothered with a major problem like this?

It didn't make any sense.

Unless he was avoiding something in Spring Forest. Or someone.

Chapter Fourteen

This was the first time Grant had flown into Spring Forest and immediately hadn't gone by Furever Paws to see Rebekah.

Well, at least the first time since they initially slept together.

He drove his rental car to the Main Street Grille, where he was meeting his aunts and Megan Jennings.

When they'd called him earlier this week about the drainage issue on their creek, it had taken every ounce of strength to stop himself from coming running. But unless his aunts or Rebekah specifically said that they needed his help, he'd vowed not to rush in and rescue anyone again.

Then, last night, Birdie had told him that they needed to talk to him about their financial situation, and that was all it had taken to get him to hop on a plane.

"Hey, Whitaker," a voice said when Grant exited his car. He turned and saw one of his old buddies from his summer visits to his aunts.

"Zeke Harper." Grant smiled as he met the man halfway across the parking lot. They shared a handshake. "I'd heard you'd come back to town after getting out of the Army."

"I keep thinking I'll run into you over at the shelter one of these days." Zeke studied him with avid interest. The psychologist was involved with local veterans' groups and he and his fiancé had even started a therapy dog training program matching pets to soldiers with PTSD. "Mollie says you've been flying into Spring Forest quite a bit lately."

"I bet she says a lot of things to you now that you guys are finally engaged." Mollie McFadden and her brother had grown up with Zeke and, while Grant had usually only hung out with the older guys, he now saw Mollie holding training classes over at Furever Paws pretty regularly. "Took you two long enough, huh?"

"All good things are worth the wait," Zeke said, then lifted a single brow. "How's your own wait going?"

"Since you're a head doctor, should I even bother pretending that I don't know exactly who you're talking about?"

"Doesn't take a psychology degree to know that you've got a thing for Rebekah Taylor."

"Can I take that to mean that people are already talking?" Grant asked, wondering how much everyone knew. Did they realize she was pregnant?

"Spring Forest has grown a lot since we were kids,

but it's still a small town at heart. However, if you ever want to swing by my office in Raleigh for some relationship advice, I can invoke doctor/patient privilege, so you don't have to worry about the gossip."

"I just might take you up on that," Grant said as he spotted his aunts walking along the sidewalk with their attorney. "I've gotta go, but I'm sure we'll run into each other soon."

He and Zeke exchanged another handshake and Grant had just enough time to make it to the restaurant's entrance to hold the door open for the trio of women.

"Grant, you remember Megan Jennings," Aunt Birdie said. "She lives out at Battle Lands Farms with her boyfriend, Cade. I'm sure Rebekah's already told you how Megan and Cade have the best luck placing all the animals they foster."

"Of course." Grant shook the young woman's hand, not revealing that Rebekah hadn't told him anything of the sort. They'd barely been willing to discuss their own relationship, let alone anyone else's. "I hear you might have some news for us."

Megan exchanged a look with his aunts and Grant's stomach dropped. He had a feeling he wasn't going to like what he was about to hear.

"Let's get a table and we can talk about everything," Aunt Bunny suggested. "I've been craving a tuna melt and a chocolate shake all week."

They were seated at a booth in the corner, away from the other customers, and Grant realized that someone had called ahead to reserve this particular table. That meant his aunts wanted privacy, but they also planned to tell him something in a public place. Did they think he was going to get upset?

"Just lay it on me," he finally said when the server left with their order.

Birdie looked across the table to Bunny, who nodded. The older sister took a deep breath. "Megan came to us a while ago with some information and we've been going back and forth on what we should do with it."

Grant pinched the bridge of his nose, already knowing what they were going to say. "It was Gator, wasn't it?"

Megan began speaking. Apparently, his uncle had gotten himself into some serious financial trouble and dipped into his sisters' financial interests to cover his own bad debts.

"When Gator pocketed those insurance premiums, his embezzlement affected Furever Paws, which operates as a nonprofit organization. Bunny and Birdie have a fiduciary duty to protect their nonprofit's assets and provide their promised services. Grant, if your aunts don't file charges to get that money back, not only do they breach that duty, they also risk losing the trust of their donors. They could pretty much kiss all future grants and zoning approvals goodbye, as well. If they want to keep Furever Paws open, they have to bring a case against your uncle and at least attempt to recoup their losses."

Grant felt all the air leave his lungs as his whole childhood deflated. "Have you talked to Gator?"

"That's the thing," Birdie said. "Nobody's seen him since the investigation started."

"Before we formally file the charges, we wanted to talk to you and your cousins first," Bunny explained. "Wanted y'all to see why we have no choice."

"What do Gator's kids say about this?" Grant asked.

"Well, they aren't very happy with their father, obviously. They think he should turn himself in."

Grant stared at Megan. "Is there any way to prosecute my uncle without my aunts having to be the ones who point the finger? I just don't want Gator to think his family betrayed him."

Birdie shared the bench seat with Grant and he could feel her sit up straighter. "Gator betrayed us first by taking our money. We trusted him to manage our affairs and instead of making insurance payments, he covered his own behind, leaving us with no resources when the tornado struck. His deception got us into a mountain of debt that we'll probably never get out of as far as our personal finances. As far as the animal shelter goes, we're left with a shoestring budget based on charitable donations. But how long will those keep coming in? Especially if folks find out that we aren't doing right by their donations?"

Grant was the source of several large donations—anonymously, of course—but the shelter needed the support of the whole community.

"If your aunts hope to recoup any of their lost money," Megan explained, "then they need to press charges. Otherwise, the insurance company won't reimburse them because there would be no evidence of a crime committed."

"I'm hearing everything you guys are saying." Grant

let out another rush of air through his nostrils. "And from a legal standpoint, it makes perfect sense. But I'm just having a hard time wrapping my head around the fact that Uncle Gator could do something like this. Growing up, he constantly preached to me about taking care of family. What about all those comments he used to make about my dad ditching his family to move to Florida?"

"I never really understood why he was so sore about that," Bunny said, shaking her head. "By moving to Florida, Moose *was* taking care of his family. His new family that he was creating. That's where your mom lived and she was already pregnant with you. It's not like he abandoned Whitaker Acres or anything. Moose sent you kids to us every summer so that you'd love the land as much as we do."

Their lunch arrived, but Grant had a difficult time swallowing his food. He only made it halfway through before his fingers began twitching. He rose to his feet and pulled his wallet out of his pocket. "I really should be heading back."

He dropped some bills on the table, then promised his aunts that he'd be back in town soon and kissed each of them on their weathered cheeks.

He didn't feel much like driving back to the airport in Raleigh–Durham, though, so he decided to walk around downtown Spring Forest for a bit.

His thoughts were so consumed with the weight of accepting Gator's involvement in embezzling from his aunts that he didn't quite know how long he'd been wandering around until he found himself standing in front of the abandoned house on Second Avenue. The one he and Rebekah had followed Angus to.

As he stood in front of the overgrown yard, Aunt Bunny's words kept replaying in his head. His father had left Spring Forest because he was expecting a new family.

Could Grant make the same sacrifice?

So Grant had been in town yesterday and hadn't sent her so much as a text, let alone stopped in to the shelter and said hello. Rebekah looked at Angus, who was now sitting in the front passenger seat of her car as she drove to work the following morning.

If the guy wanted to avoid her, that was one thing. But why hadn't he wanted to see Angus? Back at the townhome, the dog had dragged that stupid T-shirt out the front door with him this morning and Rebekah had had to wrestle it away before they got out of the car in the Furever Paws parking lot.

Rebekah should've known by the way Angus's ears perked up that something was going on besides a simple game of tug-of-war. But it wasn't until she was opening the passenger door for the dog that she realized the person getting out of the blue SUV next to her was Grant. Angus dashed out of the door before she could clip his leash on him. Her heart slammed into her chest and she sucked air into her lungs before yelling, "Angus, come back!"

But instead of taking off, the dog danced around Grant's feet, yipping and barking and wagging his tail.

"Did you miss me, boy? Huh? Did you?" Grant knelt

down to pet Angus, who immediately rolled onto his back and exposed his belly. "You missed Daddy."

Rebekah wanted to shout that he wasn't anyone's daddy. At least, not yet. But she held herself back and instead jerked her chin toward his full-size SUV. "Did they give you a free upgrade at the rental counter?"

"Oh, that's not a rental car. I drove up from Jacksonville…" Before he could finish, another vehicle pulled into the lot so quickly it kicked up gravel behind its tires. "Can you excuse me for a second?"

She recognized the person behind the wheel as Gator Whitaker and Rebekah's heartbeat picked up speed. Nobody had seen the man for a while, so if he was showing up now, something big was going on. Grant hadn't wanted to believe anything bad about his uncle the last time Rebekah brought up the subject. Had anything changed since Grant's meeting with the aunts and Megan Jennings yesterday?

"Thanks for agreeing to talk," he said to his uncle through the open truck window.

Of course Grant hadn't actually come to see Rebekah. He was here to meet with his family, to probably plead his uncle's case and get his aunts not to press charges. Judging by the idling engine, Gator had no intention of coming inside. She could only make out a few words of what the man was saying to his nephew, but his face was red and his hands were gesturing wildly.

"Come on, Angus." She scooped up the dog in her arms. Neither one of them needed to be a witness to the family drama unfolding out here.

When she got to the building's entrance, Bunny and

Birdie were already coming outside and their attorney was behind them. Despite the emotionally charged situation occurring in the parking lot, the older women still managed to say hello to Angus as they walked toward the idling truck.

"Let's move over here," Megan said to Rebekah.

"Actually, I was heading inside," Rebekah told the woman who had her smartphone out and was discreetly aiming it at Gator's truck.

"The police have already been called and are on their way," Megan whispered. "But it would help to have plenty of witnesses out here, just in case Gator admits anything."

Rebekah didn't want to be a witness. And she especially didn't want to hear Grant stick up for his uncle again. But she reluctantly let Megan lead her closer so they could hear the heated conversation.

The voices grew louder and Rebekah shifted from one foot to the other, wishing she'd just let Angus keep the T-shirt when they first arrived. She would've already been inside the building when Grant had pulled up and someone else could've been a witness.

"Now, Gator, you've left us with no choice," Bunny said. "If we want to recoup our money and protect our fiduciary duty, we have to press charges."

"This is the thanks I get?" she heard Gator yell at his sisters. "Neither one of you could find husbands of your own, and I was the only one who stuck by you two when everyone else in the family deserted you."

Rebekah's indrawn breath made Angus squirm in her arms. "Shhh. It's okay. Hold still."

She wished she hadn't dropped his leash when he'd darted out of the car. There was no way she was going to walk all the way back there now to get it and draw any more attention to herself or Megan, who was still recording the argument.

"That was a low blow," Grant warned his uncle, and Rebekah was relieved to hear him defend the older women. Bunny had been engaged when she was younger and still spoke fondly of her fiancé, who'd died tragically. Birdie...well, Rebekah wasn't sure if Birdie had ever been married or in any type of romantic relationship because nobody had ever said one way or the other.

"We didn't *need* you to take care of things for us." Birdie crossed her arms over the front of her work shirt. "You insisted that you could double our investments. I believe your exact words were, *I want you gals to focus on your animal shelter. I'll handle the bills*. But you handled that money straight into your own pocket, Gator."

"You think I wasn't planning to pay you guys back?" Gator pounded his steering wheel. "I kept track of every single penny I borrowed. But I'm telling you right now that if you don't drop these charges, you'll never see that money again."

"Bingo," Megan whispered.

Grant stepped in front of Birdie and was only inches away from the truck window. "Gator, if you ever threaten my aunts again..."

Rebekah could see Grant's lips moving, but the approaching sirens drowned out his words. Gator's response was equally muted but the beefy fist raised in his nephew's direction left little doubt as to what was going to happen next.

Angus gave a fierce bark and leaped out of Rebekah's arms, tearing across the parking lot in Grant's direction. She ran after him, but the truck tires were already spinning and it felt as though everything after that happened in slow motion.

Rebekah didn't hear the roar of the engine or the wail of the sirens or the cries of the Whitaker sisters. The only sound was the blood pounding in her ears as she raced toward Angus.

But she was too late. The poor gray dog bounced off the front wheel as Gator accelerated out of the parking lot.

Chapter Fifteen

"Have you heard anything?" Grant tried to keep his voice low as he slipped into the small room outside of the veterinarian's surgery.

Rebekah's eyes were puffy and her cheeks were still stained with tears when she lifted her head. "Not really. Lauren didn't think that his legs were broken, but, oh, Grant, there was so much blood all over his little head."

"I know, sweetheart." Grant lowered himself into the chair beside her and pulled her into his side, stroking her back as she shuddered several times. "But Angus is our Scottish warrior, remember. He's tough. He's going to get through this."

"He was trying to protect you," Rebekah said before sniffing. "When it looked like Gator was going to punch you, that's when he took off running. He thought he could save you."

Grant's head fell back against the wall and he pulled Rebekah tighter to him. "I'm so sorry, Rebekah. I should've known that I couldn't talk any sense into my uncle. I thought that I could reason with him and that he'd simply turn himself in to the authorities. Instead, I put you and Angus and even my aunts in a horrible situation. I didn't expect him to be that angry. That hostile."

"That's who you are, Grant." She lifted her face to his. "You always expect the best from people. And I always expect the worst."

"Well, in this particular situation, you were right. I should've listened to you."

"So what happened with your uncle? Did the cops ever catch up to him?"

"I'm sure they will." He shrugged.

Rebekah stiffened against him as she sat up straighter. "Why aren't you out there searching for him?"

He pushed the hair back from her face and kissed her softly on the forehead. "Because you and Angus are the ones who need me right now."

Two hours later, Dr. Lauren came into the waiting area, pulling a surgical mask off her face. "Unfortunately, the left eyeball was completely perforated by the impact and we had to remove it. I'm going to send him home with some pain meds and a list of concussion protocols I want you to follow."

"You're sending him home? With me?" Relief washed through Rebekah. "You mean he's going to be okay?"

Lauren nodded. "It's going to take him a while to adjust to having just one eye. So his balance and his steering, so to speak, might be a little off at first. You'll have to apply an ointment on the area to keep it infection free and I'll need to see him again in about a week to remove the sutures."

Rebekah stood up and threw her arms around the veterinarian, who returned the hug. It wasn't Rebekah's most professional moment, but she wasn't here as a professional. She was here as a mom.

Grant rose to his feet and extended his hand. "Thank you so much, Doc."

"Oh!" Rebekah turned to the tote bag under her chair and pulled out a scrap of cotton. "Could you put this beside him so that when he wakes up, he has it with him?"

"Was that my favorite T-shirt?" Grant asked when Lauren returned to the surgical area.

"Yeah. You left it at my house. Angus found it under the bed and has been carrying it around with him everywhere."

"Poor guy missed me that much, huh?"

"He didn't know if you were going to come back." Rebekah instinctively lowered her eyes, but then she caught herself. No. It was time to have an honest conversation with the man, once and for all. She lifted her face to his. "Actually, Grant, neither one of us knew if you were coming back."

"Of course I was planning to come back. I told you that I was committed to being a father to the twins."

"But you're always on the go and I don't want our

children growing up never knowing when they'll see you again."

"I'll see them as often as you'll let me. Rebekah, I've tried like hell to give you space, to let you come to your own conclusions about the kind of guy I am."

"Is that why you didn't come see me the last time you were in town? You were trying to give me space?"

"Well, recently it was pointed out to me that I have a tendency to rush in to help people who don't always need my help."

"I don't know what I need yet, Grant. But I don't want to start depending on you if you're going to fly off anytime it suits you."

"Sweetheart, you have no idea how much I hate planes. I would gladly give up my frequent flyer card if it means you're finally willing to let me be a part of our children's lives."

When he called her sweetheart and made promises like that, Rebekah's head fought to keep her emotions in check. And the thing her head kept telling her was that he'd only committed to being a part of their children's lives, not hers. Sure, as their mother, he couldn't very well be active in their lives and not hers. But he'd yet to say anything about being a boyfriend, let alone a husband. Not that she'd given him the opportunity to do so.

Davis, the vet tech, opened the door, causing Rebekah to jump back from Grant's embrace. "He's starting to come out of the anesthesia if y'all want to step on back."

Rebekah cleared her throat and rose to her feet.

"Hey," Grant said, slipping his hand into hers as he

followed her into the operating room. "I'm not leaving town again until we finish this conversation."

It turned out that Grant didn't get on a plane again. At least, not that week. Or the one after.

But they only spoke about the babies in terms of the immediate future. They didn't commit to any sort of long-term plan.

As if by unspoken agreement, he stayed at Rebekah's place with her and Angus, who was not very happy about having to wear the protective cone of shame to keep him from using his front paws to scratch at the healing incision where his eye used to be.

Rebekah went into the office during the days and Grant stayed home with the dog, setting up a command post on her kitchen table with his laptop, tablet and smartphone. He sent emails, walked the dog, attended video conferences, applied the antibiotic ointment the vet recommended, studied marketing trend reports and used his Bluetooth headset to make phone calls while simultaneously doing the online grocery shopping.

And then he slept in Rebekah's bed with her at night.

"You know, I could get pretty used to this stay-at-home dad life," he said, stretching in her bed as he watched her get dressed for work the following Friday morning.

"I'd like to hear that again in seven months when it's a dog *and* two babies." Rebekah's smile revealed her two adorable dimples. But her face soon turned down into a frown when she tried to zip up her dress.

"Here, let me help you," he said, getting up out of bed.

"Ugh." She dropped her arms in defeat. "I think I'm

going to need to start investing in maternity clothes pretty soon. I don't know how much longer I can hide it."

"If it were up to me, you wouldn't be hiding it all," he reminded her, slipping his arms around her waist and resting his hands over the still small bump under her midsection.

She leaned her head back onto his shoulder and sighed. "I have that appointment with Dr. Singh next week. Maybe we can start telling people after that."

"Good. Because I'm ready to stop sneaking around." He felt her stiffen, but he wasn't sure if it was in response to his words, or to the sudden ringing of her cell phone on the bedside table.

He watched her walk across the room to retrieve it, her smooth skin exposed from the unzipped back of her dress.

"It's for you," she said a few moments later, handing him her device. "Apparently everyone knows where to find you when you don't answer your own phone."

Which was exactly why he thought they should no longer be referring to their relationship as pretend. Everyone knew he'd been staying here and that something had been going on between them for a while. And there was certainly no faking the attraction.

"Hello," he said, then listened to Birdie's rapid-fire questions about the cell tower contract he'd sent his aunts last night to peruse. Rebekah had already laid the groundwork with the city council to get the zoning approved. But now the contract needed to be negotiated. With Gator's recent arrest and vows to fight them in court, his aunts were eager to have more income.

"Yes, the tower company would have full rights to that half acre of land, but you can stipulate in the contract that you get a percentage of any money they make from any secondary service providers. If you go through an agency that represents landowners, they can negotiate the best deal on your behalf."

He answered a few more questions and then disconnected. Rebekah was still standing there, although she'd put on a looser dress that showed her rounded shoulders.

He leaned his elbows back on the bed and appreciated the view. "Well, my aunt needs someone to fly to D.C. to meet with the agency that will negotiate the contract for the cell tower."

"So, when do you leave?" Rebekah asked.

"That's the thing. You're going to have to go instead. Dr. Singh didn't say anything about you not being allowed to fly, right?"

"Why would I go? I only manage the business deals that have to do with the shelter, not the Whitaker property."

"Because I just found out that my Uncle Gator finally turned himself in and I want to be there to support my cousins when they attend his arraignment." He saw the sympathetic look in her eye and before she could tell him for the hundredth time how proud she was of him for defending his aunts, he added, "Plus, I promised to turn in my frequent flyer card, remember?"

"You don't really expect me to hold you to that, do you, Grant? Obviously, you're going to have to return to Florida eventually."

"Eventually," he agreed. "But not until I put all your doubts about me to rest."

* * *

Grant and Angus drove her to the airport and Rebekah was able to meet with the cell tower representatives, as well as the landowner agency, to work out the specifics for the deal that would give Whitaker Acres an added boost to their monthly income.

She'd been a little surprised that both he and his aunts trusted her to make the best deal for them after they'd recently been burned by an actual family member. Grant's confidence in her made her go into that negotiation with the desire to accept nothing less than top dollar for her bosses.

Just like he had this past week when Rebekah was gone for the day at work, Grant sent her pictures of Angus carrying around whichever discarded item of her clothing he'd been able to find that day. And with the amount of time that she and Grant had spent getting out of their clothes lately, it was usually whatever had ended up closest to the bed.

So that night, as she lay in the hotel room, the picture that came in was of the dog curled up on the white sofa with one of her favorite bras as his pillow. She made a mental note to get a laundry hamper with a lid.

It was weird to think that a little over a month ago she'd been living on her own, perfectly happy and comfortable in the quiet, organized world she'd created for herself. Yet now a man and a dog were taking up residence in her townhome and it almost felt normal.

The following day, after her plane landed, she missed the bottom step off the escalator because she was so surprised to see Grant standing in the baggage claim area, a bouquet of plumeria in one hand and Angus's leash in the other.

She immediately bent down and greeted Angus first. "What are you doing here, big guy? Did you miss me?"

"Well, we both missed you," Grant said, then shot Angus a playful look of chastisement. "But some of us know better than to yip and prance around and draw attention to ourselves in a public place."

"Nothing draws more attention than a bouquet of flowers and a cute dog," a familiar voice said behind Rebekah.

"What are you doing here, Aunt Birdie?" Grant asked the woman who had a bright pink carry-on case at her feet. Then he looked at the man behind his aunt. "And why did you ask Doc J to pick you up from the airport? I could've given you a ride."

Rebekah smiled at the appearance of the retired veterinarian, then bit back a giggle when she saw that he had his own small duffel clutched in one of his hands. The doctor knelt down to greet Angus. "I've heard all about you, my friend. Running all over town and causing quite the stir. But I see my daughter did a heck of a job sewing up that incision. We'll need to get you a little pirate patch to complete the look."

While the two older people were distracted fussing over the dog, Rebekah used her elbow to nudge Grant. When she finally got his attention, she nodded toward the boarding passes in Doc J's free hand.

"You mean…you guys are here together?" Grant's voice was loud enough to make Rebekah wince.

Doc J grinned sheepishly at Birdie. "Guess the cat's finally out of the bag."

"Oh, don't look so shocked, Grant. Richard has always been sweet on me. Now that he's retired and we no longer work together, I figure why not kick up my heels while I'm still young enough to kick 'em."

"So you two…" Grant pointed at his aunt's suitcase. "Are you moving down to Florida, too?"

"Not permanently. I just go down for the occasional weekend getaway with my man."

Her man, indeed! Rebekah wanted to give her boss a high five. There'd been rumors about Doc J having some sort of secret crush, but nobody had been able to figure out which Whitaker sister it was since he spent time with both of them.

This time, Rebekah got to be the one smiling at Grant's look of confusion instead of the other way around. He opened his mouth several times, only to close it again.

"But what about Bunny?" Grant finally got the words out.

"What about her?" Birdie put her hands on her hips.

"It's always been the two of you together," Grant said, then looked to Rebekah for confirmation. Nope, he wasn't getting any support from her. She remembered how he'd sat back in his chair at the barbecue restaurant, practically egging her parents on as they'd asked her all those embarrassing questions. "Isn't Bunny worried that a man might come between you?"

"Psh." Birdie waved a hand at him. "Bunny has been talking to her own gentleman online for the past five years."

At this, Rebekah really did give the older woman a high five. She wished Bunny could've been there and gotten one, as well.

"Did you know about this?" Grant tilted his head at Rebekah.

"I had no idea." Rebekah grinned. "And usually I know everything that's going on at Furever Paws."

"Well, you've been so busy keeping your own secrets—" Birdie glanced down at Rebekah's waistline "—you haven't had time to notice mine."

Heat flooded Rebekah's cheeks and her hands immediately shot to her stomach, which probably only confirmed his aunt's suspicions. Well, that and the fact that Grant shifted the flowers to the hand holding the leash and protectively slipped his free arm around her waist.

"Just for the record..." Grant cleared his throat. "We were planning to tell you guys about the pregnancy after the doctor's appointment next week."

Birdie winked at her nephew. "Good. This means you'll be in town more often and can help out with planning the Paws Under the Stars event."

"Paws Under the Stars?" Rebekah lifted her eyebrow.

"That's the name Grant came up with for our fundraiser gala. We both thought Fur Ball sounded too stuffy." Birdie's hands were clasped together in excitement. "Now, Richard and I have a plane to catch, so you two rest up this weekend and let me know what time our doctor's appointment is next week."

Rebekah's eyes widened in concern. There weren't enough chairs in the obstetrician's office for all the Whitakers.

Chapter Sixteen

The Paws Under the Stars event wasn't only a fund-raiser, it was also a huge celebration of the recent additions to the Furever Paws facility. Grant had never thought of himself as a party planner, but working with Rebekah handling the dinner, dance and silent auction, he'd never been more certain that he could easily work with her for the rest of their lives.

It had been a month since they'd run into his Aunt Birdie and Doc J at the airport, and Grant had only been back to Jacksonville once, to hand in his resignation and to tell his mom and his sisters about his future plans. He hadn't moved in officially with Rebekah, but she and Angus also hadn't kicked him out of her place.

Uncle Gator had reluctantly agreed to a plea deal earlier this week and yesterday's ultrasound at the doctor's revealed that he and Rebekah were having a boy and a girl. They had so much to celebrate, Grant was determined to make tonight's gala the party of the year.

He drove Angus to the animal shelter later that morning and, when he walked into Rebekah's office, he handed her the chocolate croissant and decaf latte she'd sworn off yesterday after getting on the scale at Dr. Singh's office. If you asked Grant, though, Rebekah's new pregnancy curves made her look even sexier.

"Looks like the white tents are being set up now," he said after kissing her cheek. "Angus and I are going to take a walk and make sure they get those little twinkly lights up in all the trees."

"Grant, are you sure we needed to rent tents? I keep crunching the numbers and, at this rate, our only profit is going to be from the silent auction donations."

"Well, we sold way more tickets than even I expected and the newly built party pavilion—which was a brilliant decision on my part, by the way—isn't going to be big enough to hold everyone."

"Fine," she sighed, then bit into her still-warm croissant, pleasure written all over her face. It was the same expression he'd left her with this morning in bed after he'd—

"I trust you know what you're doing," she said around a mouthful of pastry.

Grant's lungs stopped working for a full fifteen seconds. While they'd been practically living together for the past month and she'd slowly been opening up to him more every day, having Rebekah finally say that she trusted him left him completely speechless.

When they walked outside, he looked down at Angus. "Did you hear that, boy? Mommy trusts me."

Angus replied with a yip.

"That's right." He scratched the dog's ears. "Tonight is definitely going to be a time for celebrations."

"Amanda, the food tastes fabulous," Rebekah told her friend, who still made time to walk dogs at the shelter despite having a new relationship and a new catering business.

"That's because all the fresh produce came from Battle Lands Farms," Amanda replied, having to raise her voice over the sound of the band that had just invited everyone out to the dance floor.

"Is Ryan around?" Rebekah scanned the formally dressed partygoers as they began dancing to a rendition of Elvis Presley's "Hound Dog." "I wanted to thank him for giving us that front page feature in *The Spring Forest Chronicle.*"

"He's over there with Dillon and Tucker." Amanda pointed to where her boyfriend was standing with his son and their pet, a Chihuahua/dachshund mix. The boy and dog were wearing matching polka-dot bow ties.

Rebekah noticed the woman's hand immediately drop to her waist. It was the same motion Rebekah made whenever she felt one of the twins kicking. "Amanda, are you...?"

She let her question hang in the air, but her friend smiled as she gave a slow nod. "Ryan and I eloped last month. Tonight, Dillon has been walking around telling everyone that he and Tucker are going to be big brothers."

"Rebekah, can I borrow you for a sec?" Grant said in her ear as his hand slid over her elbow. Then he smiled at Amanda and added, "The food looks amazing, by the way."

"So do you two," Amanda said, giving Rebekah a subtle wink before waving goodbye. Amanda had been one of the women at happy hour with her the night she'd gone home with Grant. Rebekah slowly realized that Mollie and Claire, who'd also been there, probably had known about her and Grant the whole time.

When they were alone, Grant kissed her temple before whispering in her ear. "Aunt Bunny and Aunt Birdie were hoping that one of us would make some sort of speech thanking everyone for coming out tonight and supporting the shelter."

"But I didn't prepare a speech."

"Don't worry." Grant grinned. "I have us covered. Just come stand on the stage next to me."

Rebekah could feel the crowd's eyes on them as Grant held her hand, leading her to the raised dais inside the party pavilion. She tried to stand behind him as he took the microphone from the bandleader, who'd just finished singing Blake Shelton's "Ol' Red," another song about a dog. She was sensing a theme with the music selection.

"Thank you all for coming to Paws Under the Stars tonight and for supporting my aunts and all these wonderful animals," Grant started and the audience applauded.

"Many of you know Rebekah Taylor, the director of Furever Paws," he said, trying to urge her out from behind him. Embarrassment flooded her and she could only manage a small wave as the guests applauded again. "But what you might not know is that Rebekah had never had a pet before. And yet, just like many of you, she now has her own success story with fostering a dog."

It was then that Rebekah saw Lana Whitaker, Grant's mom—who she'd met earlier that afternoon—standing next to Rebekah's own parents at the side of the stage. Sheila held Angus's leash and walked the dog to greet them. Her dad stayed a few feet behind and let out a hearty sneeze.

"This is Angus," Grant continued. "His owner died and he'd been left to wander the streets of Spring Forest, evading capture for quite a while. But Rebekah spent time talking to Angus and leaving little treats for him. She eventually got him trust her and, well, Angus has a little gift he'd like to give his new mom to thank her for being so patient with both him *and* his new dad."

Rebekah's throat constricted and she forced herself to swallow her emotions.

"What's going on?" she whispered to Grant.

"This would've worked better if he hadn't refused to wear the kilt costume I got him for tonight," Grant announced into the microphone. Then he whispered to Rebekah, "Check out his plaid collar."

Rebekah's knees wobbled as she unsteadily knelt beside the dog. Hanging on a little silver loop near the buckle was a very large, very beautiful diamond ring.

She gasped and jerked her face up to look at Grant, only to find him on one knee beside her.

"I love you, Rebekah Taylor. I can't wait to be a father to our twins," he said, and a ripple of murmurs came from the dance floor. "But more than anything, I can't wait to be your husband. If you'll have me."

Rebekah's heart threatened to beat out of her chest. "Of course I'll have you, Grant Whitaker."

The crowd erupted in a cheer and Angus let out several yips and wiggled his tail as Grant tried to free the ring from the loop on his collar. When he finally slipped it onto Rebekah's finger, she lowered her voice and asked, "But what about your job?"

He handed the microphone back to the bandleader. "I gave them my resignation. I've already been hired for my first consulting job and I have it on good authority…" he jerked his chin toward Rebekah's father "…that plenty of men are now working from home and raising their kids."

All the blood rushed to her head, or maybe to her heart, and she got a fuzzy feeling of excitement. "You mean, you're going to move to Spring Forest?"

He squeezed her hand in his. "Look down at Angus's collar again."

There was a second loop that had been blocked by the leash clip. When Rebekah saw what was hanging there, her eyebrows slammed together. "Why are you giving me a key?"

"It's the key to that old brick house on Second Avenue," he explained, and Angus put his front paws on

Rebekah's thighs, causing her to sink from a kneeling position straight onto her rear end.

"You bought me that house?" If Rebekah hadn't already melted into a puddle of happiness, she certainly would have at his thoughtful and surprising gift.

"Well, I bought it mostly for Angus, but also for us. And the twins. I figure we're going to need that big yard for them to run in while I'm working from those patio benches you already have picked out in your mind."

"But what about your surfing?" She couldn't believe that he was giving up so much to be with her. How had she ever doubted him?

"We'll have to take lots of trips to the Outer Banks. In fact, my mom already brought Angus a custom life vest."

"Oh, Grant," she said, awkwardly trying to stand up. He held out his hand and pulled her to her feet. As soon as she was off the ground, she flung her arms around his neck. "I love you so much."

"You have no idea how long I've been waiting to hear that." He squeezed her to him and Angus let out another yip. Holding Rebekah with one arm, Grant bent down to lift up the dog to join them.

"Apparently, your aunt was right," Rebekah said around Angus's eager licks as the pup took turns kissing both of their faces.

"Right about what?" Grant asked, dodging a little pink tongue.

Rebekah's gaze swept across the gala guests lining up their animals for the much-anticipated pet parade, taking in all the familiar faces she'd met since moving to Spring Forest.

Her eyes returned to Grant's and she couldn't stop smiling. "It's amazing how much love your heart can accommodate once you decide to open it up."

* * * * *

COMING SOON!

We really hope you enjoyed reading this book. If you're looking for more romance, be sure to head to the shops when new books are available on

Thursday 27th June

To see which titles are coming soon, please visit

millsandboon.co.uk/nextmonth

MILLS & BOON

Coming next month

A WEEK WITH THE BEST MAN
Ally Blake

Harper turned to Cormac and held his gaze, despite the fluttering inside her belly. 'Where *is* my sister?'

'Catering check. Wedding dress fitting. Final song choices. None of which could be moved despite how excited she was that you were finally coming home.'

Harper bristled, but managed to hold her tongue.

She was well aware of how many appointments she'd already missed. That video-chatting while wedding-dress-hunting wasn't the same as being in the room, sipping champagne, while Lola stood in front of a wall of mirrors and twirled. That with their parents long gone from their lives she was all Lola had.

Lola had assured her it was fine. That Gray was *such* a help. That she understood Harper's calendar was too congested for her to have committed to arriving any earlier.

After all, it was Harper's job in corporate mediation that had allowed Lola to stay on in the wealthy coastal playground of Blue Moon Bay, to finish high school with her friends, to be in a position to meet someone like Grayson Chadwick in the first place.

And yet as Cormac watched her, those deep brown eyes of his unexpectedly direct, the tiny fissure he'd opened in Harper's defences cracked wider.

If she was to get through the next five minutes, much less the next week, Cormac Wharton needed to know she wasn't the same bleeding-heart she'd been at school.

'You sure know a lot about planning a wedding, Cormac,' she crooned, watching for his reaction.

Harper played chicken for a living. And never flinched.

There! The tic of a muscle in his jaw. Though it was fast swallowed by a deep groove as he offered up a close-mouthed smile. 'They don't call me the Best Man around here for nothing. And since the Maid of Honour has been AWOL, it's been my honour to make sure Lola is looked after too.'

Oh, he was *good*.

But she was better.

She extended a smile of her own as she said, 'Then please accept my gratitude and thanks for playing cheer-leader, leaning post, party planner, and girlfriend until I was able to take up the mantle in person.'

Cormac's mouth kicked into a deeper smile, the kind that came with eye crinkles.

That pesky little flutter flared in her belly. She clutched every muscle she could to suffocate it before it even had a chance to take a breath.

Continue reading
A WEEK WITH THE BEST MAN
Ally Blake

Available next month
www.millsandboon.co.uk

LET'S TALK
Romance

For exclusive extracts, competitions
and special offers, find us online:

- facebook.com/millsandboon
- @MillsandBoon
- @MillsandBoonUK

Get in touch on 01413 063232

For all the latest titles coming soon, visit
millsandboon.co.uk/nextmonth